Note Man pulled out a
base of the wind turb

"Ohhh," Daley said with relief. The door cut the turbine noise by about half. "I can hear myself think." She looked around. "Is this the 'wonder' you promised to show me?"

"It's through that door."

Unlike the outer door, this one wasn't locked.

Daley frowned. "What's in there?"

The building had looked about thirty by thirty from the outside, almost the same as this empty room. Where could the door go? A storage locker?

"Something interesting. Try it."

Daley opened the door and found herself in a small vestibule facing another door. With his flashlight on, Note Man stepped in and closed the door behind them.

"Now, open that one," he said.

She grabbed the handle, pushed…and gasped.

"Holy—! What the—?"

A vast, well-lit, warehouselike space stretched away before her. Strips of some sort of glowing material ran along a ceiling at least thirty feet above, illuminating a wide floor lined with boxcar-size blocks of putty-colored…what?

Daley squeezed her eyes closed for a few heartbeats, then opened them for another look. Nothing had changed.

"Wait-wait-wait! This is impossible."

"It's not an illusion. It's quite real."

"But-but-but…" She jabbed a finger at Note Man. "Wait right here. Do. Not. Move."

She went back through the first door, backtracked across the room, and exited by the outer door. Assaulted again by that godawful noise, she trotted around the side of the base to the rear. The side wall ran thirty feet at most, and the rear was the same across. Thirty feet. No more.

Where's that huge building? How can it be there and-and-and not there at the same time?

She hurried back inside and rushed straight through the vestibule to the third door…

No change: the giant space still loomed before her.

DOUBLE DOSE

BY F. Paul Wilson

Dedication

again for
Chris Morgan
Thanks for the inspiration

ACKNOWLEDGMENTS

Thanks to my wife Mary and my beta reader Kim Bryson

Author's Note

As before, I have to thank Chris Morgan for triggering Double Threat and this sequel. Thus the continuing dedication to Chris.

But since earthquake science plays such a big part in *Double Dose*, I must reiterate my thanks to Rick Loverd, program director of the National Academy of Sciences' Science and Entertainment Exchange, who put me in touch with John Vidale, Ph.D., a seismologist at USC and a member of the National Academy of Sciences. He eventually put me in contact with Egill Hauksson, Ph.D., Research Professor of Geophysics at Caltech's Seismology Lab in Pasadena. Dr. Hauksson showed me around the Southern California Earthquake Center at Caltech and gave me ideas and a ton of info on earthquakes. Any errors herein are mine, either out of ignorance or because I needed to stretch the truth.

SUNDAY—March 8

1

"Home sweet home." Rhys said as he guided their Land Rover past the *Welcome to Nespodee Springs* sign.

Elis couldn't miss the sarcasm in his son's tone. Well, the desert town of Nespodee Springs was the antipode of a metropolis and didn't offer much at all in the way of culture or entertainment for a twenty-eight-year-old, but it had served as a good home to the Pendry clan for generations.

Elis Pendry was looking at beginning his sixty-sixth year in a few months, but keeping his weight down helped make him look younger. He combed his longish hair—dark with some gray at the temples—straight back. People often remarked on the resemblance between him and his son.

Rhys yawned. And then yawned again.

"Didn't sleep well?" Elis said.

Rhys shrugged. "Not really. Not a fan of hotel beds, and this damn Daylight Savings switch just adds to the problem. I didn't need to lose an extra hour of sleep and then have you waking me up at the crack of dawn."

The clocks had sprung ahead an hour this morning. It had never bothered Elis in his younger days, but now that he'd passed sixty, he felt it. Not that he'd ever admit it.

"Never attend a morning meeting on an empty stomach," he said.

"Except there was no meeting."

"I'm quite well aware of that. I was there, remember? And

I couldn't possibly know he wouldn't show up until, well, until he didn't show up."

"Yeah, but the bottom line is: This whole trip was for nothing."

"At least we had a nice dinner last night."

The halibut with crab meat in the Gaslamp District's Oceanaire Seafood Room had been extraordinary.

"Okay, no argument there. And, frankly, I'm glad the meeting didn't happen. The whole setup stank of scam."

Elis gave a sage nod. "Now that I've had time to think on it, I do believe you're right."

But Elis had known that all along. After all, he'd designed the scam. But not to buy a piece of lost Tesla technology from some mysterious crackpot—also an Elis creation. No, the whole purpose had been to get them both far out of town—to put a mountain range and a hundred-plus miles between them and whatever befell the Duad last night.

Yesterday he'd given his foreman, Jeffrey "Karma" Kendrick, a hefty down payment to arrange for her disappearance. How had he phrased it? Oh, yes. He'd said he wanted her "whereabouts to become a mystery." Kendrick, a former enforcer for the Gargoyles biker gang, had understood.

It had all seemed rather abstract then. But now, as they approached the town, as the white poles and spinning blades of Tadhak's windfarm appeared ahead, the reality of it came into sharp focus. He'd ordered another person's death...contracted for cold-blooded murder...he'd never dreamed he'd have something like that on his conscience...

They passed the mobile home neighborhoods—where Kendrick lived—and the solar array owned by the clan. And farther to the south, the struts and trusses and gleaming domed crown of the clan's Tesla tower jutted up from the valley floor.

And then the town: Nespodee Springs, plopped between the desert and the Saw Tooth Mountains, a good drive south from Palm Springs, and a short drive north from the Mexican border. The spa up the hill, shrouded in palm trees, had been a destination back in the days when hot mineral baths were the rage. The place still did business, but nothing like in the past.

And now two parallel rows of one- and two-story buildings flanked the road. People often remarked how the planked boardwalk along the storefronts made Nespodee Springs look like a Wild West town. A number of units had blue tarp hung where their front windows used to be before last Thursday's earthquake. Rhys cruised past the gas station with its car wash, the market, the café, the liquor store, the Thirsty Cactus bar, the laundromat, Doc Llewelyn's office, and assorted empty units. Nespodee Springs was in the middle of a long, slow, slide.

But only one unit held any interest for Elis today...the one that called itself *Healerina*...the one run by the Duad. The name on her birth certificate read Stanka Daley, but she wanted to be addressed by her surname alone: Daley. She presented an innocent millennial's face to the world, and to the workaday population she was no danger. But she posed a deadly threat to the destiny of the Pendry clan. As head of that clan, it had fallen to Elis to remove the threat.

Her shop, Healerina, where she hawked New Age geegaws to the gullible souls who wandered by, also sported a blue tarp where its display window had been. A *Closed* signed hung on her front door.

"That's weird," Rhys said, as they passed. "Daley's almost religious about opening at ten."

He'd asked his son, only two years older than the Duad, to get to know her and learn more about her, but Rhys had become involved. Too involved. She'd seduced him—mentally and physically—into believing she was no more than what she pretended to be.

Elis kept his tone light. "Perhaps she was out carousing without you last night."

"She's not a carouser. And it's almost noon." He pulled out his phone and began thumbing the screen. "I'm gonna call."

"Not while you're driving."

"I'm doing twenty miles an hour on a Sunday morning in Nespodee Springs. Think about that, Dad."

He had a point, but Elis didn't want him calling now. Didn't want his son starting down the road toward the realization that he'd never see her again—not just yet. He noted with chagrin that he had her on speed dial.

After a short listen: "Not answering. I hope she's all right."

No answer...not today, not ever.

Kendrick had called on the burner phone last night: *It's done...she's on her kitchen floor with a knife in her heart, put there by the dead guy in her bedroom...worked out perfect. We got a fall guy. It's all taken care of. All questions answered.*

Elis couldn't help wondering about the "dead guy in her bedroom." That hadn't been part of the plan or even—

Best not to think about it. Put it into the box labeled *Problem Solved* and leave it alone. Yes...*Problem Solved*...

But the realization came with no burst of elation. A young woman had had her life cut short. Because of Elis. A woman dangerous to the clan, yes, but a fellow human being. He would never be proud of this. And he would take the secret to his grave.

"We're supposed to go out for dinner tonight," Rhys said.

Elis turned to him. "Tell me: Do people stare when they see her or remark on her appearance?"

"You mean her hair? No remarks, but they do stare."

No surprise there. She had dark hair, as dark as a Cahuilla woman's, with a stark white patch at the crown. That plus the strange golden skin of her left hand added up to a striking figure.

And it had struck Elis between the eyes last week when he'd seen her close up without the baseball cap she often wore. Because his copy of *The Void Scrolls*, composed when civilization was young, contained an ancient etching of a human figure, crude and androgynous, with no distinguishing features except a white patch centered in the dark of its hair. Her existence had been foretold.

"I'm sure she's fine," he said. "Wouldn't be the first time she vanished for a few days."

"She didn't 'vanish.' She went back to her place in LA to pick up a few things."

"You learned that when she reappeared. She gave you no warning then and maybe this is the same."

"Maybe. But why not answer her phone?"

"Let's head home and worry about that later. I'm salivating for Maria's Sunday brunch."

Elis couldn't tell him the real reason he wanted to get home was to unlock his older brother's door. He still found it hard to believe Cadoc had allowed the Duad into the family home and shown her the film that only the clan Elders were allowed to see. A monstrous betrayal.

But now, with the Duad removed, she could never act on what had been revealed to her in that film, so Cadoc's betrayal had become moot. He would forgive Cadoc and everything would return to normal.

But not for long. Come the equinox, Elis and the clan would change the world by opening a path for the return of the Visitors. He'd led Rhys to believe that they'd be waiting for the summer solstice, but the real target date, when the heavens would properly align, was the afternoon of March 20, a mere dozen days away. With Rhys becoming infatuated with the Duad, he hadn't dared to let him know the real plan. No telling what he might let slip in the throes of passion.

But now the path had been cleared. Nothing could stop the Return. The last obstacle—the young woman who called herself "Daley" but whom Elis knew as the Duad—had been removed.

2

Daley lay in bed and stared at the ceiling as she contemplated her recent death.

Very recent. Less than twelve hours ago Karma Kendrick had stabbed her in the chest, stopping her heart cold. But she hadn't died, thanks to the sandy-haired guy sitting on the edge of her bed. He wore his usual ensemble of jeans, plaid shirt, and snakeskin cowboy boots.

Not a guy, really. And not really sitting on her bed, either. She reached out and her hand passed through him. Just an image existing only in her visual cortex.

("Why'd you do that?")

Not a real voice, either. Just thoughts translated into words in her auditory cortex.

He wanted to be called *Pard*—how lame was that?—and preferred to appear as a male. But Pard was neither male nor female but rather an *it* who hadn't experienced sentience until it invaded Daley's brain. How she'd hated it—denying its existence at first, calling it a hallucination. And even when she'd come to accept its existence, she'd hated the fact that she was never alone.

But now that thing she'd so hated had become a real person to her...had saved her life not too many hours ago. And in the process, saved its own life too, of course, because if Daley died, Pard died. Pure self-preservation when you got down to it.

But the fact remained: If not for Pard, Daley wouldn't be lying here ruminating in her bedroom. She'd be starting to stink as she rotted on the kitchen floor in a pool of congealed blood.

"Just thinking," she said.

("About what?")

Her phone rang before she could answer. When she saw *Rhys* on the screen, she flopped back on the bed.

("You're not answering?")

"Not sure what to say. I'm sure his dad put Karma up to it. The question is: How much does Rhys know?"

("I think it's safe to say that if he knew you were to be killed, he wouldn't be calling you.")

"Not necessarily. If the San Diego trip was to establish an air-tight alibi, it would look suspicious if he didn't call me when he got back."

Pard jabbed a finger at her. ("*You* are devious. But you do realize, don't you, that the plan had not been to murder you in your bed. Karma brought along duct tape, which is a sure indication that you were to be subdued and carried off.")

Daley couldn't suppress a shudder. "I don't want to think about that."

("Can you really imagine Rhys approving of the violations that Karma and Benny obviously had planned?")

No...she couldn't. She liked Rhys—genuinely liked him— and couldn't see how he could have the slightest inkling of what Karma had been up to. But his father...totally different story with that guy.

"So how do I play this?"

("The only way you can: Pretend nothing happened.")

"That works if neither of them had anything to do with it."

("Even if Daddy Pendry was involved, it still works if Karma keeps his promise to you to disappear.")

"What if he didn't? What if he tells Daddy Pendry what happened?"

("I can't see that. You appeared outside his trailer in the moonlight with the handle of that knife jutting from your chest. That alone might have been enough to scare him off, but then I gave him such a taste of the horrors—I mean, *he wet his pants*, Daley. He's going to run and keep running.")

"Let's hope so." She shuddered and touched the healing wound in her skin where the knife had rammed into her chest. "He's totally psycho."

("But he's now a totally *terrified* psycho.")

She tried to take comfort in that but couldn't help flashing back to waking right here in this bed with a bright flashlight beam blinding her and an arm going around her neck in a choke hold. She'd kicked and flailed and pulled at the strangling arm as she heard Pard's voice yelling in her brain to hold onto him and don't let go. She struggled on for maybe half a minute that seemed so much longer until the arm loosened and pulled away as her attacker slid off the bed and thumped to the floor.

Pard had slipped into the man—Karma had called him "Benny"—and done something to his heart. Benny would never hurt anyone again.

The no-brainer choice she'd given Karma was either take Benny's body and never show his face again, or die like Benny and spend eternity in the hell he'd just sampled.

"Enough about that creep," she said. "Rhys and I had a tentative date for dinner tonight." He'd said he knew an Italian place in Brawley that served Sunday gravy on, well, Sundays. "I don't know if I can go through with it—you know, act normal like nothing happened."

("Then don't. But just think: If his father sent Karma, the realization that not only are you still alive but having dinner with his son will drive him insane.")

Daley had to smile—the first time in what seemed like forever. "Yeah, there's that."

3

Elis fished the old key out of his pocket as he approached Cadoc's door on the Lodge's second floor where he'd locked him in yesterday. No one would have missed him. No one would have asked, "Where's Cadoc?" because Cadoc never showed himself. Cadoc was a wraith, a phantom who moved about only under cover of darkness. He certainly wouldn't have banged on the door to be let out. Oh, no. That would have called attention to himself. He'd suffered no discomfort, what with his quarters outfitted with an en-suite bathroom and a mini-fridge. And Maria the cook would have slipped his breakfast through the door slot on the floor this morning as she did six days a week.

So, Cadoc's brief imprisonment was just between him and Elis.

Elis could well understand his son's self-consciousness about his appearance. Every member of the clan carried a patch of scaly gray skin somewhere on their body. They called it "the Pendry Patch." Something had gone wrong with Cadoc, however. He'd been born with an unusually large patch on his back, but instead of remaining stable in size, it began to grow and spread until he was covered head to toe with dry, gray, peeling skin. He left a trail of flakes wherever he went. The condition had somehow affected his voice as well, limiting his speech to grunts.

Elis could see why anyone so afflicted might evolve into something of a recluse. But Cadoc had taken it to an extreme, becoming a dweller in darkness, fitting his quarters with room-darkener shades and venturing out only under cover of night. Hardly anyone outside the immediate family knew he existed.

Elis knocked on the door.

"Cadoc? I'm going to unlock this now. I've had time to think and I'm going to forgive your betrayal. However, I must forbid any further contact with that woman."

A moot point now, of course, but he had to engage in the charade of still believing the Duad was alive.

He heard a faint "*Ungh*" from the other side of the door.

One grunt meant yes, two meant no.

He inserted the heavy brass key into the old lever tumbler lock and gave it a twist. The latch snapped back with a *clank* and then Elis pocketed the key. He couldn't see how he'd ever need it again, but one never could tell.

To reinforce the charade, he added, "Just remember: Stay away from that woman or I'll be forced to banish you from the clan."

Just then he door was yanked open and there stood Cadoc— naked. All the room lights were on and the window shades were up, flooding the room with bright, midday light. His gray, peeling skin hung off him, giving him the appearance of a dead tree shedding its bark. His expression—what Elis could read of it in that distorted face—was furious as he thrust a slip of paper at Elis, then slammed the door.

What?...*What?*

Elis stood in the hallway, stunned. Cadoc rarely if ever showed himself fully clothed, and yet here he'd shown himself in the altogether.

The note—Cadoc's customary means of communication— fluttered to the floor. Elis retrieved it.

See what you did to me!
NEVER speak to ME of betrayal!

Elis stared at the words, repeating them in his mind, trying to make sense of them, and then the confusion segued into growing horror as it began to dawn...

His skin...Cadoc was blaming Elis for his skin.

But how could he know? How could Cadoc *know?* Only the head Elder of the clan was supposed to know the source of the Pendry Patch, only Elis.

Cadoc wandered the Lodge and crept through the town at night. He saw things and heard things. Elis had digitized most of the Scrolls for easier access, and had encrypted the parts that needed to be kept secret from the hoi polloi of the clan. Cadoc, in the course of his sneakings and spyings, must have come across the key to the encrypted sections and learned things he should not be privy to.

But it was hardly fair for Cadoc to blame him for his condition. Elis, just like every Head Elder before him, had only been following tradition as laid down in the Scrolls.

Elis raised his hand to knock—he had to explain.

But what could he say? *I would never betray you? I was only doing my duty? I never dreamed this would happen to you and I regret every day that it did?*

All true. But then he remembered the rage in Cadoc's eyes just a moment ago. It would not have abated. Not yet. Maybe never.

He lowered his hand. He'd better give Cadoc some time to cool down. He'd make this right. Once the Visitors returned, an unsightly skin condition would dwindle to insignificance in the face of the wonders of a transformed world.

Elis made his way back toward the front of the Lodge, following the enticing odors of Maria's brunch wafting from the kitchen. The first floor, where Elis conducted the business and investments of the clan, would be deserted on a Sunday, but the living quarters were alive and redolent of frying bacon.

He put on a composed expression as he strolled into the dining room where he found Rhys on the phone. His son's smile brought him to a stuttering halt. But only for a second. He forced himself forward again, toward the serving table where he poured himself a cup of coffee while eavesdropping on Rhys's conversation.

"...and yeah, I'm kind of tuckered myself, so why don't we make it an early night?"..."Absolutely"..."I'll pick you up at six and we'll head for some Sunday gravy"..."Deal. See you then."

He ended the call with that smile stuck on his face. He didn't seem aware that his father was there. Elis put down his coffee cup before he dropped it.

Making a dinner date...he knew from that smile that it wasn't with Fflur, the young clanwoman the Elders had chosen for him. It could only be...but that meant...

He opened his mouth to speak but no words came. He cleared his throat but Rhys beat him to it.

"Oh, hey, Dad. Didn't see you there."

A swallow, then, "Dinner plans?"

"Yeah, that was Daley."

No! This couldn't be!

"She's...she's all right?"

"What? Oh, yeah, no worries. The time change hit her and she slept in."

How was this possible?

"So...no problems?"

Rhys frowned at him. "You all right, Dad?"

"Yes. Fine."

He jumped as Maria spoke behind him.

"And what would you like today, señor?"

Eat? He couldn't think of eating.

"You know, Maria, I think I'll pass. I'm feeling a little tired."

Giving a little bow, she returned to the kitchen.

"You sure you're all right?" Rhys said. "You look a little pale."

"I'm fine, fine," he said with a more snap than he'd intended. "I'm going to putter around the office for a while."

With that he hurried away before the crushing disappointment and the anger it spurred could show. The *Closed* sign on her store had drawn him down this path, leading him to believe his problem had been solved. That and Kendrick's lies...

...*she's on her kitchen floor with a knife in her heart...it's all taken care of...*

Something must have interfered with Kendrick's plan. But what? Elis supposed even the best plans fell victim to unforeseen circumstances. She might have left town unexpectedly and Kendrick had been unable to locate her. A million possibilities. Why lie? He had to know he'd be found out.

Elis shut his office door behind him and pulled out his phone. He'd disposed of his burner and hated calling Kendrick on his own. Yes, the man was his foreman at the solar array so he had many plausible reasons to call him, but it spun a web of connection between them, and he wanted as little connection as possible. But he had to know what went wrong. Now.

The call went straight to voicemail. No rings, just an automated voice telling him to leave a message after the tone.

Well, that wasn't good. It meant the phone was either turned off or the power drained. The Duad blithely going about her business and Kendrick incommunicado. It should have been the other way around.

Something very wrong here.

4

("When do you want me to start my time-out?") Pard said.

Dressed in his usual, he sat atop a glass case where she displayed the local Cahuilla tribe's dreamcatchers and some other New Age paraphernalia. Daley figured if he weighed anything he would have crushed them and cracked the glass.

"I don't," she said as she loitered in the shadows a few feet back from Healerina's open front door, waiting for Rhys to take her to dinner.

Yesterday at five thirty the sun would have been well down below the mountain peaks and the street darkening. Today it was still up and shining. The wonders of Daylight Saving Time.

"Usually you want me gone when you're out with young Pendry."

Pard had figured a way to cut himself off from all of Daley's sensory inputs and allow her the alone time she craved every so often, and some privacy when the situation required it—like going out with Rhys.

"But this time I want your input on whether you think there's anything off about him."

("I told you I like him.")

"I believe you said he had a core of decency you found very attractive."

("Very good. My words exactly. And then you asked me if I was gay.")

"A logical question, I think."

("As a being of pure intellect, I am happy to be free of such mundane distractions as sex. I can't say the same for you, however, which is why I assumed you'd want me to take a time-out.")

Daley shook her head. "In case you forgot, someone murdered me at three o'clock this morning. That tends to take a girl out of the mood."

("So young Pendry's not going to get lucky tonight?")

She sighed. "Neither of us are."

("'Is.'")

"Is what?"

("Neither of us *is*. 'Neither' is a single noun.")

Pard's analness—she wondered if there was such a word— used to tick her off. But last night his anal nature had saved her life. So as far as she was concerned, he could be as anal as he pleased.

The weird white Tadhak worker bus rumbled past on its way uphill from the windfarm to the even weirder Tadhak family compound. She guessed the wind turbines didn't take Sunday off so neither could the workers. The dark windows always creeped her out. If someone was staring at her, she wanted to see his face.

Just as it passed, Rhys's Highlander pulled to a stop before the store. Daley stepped out and, as was her practice, got in before he could scoot around and open the door for her.

He leaned toward her for a kiss but she held up a hand. "No PDA, remember?"

("You *really* aren't in the mood,") Pard said from the backseat. *Hush.*

Everybody knew everybody in this tiny town and every one of them talked. She was determined to be known as a local business woman, not "the Pendry kid's girl."

"Oh, right, right."

"So how was San Diego?" she said, pushing the conversation to neutral ground. "Did your father get taken to the cleaners?"

She'd warned him that this fellow wanting to sell secret Tesla technology stank of a scam, and he'd agreed, but his father had insisted on going to San Diego and talking to him.

"Fortunately, the guy never showed."

"Maybe he found a bigger fish."

"Maybe." He gave her a close look. "You okay?"

"Why do you ask?"

"I don't know. You seem kind of..."

As he groped for a word she said, "Stressed?"

"Yeah, maybe."

"It's been a stressful day."

("The understatement of the century!")

"Anything I can do?"

"No. It's all taken care of." She turned the topic back to him. "I'm glad San Diego turned out okay."

"Yeah, well, I don't know if my father would have been taken in or not. I'm thinking yes. His bullshit detector is a little weak—no, make that a *lot* weak."

"He's into wild conspiracy theories and all that?"

Rhys shook his head. "Worse."

"Religion?"

("Carefullll...you know things you're not supposed to.")

I'm well aware. Let's watch his reaction.

Rhys gave her a slow, sidelong look. "Why do you say that?"

"Something Doc Llewellyn said when he dropped by the shop: 'The clan has its own unique religion.'"

"Did he tell you about it?"

"Nothing beyond 'We keep it to ourselves.'"

"Yeah, we do."

"Care to elaborate?"

"I'd rather not. Certain aspects make Scientology look sensible."

"You sound like an apostate."

Where had that word come from?

("From yours truly, naturally.")

Naturally.

He shrugged. "I took a comparative religion course once and found that every religion has a core belief that you have to buy into in order to be a True Believer, and I never came across one that I didn't find a little ridiculous at its heart."

"Including your clan's."

He laughed. *"Especially* the clan's."

("I told you I liked this guy.")

But can we believe him?

("I could take a look inside. I won't be able to read his thoughts but I can gauge his emotions.")

Sounds like a plan.

("Okay, but I need contact.")

Easy.

Daley laid her left hand, the golden one, palm up on the seat console between them.

"Hold my hand?"

He gave her a surprised look but never hesitated.

"This isn't a PDA?" he said as he wrapped her hand in his.

She nodded at the empty desert road stretching before them. "I don't call this public."

("Okay, going in.")

Rhys gave her hand a squeeze. "This is nice. So simple but... nice."

Daley only smiled and waited for Pard. She didn't have to wait long.

("All done.")

That was quick.

("Well, his emotions are all up front.")

And...?

("He is suffused with happiness being with you and holding your hand.")

Aww...really?

("Really.")

Daley felt bad now for doubting him.

("You have nothing to fear from this man, Daley.")

She returned Rhys's hand squeeze. "Yeah, this *is* nice."

Nicer than you'll ever know.

5

Elis waited until after sundown before driving down to the trailer park, cursing himself for his compulsiveness. But he had to *know*.

He would have preferred full dark because he knew his Land Rover would stick out among all the residents' economy cars. But he'd never been to Kendrick's home, and he'd need some ambient light to find it.

The so-called streets in the park were little more than narrow sandy lanes, and poorly marked, but eventually he found 46 Iguana Lane—a double-wide mobile home with no signs of life. He stopped in front of it, got out, and knocked on the door.

"He ain't home," said a male voice behind him.

Elis turned to see a portly, bald, elderly fellow standing by the rear of the Land Rover.

Damn. He'd hope to bring this off without being noticed. Well, he couldn't very well ignore the man, so...

"Are you sure?"

"Absolutely. Truck's been gone all day. Reason I know is we share a parking area that he usually hogs."

This was more information than Elis needed or cared to know.

"Do you know when he'll be back?"

"He don't clear his schedule with me, mister. What you want with him? Gonna send him back to jail?"

From the man's tone Elis gathered that news like that would make his day.

"Why would you think that?"

"Because he's a mean sonovabitch and it's only a matter of time before he fucks up again."

"Well, I assure you, I have no such authority and none of that is any of my concern." Elis climbed back behind the wheel. "Good evening to you, sir."

As he drove away he checked the rearview and saw the man staring after him, shaking his head. No surprise that Jeffrey "Karma" Kendrick was not a good neighbor, but where had he been all day? He certainly hadn't spent it disposing of the Duad's remains. And where was he now?

The possibilities seemed endless. Elis had given him five thousand as a down payment. Had that much cash in hand proved too much of a temptation? Had he driven to Vegas or the like for a bender of gambling and whoring?

Elis almost hoped that was the explanation, because he found the current situation more than a little unsettling: He'd sent out a killer to make the Duad disappear and the killer had disappeared instead.

Who was this woman? Really...who *was* she?

6

The full moon was high as Rhys drove them back into Nespodee Springs. Dinner had been sumptuous. Great flavor and great big portions of meatballs, hot and sweet sausage, spaghetti, and Sunday gravy. Mama's Meatball in Brawley... Daley made a point to remember that place.

"Oh, I meant to tell, you," he said. "Remember that teenager who collapsed outside the café on Friday?"

"Hard to forget." Yeah...Wynny. She especially remembered how her friend had screamed at Daley not to touch her—*Get your hands off her now!* "Is she all right?"

"She seems to be fine, but the weird thing is...you know that scaly patch on my back?"

"You called it 'the Pendry Patch.'"

"Right!" He grinned. "You remember. Well, anyway, she came home from the hospital yesterday and noticed hers is gone."

Why was he telling her this?

"You're probably wondering why I'm telling you this—"

She laughed. "You just read my mind."

"Well, she's blaming you."

Daley hadn't seen that coming. "Me?"

"Yes, you. She says while you were pretending to help her you were really putting a spell on her."

"I'd think she'd be thanking me."

"Well, no. Not in our family. If you don't have the Pendry Patch, you're not a real Pendry. So she's starting to get shunned by the other kids."

Daley shook her head in dismay. "Teenage girls can be brutal."

She remember the minor hells she passed through as

the new kid with the funny first name—she quickly became "Skanka Daley"—who didn't belong to everyone's online hang at the time, Myspace.

"I just thought you should know that you're now officially a witch," he said as he pulled around to the rear of Daley's building.

She remembered how Pard had gone into Wynny to try to help.

Pard? Did you do anything while you were in her?

("I started dissolving that clot in her lung.")

Anything else?

("Well, I noticed this little anomaly that was impacting her skin so I corrected it.")

Can't resist, can you?

("I'm still determining my abilities and limits.")

So now I'm a witch.

("You've been called worse.")

Yeah, she had.

"Great dinner," she said as she kissed him on the cheek. "Thanks."

"How about I walk you to your door."

"That's okay," she said.

"Sure?"

She sensed his desire. She'd taken him to her bed just three nights ago and it had been good until the earthquake had interrupted. She hated to disappoint him, but it simply wasn't in her tonight. She couldn't tell him the real reason, so she made up a lame one.

"Just too tired tonight. Call me in the morning."

She hurried up the steps, waved from the door, then went inside. She watched from the kitchen window as he waited a few heartbeats, then drove off.

"Think he'll call?" she said.

("Only death or dismemberment will stop him.")

She sighed. "Okay, then. Let's find something mindless on TV."

She needed to shut down her brain and just veg before trying to find sleep in the bed where she'd been attacked.

7

"Checkmate," Rhys said.

He'd been looking forward to another bout of fantastic lovemaking with Daley tonight, and had been crushed when she'd shot him down. He should have seen that coming because she'd been...what? How to describe her tonight? Not cool, not aloof...distracted. That was it. She'd said she'd had a stressful day, and maybe she had, but tonight she'd been like not all there, like a part of her had been somewhere else.

God, he was drawn to her, like the proverbial moth to a flame. So many little things about her turned him on. Her knowing eyes, that enigmatic Mona Lisa smile, and, like tonight, the way she dunked her biscotti into her cappuccino and bit off the foamy end, and dipped again...he'd wanted her *so* bad. But, alas...

So he'd come home with the intent of indulging in a little tequila. Okay, maybe a lot of tequila. But as he was ferrying the bottle of Patrón Silver toward his room he passed Cadoc's door and realized they'd missed their regular Saturday night chess game. Well, why not? He'd knocked and they'd started playing.

As usual for their games, the light in Cadoc's heavily curtained suite was limited to one small gooseneck lamp with a high-intensity bulb sharply focused on the board.

"Ungh?" Cadoc said. His flaking, papery, gray-skinned hand floated out of the shadows, hovered over the board, then tipped his king onto its side. "Ungh!"

Rhys didn't beat Cadoc very often. He'd seemed distracted tonight, just like Daley. Was it catching?

"You didn't play to your usual level, dear brother," Rhys said as he began to set up for a second game. "And I'm the one who's drinking. Anything wrong?"

A note dropped onto the board.

Things on my mind

"Oh? Anything I can help with?"

No worries.
How was your date?

"Oh, you know about that?" Rhys wasn't surprised. Cadoc knew more than he should about many things. "It was fine, although her mind seemed somewhere else. Much like yours tonight, and Dad's all day. What's the matter with everybody?"

Papa?

"Yeah. He was fine all the way back from San Diego but fell into a black mood as soon as we got back here. When Elder Baughan showed up with a problem he wanted to discuss, Dad wouldn't even see him. I wound up listening to him."

Problem?

"Yeah, his granddaughter Wynny—you know, the one who wound up in the hospital with that clot on her lung? Well, when she got home from the hospital yesterday she discovered that her Pendry Patch was gone. The Elder is all upset because her sibs and her friends are shunning her, and he wants Dad to do something about it. I made nice-nice and promised Dad would be in touch, but really—what can anyone do about that?"

Her patch is gone?

"Yeah, completely, according to her grandfather."

Did the hospital do
something to her?

Rhys shrugged. "Who knows? She blames Daley."
No note this time, just a higher pitched "Ungh?"
"Apparently Daley was trying to help her after the clot hit and she couldn't breathe, and she says Daley put a spell on her."

Daley touched her?

"I guess so. I wasn't there so I don't know. Why do you ask?"

No reason

Another note immediately followed.

*I'm not up for another game
Let's call it a night*

"You sure?"
"Ungh."
As Cadoc began to sweep the pieces off the board into their storage box, Rhys gathered up the notes and handed them across. Then he grabbed his bottle of Patrón.
"Our usual Saturday night game still on?"

Unless I get a better offer

A crummy end to a crummy weekend, Rhys thought as he closed Cadoc's door behind him. A wasted trip to San Diego, then Daley leaves me high and dry, and now my brother craps out on me.
He cradled the Patrón in his arms. Just you and me, baby. Just you and me.

☐

("Someone's at the door.")
Pard's voice jarred her from her snooze in front of the TV. She'd come across *Galaxy Quest* while channel surfing and stopped to watch. Though she'd seen it at least thirty times, she never could pass up *Galaxy Quest*. With adventure, laughs, visuals, and tons of heart, it had relaxed her so much she'd dozed off half way through.
She shook herself awake in time to hear a *knock-knock-knock* from the kitchen. A sudden fear seized her.

You don't think it's Karma, do you?

("I told you, he's gone. It's our guide from Saturday morning.")

You're sure?

("Well, I'm reasonably certain, but I can't be sure until we walk into the kitchen and see a note on the floor inside the door.")

She glanced at her phone—almost midnight—then noticed what Pard was wearing: striped flannel pajamas and a matching night cap.

What's with the weird getup?

("Well, you'd fallen asleep so I prepared for bed.") He morphed into Jason Statham. ("But if you feel you need protection—")

How about just your usual self?

("You're no fun.")

He reverted to his customary sandy-haired, jean-clad self.

Can't leave you alone for a minute, can I.

("Well, I had no one to talk to so—")

She started for the kitchen, praying Pard was right about who was knocking, and sighed with relief when she saw a now-familiar sheet of note paper just inside the door.

Can we talk?

"Hello, there," she said. "I expected you to come by last night."

She wished he had. If he'd been around, Karma would have had to make other plans.

I was indisposed

That could mean anything, but she didn't pursue it.

"Yeah, so was I. But now that you're here, I have so many questions after seeing that video."

Of course.

For instance?

"Like what are the Visitors? Aliens?"

"Others"

Well, that had been obvious, but she took it to mean that he didn't know. Maybe no one knew.

"And why were they so blurry? No one knows what they look like?"

Our eyes can't see their color

Another note quickly followed...

Or their shape
Different geometry

What's that mean?

("I think he means their colors are ones our retinas can't perceive and our brains can't reconcile their shapes with anything we know.")

So the filmmakers took a shortcut and just blurred the images?

("So I would assume. Ask him when we can see disk two.")

"What about the rest of the film?"

Sorry
not possible

"Why not? Can't we just sneak back like we did Saturday morning?"

films taken away

What did that mean? Had their little excursion been discovered?

"Who took them away?"

*Wynny Baughan
says you're a witch*

"Don't change the subject. Are you telling me I won't see disk two?"

*Working on it
Patience*

Not one of my strong points.
("I know, but let's give him time.")
As if we have a choice.
Another note slipped through.

Wynny?

"Okay, okay. Yes, I heard. She says I cleared her Pendry Patch."

*You know about
Pendry Patch?*

"Obviously I do."
She didn't feel a need to explain that she'd seen one on Rhys's back when they'd been in bed.

Did you clear it?

What do I say?
("Feel free to lie if you want.")
I'd rather not. He's been pretty straight with us.
("Except about who he is.")
"Do you believe that's possible?" she said.

*Not an answer
I know you can heal*

Oh, crap.
"Why do you think that?"

Told you
I watch
I listen

("Yes, he did tell us that.")
"And just what have you heard?"

A healed ulcer

Another note:

Deputy thinks you
cured daughter's tumor

("He's got good ears.")
So what do I tell him?
("The truth, I guess.")
The truth is overrated.
("This is the new you, remember?")
Ah, well. Okay...here goes...
"I can, in a way, under certain conditions, heal certain things."
She'd never uttered those words before.

You healed Wynny's Patch?

"In the course of starting to dissolve her lung clot, yeah. It sort of happened."
("'Sort of'?")
A long pause followed...to the point where Daley wondered if Note Man was still out there. She was about to call out to him when...

I have Pendry Patch all over
Severe

"Oh. I'm sorry."
("Now we know why he hides.")

Ruined voice too

I have a feeling I know what's coming next.
And sure enough...

Could you heal me?

Well, Pard...can you?
("Total body...that's a big order. I can make the attempt. But he'll have to show himself and face you. I can't get in without physical contact.")
"We can give it a try," she said. "But there has to be contact between us. I have to touch your skin to make this work."

You would not like.
Repulsive

"Let me be the judge of that. Anyway, it's my worry, not yours. Tell me when."

Tonight?

Doesn't want to waste any time, does he?
("I gather he's been afflicted all his life. I'm sure he's had enough. More than enough.")
"Sure. I guess."

Please turn out lights

"How will we see?"

Moonlight

"Okay."

She turned off the lamp in the front room, then doused the kitchen overhead. Her hand rested on the doorknob but didn't turn it. Not yet. Standing in darkness, letting a stranger into her house near the midnight hour. It seemed reckless. But in this instance it seemed right. She pulled open the door...

A tall, hoodied, rail-slim figure stood on her landing. As was his habit, he'd loosened the bulb over the doorframe, but the high, bright moon outlined him in pale light. He held a pen in one hand and a note pad in the other. His face was invisible within the shadow of the hoodie, just as it had been on Saturday morning.

The moonlight coming through the door and the window over the sink, augmented by the glow seeping in from the big front window, rendered the kitchen table easily visible. She gestured to it.

"Come in. Have a seat. Make yourself comfortable. Can I get you something to drink?"

My God! she thought. *I sound totally inane.*

He grunted "Ungh-ungh."

Pard had taken a position by the kitchen sink. ("That sounds like an 'Uh-uh.'")

Pocketing the pad and pen, the figure stepped in and dropped onto one of the chairs along the long side of the oblong table. He kept his hands out of sight on his lap. His face remained in the deep shadow within his hoodie. Daley left the door open and sat opposite him. She realized if she was holding his hands while Pard went in, he wouldn't be able to write on his pad. Well, they'd just have to wing it.

Here we go. Ready?

("Ready.")

"Okay..." She laid her hands, palms up, in the flood of moonlight lighting the table top. "Give me your hands."

A long pause...long enough that Daley began to wonder if he might blow her off and bolt for the door. But then his fingers appeared above the edge of the table and slowly slid forward.

They lifted as they reached hers, then hovered above them, like drones afraid to land.

She'd never seen a mummy's hands, but she imagined this was how they might look: dry, gray, papery skin hanging off like bits of peeling wallpaper. They weren't descending, so she lifted hers and closed her fingers around his. Like holding dry, flaking papier-mâché. Daley was pretty sure she wouldn't want to be caressed by such hands, but holding them was no biggie.

Not bad at all.

("Well, he told us right from the get-go he was vain.")

"Okay," she said softly, trying to ease the tension she sensed coursing through him. "I've got you, and it's not 'repulsive' at all. If they were cold and wet and slimy, that would be a whole other thing altogether. But this...like you're in dire need of hand lotion, that's all."

She felt the tension release as his hands relaxed.

("You continue to confound me.")

What?

("You'll scam people without a shred of remorse and yet here you are, soothing his feelings, putting him at ease...this kind of compassion isn't you.")

Maybe it is. You don't know me.

("Oh, I know you better than *you* know you.")

Well, he's become a kind of weird sort of friend, and I don't have many friends.

("You can say that—")

Will you get the fuck in there and do your thing!

("Going, going, gone.")

"Okay," she said aloud as she realized she was going to have to put on a bit of a show, "we're gonna have to stay like this a little while as I concentrate on what I'm doing."

She closed her eyes and sat very still as she waited for Pard to finish whatever he was doing inside.

And waited...

He usually didn't take this long.

Finally... ("Okay. A lot of work, but I did the best I could do.")

She kept her eyes closed. *"The best I could do"? You mean*

you're not sure this is going to work?

("I think I got it all but, if not, I can always go back for a second pass. Weird, though.")

What do you mean?

("Tell you later. Open your eyes so I can see.")

She felt a burst of...what? Excitement? Alarm?

You mean he's going to change instantly?

("No chance. It's going to be a slow change as normal skin cells start to replace the abnormal. Tell him to be patient.")

Daley opened her eyes and released his hands. "There. I did what I can."

"Ungh?"

He pulled out his pad and pen, scribbled, then pushed the note across. She had to squint to see it in the moonlight.

When do I see results?

"Slowly. Your old cells have to slough off before the new ones can show."

If this works...

A short, sharp sob issued from the shadow within the hood. The sound was so full of anguish, Daley felt her own throat thicken. She reached out and squeezed his hand.

"I know, I know. Just be patient."

("There you go again...")

Stuff it!

"One thing I need from you is a promise to keep this just between you and me. When you skin starts to improve, you can make up any explanation you please, just don't mention me."

Why not?

"Because that's the way I want things for now. Later on, maybe you can give me credit, but for now...it's our secret."

("Ask him if it affects all the Pendrys.")

She did and he scribbled.

All the ones
Living here

What?

("An odd response. An odd condition. If all the members of the clan have a Pendry Patch, it should be genetic, but I discovered that it isn't.")

I don't follow.

("If it's handed down from generation to generation, the defect or anomaly should be in the germline cells—the cells that produce sperm and eggs—but it's not. Which means it's not an inherited trait, it's acquired. The defect seems to have been introduced *after* conception.")

How does that happen?

("I have no idea.")

Daley figured as long as she had Note Man here, she'd ask him.

"The Pendry Patch doesn't seem to be genetic," she said.

He scribbled.

It's not

("He *knows*?")

"What is it then?"

An ugly secret known
only to a very few

"Can you tell me?"

No
Too awful

I can't imagine…I mean, "Too awful?" How awful can it be?

("Push him. I'm curious.")

"Don't you think you owe me?"

Not yet

("I think he means he doesn't know if he's cured.")
Fair enough.

Thank you

"Don't thank me yet."

You tried
You are a friend

Now her throat was getting all tight again. She nodded, not daring to speak as he gathered his notes and rose, waved, then went out the door, closing it behind him.

Just when I'd thought I'd maxed out all the possible strangeness in life...

("I do hope it works—for his sake, if nothing else.")

If his skin clears, it will change his life. Will he be able to adjust to being with people?

("Maybe we'll finally find out who he is. And maybe he'll tell us the mystery of the Pendry Patch.")

Whatever. I'm going to bed. The last twenty-four hours have been the weirdest of my life—of anyone's life, I'll bet.

("Yes, but who knows what tomorrow will bring.")

MONDAY—March 9

9

Rhys stopped in the doorway to his father's office and watched him. Usually Dad was hyper-busy on a Monday morning, dealing with the markets as they returned to life after a weekend. Instead he sat quietly, staring at nothing through the big front windows, his thoughts apparently a million miles away.

"Hey, Dad," he said and watched his father start and snap back to the here and now, then spin in his chair to face him.

His smile looked forced. "Rhys...what is it?"

He'd run last night's celestial scans through the Scroll program as he did every weekday so his father could apply the results to guide the investments of the Pendry Fund. And as had happened for the last two weeks or so, a message popped up at the bottom of the printout.

"We're getting the same message as before: *The Duad must cease.*"

He nodded absently. "No surprise there."

"What do you mean?"

"Hmmm? Oh, I mean nothing has changed—the Duad is still here, we've learned nothing of any substance about her, you're still infatuated with her—so why should the message change?"

"Well, you're in an odd mood today. What put you there?"

His father shrugged. "Nothing...everything."

Rhys had no patience for this crap this morning. He had a headache—not a bad one, just enough to be annoying—from last night's tequila, and he needed more coffee.

"Whatever. The other news is that Kendrick didn't show up for work this morning and he's not answering his phone."

"No surprise there either."

Again with the "no surprise"?

"Well, yeah, it *is* a surprise since he's never missed a day's work since you hired him."

Rhys didn't think much of Kendrick as a person, but he'd proved to be a dependable worker and a good foreman. He seemed to like bossing people around and kept the solar array running smoothly.

"It's no surprise when you give an ex-con responsibility and he lets you down."

Seriously? This made no sense. He'd hired the guy *because* he was an ex-con. And then bragged about what a good decision he'd made.

The only thing Rhys was accomplishing here was making his headache worse.

"I sent someone around to his place but he didn't answer his door. Maybe I should go."

Suddenly his father came to life—out of his chair and shaking a finger at Rhys. "No-no. You stay away from that man. He'll either show up eventually or he won't. If he doesn't, we'll promote someone else to foreman. As for now, give me some space. I've got decisions to make."

Shaking his head, Rhys headed back to his own office. He didn't know if he was more baffled or annoyed. And he didn't want another foreman. He'd seen the way Kendrick had driven the men when they were laying the cable from the Tadhak transformer to the tower—on a Sunday, no less—and liked the way he'd operated.

Forget what Dad said. Kendrick might not answer the door for one of his underlings, but if he was there, he'd open it for Rhys.

10

Daley walked into Arturo's Cozy Coyote Café for her morning coffee and traded waves and hellos with all the regulars. She hadn't wanted to stay in Nespodee Springs when Juana had first brought her here, but Pard—for reasons that still weren't clear to her, and maybe not even to him—had pushed for it. Now she was glad she'd listened. Jason Tadhak had proven himself a generous, conscientious landlord, and the local folks had accepted her as one of their own. Arturo especially.

As she arrived at the counter, the big guy pushed a twenty-ounce coffee container toward her. Like every other day, he wore a backward Padres cap and an apron that was long overdue for a swim in some hot soapy water.

"The usual," he said, and winked. "I saw you crossing the street. Any food?"

The usual...how great was that?

"Maybe later. I don't know what I'm doing today."

"That's right. You're closed Mondays. I were you, I'd get outa town. Nothing doing here."

"Not a whole lot doing anywhere in the valley."

"Well, you got that right."

"Hey, Arturo," someone called from down the counter. "I know I ain't as pretty as her, but you think you could start that Taylor Ham frying before I starve to death?"

"'Taylor Ham'?" Daley said.

"Pete's from New Jersey. That's what they call pork roll where he comes from."

"Pork roll? People really eat something called 'pork roll'?"

"Delicious. You should try my breakfast special sandwich sometime." He winked and headed for the grill. "Gotta go."

His departure gave Daley a view of the small TV playing low behind the takeout counter. A newsreader was talking about the horrors.

"*...and the plague continues to ravage Southern California. With no known cause and no cure, hospitals are reporting bed shortages due to the steady influx of screaming unconscious patients who need skilled nursing care and constant sedation.*"

("Which gives me an idea of what we can do on our day off,") Pard said.

Good. Because I'm at a loss.

("Well, unless you object, I'd like to check on that horrors victim. Remember him?")

The guy from Saturday? Hard to forget.

The guy had been spending the weekend at the spa with his wife. They'd been sightseeing in town when he collapsed in the middle of what passed for Main Street here and started screaming.

"Happy Monday," Daley called to the breakfast gang as she waved and headed back across the street to Healerina where they found a glazier's truck parked in front of it and Jason Tadhak talking to the driver.

"Oh, Daley," Jason said. "I was looking for you. I know you close Mondays so I thought now would be a good time to replace your front window."

"Absolutely," she said. "I'll leave the place unlocked."

This was perfect. The store had been bright and airy before last week's quake broke the big front window. The blue tarp had turned it dark and creepy.

Jason Tadhak—the best landlord anyone could ever want.

("Okay,") Pard said as she unlocked the store door. ("Let's get back to the subject of our horrors guy. He's an itch I need to scratch.")

You don't have any skin.

("You know the kind of itch I mean.")

I do. I remember you saying the horrific images in his head were from "outside," whatever that means.

("It means they're unrelated to human experience. Nightmares and such come from experience or a mash-up of images you've been exposed to. From my brief look inside— before that fascist EMT forced you to break contact—I gathered that these horrors are not being drawn from the victim's unconscious but being fed to him from elsewhere.")

His wife called him Timothy.

("Okay, then. Do you mind if we go look for Timothy? I'd like another peek inside.")

Got nothing better to do. Why not?

With a wave to Jason, she walked around back and up the stairs to her apartment.

("And who knows? I might be able to help him.")

"Oh, wait," she said aloud as she closed the door behind her. "That might bring too much attention. I'm not ready for that."

("You can play dumb.")

"As the owner of a shop called Healerina? Think about that. I've never been in the medical center, but I bet it's got cameras all over the place."

("Good point. Well, then, we'll have to disguise your more prominent features.")

"Like my hair."

("Definitely your hair. And not with your Dodgers cap— that's all but a signature look for you. We need to hide that golden left hand as well.")

"Gloves?"

("It's going to be in the seventies.")

"One glove? It worked for Michael Jackson."

("We're trying to deflect attention, not attract it.")

"Makeup, then. I'll buy a floppy sun hat and some heavy-duty makeup for my hand."

("And big sunglasses.")

"Those I already have."

("Well, then, let's be on our way.")

11

Rhys banged on the door of Kendrick's double-wide mobile home and got no answer.

"Mister Kendrick!" he called. "It's Rhys Pendry. Just checking to see it you're all right."

Still no response, so he banged again. What if he'd overdosed on something and died? He spotted an elderly gent stepping out of the trailer next door.

"Excuse me? Do you know if Mister Kendrick's home?"

He shook his bald head. "Ain't seen him since Saturday."

"He didn't show up for work today and I'm wondering if he's all right."

"Truck's gone so that's a pretty good sign he's gone too."

Rhys absently tugged on the door handle and it swung

open.

"Doesn't he lock his door?"

"We ain't buddies, mister. We've lived next door for years, but if you know him at all, you know he ain't exactly the warm friendly type."

"Agreed," Rhys said. Anything but.

"But I gotta say, pretty much everyone locks their doors here in Mobile Jungleland."

"Is that what it's called?"

"That's what *I* call it."

Rhys gestured toward the open door. "I'm just going to take a quick look to make sure he's not in there."

"Knock yourself out."

Up the three steps and inside—first thing Rhys noticed was a urine smell, which did not bode well. But a quick search of the double-wide revealed an unmade bed, a sink full of unwashed dishes, a pressing bench with massive weights in the second bedroom, but no Kendrick. He noticed Kendrick's last paycheck on the kitchenette counter, and took that to mean he intended to come back. But it didn't rule out the possibility that he'd driven off and fallen victim to foul play. He could be lying in a ditch somewhere.

He stepped back outside and latched the door behind him.

"Nobody home."

"Why's he suddenly so popular?" the codger said. "You're the second fella come looking for him in two days."

"Second?"

"Yeah. Fella in a Land Rover last night. Couldn't see him too well in the dark, but there was still enough light left in the sky to see he coulda been an older version of you."

An "older version" of Rhys in a Land Rover...that could only be his father. Why was he looking for Kendrick last night? And why didn't he mention it earlier when Rhys told him Kendrick was a no show?

And where the hell was Jeffery "Karma" Kendrick?

12

Karma stared up at Salvation Mountain.
      He'd driven the desert roads and the highways all day Sunday and into Monday, south to Jacumba Springs, east to the outskirts of Yuma, north to Palm Desert, south again to circle the Salton Sea until he wound up here at this giant pastry mountain. A big dune bulked up with mounds of sand and bales of hay to a height of five stories or so, all smoothed over with a truckload of plaster and slathered with a small ocean of brightly colored paint, then decorated with spiritual sayings and quotes from the Bible and "GOD IS LOVE" in huge pink letters, all topped with a skinny white cross. If Godzilla was some crazy-ass preacher, this was what its birthday cake would look like.

Karma didn't know nothing about the Bible or this "God is Love" bullshit. He'd been raised without religion. His father had been a stupid, violent drunk and his mother had been from the local Cahuillas. Both were gone now, and he'd never missed them for a minute. The only real family he'd ever had were the Gargoyles—his brothers, man, his real brothers. And all they'd ever worshipped was whatever they could smoke, drink, or snort to get high. He'd been right there with them. And now even they were gone.

So "God is Love" and the Bible quotes meant nothing to Karma, never had and he knew they never would. The Bible thumpers all talked on and on about Jesus rising from the dead, but those were just words in a book. He'd met a real, live goddess and he'd killed her himself, and she didn't wait no three days to rise from the dead, she'd knocked on his door, like, just minutes later and she showed him the hell she'd send him to if he ever crossed her path again. So he had to stay away from her. He wasn't worthy of her so he had to become someone else.

He walked back to the parking area where he sat in the oven-hot cab of his truck and stared through the windshield at Salvation Mountain. He hadn't slept in forty-eight hours but he wasn't tired. He just didn't feel like driving no more. Couldn't stay here though.

He returned to the road and followed it farther uphill past some ramshackle structure calling itself "The Church of Enlightenment." What was it with religion around here? A sign along its side read "All You Need Is Love." Really? That's all you need? Did anybody really believe that hippie bullshit?

The road ended at a fence decorated with signs that directed him left to East Jesus and right to the Slab City Library. East Jesus sounded like more religion and not a place for him, but he'd heard of Slab City so he turned right.

He didn't have to go too far before he saw a scattered collection of trailers and RVs and campers parked here and there. Some had a solar panel or two for power, and they all had litter around them. He saw a scrawny old fart walking along the side of the road using a walking stick taller than him. He was rockin' the Willie Nelson look with the beard, the braids, and the bandana, pulling a banged-up Radio Flyer wagon behind him.

"Hey, man," Karma said as he pulled alongside. "I heard of Slab City before but never heard why they call it that."

The guy glanced at him and kept walking. "Use to be a Marine camp—Camp Dunlap back in World War Two. When the war ended they packed up and left, taking everything with them 'cept the concrete slabs the buildings was on. Now we live on them."

"Who runs the place?"

"Ain't nobody runs it. We all run it."

"Hey, it's a city. No mayor?"

"Fuck that shit. No mayor, no city council, no electricity, no running water, no sewers neither. You stay here you gotta figure all that out for yourself."

Karma was kinda liking this place—liking it more and more.

"Who do I see about getting myself a slab?"

"You find yourself an empty one and park on it."

"That's it? No rent?"

The guy gave him a scathing look. "Anybody tries charging rent around here won't be around here for long. This here's the Last Free Place in America, buddy."

"Awright!" Karma shouted. "Awright!"

Maybe he'd found a new home, a place to become the new Karma Kendrick.

13

El Centro Regional Medical Center…a big, sprawling collection of pastel-colored buildings occupying several square blocks on South Imperial Avenue. Like most structures in El Centro, its buildings were one story except for a second floor on the main building that housed the ICU and medical-surgical beds. Fortunately, Daley had never needed the place.

Before entering, she stopped under the portico to check her reflection in the tinted glass door of the main entrance. She'd bought a floppy, wide-brimmed sun hat in Brawley, along with some skin-toned makeup for her left hand. She wore loose jeans and a white, three-quarter-sleeve peasant blouse.

You don't think I look too mysterious, do you?

Pard appeared beside her dressed in a white lab coat with a stethoscope draped around his shoulders. *Dr. Pard* was embroidered over the breast pocket.

Doctor Pard? Really? I wish you'd take this a little more seriously. You know, I'm not comfortable doing this. I doubt the hospital is keen on strangers sneaking into patient rooms.

("Trying to keep things light is all. And you look very ordinary, except wearing those big sunglasses indoors will look kind of affected.")

Can't be helped. They hide lots of my face.

She'd remembered the horrors victim's wife saying his name was Timothy Blaine, so Daley had called earlier and learned his room was on the second floor of the East Wing. Visiting hours were from noon to eight. She'd waited until two to make sure all lunches had been cleared away and the staff was occupied getting all their notes done before the end of shift.

She strolled through the lobby as if she belonged there, passing a table displaying flyers about local events.

("Pick up one of those flyers.")

Which one?

("Any one will do. Use it as a prop you can look at as an excuse to keep you head down. Plus humans are a curious lot, so their attention will tend to be drawn more to what's in your hand rather than your features.")

Think you've got us all figured out, dontcha.

("I'm working on it. The irrationality that runs rampant in your species does not make it easy.")

How's the air up there on your high horse?

("No need to get touchy. I'm just an impartial observer. Now...where's that elevator?")

She spotted one down the hall but the doors closed before she could reach it. She pressed the UP button and as she waited, people began gathering around her.

("Might be best if you weren't crowded into an elevator car with all these folks.")

Good thought. Where are the stairs?

The door next to the elevator was labeled with a stairway icon. She broke from the crowd and climbed to the second floor, which was also the top floor. As she stepped out into the vestibule she did a quick scan of the ceiling.

Pard said, ("A camera bubble to watch the elevator. Let's wander. Just keep your head down.")

She made a couple of turns and came to the ICU.

Information gave me a room number for Timothy and never mentioned ICU. Let's go back.

("Camera bubbles at regular intervals, covering the hallways and the nurses station. Let's check out the medical-surgical section.")

Daley found Timothy Blaine's room and strolled past it. She recognized his wife sitting next to the window bed, holding her husband's hand and looking miserable. After a brief pause, she kept walking.

Okay, we've found him. Now what?

("Not sure. No obvious CCTV in the room. I'd like to go back into him since I've already been there and know my way."

Well, I can't just walk in there. That would be totally weird.

("Agreed. Damn. I need another look inside.")

How about this? Visiting hours are till eight. She's not going to sit

there for eight hours. *She'll need a cup of coffee or something to eat. I
saw a coffee shop downstairs. Why don't we set up watch there? When
she comes down, we go up.*

("Excellent idea.")

With her eyes fixed on the flyer, Daley strolled back to the
stairs. She settled herself at one of the tiny tables in the coffee
shop with a Diet Mountain Dew and a copy of *People*. Pard sat
opposite her, sans doctor getup.

I'm so out of it, she told Pard as she paged through the
magazine. *I don't know anyone in here. Wait, there's Taylor Swift—I
know her. And here's J-Lo. But who are all these other people?*

("Are you sure it isn't because you're reading indoors with
sunglasses.")

Quite sure.

("If you don't know them, I don't know them. I believe
they're called 'celebrities'—famous for being famous. You don't
watch enough reality TV.")

Because I can't stand reality TV. Consider my *reality for a minute.
Do I need to watch somebody else's?*

("Point taken.")

Daley pretended to read while she kept an eye on the
customers. She'd been at it a good hour before she spotted Mrs.
Blaine walking toward the shop.

That's her!

("Go-go-go!")

Daley kept the magazine as a prop as she quick-walked to
the stairwell and back up to the second floor. She made a beeline
for Timothy Blaine's room.

What about his roommate?

("According to my research, hospitals have been rooming
victims of the horrors together since they're all heavily sedated
and not very good company for anyone else.")

A nurse exited Blaine's room as they approached. She wore
blue scrubs and a surgical mask.

Why the mask, I wonder?

("A holdover from COVID, I guess. Besides, it's still flu
season.")

I wish I'd thought of a mask.

("Next time.")

Next time?

("Just get us into that room.")

Daley made a point of looking down at her magazine cover as the nurse passed, then turned into the room. Apparently the nurse had drawn a curtain between the two beds. The roommate was out cold and alone. A careful check showed no CCTV in the room.

Looks like everything's go.

("Then get us to the bed and hold his hand, just like the wife did.")

What if she comes back?

("Do it! Do it! Do it!")

Okay!

Daley hustled over to the window bed and grabbed Timothy Blaine's hand. An IV was running into his opposite forearm. His palm felt sweaty and the fingers trembled.

I thought he was supposed to be sedated.

("Maybe he's due for another dose and he's getting light.")

Well, hurry up, then. I don't want to be here when he comes out of it.

She remembered his piercing screams of terror when he collapsed in the street back in Nespodee Springs.

("All right—going in,") he said and disappeared.

Be quick.

She also didn't want to be here when the wife returned. The room faced south and afternoon sunlight flooded through the window, making her feel like she was standing in a spotlight. How would she explain standing here holding her husband's hand?

Timothy whimpered and twisted slightly under the covers as if he were trying to get away from something. Was that a result of the horrors or from whatever Pard was up to inside him?

And what *was* Pard up to?

The trembling is his hand increased. His whole body began to shake.

Pard...wherever you are...we need to get out of here before he starts screaming and brings people running.

His voice sounded faint. ("Hang on out there. I'm merged. I need just a little more time.")

Timothy was starting to writhe now.

Hurry!

His movements became more pronounced, almost violent. His features twisted into a tortured grimace.

Oh, crap, he's gonna scream!

And suddenly he froze in mid-spasm, as if he'd been hit with some sort of paralyzer ray.

What just happened?

Then, slowly, gradually, he began to relax. His knees and arms straightened and his features became almost placid.

Pard reappeared beside her. ("I think I accomplished something in there.")

Something good?

("Hope so. There's a pathway—")

He's opening his eyes. ·

Timothy Blaine stared at the ceiling but didn't seem aware. He looked dazed.

("He may be coming out of it.")

The sedation?

("No. The horrors. Or so I hope. Let's get out of here. If he's free, we don't want him to see you. And if he's not, we don't want to be here when the screaming starts.")

Daley released his hand and rushed toward the door, stopping at the threshold to gather herself. Needed to look calm and composed when she stepped back into the hall. Behind her she could swear she heard a sob.

What was that?

("A good sign, I think.")

Pretending to be interested in the cover of *People*, she made her way back to the elevator. No one was waiting and the door opened immediately when she pressed the button, so she stepped in, with Pard close behind.

What was that about a "pathway"?

("While I was exploring our friend Timothy I discovered he has a unique neural pathway from his pineal gland to his amygdala.")

Other people don't have it?

("I don't have enough experience with other people's brains to say that, but I do know you *don't* have it. The pineal gland has been called 'the Third Eye' in some religions, and the amygdala is where we perceive emotions—like fear. I believe the horrors are being fed through Timothy's pineal gland into his amygdala, triggering uncontrollable fear.")

Fed by who?

("'Whom.'")

Now? Really?

("Sorry. I can't help myself. But anyway, perhaps I should not have said 'being fed.' More like 'flowing' through his pineal into the amygdala via his unique neural pathway. If that pathway is the key, then anyone who has it is susceptible to the horrors.")

The elevator doors started to separate and so Daley again feigned interest in her magazine as she stepped out and headed for the main entrance.

And anyone—like me—who doesn't have it will be immune?

("That's my hypothesis. I tested it by blocking Timothy's pathway. We'll see what happens. If he comes out of it, then we may have found a cure for the horrors. That's the good news.")

There's bad news?

("Of course. Every yang has a yin. If we can indeed work the cure, we'll be the only ones who can. Which means you're going to become an instant national figure and the most in-demand human being in all of Southern California.")

She stopped dead as she stepped outside into the bright afternoon sunlight.

Well, I definitely don't want that. No way.

("But there are hundreds—maybe thousands of people suffering terribly.")

Yes, and more falling victim every day. It will take over my life... indefinitely.

("How do you say no?")

How do you say good-bye to the last shred of whatever passes for privacy these days?

("I repeat: How do you say no?")

Let's just wait and see if your fix worked. If not, this whole discussion is moot.

There—she'd gone and used "moot" again. Pard's effect on her vocabulary.

("Okay. We'll wait and see what happens.")

Good. I'm hungry.

("Our favorite In-N-Out is just a hop and a skip away.")

Her mouth started watering. *Say no more.*

14

Freshly showered, Karma Kendrick stood naked before the bathroom mirror. After a burger and fries at the Buckshot Deli and Diner, he'd walked around the corner and rented a room at the Niland Inn.

He gave one last look at his beard before picking up the knife. He'd taken it into the shower with him and washed off all the goddess's blood. Now the blade gleamed in the bathroom light. He grabbed a handful of beard and began sawing at it with the blade. Slowly, tuft by tuft, he reduced the bushy growth from a wheat field to a lawn. When he was as close to the skin as he dared, he lathered up and attacked it with the razor he'd picked up at the Soco mini-mart down the street.

After a final rinse off, he hardly recognized the face staring back at him from the mirror. The lower half was relatively pale where the beard had been. He couldn't remember the last time he'd seen his jaw.

The Karma beard was gone—and only fair that the goddess-killer blade had done most of the work. Yeah…Goddess Killer…a good name for that knife. But too long. He'd just call it "GK."

Yeah, Karma Kendrick gone, leaving Jeffrey Kendrick to deal with the world. Everything else remained the same on the outside—the bulging muscles, the tats. Couldn't do much about those. But he could change inside and become worthy of the goddess.

He looked longingly at the bed. He was bone tired but didn't deserve a soft mattress. Not yet. He had to earn it. Until he became worthy, his truck would be his home. Time to get dressed and back up to Slab City.

15

His father wasn't in his office, so Rhys went looking. He found him on the second floor, sipping a drink—bourbon, judging by the color—in the family room on the second floor. It sat above his father's first-floor office and sported a similar panoramic view of the valley. No TV, no music, just sitting and drinking and staring at the empty sky beyond the wide windows. He usually waited till after five. Rhys thought about mentioning it, but he had other topics he needed to discuss. And what the hell, the US markets had ended their trading day.

Clearly something was bothering him.

"Someone tried to hack our servers earlier," Rhys said.

He nodded without looking up. "I know. Garth called me. He said no worry. Our firewall is impenetrable."

Garth Mostyn acted as the clan's IT authority, and he knew his stuff.

"No firewall is impenetrable, Dad, but if Garth is confident it'll hold, that's good enough for me."

Now he looked up. "Anything else?"

"Yes. I went looking for Kendrick."

His father's face darkened. "I told you to stay away from that man. He's an ex-con."

"He's also our foreman. If he were just another worker, I wouldn't give it a second thought. But he runs things for us."

"No one is more aware of that than I, but—"

"I think he may be in trouble."

"Well, if he is, I'm sure it's his own doing." He frowned. "What sort of trouble?"

"His truck was last seen Saturday night, his mobile home was unlocked and empty, and he hasn't cashed last week's check."

"Why do you think that spells trouble? He's a ne'er-do-well who makes decent wages and has no family to support. I'm not surprised he's in no hurry to cash a check. If there's a red flag here, I'm not seeing it."

"The check tells me he was planning on coming back, and he hasn't."

"I don't understand this sudden concern over an ex-con."

And I don't understand all this push-back, Rhys thought.

"Very simple, Dad: If he's not coming back, we have to appoint a new foreman."

"Then appoint one. You're in charge of the solar array. Do what needs to be done to keep it cranking out the wattage."

"Fine. I'll do that." Now the dicey part. "Someone else was checking on Kendrick's whereabouts. His neighbor said a man in a Land Rover who looked like an older version of me come looking for him yesterday. That pretty well fits your description."

A pause, then, "Really...how old was this neighbor?"

"He was on in years, but—"

"I can assure you it wasn't me. I never left the Lodge after we returned from San Diego. I doubt anyone down in that mobile home village knows a Land Rover from a Jeep. And how an aging pair of eyes could draw a comparison between us in the dark is beyond me. Look elsewhere for your mystery man."

It had to be him, Rhys thought, but wasn't about to call his father a liar to his face.

Dad rose and headed toward the doorway. "I'm going to see if Maria can serve dinner early tonight. I'm tired."

Rhys stayed where he was. He turned and stared out the windows. Something his father had said...

And how an aging pair of eyes could draw a comparison between us in the dark is beyond me...

And then he realized: He'd never said what time of day it was. He'd said "yesterday." But the codger this morning had said the Land Rover was there *last night*.

Dad was flat-out lying. What was his connection to Karma Kendrick?

16

A ll Lucy's doctors say she's "on the spectrum."
    She never had a problem with that. Seemed perfectly
fine with it. Her brother Tom wished he could say the same. As
far as he was concerned, "on the spectrum" was a wastebasket
term the lazy bastards used for hard-to-classify disorders like
Lucy's, which was a clear case of Anti-Social Pain in Her Big
Brother's Ass.

Fuck 'em. Fuck 'em all.

When their folks died back in 2016, Tom was twenty-two,
just out of college, Lucy was eighteen and still going to her
special school. Suddenly they were the sole residents of their
Pasadena home. Lucy took it lots better than Tom, but then, the
real world had never affected her like most people. She didn't
feel things like most people. Tom had heard a number of her
psychologists mention "flat affect." But that wasn't true. She had
one emotion she could show pretty well: anger.

Tom, on the other hand, had wandered around in a shocked
daze for months after the accident. Consider: Your folks go out
to dinner with friends and never come back, all because some
drunk asshole in a pickup blows through a stop sign.

Lucy had just stayed online, where she tended to spend her
life. Never liked strangers, which covered pretty much everyone
except her brother, and Tom was pretty sure she wasn't too
crazy about him. It was mutual.

They were both of a generation that couldn't remember a
time when they didn't have easy access to some sort of computer.
Tom would admit he'd be lost without his iPhone, but Lucy *lived*
online. She had a powerful desktop and one of those laptops
with the detachable keyboards so she could sit or lie anywhere
and use it like a tablet. And when not into that, she was on her
phone. Not talking to another human being—God forbid. And
not on social media—she was totally asocial—just...exploring.

The million-dollar proceeds from his father's life insurance
policy had snapped Tom out of his daze. The will had left the
estate to him. He was in charge. He'd become the default man of

the house, which made him responsible for Lucy. The last thing he wanted.

The payout meant he and Lucy were set for the short term. But a million wasn't what it used to be, so the long term was looking a bit shaky. Because really, all their future income would rest on Tom's shoulders and what were the income prospects for an Art History major? Lucy couldn't be counted on to contribute a cent. Or so he'd thought.

He'd have been the first to admit he was floundering. Toward the end of that year Lucy lifted her head from her monitor and began to browbeat him into investing half of the insurance money in Bitcoins. Officially he was in charge, but she said since she was half the family, she deserved a say in half of what they owned. And rightly so, he guessed. She wasn't a minor.

He checked out Bitcoins and they'd been creeping up in value, so it seemed low risk with modest profit potential, but still he hesitated. Really...*half* their money? And what the fuck was a Bitcoin anyway? But Lucy said she understood them and wouldn't let up. Once she got a bug up her butt she was absofuckinglutely relentless. And Tom hadn't been in a good place mentally and emotionally, anyway, so just to shut her up he agreed and took the plunge, investing in 500 Bitcoins at $940 apiece. Their financial advisor—Dad's old accountant— screamed like a banshee, but he didn't have to live with Lucy.

Just a year later, when the price had spiked to over $16,000 apiece, Lucy said to get out. They missed the peak—something like $18K—but no matter. With eight million-plus in the account they were set for a good long term.

Tom wanted to celebrate the windfall. Lucy didn't see the point. She acknowledged it with a shrug.

"As long as we're imprisoned in these flesh traps, we might as well make the meat comfortable."

Here we go again, Tom thought.

Along about age twelve, much to the dismay of everyone who had to deal with her—which meant Mom, Dad, and her dear brother—Lucy came across a bunch of obscure online tracts and devoured them. She began referring to her body as "cursed flesh"—using the two-syllable pronunciation of "cursed"—along with other less savory epithets, and called her parents sinners for procreating. Not the most pleasant dinner conversation, as one might imagine. They all thought it just a phase, but it turned out his dear sister had discovered an extreme worldview and cradled it to her breast, as it were.

Anyway, the Bitcoin windfall allowed them to keep their folks' Pasadena McMansion and add a pool. Lucy was comfortable in the house and so was Tom. The place was rich with memories, at least for him. He kept his old room and gave Lucy the huge master suite.

Tom wished he could travel, though—see the country, the world. They had all this money but he was afraid to leave Lucy alone and they had no family to stay with her. She wouldn't consent to having a stranger in the house. He'd have to bring her along with him but she wouldn't leave the house if she thought she'd be among strangers. So he was stuck.

Around noon, Tom knocked on her bedroom door. He got no answer, but the *thwack!-thwack!-thwack!* from the other side told him what she was up to—probably with earbuds blasting K-pop. Yeah, she was way too old for K-pop and it was long past its peak, but Lucy was her own demographic. She liked what she liked, and when she liked something, she liked it a *lot*.

Like Miho. Way back when, she saw *Sin City*—on her TV, of course, since going out and sitting in a theater with other people was unthinkable—and became obsessed with the character. Tom didn't know Lucy's sexual orientation—she'd never dated anyone and, true to her anti-natalism, had vowed never to procreate—so he never figured out the attraction. Well, sure, he thought Miho was hot, and definitely cool too, but once the film was over, he pretty much forgot about her. Not Lucy.

Knowing she'd never hear his knock he pushed in and found her as he expected—dressed in a black kimono, her ponytail flying as she whirled and slashed away with a katana at the wooden karate practice post in the center of the room. She knew the post was not for sword practice but didn't care. She'd dyed her hair jet black and cut it—herself—into thick bangs down to her eyebrows. She had a good appetite and got no exercise other than her swordplay, so she'd grown a bit hefty. But she was clean. Had a thing about body odor and showered three times a day.

No one would mistake her for autistic. She'd look you in the eye and have a conversation when she wanted to. The thing was, she hardly ever wanted to. And the conversation had to be about something she was into, otherwise she shut down. Let her get started on some aspect of her *Weltanshauung* and she wouldn't shut up, though any sane listener quickly wished she would.

She had very little need of face-to-face human interaction. All her interactions took place online, usually in pursuit of her *obsession actuelle*. That meant life for Tom was pretty much like living alone. An exception occurred last month when the whole Internet crashed. Tom had been inconvenienced like everyone else, but Lucy damn near went 'round the bend. She cried, she ranted, she blamed Tom and demanded he fix it. Right, like he could wave a hand and accomplish what all the world's governments were scrambling to do. When it did go back up, she disappeared into her room again, leaving him with the realization that maybe living alone wasn't so bad.

Mostly they saw each other at meals. Neither of them cooked—although Tom wished she'd take it up because if she got into it she'd be fantastic—so they ordered in. Living in Pasadena as they did, absolutely everything was available in minutes via Grubhub and DoorDash and the like.

Tom stood in the doorway of her bedroom waving his arms until she noticed him. She sheathed the katana in the scabbard slung across her back and removed the earbuds.

"Tommy."

No smile, just the name he didn't like, spoken in her squeaky voice that never failed to set his teeth on edge.

As a kid he didn't mind being called that. As an adult he preferred Tom. An adult called Tommy should be in the mob. Like: *Yo, Tommay!*

But she'd called him "Tommy" as a child and never stopped. Lucy got a pass. Mostly because he couldn't change her anyway.

"You texted me?" he said.

God forbid she'd leave the room to come downstairs and tell him in person, even if it meant hearing her voice.

"Yeah. I found something really interesting."

Well, this was odd. He was sure she found something "really interesting" online every day but she never included him. He followed her to her desk computer where she dropped into the wheelie chair, wiggled the mouse, and watched the 36-inch monitor come to life. As usual, the desk was littered with numbered lists. He didn't bother reading them. She'd started making lists of everything—*everything*—as a kid and never stopped. He was sure one of those lists was a list of all her lists.

"I was looking for investment opportunities."

After her Bitcoin coup she'd added moneymaking to her obsession list, especially after she missed out on the insane Bitcoin run up in 2021. Whatever this was, Tom didn't want to hear it.

He said, "The T-bills are safe and—"

"—and they're marking time at best or losing ground to inflation. But I don't want to talk about money per se."

Okay, relief. "But you just said—"

"The investment search led me to the aforesaid interesting stuff. I found this private fund—exclusive to members of this Welsh clan living out in the desert—and it has an amazing track record in equities. They buy low and sell high and, somehow, they've managed to divest right before every major sell-off...as if they knew it was coming."

"Some people are good at that sort of thing—and I thought you said this wasn't about investments."

"Well, it is and it isn't. They're selling off now, but doing it slowly, like they don't want anyone to notice. They know something I don't know, Tommy."

"Maybe they do, but so what? We're not in the market so a big drop won't matter to us."

"*They know something I don't know, Tommy,*" she said with extra emphasis, sounding annoyed that she had to repeat it. "I don't like that. I want to know what they know. I want to know who was picking the stocks and what criteria were being used. I want to know why they're selling off."

"Again: So what? Who cares?"

"I care, Tommy. If the market's going to tank, we can cash in by selling short."

*Cash in…selling short…*all of a sudden she thought she was a hedge fund manager? But he wasn't going to get into this with her.

"So…find out. What's the problem?"

"It's all encrypted up the wazoo. Can you believe that?"

Her tone got all scandalized and how-dare-they? Like she couldn't believe anyone would want to keep anything from her.

Tom couldn't resist: "So, of course, you just moved on to other matters, right?"

She frowned. "You've *got* to be kidding. I was just barely interested until I ran into their firewall. I did a little poking and found out the family has its own server where everything's massively encrypted."

"What are they hiding?"

She jabbed a finger at me. "Exactly my thought. So, FYI, it's now my mission in life to break through their firewall."

Well, Tom knew if anyone could do it, Lucy was the one. The "O" in her OCD was italicized and bold-faced.

17

Rhys sat opposite his brother at their chess table. All was the same as usual—the darkened room, the single tensor lamp focused on the table—except no chessboard.

"Sorry to bother you like this but I've got some questions I need answered. I assume you were here in the house before our chess game last night."

Cadoc scribbled, then a note landed on the table.

*All day and
most of the night*

"'*Most* of the night'?"

*I went out for a wander
after our game*

"Oh...after." Rhys was disappointed. He'd been hoping he might have seen Dad arriving or leaving. "You don't happen to remember Dad leaving the house, do you? Before our game, that is?"

No
Why?

...still enough light left in the sky to see he coulda been an older version of you...

With that description of the sky, Kendrick's neighbor had pretty much placed the visit to Kendrick's place by the man in the Land Rover at shortly after Rhys and Daley had left for the restaurant. How convenient. With Mom in her perpetual tranqued-to-the-eyeballs state and Cadoc in his self-imposed exile at the rear of the Lodge, he could leave and return with no one the wiser.

"Dad said he didn't leave the Lodge at all after we returned from San Diego yesterday, yet I talked to a guy who said a man fitting his description was out looking for Karma Kendrick last night."

Maybe not Papa

Cadoc always called him "Papa."

"A guy who drives a Land Rover and looks like an 'older version' of me?"

That's Papa
He lies you know

"Yeah, I know. But why would he lie about seeing Kendrick?"

He lies a lot

Another note dropped.

Also unhinged

"Tell me about it. This Duad thing..."

Thoughts were colliding in Rhys's brain. Kendrick had a history of violence, and Dad thought Daley was a danger to the clan...

"I just had a horrible thought: Dad wants Daley gone. Would he try to use Kendrick to drive her out? Do you think that's a possibility?"

"...*esss.*"

"Aw, man, I don't want to think that. I just—" He froze. "Wait. Did I...did you...was that 'yes'?"

A pause, then a very soft, sibilant, "*Yesss.*"

Rhys leaped to his feet, almost knocking over the table.

"You can speak? When did this happen?"

"Ungh!"

Cadoc scribbled. Was "yes" all he could say? But even that was momentous.

> *Just now*
> *shocked self*

"Cad! This is fantastic! How did it happen? We've got to tell Dad! Mom too!"

> *No-no-no!*
> *Tell no one!*

"Why not?"

> *May not last*
> *Yes may be all*

"But-but-but how did this happen?" He was so happy for Cadoc he was sputtering.

> *Can't say*

"Can't say or won't say?"

"*Yesss.*"

"That's not an answer."

"*Yesss.*"

Need be alone now

As Cadoc began gathering up his notes, Rhys said, "Okay, I can understand that."

"*Yesss.*"

But he couldn't understand why his brother was being evasive about the explanation for this momentous breakthrough. Had it just happened? Or had he done something? Or had something been done to him? And it truly was momentous. For much of his childhood and all of his adolescence and adult life, Cadoc's vocal communication had been limited to monosyllabic grunts. Now...

"*Yesss.*"

Still monosyllabic, but a word...a real word.

"*Yesss...Yesss...Yesss...Yesss...*"

Cadoc kept repeating it. Was he afraid he'd lose it if he stopped? Or was it simply the sheer joy of being able to speak a word...a real word after so long?

"*Yesss...Yesss...Yesss...*"

Rhys closed the door and left his brother alone with his breakthrough.

("You might want to turn on the TV.")

Daley had been lying in bed, wondering what time it was. She could tell the sun wasn't up yet, but beyond that...

"That would require getting out of bed," she mumbled into her pillow, "and I'm not even ready to open my eyes yet."

("You'll want to see what's on the news—*all over* the news. Trust me.")

Since Pard couldn't walk to the front room and turn on the TV himself, where was he getting his info? She opened her eyes and saw him sitting on the edge of her bed.

"And you know this how?"

("Your phone. The news broke last night while I was reading up on neural pathways.")

She spotted her phone lying next to her pillow.

"Haven't I asked you—?"

("After my little sojourn in Timothy's brain yesterday, I needed to do research and we both know damn well the subject matter would bore you silly if you were conscious.")

"Yeah, but my eyes..."

Her eyes always burned after one of Pard's all-nighters.

("Fix your eyes on the TV.")

She checked her phone: 6:32.

"It's the middle of the night!"

("It's important.")

"It better be. Will I thank you later?"

("I can assure you you won't regret it.")

Groaning, she threw off the covers and stumbled from her

bedroom to the front room—only a few steps—and found the remote on the couch.

"What am I looking for?"

("Any news. Try that San Diego station.")

She found *News 8 This Morning* and saw a reporter with a microphone standing outside a lit-up building she immediately recognized as El Centro Regional Medical Center.

"—have any more information until the nine a.m. press conference when Doctor Alfred Milton, the chief of medicine, will answer questions. Right now we have nothing official, only what we've heard from staff, which might otherwise be attributed to rumor were it not for direct confirmation from the victim's wife. We know now that the victim's name is Timothy Blaine and here is the conversation my fellow reporter Jamie Robinson had with Mrs. Blaine earlier."

"Timothy Blaine?" Daley said, feeling a rush of excitement. "That's our guy!"

("I'm ready for your 'Thank-you' anytime you're ready to express it.")

"Hush, I want to hear this."

After a brief, somewhat awkward pause during which the live reporter stared mutely from the screen, the picture scrambled for an instant and then a woman reporter was standing by the hospital entrance speaking to a woman Daley recognized and Mrs. Blaine. Her eyes were wet and red and she'd obviously been crying. The sky was still light so this had to be sometime yesterday.

REPORTER: *—so as we understand it, your husband was struck down by the horrors on Saturday afternoon, is that correct?*

MRS. BLAINE (nodding): *Yes. We were visiting Nespodee Springs when all of a sudden Tim collapsed in the middle of the street and started screaming.* (dabs at her eyes with a tissue) *It was awful!*

REPORTER: *He was rushed here, correct?*

MRS. BLAINE: *Yes. Nespodee Springs doesn't have its own first aid squad so we had to wait for an ambulance from El Centro, but we finally got him here.*

REPORTER: *Where the doctors confirmed that he had the horrors, correct?*

MRS. BLAINE (sobs and dabs at eyes): *Yes! I thought I'd lost him! No one has ever come back from the horrors.*

REPORTER: *But we understand your husband did.*

MRS. BLAINE: *Yes! It's a miracle!*

REPORTER: *Tell us about it.*

MRS. BLAINE: *Well, I came here as soon as visiting hours started, just like I've done since he was admitted. You know, just to be with him and hold his hand and talk to him. I don't know if he could hear me but I just wanted him to know I was there for him and he wasn't alone.* (sobs)

REPORTER: *Take your time, Mrs. Blaine.*

MRS. BLAINE: *Well, after a couple of hours I needed a bathroom break and went down for a cup of coffee. When I got back…*(sobs)

REPORTER: *When you got back…?*

MRS. BLAINE: *When I got back he was sitting up in bed looking lost. When he saw me he said, "Where am I? How'd I get here?" It's a miracle! A miracle!*

REPORTER: *Do you have any idea what brought him out of it?*

MRS. BLAINE: *None at all. And neither does Tim. He vaguely remembers having what he calls "the worst nightmares ever" and being frightened out of his mind, but he didn't realize he'd had the horrors until I told him.*

REPORTER: *Did he receive any different treatment?*

MRS. BLAINE (shrugs): *The doctors say they were giving him the same sedation as everybody else.*

REPORTER: *Did you give him anything? An old family remedy or the like?*

MRS. BLAINE: *Absolutely not. Anyway, he wasn't swallowing anything. Everything went through his IV.*

REPORTER: *Do his doctors have any explanation for it?*

MRS. BLAINE: *They're baffled because, like I said, he had the same treatment as the others. They won't say it's a miracle, but that's what it is. Oh, look, I've got to get back to him. He wants to go home and he can't leave yet.*

REPORTER: *Yes, of course. Thank you so much, Mrs. Blaine.* (turns to camera) *And there you have it. Timothy Blaine is the first confirmed case of the horrors to recover. We've tried to get opinions from the medical staff but so far they're not commenting.*

As the image returned to the original reporter, Daley hit the *MUTE* button.

"It worked! Whatever you did, he's back to normal." A white lab coat suddenly replaced Pard's flannel shirt and he was back to Dr. Pard from yesterday, with the addition of a pair of tortoise-shell eyeglasses. ("But can I do it again? My hypothesis needs more experimental data before I can call it a theory. I must return to the field.")

"Let's wait and see what the real doctors say."

("Agreed, but eventually I do want to go back and investigate some other patients.")

Daley wasn't crazy about that.

"Well..."

("I'm sensing some hesitance. Perhaps maybe even a little anxiety?")

"Maybe more than a little. I don't want to get caught sneaking around the hospital. I especially don't want to be presented to the world as the cure for the horrors."

("But I thought this was what Healerina was all about— starting on the road to becoming a recognized healer.")

"Yeah, well, sometimes the thing you want most in life can look totally wonderful in the abstract but change to something totally terrifying when it becomes a real possibility that you're going to be forced to deal with on a day-to-day basis."

("I seem to remember it was just a few weeks ago when you said, 'I see us on network TV with worldwide syndication.' Remember?")

"That was before I had a small mob outside my door that made me a prisoner in my own apartment." She held up her golden-skinned left hand. "I lost a hand because of that mob. I'd have been maimed for life if you hadn't been able to grow me a new one. All because of just two healings in that little medical arts building. Think of the mob outside Healerina if I'm revealed as the only person who can conquer the horrors." She shuddered at the thought.

("We had this discussion yesterday. We don't need to rehash it now. I'll just sum up my position by quoting Winston Churchill: Where there is great power there is great responsibility.")

"I thought that was from Spider-Man."

His expression turned annoyed. ("Must you? Must you?")

"No, seriously. I really did. But anyway, I get it. I get it. You need to find out if you can do it again."

("Reproducibility is key to establishing a theory.")

"Please don't get all sciencey on me. It's too early in the morning and I haven't had my coffee yet. We'll go back, but not today, okay? We need to let things settle down over there before we stir them up again."

("I agree.")

"But I'm going to need a new look. I don't think the lady with the big hat and sunglasses should show up again."

("You have another look in mind?")

"I do. I just need to find a place to sell it to me."

19

Rhys ambled into Elis's office and dropped into a chair. Elis swiveled his own chair to face him. His son looked wound up, distracted. Something was on his mind. Elis had a pretty good idea what.

He'd lied to Rhys about being at Kendrick's place Sunday night. A transparent lie, considering the accurate description from Kendrick's neighbor. But he had no plausible excuse. What could he say? *I was wondering why he hadn't killed your girlfriend like I hired him to do?*

So things had devolved into a situation of, *I lied; you know that I lied; I know that you know that I lied, and let's just leave it at that.*

"What's up?" Elis said.

"Kendrick didn't show up again today. I think we're going to need another foreman."

Elis knew that was a waste of time. When the Visitors returned at the equinox—just ten days away now—everything would change and the clan would no longer need the solar array running at peak efficiency. But maybe searching for a replacement would distract Rhys.

"Do you have any prospects in mind?"

Rhys shook his head. "Not particularly. Benny Mendoza's

gone missing for two days as well."

"And who, might I ask, is Benny Mendoza?"

"Just a solar laborer I did some checking. He and Kendrick used to hang out at the Thirsty Cactus. Benny's car is still at his place. I'm wondering if the two of them drove off in Kendrick's truck Saturday night and something happened to them."

When Kendrick had agreed to make the Duad disappear, he'd said he needed to get someone else involved.

...I might need a little help...This gal won't go quiet. Might involve some getting rough...

Elis hadn't wanted to know the details, but now he wondered if that someone else had been this Benny Mendoza. If so, that cast doubt on Elis's theory that Kendrick had run off with the money, which had already been doubtful, considering the uncashed paycheck he'd left behind.

But if he did take Benny along to dispose of the Duad, that meant *two* men had gone after her and now both were missing.

Who *was* this woman?

He forced a smile. "You seem to like playing detective. When do you don the deerstalker hat?"

"The what?"

"Sherlock Holmes wore one."

"Not funny, Dad. This is all a major annoyance. By the way, what did the star-scan analysis say today?"

"To keep divesting."

"Are we on schedule?"

"Absolutely. We will be completely liquid by the end of the week."

"That's a lot of cash."

"Yes. A *lot*. We'll start buying gold and silver next Monday."

Rhys blinked as if unsure he'd heard correctly. "You mean mining stocks?"

"No. Gold and silver—hard assets."

A baffled look. "Why?"

The honest answer was *I don't know.*

The Void Scrolls, the source of all Elis's knowledge about the Visitors, explained that when gravitational and celestial forces were in the proper alignment, a path could be opened through the Void to allow the Visitors to return. Those who opened the path—in this case, the Pendry clan—would be rewarded. Those forces would be properly aligned in ten days. All this was made perfectly clear in the Scrolls. What was not clear was how much of an effect the Visitors would have on life as humanity presently knew it.

Elis believed the effect would be profound. And now the stars were telling him to flee equities. That told Elis that the Visitors would actually come through this time. Their arrival would panic the markets, causing a catastrophic meltdown. Normally, cash was the place to be during a meltdown.

But...

But what if the societal effect was so catastrophic that governments collapsed? Currencies were the products of governments. Without a government to back it, a currency stops being a medium of exchange and is reduced to slips of paper adorned with the images of dead politicians, handy in the outhouse but of little value anywhere else.

Ah, but gold has always been a medium of exchange. Silver too. So, just to be safe, just to make sure the Pendry clan occupied the catbird seat, Elis was going to move the cash into those two precious metals.

But how could he tell Rhys that? How could he say, even though he didn't know for sure, even though he had no proof, that he feared currency might become worthless? The poor boy would think his father had gone totally mad. So that engendered another lie.

"Why? Because the stars tell me to, and they've yet to steer me wrong."

Rhys stared at him a moment, then shrugged. "I can't argue with that."

No, he couldn't. The fund's track record was impeccable.

"Is there anything else?"

"Garth says someone is still trying to crack our firewall. Says they're very determined, but it's holding up."

"Can't he find out who it is?"

"He's trying but they're going through anonymizers."

"Why us? We're hiding nothing of value on the server."

"Could be a hedge fund or the like looking to steal the secrets of your success."

"Won't do them much good. That's all in the Scrolls, which are heavily encrypted. And no one outside the clan knows we even have the Scrolls."

Rhys looked like he wanted to say something else—was *dying* to say something else—but was holding back.

"That's all?" Elis said.

He rose. "That's it."

"No new message at the end of the scan analysis?"

He shook his head. "Still '*The Duad must cease.*'" He waved and headed for the door. "Later."

The Duad must cease...

The words had an imperative cast, but really...cease what? Living? Elis had sent Kendrick to accomplish just that, yet she persisted. Maybe it meant cease nosing around. The message had appeared after she'd seen the film—or at least Elis assumed she'd seen it. All evidence pointed to Cadoc betraying the entire clan by bringing her into the Lodge and showing it to her. But where was the threat there? Even if she believed the film's scenario had a possibility of becoming reality, she'd yet to speak of it to anyone. Hadn't gone running to the media—hadn't even told Rhys about it, from what Elis could gather. She acted as if she'd never seen it.

What was her game? Did she know the Visitors would be returning with the equinox? If so, she didn't learn it from Rhys. Elis had been feeding him and everyone else—including the Elders—disinformation about the date, telling them the proper alignments would coincide with the solstice. He would spring it on them at the last moment.

"Oh, did you hear?" Rhys said, ducking his head back through the door. "One of the horrors victims has come out of it. First one ever—right down there in El Centro."

"Glad to hear it," Elis said. "Does that mean they have a cure?"

"Nah. They're as clueless as ever." And then he was gone again.

The horrors...Elis couldn't help but think the mysterious

malady was somehow connected to the impending return of the Visitors. But how? Were the Visitors, for some arcane purpose, reaching across the Void and through the Veil to beam these horrors into their minds? Or were the victims somehow sensitive to what was coming?

Elis much preferred the former explanation to the latter.

20

Karma jumped at the rap on his pickup's passenger window. He levered up from where he'd been lying on the front seat and looked around. The skinny Willie Nelson wannabe from yesterday stood outside the door.

What was this fucking weasel-faced rat bastard thinking, sneaking up on him like that? This'd be the first and last time he'd ever do that because Karma Kendrick was gonna tear him a brand new—

Wait-wait-wait. That was the old Karma. He was going to bury the old Karma and become someone else, someone the goddess might allow back in her presence. And that meant shedding the old name...scraping it off like an old snakeskin. He was "Jeffrey" now.

"Rise 'n' shine, big guy," the old coot said. "Hey, didn't you have a beard yesterday?"

"What's it to ya?"

"Don't make no nevermind to me." He held up a travel mug. "Made a pot of coffee. Want some?"

Well, that put a different face on it, now, didn't it. See? Already the new him was getting rewards.

He slid out from behind the wheel and came around the front of the truck.

"You oughta be more careful comin' up on people like that."

"Well," the coot said as he handed him the cup, "with the sun up and all, I figured you'd be awake. That's high octane, by the way."

"Can't make it too strong for me." He took a sip. Damn, that was *real* strong. "You the Slab City coffee man or something?"

"Just being neighborly. You picked a slab right next to mine."

He jerked a thumb over his shoulder at the small camper trailer behind him. It sported a couple of solar panels on its roof; a hibachi and some aluminum porch chairs sat out front. "We're neighbors."

After leaving the Niland Inn yesterday, Jeffrey had driven around Slab City until he found this empty slab and parked on it. He'd been wiped out so he'd stretched out on the front seat and conked out. Wasn't the first time he'd spent a night in his truck, and it sure as hell didn't look like it would be the last. The old Karma would have loved to have snuck back to his double-wide, but wouldn't have dared. The goddess would be watching...he just knew she'd be watching. Jeffrey, on the other hand, knew he belonged out here.

"I'm solar powered," the coot was saying. "Got more than I need, so if you ever want to charge your phone or anything, feel free to come over and plug in."

Jeffrey was trying to figure this guy's angle. What did he get out of it? Maybe he was just one of those do-gooders. A peace, love, and share-the-world geek. Whatever, his coffee was good.

"Don't get too used to me."

"Why? Figuring on movin' on?"

"Ain't decided yet."

"Ain't a bad place," he said, looking around. "Allows me to stretch my Social Security check like nowheres else. And there's something to be said for livin' in the desert...a kind of spiritual cleansing takes place once you get away from the noise of other people. All the prophets of old used to go to the desert to find clarity and purification."

...spiritual cleansing...purification...

Just what he'd come for.

The coot stuck out his hand. "I'm Jimmy Fries, by the way. You?"

He almost said *Karma.*

"Jeffrey...I go by Jeffrey."

*Cleansing...*Jeffrey thought as they shook hands. *The purification begins.*

21

The press conference at ECRMC was delayed and didn't get rolling until nine twenty. All the local stations broke into their regular programming to carry it, with Fox News and CNN on board as well. Daley settled herself front and center before her TV screen when the medical center's chief of medicine, Dr. Milton, read a statement, then started taking questions.

All the blather boiled down to *We're as baffled as you are.* Dr. Milton categorized Timothy Blaine's recovery as "spontaneous remission." When asked to elaborate on that, Daley found his explanation intriguing:

"As we immerse ourselves in the mechanisms of disease and the interventions we can use to combat it, we tend to forget that the human body has a tremendous capacity to heal itself."

"Well, if that doesn't sound like a plug for Healerina, I don't know what does."

("But we both well know that Timothy Blaine did not heal himself.")

"Of course, but that's the exact line I've been peddling downstairs. You're providing the actual cure while I'm deflecting credit by giving them palm stones and pushing them to think their body is healing itself."

("A perfect partnership: I'm in charge of cures and you're in charge of mumbo-jumbo.")

"Right. But that's why this curing-the-horrors thing has me on edge. I can't say, 'Just get out of the way and let your body heal itself,' and then days later they're cured. I've got to be right there with my hands on the patient when the cure goes down. And suddenly I'm a miracle worker. Or, à la the Pendry clan, a witch."

("We'll figure out something.")

"Let's hope so. Now it's time to get downstairs and open Healerina."

The new front window was spotless, and the glazier had even rehung the *Healerina* banner front and center. The daylight through the window lit up the crystals and the geodes and the rest of the New Age junk.

"This is great," she said, spreading her arms as she walked in. "It doesn't look like a dungeon anymore."

"Talking to yourself again?"

Daley turned to find Juana, bib denim overalls and all, standing in the doorway. This was the second time she'd caught her talking aloud to Pard. But she and Juana had something else to deal with right now.

"You!" Daley said, charging her. "I've got a bone to pick with you!"

Juana stood her ground. "Yes?"

("She doesn't look terribly surprised,") Pard said.

The old Cahuilla woman had probably spoken to her sisters by now and they would have told her that her phony story had been outed, so she'd been no doubt expecting a little confrontation.

No matter. Daley needed to get this off her chest.

"I saw your sisters on Saturday and they told me your mother's been dead for a long time."

"This is true."

"So that story about her being in the hospital with the horrors was all bullshit."

"Obviously."

"Which means you were stalking me."

"I prefer to think of it as watching out for you...doing my duty."

"To 'help and guide' me, right?"

"Right."

Her calm expression and matter-of-fact tone were derailing Daley's intended rant about being straight with each other.

"You could have told me what you were up to."

"You would have thought I was a stalker and told me to get lost. I needed to keep watch and put you on the right path."

"Path to where? Nespodee Springs?"

Juana waved her arms around. "Is it so bad?"

Daley glanced at Pard who'd assumed his position on the front window shelf like a bookstore cat waiting for a ray of sunlight.

Where do I go from here with her?

("Maybe it's time to start demanding answers to the tough questions.")

Past time. Here goes.

"Okay, Juana. Time to come clean. You told me I was struck down by an alaret in that cave and how nine hundred and ninety-nine out of a thousand victims die, but I didn't. It turned a patch of my hair dead white. Blah-blah-blah. But there's a bigger picture, isn't there? You don't camp out there by that cave just for the hell of it. No one else has ever heard of an alaret—you can't find the word anywhere. So what's going on, Juana? I want to know what *you* know—everything."

Juana closed the door behind her, saying, "No one else needs to hear this." Then she shrugged. "I don't know everything. I don't think *anyone* knows everything."

Pard said, ("Ask her about me. Press her about alarets.")

Must it always be about you?

("We're in this situation because of me.")

Daley couldn't argue with that.

She said, "Okay, then let's stick with what *you* know. Like alarets. What the hell is an alaret? Where did they come from?"

"They're from the gods."

("Divine origin!") A halo suddenly glowed above his head. ("Knew it.")

Be careful what you wish for.

"And just what gods would those be?"

"The gods who dwelled in the ancient ocean. They departed when the ocean dried up and they left the alarets behind."

"But *why* did they leave them behind? To hang out in caves and drop on a poor unsuspecting girl's head. Or were they just litter?"

("Now *that's* hurtful.")

Sorry. It was just too easy. But what she's saying dovetails with the film Note Man showed us. You're related to the Visitors, which makes you...an alien.

She had an alien living in her brain. She'd gotten used to Pard—grown fond of him, to be honest—but when she put it like that...

"I don't know," Juana was saying. "The fables don't tell. But they say anyone who survives an alaret is very special."

"What fables?"

"We have traditional fables in my family—not true Cahuilla tribal fables, but specific to my family, and somehow related to our dwelling for so many generations in what used to be the bottom of a sea." She looked into Daley's eyes. "Your coming was foretold."

"You're talking about that Cahuilla art stone—the one with the drawing that looked like me?"

Juana had shown Daley the stone just before she'd opened Healerina: a drawing of a crude, vaguely androgynous face framed by black braids. Daley might have written it off as typical native stone art except for the white patch in the hair at the top of its head.

"It's not just the image. The story that goes with it tells of a wondrous healer."

That struck a little too close to home.

"A healer, huh? Is that why you pushed me to get out of LA and come here to open this place?"

"As I recall, I did not bring up healing. I saved you from a bunch of ladies who thought you could cure their ills. And then the matter of your hand…you told me then that the yellow color was left over from your injury. But as I watched and waited in the hospital after your accident, word was out that your 'injury' was so severe they couldn't save your hand…had to amputate…and yet…" She pointed to Daley's golden left hand. "There is it."

Daley raised it and rotated it back and forth.

What do I say…?

("You could tell her the report of your hand's death has been greatly exaggerated.")

Yeah, probably best. I don't see any other options.

("You could try the truth.")

Nah.

"You should know by now, Juana, that you can't believe everything you hear."

"What I do know is that it was foretold that a healer will come to us in a time of need." She pointed again to Daley's hand.

"You healed yourself when you had to, and now you must meet your destiny of healing others."

Destiny...now there's one scary word.

("Don't let her sidetrack you with generalities. Stay on topic.")

"But why am I *here*, Juana?"

"You told me you wanted to try healing. And so I suggested Nespodee Springs."

("There's got to be more to it than that,") Pard said. ("I get the feeling she's holding back.")

That makes two of us.

"But *why* Nespodee Springs, Juana?"

She shrugged again. "It's small, out of the way—"

"No-no-no," Daley said, wagging her finger. "That's not going to fly anymore. This looks like just another desert town built around a hot spring, but it's more than that, isn't it. There's a lot more going on here than meets the eye, isn't there. I mean, this place is a freaking mishmash of cross-currents."

("You're mixing metaphors.")

And you're interrupting.

Juana said, "But—"

"No buts. The Pendrys are rich and crazy as loons—'away with the fairies' as my Gram likes to say. Rhys is okay but the rest? They dress like Mennonites or whatever and they home school everybody and they tell their kids I'm a witch and to stay away from me. Well, that's fine with me, but you've got to admit it's really, really weird."

("Actually, only the Pendry women have a Mennonite look. The men—")

Zip it. I'm on a roll here.

"And the Tadhaks? The whole family lives behind a ten-foot wall of rock-hard mocha whipped cream and none of them are ever seen close up except for Jason, because when they're trundled back and forth to work at the family windfarm they're hidden away inside that creepy white bus with its super-tinted windows. Does anyone know for sure if there's really anyone on that bus?

"And as long as we're on the subject of the windfarm, we've

got one family harvesting the wind and the other family with a huge solar array. What's with this fixation on electricity? Between the Pendrys and Tadhaks, they could light up San Diego."

("Well, actually that's not—")

Zip!

"And then there's the Pendry's Tesla tower. It's a couple hundred feet above ground and anchored hundreds of feet into the Earth and they funnel all sorts of electricity into it for huge light shows. I mean really, what's going on here? Oh, and on the subject of *'going on,'* what's going on between you and Jason? You two seem to have an awfully cozy relationship. Something going on there I should know about? Why am I here, Juana? Why did you choose this place out of all the small towns in Southern California? *Why the hell am I in Nespodee fucking Springs?"*

Daley stopped to take a breath. She'd worked herself up a little more than she'd realized.

"Very well," Juana said softly. "I don't know how you'll take this, but Nespodee Springs has long been known to us as a place of power."

"Those are just words, Juana. 'Power'? What kind of power? What does that *mean?"*

"I wish I knew. There's a tradition that some lines of magic converge here—not as many as in the Salton Sea, but enough to matter. The Salton is too strong. Here is better"

"'*Lines of magic'*? What if I don't believe in magic?"

Another of Juana's shrugs. "It might mean something else. The tradition has come down through the generations and that's the word that came down to me."

("Her 'magic' lines could be analogous to ley lines.")

Ley lines...why does that sound familiar?

("I came across them in my late-night reading. It's a New Agey belief that an energy grid encircles the globe, linking historic and supposedly sacred sites like Stonehenge, the Egyptian and Mayan pyramids, Native burial mounds in North America, and so on. Pure poppycock, of course. But I sense Juana believes her statement about lines of magic.")

"Okay," she said to Juana. "Doesn't matter what I believe.

You're saying that you brought me to Nespodee Springs because these lines of magic converge here. Is that right?"

"Jason thought it would be a good place for you to gain power."

"Jason? Okay, now we're getting somewhere. How does Jason Tadhak get involved in my life?"

Juana sighed. "It's a long story."

Daley folded her arms and leaned back against a display counter. "I've got time."

"The Tadhak family has lived in the valley as long as anyone can remember and have always had a good relationship with my people. Jason's father was there to help after the 1940 quake damaged what little infrastructure exists at the Torres-Martinez Cahuilla reservation. I wasn't alive then, but I was around for the quakes in 1968 and '79 and '81, and the two last month, of course."

"Help? You mean financially? Where does he get his money? Not from rentals in Nespodee Springs, I'm sure."

"Batteries. The Tadak family makes dry-cell batteries for all the major companies, and have patents on energy storage technology. They're quite wealthy, I'm told. They supplied us with hundreds of free batteries when our power was down. During his involvement, Jason became familiar with my family and its fables. When I told him that I thought the healer we have waited for might have come, he said to bring you here and he would take care of you."

"Take care of me? I'm not so sure I like the sound of that."

Juana gestured around. "You have a place to display your wares—and yourself, do you not? You have a place to live. You have made friends."

And enemies, as well, she thought.

"You even have a lover," Juana added.

"Oh, hell. Does everybody know about that? I mean, it was one night."

"My point is: Life had been good to you since you came to Nespodee Springs, hasn't it?"

Obviously she doesn't know about Karma Kendrick.

("Obviously. But I'm a little concerned about your being

identified with this messianic prophesy. Events tend not to work out well for messiahs.")

Well, I've already been murdered. I figure it's got to be all uphill from there.

("Don't be so sure.")

Now who's Little Miss Sunshine?

"Yes, Juana, I have to admit I like the place."

"Then why are you so angry at me?"

"I'm not angry. I know you only meant well. I just don't like being lied to."

("Yes. *You* prefer to do the lying.")

Exactly.

But she wasn't through with Juana.

"A minute ago you said Jason thinks Nespodee Springs is a good place for me to 'gain power.' What does that mean?"

"Jason believes in the ancient tales of converging lines of magic. Or at least he says he does. He thought this was a place where you could come into your own and hone your healing powers."

"Who says I have healing powers?"

Juana's look became reproachful. "You know you do. I know you do. Those women in LA know you do. Deputy Alvarez is convinced you do. You may want to deny it to others, but don't deny it to me."

What do I say here?

("Well, as she says, it seems futile to deny it to her. She knows too much.")

But I can minimize it.

"It's not as magical as you might think, Juana. I can do certain things but there's lots of limitations."

Juana nodded. "Okay. I can see how that would be true. Which brings me to why I came today. I assume you've heard about the cure in El Centro yesterday."

Uh-oh.

"The horrors victim? Sure, who hasn't?"

"I know Monday is your day off. Were you in the medical center yesterday? Did you cure that man?"

("You can't say 'yes.' Not yet.")

I know.

"I'm going to put it to you this way, Juana: I am honestly not sure yet if I can cure the horrors."

She stared at Daley for a long time, then gave a slow nod. "Very well. I accept that. When will you be sure, if ever?"

The answer seemed important to her. Maybe some members of her tribe had been struck down.

"Within the next few days, I hope."

"That is good." She opened the door. "I need to get back to my people now. I will be watching."

Daley had to laugh. "Oh, I've no doubt of that."

22

Rhys stopped by Cadoc's room on his way to bed.

He'd spent the day shuttling back and forth between the Lodge and the solar array. With no foreman, somebody had to oversee the crew and make sure the power inverters maintained their AC output.

Goddam, he was beat. He blamed it more on stress than physical exertion, although he was the first to admit he was woefully out of shape. Whatever, he was hitting the hay early tonight.

He'd called Daley earlier to touch base to explain how he'd be tied up for the next few days until he found a replacement for Kendrick and she'd been okay with that. Maybe too okay for his liking, but she explained that she was working on a project of her own, though she'd been cagey when he pressed for details. She said she'd tell him all about it when she'd wrapped up it up.

But before he got some rack time, he wanted to check on his big brother.

The door opened two inches in response to his knock. All was dark in the room and the hall was fairly dim as well, so he saw nothing.

"Got a minute, Cad?"

The door opened wider and Rhys slipped through. It closed behind him, leaving him in total darkness. No problem. He was used to this.

"I didn't want to ask out in the hall because you said to tell
no one, but how's the voice? Still working?"

"*Yesss.*"

"Great! You've been exercising it?"

"*Yesss.*"

"And you still don't want me to say anything?"

"*No-no-no!*"

"Hey, that's two words now. I'm so happy for you, Cad. I
can't tell you how good this makes me feel."

The invisible hand that squeezed his shoulder in the
darkness said more than any words ever could.

23

"That's the place," Daley said as she stared at her laptop
screen. "Bracco Medical Equipment."

("It's down in Calexico,") Pard said. ("There's got to be
someplace in El Centro that sells surgical scrubs.")

"Don't want El Centro. Don't want to leave any trail to trace
me."

("Speaking of traces, do I detect a trace of paranoia? That's
my department. Anyway, we're not planning to rob a bank,
we're simply going to walk into a hospital.")

"Not just 'walk in.' I'm going to be impersonating a member
of the staff. Do you know the kind of grief coming down on me
if I get caught, what with all this paranoia about opioids and
such? What's my explanation? 'Oh, I just popped in to cure a
few horrors patients.' Yeah, that'll fly."

("Point taken. I just—") A knock on her door interrupted
him. ("Three guesses who that is.")

*It's been forty-eight hours since you did your thing. Do you
think...?*

("Only one way to find out.")

Daley shut off her laptop and hurried to the kitchen where a
note awaited on the floor inside the door.

Can I come in?

"Sure. You want the lights out again?"

Please

She doused the front room lights, followed by the kitchen overhead—the moon was waning so there wasn't as much wash as before.

"I think I'm going to need a flashlight to read your notes."

With Pard leaning against the sink counter as he had before, she retrieved her keychain with its mini Maglite from the hook on the wall, then pulled the door open. A hoodied figure stepped in and went straight to the kitchen table but didn't sit.

"How are you doing?"

"Betterrr."

The word was soft, rough, faint, but definitely a word

"Ohmygod! Ohmygod, you spoke! You can speak?"

Daley's throat tightened.

"Very little, but…" And then he sobbed. *"But…yesss."*

He'd sobbed once Sunday night too, but that had been full of anguish. This sound was full of hope. Daley tried to hold back a sob of her own but it broke free.

"Oh, God, that's wonderful!"

("We did it, Daley,") Pard said softly. ("He's on his way.")

Note Man started scribbling. Daley lit up the note.

You sound surprised

"I…I'm still new at this. Shouldn't you keep using your voice?"

Hurts
Then fades out

A new note…

But better
than yesterday

...quickly followed by another.

And still better
Tomorrow

"That's the spirit!"

She bit her lip to keep herself from breaking down and totally bawling. To do this for someone, to...to change their life for the better like this...it felt so damn *good*.

Another note.

Give me flash?
Show you something?

"Sure."

She laid it on the table; he did something with his sleeve, then picked up the light and turned it on, illuminating his forearm. His skin looked like it had felt to her when she'd taken his hands Sunday night: like peeling tree bark. But there in the crook of his elbow...a clear patch. She reached out and touched it with a fingertip.

"This is new?"

"Yesss."

"That's just super."

"It continues?"

What do I tell him?

("Tell him yes. But as I said on Sunday, I might need to go back in for a second round to clean up.")

"It should continue clearing but I may have to give you a second treatment to finish the job."

Another sob as he handed her the light.

"Owe you. Whatever you want."

"You mean money?" She shook her head. "Oh, no, your money's no good here. I want to see the rest of that film. That's my fee: Part Deux."

"Working on—" His voice cracked and he started scribbling again.

Working on it
Need 1-2 days

"Okay," Daley said. "I'm going to trust you."

Have wonders to show you

"What wonders?"
Two notes fell in rapid succession.

Must prepare the way
Be ready to walk
Thursday night

"Thursday night? Are you asking me out on a date?"

"Date?"
How old are you?

("He's got a point.")
I blame the old Irish lady who raised me through high school.
"Ancient, I guess. You should know a woman never tells her age."
The next note hit her like a punch in the gut.

Never been on a "date"

Daley's throat tightened again. Damn! What was happening to her?
She swallowed and said, "Well, it's about time you went. Thursday night. It's a *date*."

See you then

He gathered up his notes but paused as he opened the door.
"Good night."
And then he was gone.
("'Have wonders to show you'…sounds interesting.")

"But he said I should be ready to walk. That means the wonders are close by. I can't think of anything even remotely 'wonderful' in Nespodee Springs."

("Except for me.")

"Riiiiight."

WEDNESDAY—March 11

24

"How do I look?" Daley said, checking herself in the rearview mirror.

("You may perceive me here in the passenger seat,") Pard said in his Do-I-have-to-explain-this-again? tone, ("but I'm really in your head and can see only what you're looking at.")

"Okay, I know that. But I see you sitting there and the question pops out."

She'd driven down to Calexico early so she could enter the surgical supply shop as soon as it opened. She remembered the nurse she'd seen in the hospital hallway on Monday had worn dark-blue scrubs so she bought herself a set in the closest matching blue they had. Then she added a surgical mask and a flowered surgical scrub hat. She found a Dollar Tree just up the street where she bought a pair of glasses with the thickest rims and the weakest lenses available, and added a plastic clipboard as her pièce de résistance.

She'd changed in a Calexico McDonald's, then drove to El Centro. She parked in ECRMC's visitor's lot where she tucked all her hair up inside the surgical scrub cap.

("Make sure you cover your ears as well,") Pard said.

Daley pulled the cap lower and checked the result. "That looks dumb."

("I've read that ear biometrics surpass facial features when it comes to identifying people. Not that I believe you'll ever be the subject of facial-recognition software, but—")

"And you were calling *me* paranoid yesterday?"

("I always say: Anything worth doing is worth doing well.")

"You don't always say that. In fact you've never said that."

("Well, I'm saying it now.")

Daley left her ears covered, then tied the surgical mask around her neck so it dangled between her breasts.

("Once you put on those awful glasses I think we can safely assume that you'll have erased the Daley we know and love, and adopted an entirely new persona.")

"Let's hope so."

("I sense your anxiety.")

"Well...it's a small hospital. Like a hundred beds or so. All the staff will know one another."

("Like any hospital, it's got multiple shifts. Nobody can know everybody. Let's go. Get in, get out, get home.")

"I'm all for that."

Pard winked out as she grabbed her clipboard and put on her glasses. The lenses were weak enough that they didn't affect her depth perception and made the world look only slightly distorted. She pulled out a pen as she quick-walked to and through the emergency exit with her head down, jotting some random squiggles on the paper on her clipboard. She continued straight down the hall toward the surgery section but took the stairs up just before she reached it.

She tied the surgical mask over her face on the stairs and emerged onto the second-floor hallway with her head down, still studying the clipboard. She passed two nurse's aides along the way to Timothy Blaine's old room but they were both staring at their phones and didn't even register her.

In Blaine's former room she spotted another unconscious male in his bed. Since horrors patients didn't get meals and visiting hours didn't start till noon, she was the only conscious occupant. Daley stepped between the beds and went to the closest. A very dark-skinned Hispanic man lay flat on his back, hooked up to an IV and a heart monitor. She pulled the curtain to shield her from the door.

("Quick now. Grab his hand.")

How do we know these are horrors patients?

("They keep them together and I recognize this guy. He was Blaine's roommate on Monday.")

Daley wrapped her fingers around his wrist. If anyone spotted her, she hoped they'd think she was taking his pulse, although why she'd bother with that when the monitor screen was displaying his heart rate as it registered his EKG.

Okay. Quick now.

("If he's anything like Blaine, I know exactly where I'm going in there.")

Daley maintained her grip. She could feel her palm moistening against the patient's skin as she stood and listened for the sound of approaching footsteps. With most of the staff wearing sneakers, she doubted she'd hear a thing until someone stepped into the room, which only increased her anxiety.

After a couple of forevers, Pard's head popped out of the guy's chest, startling her.

("Okay, I'm out. Quick to the next.")

Jesus, don't do that! What's the matter with you?

He reappeared on the other side of the bed. ("I know you enjoyed *Alien* so—")

So you thought you'd pop out of this guy's chest?

("Well...")

Alien scared the crap out of me and you nearly did the same. Did you finish up in there?

("Yep. He had the same neural pathway as Blaine. Now... grab the new guy.")

She stepped over to the window bed and held his wrist, again trying to look like she was taking a pulse. Pard merged and in no time was out again, visible this time in his Dr. Pard lab coat.

("Cheers for us. I think we just cured two more victims.")

But they don't look any different. Last time Timothy was starting to—

("Go-go-go! Time to get out of here.")

Daley wasn't going to argue that. She quick-stepped toward the door, then eased out into the hall as she jotted on her clipboard. The coast was clear so she retraced her steps to the stairs.

But—

("Blaine was getting light on sedation when we saw him,") Pard told her as she hurried down the stairs. ("From what I could tell, these two received their morning dose not too long ago, so it'll be a while before they start showing signs of recovery.")

Out of the stairwell she headed straight down the hall toward the Emergency Room, but skidded to a halt.

Crap!

("Yes, I see him.")

Deputy Alvarez was filling out a form at the Emergency Room front desk.

He must have come in with an emergency. Can't let him see me.

She did a quick about face and followed the hallways to the main entrance where she exited to the front parking lot. She was now on the opposite side of the building from her car, so she walked around the south side, past the ambulance entrance, and into the rear lot. No one gave her a second look.

When she reached her car she dropped behind the steering wheel and closed her eyes.

"Made it!"

Pard appeared in the passenger seat, sans lab coat. ("That was close. If Alvarez had seen you—")

"It would have blown everything."

("It's those unpredictable variables that screw up the best plans. But I've got to hand it to you, Daley, that was one efficient mission. Your disguise was perfect. No one raised an eyebrow. You might as well have been invisible.")

"Well, thank you, Pard, but your quickness was a big factor. The longer we stayed in that room, the greater the chance of discovery."

("Do you think we've stroked each other enough?")

"I think so. It's beginning to make me feel a little nauseous. Would that be an indicator?"

("'Nauseated' would be the more correct term.")

Well, damn. The tight ass strikes again.

"Had to go and ruin it, didn't you," she said as she started the car. "We had a nice mutual admiration society started there but you had to go and pull your Grammar Nazi schtick."

("It's not a *schtick*! There's proper usage and improper usage.")

She knew she shouldn't let him aggravate her. He couldn't help being a perfectionist. She steered out of the lot and got them headed north on Imperial Avenue.

"Whatever," she said finally. "When do we find out if this worked?"

("The sedation should wear off in four to six hours, I should think. We'll have to keep a close eye on the TV.")

"Well, since the shop has no TV, we'll have to make do with updates on my phone. I want to be very visible in Healerina today. Too bad I can't have you watch the TV upstairs while I'm in the shop."

("That would be quite the trick, wouldn't it.")

25

This time Jeffrey didn't jump when Jimmy Fries knocked on his window. He was already awake, but the blanket was so warm, he'd remained lying down on the front seat. He sat up to see Jimmy's grinning face on the other side of the glass.

"Coffee time!"

Jeffrey turned on the ignition and lowered the window.

"Thanks for the blanket."

Last night he'd walked out into the desert to relive himself and when he got back a neatly folded blanket was waiting on the hood of his pickup with a note: *You might have use for this.*

So Jeffrey had used it.

"Just being neighborly." Jimmy handed the coffee through the window. "The days ain't bad, but winter nights can get cold out here."

"You need it back?"

"I got a couple so I can spare you one. Just bring it back when the weather starts heating up."

Jeffrey wasn't used to kindness. Made him kinda suspicious.

"What's your story, Jimmy? What you do with yourself all day?"

"Mostly I read. We got ourselfs a library here in the Slabs.

Plus I got my own books. And I walk into town a few times a week. Buy some groceries."

"You walk? To Niland? Gotta be ten miles round trip."

"Yep. Thereabouts."

Jeffrey pointed to the battered Mitsubishi by Jimmy's camper. "Don't your car work?"

"Yeah, but exercise is good for you."

Jeffrey sipped his coffee and thought about exercise. He hadn't worked any weights since Saturday. He'd be getting flabby soon.

Jimmy dipped into a purple bag he'd been holding in his free hand, came out with a reddish tube that he bit into with a crunch.

"What's that?"

He held up the bag. "Fuegos. Takis Fuegos. Little rolled tortillas coated with pepper. Want one?"

"Hot stuff for breakfast? Not my thing."

"I'm addicted to the little fuckers. The store in Niland stocks 'em in for me. They don't worry about not selling 'em 'cause I buy 'em all. What *you* do with your day, Jeffrey?"

"Right now, I'm taking inventory. I fucked up royally and I'm figuring out where I go from here."

"Yeah, most of us out here have fucked up one way or another. I won't ask about your fuck-up if you don't ask about mine."

"Fair enough." He didn't give a shit about Jimmy's fuck-up and no way in hell he was talking about his. "I wound up with a second chance. Just need to figure how to make the best use of it."

"Cool. You ever wanna talk about it, I'm always around. And when you're not taking inventory, you might try a little reading." He pulled a battered paperback from a back pocket and handed it through the window. "I've read this at least a dozen times."

Jeffrey stared at the cover in disbelief. "What the fuck? Tarzan?"

"*Tarzan of the Apes.* Great book. All about learning who you are and finding your place in the world."

Oh, yeah, right, like he was going to waste his time with this kinda shit. He'd seen bits and pieces of the movies. Some asshole swinging through the trees on a vine and yodeling at the top of his lungs. No way. Was this some kinda joke? Did Jimmy think he was too dumb to read a real book? Oughta grab him by the neck shove his fucking piece of shit book down his—

No. No-no-no. That was Karma talking. He was Jeffrey now, and Jeffrey didn't do shit like that.

He forced calm and said, "Hey, thanks. Ain't much of a reader but I'll give it a try."

Yeah. He might take a look at it. A man could do only so much inventorying in a day. After that it got boring as shit out here.

26

Despite rushing back from El Centro, Daley had been a little late opening Healerina. She wondered why she'd bothered. The morning had been dead and the afternoon's prospects weren't looking much better. Lucky for her Jason had given her the first five months here rent free.

Shortly after one p.m. Daley's Feedly app broke the news that two more horrors victims had spontaneously recovered.

She pumped her fist. "Yes!"

("'Spontaneous'?") Pard said from his perch by the window. ("I beg to differ.")

Some medical commentators were saying that maybe the horrors was a self-limiting condition, while others were questioning why, with horrors victims all over Southern California, ECRMC patients were the only ones coming out of it.

One was quoted as saying, *"What are those El Centro docs doing that no one else is?"*

("What indeed?")

"So, Doctor Pard, have you proved your theory?"

("Yes. I have no doubt now that horrors sufferers are predisposed to the condition due to a neural pathway from the pineal to the amygdala. Blocking that removes their susceptibility. The downside is that it's not an anatomical neuronal bundle, merely a pathway. Which means unless you're tuned into their brains, there's no way to detect it. Which, in turn, means only we can cure them.")

"Well, damn, that's not good. There's hundreds and hundreds of cases from Baja to LA. Are we their only hope?"

The weight of the responsibility pressed on her.

("We are until someone figures out where those images are originating and cuts them off at the source.")

"Any ideas on that?"

("If I could stay inside one of these victims long enough, I might get a clue.")

"Meanwhile there's scads of horrors victims out there and we're all they've got. Don't you find that majorly scary?"

("I would have characterized it as 'daunting,' but 'majorly scary' captures it well enough.")

"Putting all your condescension aside—and I realize it's a heavy load—do you think—"

Pard disappeared from the window and reappeared beside her. ("Sorry-sorry-sorry! I've been sentient only three weeks. I've still a lot to learn about the nuances of communication.")

"Like tone?"

("Yes, tone is something I need to work on. Don't hate me.")

"Well, considering how seventy-two hours ago I was lying on the kitchen floor upstairs with a knife in my heart, and now, because of you, I'm down here managing my shop, it's hard to truly hate you."

("Actually it was more like eighty-four hours ago.")

Daley squeezed her eyes shut in frustration. "Then, on the other hand..."

("There I go pettifogging again! I'm also working on that too.")

She knew she had to expect and accept a certain level of tight-assedness from Pard—he was who he was—but sometimes...

"Anyway, as I was saying, I think we have a numbers problem with the horrors patients."

("Absolutely. We can't possibly reach every sufferer, especially with more people falling victim every day, so the solution seems to lie with cutting off the source of fear.")

"How do we do that?"

("I haven't a clue, Daley. Not a clue.")

<h1 style="text-align:center">27</h1>

Come the dark, Daley wasn't too surprised to hear a tap on her door. Had been kind of expecting it.

Note Man's back.

("Are you sure it's him?")

She pointed to the slip of paper on the floor just inside the door. *Yep.*

Can we talk?

"Of course," she said. "Wait till I turn the lights out."

No need

"You sure?"

When no note came through she assumed he was, so she opened the door.

Note Man still wore his hoodie which shadowed most of his face, but what she could see of his features showed the barklike skin she'd seen on his hands and arms. He stepped in and closed the door behind him.

"Hello, Daley," he said in a husky tone.

She had to smile. "Your voice…it's…"

"Stronger? Yes. I can't raise it much beyond this conversational tone yet, but it's steadily improving."

"Is everything okay otherwise?"

"No, the clan is generally a mess, but things couldn't be better for me personally. I had a question and also wanted to confirm our walk tomorrow night."

"The walk of wonders? Sure. Just what wonders are you going to show me?"

She saw a flash of white as he smiled. At least his affliction hadn't affected his teeth.

"You'll have to wait and see, I'm afraid. But I guarantee they will occupy your mind long after tomorrow night."

("Now I'm intrigued. Whatever could he have up his sleeve—besides more river birch skin?")

Unkind!

("Only if he'd heard it, which he didn't.")

"I can't wait. And the question?"

"I have to ask this…it's haunted me ever since news came about the cures of the horrors down at the medical center."

("I know what's cominggggg,") Pard singsonged.

Kind of obvious.

"I think I know what you're going to say, but I'll let you say it."

"Okay. Considering the miraculous change you've done for me, and since the only known cures of the horrors have occurred just thirty miles away, it's only logical to assume you're behind them. So I have to ask: Was that you?"

("First off, I wouldn't say it's 'logical.' Secondly—")

Never mind that. What do I say?

"You're hesitating," Note Man said. "Please don't feel you have to answer."

("But not answering is an answer in itself, isn't it.")

For sure.

"I'll need your promise of discretion."

"You have it." To her shock, he dropped to one knee and bowed his head. "After what you've done for me, I'm at your command. Anything I have is yours, My Lady. Anything you want, consider it done."

An embarrassed laugh escaped her. "Wow. Now I know how Guinevere felt."

"Consider me your Lancelot," he said, rising.

"All right, yes, that was me."

("If I had a tongue, I'd be biting it.")

Hush.

"I assumed so. And considering the media frenzy around El Centro right now, I can understand why you'd want to keep the credit at arm's length. But how did you—?"

"I did what I did. Can we please just leave it at that?"

He bowed. "Absolutely."

Daley wanted to switch the topic.

"Where are we on the rest of that film?"

He sighed as he rose. "As I told you, I no longer have access to the copy at the Lodge. But I've been doing some searching and found a receipt from a service in San Diego for the digitization of home movies."

"And you think that's where Elis Pendry had it put on disk?"

"I'm reasonably sure, but this was all twenty or so years ago. The business has since been sold and the name changed."

"Well, damn!"

"Hold on. I'm on the case and homing in on an answer. I hope to have a name and address for you when next we meet. In the meantime, prepare yourself for wonders tomorrow."

"I'll have my walking shoes by the door. What time?"

"Late. Say around eleven? We'll be walking though the desert."

That didn't sound good.

"Oh, I don't know about that. On one of my stops in the desert I saw these giant lizards and—"

"They weren't lizards," he said.

"Then what—?"

"They won't be around, and even if they were, they wouldn't harm you. The film will explain them."

She suppressed a gasp. "The film? You mean they're related to those aliens, the Visitors?"

He nodded within his hoodie. "There's a lot going on around here you need to know about. I could never adequately explain it. You need to see it to grasp it. It's all in the film. Well, most of it. Still some things going on around here that I can't put my finger on." With a quick bow, he said, "Until tomorrow, M'lady," and then he was out the door and gone.

("It appears you have a knight errant to do your bidding.")

Can my life get any more weird? Can it?

("Nespodee Springs appears to be a quagmire of intrigue.")

And we're right in the middle of it.

THURSDAY—March 12

28

Daley watched the morning news shows which all carried the second press conference from ECRMC, and once again poor Dr. Milton had no explanation for yesterday's two cures.

In the Q & A section, the first reporter asked the question that seemed to be on everyone's mind—everyone but Daley and Pard, of course: Why here? Why El Centro? Horrors patients were being treated in Cedars-Sinai in LA to the Naval Medical Center in San Diego and in every hospital between with no results. Yet here in this relatively tiny hospital in a desert town in the Imperial Valley, victims were being cured. Why? How?

Dr. Milton cited "spontaneous remission" again but no one was satisfied with that.

At ten a.m. Daley went down and opened the shop.

("Looks like another slow day,") Pard said from his seat in the window. ("They can't all be as exciting as yesterday.")

"Exciting? I'd call it nerve wracking. But at least we have tonight to look forward to. What kind of wonders can Note Man show us—I mean, within walking distance?"

("Well, I don't know about you, but I'm prepared to be unimpressed. 'Wonders' indeed. We've seen all there is to be seen here.")

Daley wasn't so sure about that. "You never know."

"Never know what?" said a voice behind her.

She turned to see Rhys standing in the doorway, exactly where Juana had stood the other day when she'd overheard Daley talking to Pard. She needed to be more careful.

"Howdy, stranger. Just thinking out loud."

It seemed much longer than four nights ago that they'd had dinner at Mama's Meatball, but a lot had happened since then.

"About what?"

"Oh, the future. Has Karma Kendrick shown up yet?"

The answer better be *no*, she thought.

"Not a trace of him."

("Looks like he took your warning seriously,") Pard said.

Let's hope he keeps on taking it that way.

Daley said, "This makes four days now."

"Yeah. His buddy Benny is missing as well. I'm thinking something happened to them."

("I think that's a good bet. We can assume Benny is six feet under out in the desert. And Karma is in the wind.")

Blowing far away, I hope.

"So...started to hunt for a new foreman yet?"

"Sort of. I'm acting the part now and I hate it. As if I don't already have enough to do. I'm trying to decide whether to hire from the ranks or bring in an outsider. I'd prefer the ranks but sometimes it's hard for these guys to ride herd on their buddies."

Daley gestured around at her empty shop. "I don't think I'll ever have that problem."

"Lucky you. Anyway, the reason I stopped by is to see if you'd like to go out to dinner Sunday night. This foreman problem will keep me tied up all week and even into Saturday. How's Sunday look?"

She smiled. "I'll make room on my packed schedule."

"Mama's for Sunday gravy again?"

"Yeah, sure. You really like that place, don't you."

"It's okay. What I really like is watching you dunk a biscotti in your cappuccino."

She laughed. "I'll have to remember that."

A couple more minutes of small talk and he made his exit, blaming his foreman duties.

("He is definitely taken by you.")

I like him too, but you know that. What I'd really like to know is our next step with the horrors.

("The source...we need to find the source. As I told you: If

I could spend some quality time in one of the victims' brains, I might be able to home in on it.")

*Quality time...*that meant more exposure for Daley at a patient's side.

I don't know...we got away with it twice. A third time could be pressing our luck.

("I'll leave the decision up to you. Not that I have any real choice, but it sounds better if I put like that. I'll just sit here thinking of those poor victims and how they must be suffering while—")

All right, all right! We'll have another go at it tomorrow.

Her only consolation was that if Pard could find the source of the horrors, maybe the plague could be ended without Daley winding up in the spotlight.

29

Used to be, when Karma was living in the double-wide, he'd get up early, scramble up half a dozen eggs alongside some Jimmy Dean sausage patties, and wash the whole mess down with half a quart of coffee. Then he'd hit the weights.

Now, with no double-wide and no weights, Jeffrey tended to skip breakfast—other than the cup Jimmy brought over. But he'd get hungry come midday and head to the Buckshot in Niland for a sandwich.

Usually the only people he'd pass along the way were tourists gawking at Salvation Mountain, but today he came up on a bearded, braided dude in a cowboy hat dragging a Radio Flyer wagon behind him.

"Hey, Jimmy!" he said as he pulled up beside him. "Toss that dinky red wagon in the back and I'll give you a lift."

Jimmy kept walking. "Well, I appreciate the offer, man, but I need the exercise."

"Ten miles is a long walk. You sure?"

"Absolutely. I'm outa Fuegos. Gotta restock."

"Have it your way," Jeffrey said with a wave and continued on his way.

He found himself a table off to the side in the Buckshot

Deli and Diner. The special of the day was shrimp patties with nopales so he ordered that plus a Bud. Then he opened the Tarzan book Jimmy had given him. He'd started it earlier this morning and was surprised how much he liked it. Nothing like the yodeler in the old movies. Jimmy had given him some line about how it was about "learning who you are and finding your place in the world" or some such shit. Jeffrey didn't know about any of that. All he knew was the book Tarzan kicked ass and he liked that. Liked that a lot.

He liked the lunch special too. Liked it so much—especially the refried beans and rice that came with it—he ordered a second plate. When he was done he drove up the street to the SoCo for a fill-up, then headed back toward Slab City.

As he was crossing the tracks he saw a little red wagon lying on its side and recognized the guy sitting on the ground next to it.

Jimmy. Shit.

He pulled over and got out.

"Hey, man. What happened?"

Jimmy looked up at him. His left eye was starting to swell—he was on his way to a wicked shiner. "Oh. Hey, Jeffrey. Nothin' much. Just a little dust up."

"What kind of dust up? Hit and run?"

"Nah. Little disagreement I been having with this guy." He spat some blood. "No biggie."

He looked like he'd gone toe to toe with a couple of Karma's old biker buddies. If this was what a little disagreement looked like, what happened when it graduated to a big disagreement?

Jeffrey held out his hand. "C'mon. I'll drive you."

"That's all right. I need—"

"Fuck the exercise. Get in the truck. *Now.*"

Jimmy shrugged, then let Jeffrey pull him to his feet. Weighed damn near nothing. As Jimmy climbed slowly into the passenger seat, Jeffrey laid the wagon on its side in the truck bed.

"You're too old for this shit, Jimmy," he said as they got rolling.

"Tell me about it."

"I'll take you to the store and—"

"Already been there."

Been there? The wagon had been empty.

"Didn't you buy anything?"

"Yeah, but they're gone now."

"What? Your Fuegos? So you're telling me this 'little dust up' was really a mugging?"

"Nothing like that. Like I said: a disagreement. Let it go."

Good advice. Not his problem. Let everybody settle their shit on their own.

"Okay, we'll go get you some more."

"Can't. I bought them all out. All four bags."

"Well, then, Jimmy, I guess you're fucked."

"I guess I am."

"And what're you gonna do when you're jonesing for a Fuego later?"

"I guess I'll just have to wait until the store gets another shipment. Shouldn't be too long."

"Who did this, Jimmy?"

Not that he cared all that much, just curious.

"Nobody. Just a bully. I don't want no one else involved."

"I ain't getting involved. I'm new here. Just want to know who to stay away from."

The last thing he needed was trouble. The sheriff and his deputies had all had their share of run-ins with Karma Kendrick and Jeffrey didn't want them or anyone else to know where he was. Jimmy was an okay guy but Jeffrey wasn't here to solve anyone else's problems. He had enough of his own. Jimmy would have to deal for himself. Jeffrey just wanted to be left alone.

"Good," Jimmy said. "Stay away from him. Likes to say he's a ex-Navy SEAL but someone did some checkin' and he ain't. But he's real mean. Likes to beat on people."

"Yeah, but who do I stay away from?"

"You'll find out soon enough. He'll be pissed if I rat on him and things'll only get worse. Can we change the subject?"

"Sure. What to?"

Jeffrey had nothing. He'd leave it up to Jimmy.

"Hear about them horrors cures?"

Karma had never listened to the news and neither did Jeffrey—not on TV, not on the radio—but even he had heard about the horrors. Maybe he'd even experienced them when the goddess had shown him what waited for him if she ever saw him again. Just the memory of those few seconds in hell shook him up. He broke out in a sweat.

"You okay?" Jimmy said, looking at him strange.

"Yeah, fine. No, I didn't hear about no horrors cures. I thought they was permanent like."

"That's what everyone thought until this week."

"Well, that's great."

Like he gave a shit.

He pulled up before Jimmy's camper and lifted the red wagon out of his truck. Jimmy thanked him for the ride and limped inside.

Instead of parking on his slab next door, Jeffrey took a little cruise through Slab City. When he'd first got here Monday, he'd driven up and down the streets looking for a slab to call his own. He hadn't been paying a whole lot of attention to the campers and trailers and mobile homes parked willy-nilly throughout the area, but he thought he remembered one that stood out because—

There. Right over the door of that dirty white RV...

And sitting on a lawn chair right in front in cut-off shorts and a tank top was a hairy guy eating from a purple Fuegos bag. Jeffrey told himself to drive on but something inside pushed him to talk to this guy. He got out and sauntered toward him at a relaxed, non-threatening pace.

"Looking for someone?" the guy said.

Jeffrey pointed at the USN logo. "You in the Navy?"

Now that he was close he could see *Jake Lugo* printed under it.

"Was." He pointed to a tat on his left delt. "SEAL Team Six."

"Like on TV?"

Lugo snorted. "Hollywood pussies! I'm retired and I could take 'em all out in sixty secs."

Sure you could, Jeffrey thought. Might as well get to the point.

"Hey, where you get those Fuegos?"

Lugo's hand froze as it dipped into the bag. "What's it to ya?"

"Oh, nothing, just that my neighbor got mugged a little while ago and someone stole his Fuegos."

Lugo dropped the bag and rose from the chair. "And what? And that little faggot sent you to get them back?"

Jeffrey raised his hands palms out, and backed up a step. "Hey, no. He didn't tell me who did it. I just happened to be driving by and saw you eating them, so I figured I'd ask."

"Well, what if they *are* his? What if I happen to like them and he buys up every bag in the store, and what if I warned him about that? What are you gonna do about it?"

Jeffrey kept his hands up and backed up another step.

Karma wouldn't care about Jimmy and his stolen Fuegos, but he would never let anyone talk to him like this. By now Karma would have this guy by the back of his neck, smashing his face into the slab his RV sat on. But Jeffrey wasn't going to fall into that. Jeffrey was all about minding his own business and staying out of trouble.

"Nothing. Just asking, is all."

"You wanna piece of me, I'm here any time you wanna have a go. Otherwise, get back in your candy-ass truck and get outa here. And tell that little faggot I don't appreciate him talkin' about me. He'll pay for that."

Jeffrey kept backing up. "Hey, he didn't say any—"

"Get the fuck outa my sight before I mess you up good."

With Karma screaming inside to be let loose, Jeffrey forced himself to walk to his pickup.

I ain't that guy no more. I ain't Karma. I'm somebody else.
I'm Jeffrey, and I'm gonna stay Jeffrey.

He started his truck and drove off.

Hey, I did it.

The goddess would be proud of him.

30

When Note Man showed up at eleven sharp, dressed in his usual hoodie and jeans, Daley was ready and waiting in her jeans, knock-off Lakers jacket, and walking shoes.

"Before we go," he said as she opened her door. His voice was even stronger than last night. "I want to show you something."

With that he rolled up his sleeve to reveal large patches of normal skin spreading into the barklike areas.

"Excellent!" she said. "Does it feel any different?"

"It feels wonderful—much more flexible."

Ya done good, Pard.

("So it would appear,") he said from where he leaned against the sink counter. ("But the grammar of your encomium is giving *me* a rash.")

You don't have skin.

("A virtual rash—like hives.")

Note Man stepped back onto the landing. "All right. Ready for some wonders?"

"Absolutely."

He led her down and behind the row of buildings instead of on the street—no surprise that he was keeping off the main drag. They passed behind the laundromat and the Thirsty Cactus, among others, and into the desert east of town. They hurried across the road and continued north toward the windfarm. The moon was waning but still bright enough to light up the whirling blades which, even at this distance, were making quite a racket.

"Is that where we're going?" she said, catching up and walking by his side.

"It is."

"I'm sure we can't just stroll in, can we?"

"No. But they have minimal security at night: Someone drives a circuit of the property about once an hour and stays holed up in a shack by the gate the rest of the time."

"How do we get past the gate then?"

"We don't. I have my own private entrance."

As they neared the windfarm, the sound of the turbines grew louder and louder.

"Is it always this loud?" she said, leaning in close so she wouldn't have to shout.

He nodded. "Conversation is going to be difficult when we get in there."

He led her to one of the ten-foot posts that supported the chain-link fencing and began twisting at wires on the post.

God, it was loud. She'd need earplugs if she worked here. ("I hope this isn't one of his 'wonders.'")

Be patient.

After a moment, a section of the fencing peeled back as Note Man held it open for her.

"After you."

"Is it safe?"

"Very. I come here often."

"Why?"

"I find it...interesting. You will too. I guarantee it."

As Daley ducked through, she had to admit she was beginning to share some of Pard's skepticism about the "wonders" waiting. Note Man followed her through and she stood by as he refastened the flap to the pole.

He pointed to one of the turbines near the center of the farm and raised his voice as he leaned close. "See the one that's a little taller than the rest?"

She nodded. They were all about twenty stories high but this one poked another dozen feet or so above its neighbors. "What about it?"

"That's our destination."

She let him lead the way through the forest of white towers to the tallest at the center. It differed from the others in that it had a small windowless, flat-roofed structure built around its base.

Note Man cupped his hands around her ear and said, "Before we go in, I want to ask you to notice something."

"What?"

He pointed up. "See how the blades are all turning at the same speed?"

She looked around, then nodded.

She asked Pard, *Isn't that expected?*

("I would think so, but my wind turbine knowledge base is limited. Had I known this was our destination, I could have boned up.")

"Do you feel any wind?" Note Man said.

She didn't—nothing obvious, anyway. She wet her finger and held it up as she'd seen people do in the movies: still no wind.

"No," she said, almost shouting. "Not even a breeze."

"Don't you find that strange?"

"Very."

("I can explain some of that. Wind shear from the ground slows air velocity at lower altitudes but not at higher.")

I'll ask him.

She said, "What about—?"

"We'll talk inside." He indicated the padlocked door to the base building. "Quieter."

He pulled out a key and inserted it into the lock, then removed a small hammer from his pocket and tapped the key's bow. A quick twist and the shackle popped free. He traded the hammer for a flashlight and stepped inside. Daley followed. After closing the door behind her, he flipped a light switch to reveal a rectangular room running thirty feet or so wide and about half that deep under a ten-foot ceiling. A ladder was set into the far wall next to another door. The rungs ran up into the tower.

"Ohhh," Daley said with relief. The door cut the turbine noise by about half. "I can hear myself think. How do people stand it?"

Note Man shrugged. "They say your brain edits out noise you hear all the time."

Daley couldn't imagine her brain editing out that racket.

"Say," she said, "you're pretty handy with a bump key."

Note Man gave her an appraising look. "You're familiar with bump keys?"

Uh-oh. A bump key was a lock-picking device used by locksmiths and criminals...she'd used her share of them in the family that raised her for the first thirteen years of her life.

Me and my big mouth.

("I won't disagree. Time for a little fabrication. I suggest—")

"My uncle was a locksmith."

Note Man shrugged. "Oh, well, that explains it."

("My, you're fast with the fiction.")

Practice, practice, practice.

"But about the wind?" she said to get off the subject of bump keys. "Aren't wind speeds higher the farther up you go?"

"True, but this is not a particularly windy area of the desert like the San Gorgonio Pass or Ocotillo." He pointed to the ladder. "You can climb to the top if you like and check it from up there—or..."

"Or what?"

"Or you can take the word of someone who's been up there many times and has often found no wind, and rarely ever enough wind to turn those huge blades at anywhere near that rate."

She'd already climbed to the top of the Pendry clan's Tesla tower—almost the same height as this—but that had been in daylight. Climbing up there in the dark...no thanks.

"I'd rather take your word for it, but...I mean...no wind and yet..."

"*Eppur, si muove,*" he muttered.

"Sorry?"

("He just quoted Galileo—in Italian: 'Nevertheless, it moves.' Oh, I like this guy.")

Note Man said, "It's almost impossible to believe, isn't it?"

"Exactly. But I mean, if wind isn't moving those blades, what is?"

("Ditto!")

"Yes...what is?"

"Is that the wonder you promised to show me?"

"One of them." He pointed to the door in the opposite wall. "The other is through there."

Unlike the outer door, this one tapered to a point on top and wasn't locked.

Daley frowned. "What's in there?"

The building had looked about thirty by thirty from the outside, almost the same as this empty room. Where could the door go? A storage area?

"Something interesting," Note Man said. "Try it."

Daley opened the door and found herself in a small vestibule facing another pointed door. With his flashlight on, Note Man stepped in and closed the door behind them.

"Now, open that one," he said.

She grabbed the handle, pushed...and gasped.

"Holy—! What the—?"

A vast, well-lit, warehouselike space stretched away before her. Strips of some sort of glowing material ran along a ceiling at least thirty feet above, illuminating a wide floor lined with boxcar-size blocks of putty-colored...what?

Daley squeezed her eyes closed for a few heartbeats, then opened them for another look. Nothing had changed.

"Wait-wait-wait! This is impossible." She looked at Note Man. "Isn't it?"

"It's not an illusion. I've been in there, I've walked through it. It's quite real."

"But-but-but..." She jabbed a finger at Note Man. "Wait right here. Do. Not. Move."

She went back through the first pointed door, backtracked across the room, and exited by the outer door. Assaulted again by that godawful noise, she trotted around the side of the base to the rear. The side wall ran thirty feet at most, and the rear was the same across. *Thirty feet.* No more.

Pard—what's going on? Where's that huge building?

("I...I don't know.") Pard sounded uncertain. He hardly ever sounded uncertain. ("Truly, I don't.")

It's the size of a football field!

("Multiple football fields.")

How can it be there and-and-and not there at the same time?

("I wish I knew.")

You're not helping matters. You're supposed to know everything.

("That's an unrealistic expectation on face of it. No one can—")

Yeah-yeah, I know. But what's going on here, Pard? I mean, what the fuck is going on?

She hurried back inside and rushed straight for the pointed door, through the vestibule to the third door...

No change: the giant space still loomed before her.

"How did you ever find this place?" she said to Note Man.

He shrugged. "I have no life. I've never had a life. So I spend my nights wandering. Every barrier, every locked door is a challenge to overcome. I stumbled on this a few years ago."

"*Years?* You've got to explain this to me. How can the inside of this place be bigger than the outside?"

"I wish I knew. It's one of the wonders I promised."

She turned on him. "You have *more?*"

"No. Isn't this enough?"

"Yeah. Totally."

She gestured into the space at the boxcar blocks. "What *is* this place? How did it get here and what are those things?"

"I don't know for sure, but I have an idea."

"I'm listening."

"Come in and I'll show you."

He stepped into the space but Daley didn't follow...couldn't bring herself to pass that threshold.

"It's all right," Note Man said. "Nothing to fear."

"Nothing to fear? That place isn't really there. I know because I went outside and double-checked."

"You're right about it not being really here—there's some strange space-folding quirkiness involved here—but it's quite real."

("'Strange space-folding quirkiness'? Meaningless blather! This is all impossible!")

In case you haven't noticed, he's standing in the impossible.

("I am well aware of that.")

Note Man waved her forward. "Come on. I've been in here many times."

Should I?

("Well…he seems unharmed so…I guess so.")

Taking a breath, Daley stepped across into the space. The temperature suddenly jumped a good ten degrees.

"Warmer in here," she said.

The extra brightness of the space reached inside Note Man's hoodie and faintly illuminated his face, enough to allow her a vague sense of his features. He had what would have passed for an ordinary face except for the tree-bark texture layering it. She could make out patches of normal skin on his cheeks and forehead though.

He stepped over to one of the big blocks and pressed a hand against its side. "Because of these."

As Daley approached she heard a low-pitched hum. When she touched the block's surface she found it smooth and warm and…

"Ooh, it gives off a faint tingle."

"I think they're some sort of batteries."

"Batteries? Where'd you get that idea?"

"Consider: The windfarm is run by the Tadak family and the Tadaks have made their fortune in the battery field—energy storage. These things are connected to an electricity-generating facility. So is it so off the wall to assume that these are batteries to store the output of all those windmills?"

"Big as boxcars?"

"Why not?"

("It's a good train of logic.")

"But wait—you said there's not enough wind to turn those turbines."

"Right. Not enough wind here in Nespodee Springs—but there could be enough elsewhere."

Daley shook her head, baffled. "Okay, you've lost me."

Note Man waved his arms. "Look around you. This place isn't in Nespodee Springs. You checked yourself and saw that. It's Somewhere Else. What if those turbines are being turned by a wind from Somewhere Else?"

Daley squinted at him. "Are you high? Because that sounds like stoner talk."

"Weed?" he said with a laugh. "I used to indulge when I was younger—it helped stave off depression—but I gave it up long ago. No, as I told you, I've known about this place for years. I know every inch of it and it offers no clue as to where in time and space Somewhere Else might be. No windows and no other door besides the one we came through."

"So the only way to find out where this place is would be to break a hole through the wall."

"No way I'd do that, even if it were possible. I might not like what I'd find. But I did discover something about the turbine blades."

("This I want to hear.")

"They're coated with a clear substance that feels sticky except nothing sticks to it. A while ago I scraped some off and sent it out for analysis to two separate labs. Neither one could identify it. So, I don't know what it is, but I think I know what it does."

"Let me guess," Daley said. "Your wind from Somewhere Else...the coating makes the blades sensitive to the wind from Somewhere Else."

("You're as loony as he is!")

"Exactly! We can't feel the wind, but the coated blades can, and they turn in response."

("Madness!")

Why not? Look where we are, Pard. We're in an impossible place. If Note Man had told us about this instead of showing us, you'd have called him "nuts," right?

After a pause came a grudging ("Well, yes.")

So, is a place that exists Somewhere Else any crazier than a wind from Somewhere Else?

Even though he didn't breathe, Pard made a sighing sound in her head and said, ("No, I suppose not.")

Daley turned to Note Man. "Okay, but if these *are* batteries and all those turbines are feeding them, what's all this energy being stored for?"

"The million-dollar—or should I say, *billion* dollar question."

"No, really...who needs all this energy? I mean, look at the size of these things."

"Ten feet high, ten feet wide, and forty feet long—all guestimates since I simply paced them off, but close enough."

"Like a regular mobile home. And there's gotta be hundreds of them."

"Five hundred and forty-one, to be exact."

It took a few seconds for the enormity of that number and the scale of the place needed to house them to sink in, then Daley had to laugh. "You *counted* them? You're sure there's not five hundred forty-*two*?"

"Positive. I kept thinking that's such a random-sounding number, I must have miscounted, so I counted again and it came out the same."

("It's a prime number, but I can't imagine the significance of that.")

"Okay, okay," Daley said, "we've got a lot of boxcar-size blocks here that we're calling batteries, and we've got wind turbines that turn without wind, but the real mind-blowing aspect of all this is Jason Tadhak and his family. This is *their* place. Who are they and where'd they get this technology?"

"The Tadhaks are what you'd call an enigma," Note Man said.

"Jason seems like such a regular guy—a *nice*, regular guy. And yet…" She spread her arms. "Why aren't they sharing this with the world?"

"Jason is the face of the Tadhak family, the only one we ever see up close. The rest…have you seen their compound?"

"Just the weird wall around it. Rhys Pendry showed me."

"They travel back and forth to the windfarm—"

"In that creepy white bus with the no-see windows."

"That's the one. But other than that, except for Jason, they're never outside their compound. Has a Tadak—besides Jason, of course—ever come into your shop?"

"Never."

"Right. No one's ever seen a Tadhak at the Thirsty Cactus or the Coyote either. Total recluses."

"Which is fine," Daley said. She took a live-and-let-live approach to life. "Whatever floats your boat. Although they must be a really close-knit family to stay cooped up together all the time. But this technology they got…wouldn't you think they'd want to, you know, license it? I can't imagine what it's worth."

Note Man shook his head. "I think they've got all the money they need. Maybe there's a downside that makes it not commercially feasible. I'm neither a scientist nor a businessman, so I can't figure it."

The possibility of a "downside" wormed through Daley's gut. Here they were, standing in a place that was Somewhere Else. What if whatever technology was responsible for this suddenly developed a glitch and they wound up trapped here?

"Okay," she said, easing toward the door, "I think maybe I've seen enough."

She released a little sigh of relief when she stepped back into the relatively tiny front room and Note Man closed the door behind them—back to the real world from wherever Somewhere Else might be.

"It will take you a while to absorb all this," he said.

Daley shook her head. "I don't know…the warehouse in Somewhere Else and the wind from Somewhere Else…they're so far out they're like *Star Wars* or some other science fiction come true. They're just technology, and I can accept advanced tech a lot easier than why anyone would want to store so goddam much electricity."

"Jason Tadak made a deal with Elis Pendry to trade some of his excess electricity for an interest in the clan's Tesla tower."

"I knew they were sharing power but not much beyond that."

She remembered Rhys complaining about the rush job to connect the tower to the Tadhaks' transformer.

("Maybe the Tadhaks aren't so smart. Broadcast energy will never work.")

Maybe they know something you don't—like how to construct a building that's bigger on the outside than it is on the inside.

Which prompted a question…

"Why would people with the Someplace Else technology want to get involved in something like a Tesla tower?"

Note Man hesitated, then said, "I'm guessing they don't

know the real purpose of the tower."

Daley shrugged. "To broadcast energy, right? Wireless energy."

A slow shake of his head. "Not according to the film."

"The film! Yes! Speaking of which, you're supposed to have a name and address for me."

"I do. I'll give it to you when I drop you back at your place."

31

The walk back from the windfarm was quick and uneventful, with Pard remaining unusually silent. And now Note Man stood inside her door, offering a slip of paper.

"A Japanese fellow bought the original company and renamed it."

Daley took the slip and read the name out loud. "Daigo Digital. In La Mesa?"

"He moved it from San Diego, which is what made tracking the company so hard. I spoke to him. He has all the digital assets of the original company and he'll be glad to make a copy for a nominal fee."

"Finally. I'll check it out first thing tomorrow."

"You'll have to involve my brother."

"Your...brother?" This was a shock. "You've never mentioned him."

"As I'm sure he never mentioned me."

"I know him?"

("Uh-oh. I've got a feeling...")

"Rhys Pendry."

"*What?*"

("Knew it!")

"I'm Cadoc Pendry, Rhys's older brother."

Daley backed up to one of the chairs by the kitchen table and dropped into it.

"But he never mentioned he even *had* a brother!"

"We're actually quite close, but it's long been my wish that no one in the family mentions me. Because mentioning me will lead to questions as to why no one ever sees me and then to requests to meet me, which I've always desperately wanted to avoid."

"I can understand that, but...Rhys's brother...I had no idea."

"I want you to involve him because it's time he saw the film and learned some hidden truths about our family and its beliefs...and what the clan considers its destiny. He needs to know."

"I'll tell him as soon as I call this Daigo Digital place and—"

Cadoc waved a hand. "No-no. Not yet. Rhys has no idea you and I have been in contact. I want to be the one to tell him. I'll mention it during our Saturday night chess game. You can contact him about the film on Sunday. You'll need him along because I called Daigo Digital about getting a copy. They said no problem, but since they have it listed as a family film, they'll release a copy only to a member of the family. I'm not about to present myself there, which means Rhys has to be with you."

"Oh...okay." The question that popped into her head struck her as an awfully girly thing to say, but she had to ask. "Does he ever mention me?"

"We don't discuss women because it's not a topic to which I can contribute, but he has mentioned you in glowing terms. My brother is quite taken with you."

Daley felt a flush creep up her neck. She wasn't sure why she'd asked, but was glad she had.

"That's nice to hear. I like him too. But you never mentioned we'd met?"

"Well, until this week, we really hadn't. We've been communicating, but we've never met face-to-face until the past few days. You were new in town and something about you intrigued me. I simply wanted to contact you and leave it at that. So I took a chance. I so enjoyed our interactions, even with a door dividing us, that I kept coming back. You've made me realize how lonely my life has been."

"I'm sorry."

"You never *ever* have to apologize to me, Daley. You've given me more than I could ever give you."

"I meant, sorry you were lonely."

"I was isolated by choice, because of my skin. I know who to blame for my skin."

Daley stiffened. "Someone's to blame? I thought it ran in your family."

"It does...and it doesn't." He reached behind him and opened the door. "Good night, Daley."

("Obviously not a topic on which he wishes to elaborate.")

"Good night...Cadoc."

No longer Note Man, he was Cadoc Pendry, Rhys's brother. Holy shit.

("Well,") Pard said when he was gone, ("this has been quite the evening.")

"Wasn't it just last night that I asked you if my life could get any more weird?"

("I believe it was.")

"Well, remind me not to ask that anymore, because every time I say something like that, the weirdness only increases."

("Exponentially so tonight. I can't get that windfarm out of my thoughts.")

"I know...those turbines and that warehouse that goes on forever..."

("The Tadhaks must have discovered a different kind of geometry that the rest of us can't even dream of.")

"And to think how Note Man—I mean Cadoc Pendry—has known about this for years and never said a word."

("I've a feeling that's just the tip of an iceberg of secrets Cadoc Pendry guards. I now understand how he managed to sneak us into the Lodge—he lives there.")

"How am I going to sleep tonight?"

("I can help with that—increase you melatonin level, for instance. You need to be well rested for our return to the medical center.")

Oh, hell. She was going to have to sneak back into ECRMC again tomorrow. With all that happened tonight, it had fallen off her radar.

FRIDAY—March 13

32

"I just realized," Daley said as she eased her Subaru into a spot in the ECRMC visitor's lot, "it's Friday the thirteenth."

("Surely you're not prone to triskaidekaphobia.")

"Not a bit. I don't believe in any of that superstitious junk."

("Glad to hear it.")

"After all, I was born in May which makes me a Taurus and, by nature of our birth sign, we're a very skeptical lot."

Pard made no reply.

"Hello?"

("You set me up for that one.")

Yes, she had. Oh, yes, she had.

"I couldn't resist. And I needed something to ease this anxiety."

("I've been aware of your mood. I know you don't like placing yourself in this position...")

No, she didn't. She hated it.

"It's just that if I'm found out, I'm caught red-handed: I'm dressed as a nurse but I'm not a nurse or any sort of employee here. As a rule I'm pretty good at talking my way out of things, but how do I talk my way out of *that*?"

("But think about it: What is your crime? Visiting before visiting hours? And this is America, which means you can dress any way you damn well please. You've got no stolen property on you and so the most they can do is show you to the door.")

"Well, put that way, I guess it's not so bad. I just wish it wasn't

Friday the thirteenth because I can't help thinking something's going to go wrong."

She wasn't joking this time. She had a bad feeling this morning.

After a long pause, Pard said, ("We will not speak of the date again, understood?")

"Got it."

("And if you want to back out, it's fine. Really and truly. Restart the car and we'll head back to Nespodee Springs.")

"Nothing I'd like better, but we're all they've got."

That was the kicker. It always came down to that. People were suffering and she had no one who could step in for her. And today was extra important. Today they might discover the source of the horrors and that would put them one step closer to ending this plague.

She checked herself over. She wore the same outfit as Wednesday—blue nurse scrubs, hair tucked up under flowered scrub cap pulled low over her ears, surgical mask dangling from the neck, dork glasses, and clipboard with pen.

Just as she had Wednesday, she headed for the emergency exit. That bad feeling followed her. She knew it was irrational but she couldn't escape the feeling that something was going to go wrong today.

She lowered her head as she entered the emergency department and pretended to stare at her clipboard. An orderly had the hallway blocked with an elderly woman on a gurney, probably on her way to X-ray. As Daley waited to get by, she glanced down at a copy of one of the local papers someone had left on a chair—the *Imperial Valley Press*. The front page showed a blurry photo of a bespectacled woman in scrubs and a flowered cap walking down a hallway toward the camera. The headline blared:

IS SHE THE ANSWER TO THE HORRORS?

The figure's head was down, staring at a clipboard, but Daley knew in an instant she was looking at herself.

Shit! That's me!

("Turn around and leave. Now.")

Daley was already into a turn. Her heart pounded madly as she quick-walked through the parking lot toward her car.

What?...how?

("Obviously CCTV footage from one of the hall cameras. That clipboard was an excellent idea. Your head was down and none of your features was visible.")

But why me? Hundreds of people must march up and down those hallways every day and those cameras record every damn one of them. Why do I wind up on the front page with a headline about the horrors?

("We'll have to pick up a copy and see if they explain it. Right now you've got to get out of this parking lot and out of those scrubs.")

Daley reached her car but just as she was opening the door, she heard an angry voice behind her.

"God *damn*! I knew it was you! I *knew* it!"

Daley groaned. She knew that voice. She turned and—yep—a graying, fiftyish man stood there smirking.

Billy Marks. A member of the Family come back to haunt her. Again. She'd gone a dozen years without seeing him and now here he was again, the second time in the past two weeks. And not just any Family member, not just a distant cousin of her father's—the man who murdered her father on the day she was born.

A bad day had just got infinitely worse.

"What are you doing here?"

"Is that any way to greet your Uncle Billy?"

"If I believed for an instant I carried one cell of your blood in my veins I'd slit my wrists right here!"

("I might want to have something to say about that.")

Hush!

Billy's expression hardened. "When I saw that photo in the paper this morning I recognized you and almost choked on my coffee. You lying little bitch!"

"*What?*"

"I told you I had an angle to work the horrors and warned you off it. You told me you had no interest."

"I don't. Absolutely no interest in running a game on the horrors."

He waved a hand at her. "And yet here you are, dressed as a nurse and taking credit for these cures."

"I'm doing no such thing!"

"The headlines say different. And they've even got a picture to prove it."

She didn't care what Billy Marks thought and he wasn't worth the trouble to convince otherwise.

"We're done here," she said and slipped in behind the steering wheel.

"Oh, no we're not!" He went to grab for the door but she slammed it and hit the electric locks.

"You're working something good," he shouted, "and I want a piece!"

She started the car and backed out with him following her.

"You're getting credit for the cures and I can work that with you! We can be a team!"

"Stay away from me!"

Daley hit the accelerator and roared off.

("You're shaking. And your heart's racing—just like the last time he accosted you.")

"He does that to me, the bastard."

She calmed slowly as she drove.

"What do we do now?"

("You change into regular clothes and we find a convenience store to buy a paper.")

Daley hadn't wanted to be spotted in her scrubs in Nespodee Springs so she'd left town and changed in the desert. Changing back would prove a little more complicated here in El Centro. But she found a 7-Eleven and changed in the restroom. Out front she made herself a coffee. As she was picking up a copy of the *Imperial Valley Press* she noticed the same photo and similar headline on the front page of the *San Diego Union-Tribune.*

Oh, crap!

So she picked up a copy of that as well. Then she sat in her car and stared at the photos on the front pages. How had Billy Marks known it was her?

("Let's see what they say inside.")

She read both articles, which were remarkably similar. It came down to the administration and the staff of ECRMC desperate for an explanation for the cures and trying everything to find one. One avenue was to interview anyone—staff or visitor—who'd had the slightest passing contact with the cured on Wednesday morning. That involved a careful analysis of the CCTV images of the hallway outside the room where the two cured roommates had been under treatment. Working around the clock, they'd identified everyone entering and leaving that room except this woman in scrubs.

Despite the best efforts of the security staff and even the police, no one could isolate an image of her face.

In desperation they went back to Monday and the hall outside Timothy Blaine's room. Mrs. Blaine had stated that she'd been out of the room for less than an hour that afternoon. Analysis of CCTV images had proved more complicated because the cure had occurred during visiting hours but eventually they homed in on a slim young woman with a very similar build to the mystery scrub nurse. But she wore a broad-brimmed hat and sunglasses that completely obscured her face.

Both papers showed another blurry photo of Daley, this time in her sun hat and peasant blouse. The article ended with a plea:

If anyone can identify this woman, please contact ECRMC immediately. She is not in any trouble, she is merely a person of interest.

Daley said, "Remember the other day when you said things don't tend to turn out too well for messiahs."

("Of course.")

"Well, things tend not to end too well for persons of interest either."

("This puts a major crimp in our plans. How can I seek out the source if I can't have contact with a victim?")

"I wish I knew. One thing I do know: I'm heading back to Nespodee Springs and laying low until—"

("Can I just say, '*lying* low'?")

She damped a flare of anger. "No, you may not. I'm not a happy camper at the moment. It's been a bad morning: I've had my picture in two newspapers, maybe more, and I had to speak to Billy Marks. So I'm going to lay low for a while and wait for this to go away. Because if Billy Marks could recognize me from that photo—"

("He's a special case with a special interest in the horrors. He wants to use it to scam people, and he'd already warned you to leave the horrors alone. So he'd be intensely interested in news of anyone curing the horrors. He was primed to find you involved.")

"Let's hope so. But I can't help worrying that if Billy Marks could recognize me, someone else might too."

33

Sunlight awakened Jeffrey.

He'd parked his pickup facing west so the rising sun wouldn't shine in his face. But now it poured through the rear window. He sat up and looked around. Usually he didn't get to sleep this late because of Jimmy banging on his window.

So where was Jimmy this morning? And where was his coffee?

How quick you got spoiled.

He threw off the blanket, got out of the truck, and stretched. Then he stumbled over to Jimmy's camper and pounded on the door.

"Jimmy! Yo, Jimmy, you in there?"

Nothing.

He pounded again. "Jimmy!"

A faint sound…a groan?

Jeffrey yanked on the handle and the door opened. And there, sprawled on the floor directly in front of him, lay a very bloody and beat-up Jimmy Fries.

"Aw, shit, Jimmy!" he said, stomping up the two steps and kneeling beside him. "What happened?"

The word came out wrapped in a groan. "Nothin'."

"Yeah? Fuck that. Somebody kicked the shit outa you."

"Said I ratted on him…sent someone to see him. I didn't rat."

Well, shit. That pretty much confirmed what Jeffrey had figured the instant he saw Jimmy: Lugo.

"I think something got busted inside."

Yeah. He looked like shit. Jeffrey pulled out his phone and dialed 9-1-1.

34

"What did I say about Friday the thirteenth?" Daley said. "Didn't I tell you something bad was going to happen?"

She'd made it back to Nespodee Springs in time for Healerina's ten a.m. opening, but for once she was hoping no one would show up. Fat chance of that on a Friday when people started arriving for their weekend at the spa.

Pard gave a dismissive wave from his window perch. ("It's a matter unworthy of a moment's more discussion.")

She heard a motorcycle pull up outside. She had a pretty good idea of what that meant but asked anyway.

"Who is it?"

Pard gave her a *Duh!* look. ("How would I know?")

"Well, you're sitting by the window."

Another *Duh!* look. ("Really?")

And then she remembered: His sensory inputs were locked into hers; he could see only what she was seeing. She'd got so used to him being around she'd forget he was not a physical entity and that his image was merely…an image.

"Sorry. You should make yourself less solid looking."

She stepped over to the window and, as expected, saw Juana heading for Healerina's door.

"I see you've been busy since my last visit," the old woman said as she stepped in and closed the door behind her.

That would have been three days ago. What did she—? And then Daley saw the folded newspaper in her hand.

Oh, crap.

("Don't get upset. She's another special case. She asked you about the first cure when she was here on Tuesday, remember?")

Yeah, but still…

This put her way on edge.

"Business has been rather slow, actually," Daley said in her most innocent, whatever-do-you-mean? tone.

Juana held up a copy of the *Press*. "I'm not talking about the shop. I mean *this*: two more cures and now your picture on the front page."

Damn!

Daley put on a frown. "What makes you think that's me?"

"Isn't it? Look me in the eye and tell me that's not you."

She didn't see any point in lying, especially considering that lack of even a hint of doubt in Juana's expression.

"Okay, please keep it between us, but yeah, that's me. Is it that obvious?"

Juana turned the paper around and stared at the front page. "As soon as I heard, I was looking for you. And because I expected to see you, I guess I did."

"You 'expected' to see me?"

"Well, when I asked you if you'd cured that first one, you told me you were honestly not sure if you could cure the horrors, but you hoped to be within the next few days. The very next day two more people are cured. What else could I think?"

Daley gave a reluctant nod. "Yeah, okay, I see what you mean."

("As I said: A special case, primed to recognize you.")

Juana was staring at her with...was that awe in her eyes?

"You're the promised one...the healer. But what next?"

Daley sighed. "Not sure. I'm laying low and thinking on how to deal with this. Being the center of hysterical attention isn't exactly my thing."

"But there are more victims every day."

"Exactly. I can't get to everyone, so some people will love me and some will hate me. But no matter, if I go public I can kiss any shred of privacy good-bye. So I need to find the source."

Juana frowned. "Of the horrors? There's a *source*?"

"Yeah. They're emanating from somewhere, affecting susceptible people."

"So where better to find the source than through the victims?"

("She's right, of course.")

Yeah, she is.

Juana added, "Sooner rather than later you've got to show up in El Centro and tell them you're the one."

"But not today," Daley said. "Today's not a good day. I'll go first thing tomorrow."

"Go where?" said a voice from the door.

Daley turned to see Deputy Alvarez standing in the open doorway. She hadn't heard him come in.

"Deputy!" she said. "Good to see you! How's little Araceli doing?"

The deputy nodded to his old friend Juana, then stepped up to Daley. "What's with this 'deputy' stuff? I told you: It's *Sam*. And Araceli is doing beautiful, thanks to you."

"And I told *you*," Daley said, "Araceli cured *herself*."

Sam smiled. "You know better and so do I."

As much as Daley had tried to deflect credit from herself for the disappearance of the tumor in Sam's daughter's brain— Pard's work—he was sure she'd performed a miracle.

Sam turned to Juana. "I have something I need to discuss with Daley."

Juana folded her newspaper and said, "We've talked about what we needed to, and I was just leaving."

Sam pointed to the paper. "Was it about that?"

"What do you mean?" Juana said with a glance at Daley.

Not another one who recognized me!

"I mean the front page…are you here about the photo there?"

Juana looked like the proverbial deer in the headlights. "I… well…I…"

"You think that's Daley, don't you."

Another look at Daley and then her shoulders slumped. "Yes."

Sam nodded. "So do I."

"Oh, great!" Daley muttered.

"What do you expect?" Sam said. "I hear about a miracle cure and who do you think I'm gonna look for?"

Pard said, ("Another special case, primed to recognize you because he's expecting to see you.")

"And why are you upset?" Sam said.

"Because I don't *want* to be recognized."

His eyes fairly bulged. "Then it's really you?" He tapped the paper. "That's *you*? You're the one? You're curing the horrors?"

Daley nodded. "Guilty."

"*Madre de Dios*," he said, stepping closer. "I sort of had the thought in my head that it might be true but I never really believed...I..." His face fell. "Oh, damn!"

Uh-oh.

"What?"

"We had a lady come into our El Centro office saying she thought she recognized the mystery woman."

"Somebody *else*? Maybe I should have just hung a sign around my neck."

"She came all the way from Coachella."

Coachella? Oh, hell.

("Coachella? What's bad about Coachella?")

Something that happened before we, um, met, so to speak.

("*What* something?")

Hush. It may not be related.

"Did she give my name?"

"No. She gave another name which I didn't pay much attention to because I didn't recognize it and because she said the name was probably bogus because the woman she had in mind was a grifter who ran a car raffle scam in Coachella last month."

Oh, no.

"What did you tell her?"

Sam shrugged. "The only thing I could: We hadn't found the mystery woman yet. So the lady left her name and number and said to get in touch with her if we found her because she and her friends had a score to settle with this grifter. She also said that, if she turned out to be the same woman, the cures were probably bogus and she was no doubt running a scam on the hospital."

Shit!

Daley combed her memory for the name of the woman who'd pursued her out of Coachella...one vindictive little—Amber! That was it. Amber Seabolt.

She said, "Wow, she sounds like one angry lady."

Sam laughed. "Yeah, I wouldn't want to get on her bad side. But she's gotta be mistaken. All the docs at the hospital say those were real horrors patients and the three of them are really cured."

Daley nodded. "Yeah, obviously mistaken identity. You don't, um, happen to remember her name, do you?"

"Yeah. She left a bunch of her cards: Amber Seabolt."

Shit-shit-shit!

Still over by the window, Pard folded his arms and gave her a stern look. ("I'm getting the distinct feeling it's not a case of mistaken identity at all.")

We'll discuss it later.

Sam was staring at her, shaking his head. "You're the mystery woman...that's so great. When are you going back?"

Juana said, "She's going public tomorrow."

"Well, soon anyway," Daley said. Maybe she'd spoken too rashly, especially now, considering how Amber Seabolt was rearing her ugly head. "Real soon. But I need to choose the right time, so until then I've got to swear you both to secrecy, okay? It's very important that I control this."

"Understood, understood," Sam said as they both nodded.

"Okay, so I'm going to need a little space here to make my plans."

After good-byes and good-lucks Daley was able to usher them out. As she closed the door behind them...

("Okay, I've gone through your memory I found Amber Seabolt and I know what her problem is.")

"Good. Then we don't have to discuss it."

("Remember back in LA I warned you about these scams. They're time bombs. They never go away entirely. They're always waiting to come back and haunt you. Well, now one has.")

"If this is going to be an I-told-you-so party, you can stop right now. That was the end of my running that kind of scam anyway."

He held up his hands in a placating gesture. ("Okay. You're right. What's done is done. The question now is how do we deal with the fallout?")

"That's what I've got to figure. If I go public, my face will be on every front page everywhere, and Amber Seabolt will come charging down here with her accusations."

("Can we find some way to circumvent that?")

"Gotta be a way. We've got all day and all night. Let's work on it."

35

"What the fuck you doing in here?"

Jeffrey turned at the sound of the voice and found a dark-skinned guy standing just outside Jimmy's camper door. He had long black hair pulled back in a ponytail and looked pissed.

"Just getting my phone. Jimmy lets me charge it here."

"How do I know that's your phone?"

This guy was getting all sorts of righteous on him and Jeffrey didn't take kindly to that.

"You'll have to trust me on that. It's the one I used to call the EMTs this morning."

The guy's expression softened. "You're the one who found him? The neighbor?"

"That's me."

The guy extended his hand. "Santo. Jimmy and I moved in here about the same time—a long time ago, it seems."

He shook the hand. "Jeffrey." He raised the phone. "I was just gonna call the hospital to see how he's doing. The one in Brawley, right?"

Santo nodded. "Pioneers Memorial, yeah. But I can save you the trouble. He didn't make it."

It took a moment for that to sink in.

"Jimmy's gone? But he was talking as they carried him off."

Santo shrugged. "They couldn't save him. Whoever I spoke to either didn't know or wasn't allowed to say what the cause was, just that he didn't make it."

"He told me he thought something got busted inside, but I never thought…"

Jeffrey hadn't known that would be the last time he'd ever see Jimmy.

"He was a harmless little guy," Santo said, looking away. "Wouldn't hurt a flea."

"You know who did it?" Jeffrey said, wondering if he was the only one.

Santo nodded. "Got a pretty damn good idea. Something needs to be done about that guy."

Jeffrey tucked the phone into the breast pocket of his shirt, saying, "Well, don't look at me to do it. I got me a new leaf growing and I gotta keep off the law's radar."

"I hear you. Not that anything's gonna get done anyway. People talk tough and then nothing happens. This guy's been getting away with all sorts of shit and now he's gonna get away with murder."

"Well, I ain't been here long enough to know who you're talking about," he said as he hopped out of the camper to the ground, "and it's probably better if I don't."

He knew damn fuck well who done it, but he had a feeling he might be better off in keeping that to himself. No point in letting anybody else know.

"Smart man."

Jeffrey gestured to the camper. "What happens to all his stuff?"

"I'll see if I can find some family, but he doesn't have much that's worth anything."

"Doesn't even have any Fuegos."

Santo laughed. "Oh, you know about that."

The sun had set and a breeze was picking up.

"Yeah. His addiction." Jeffrey stared at the empty camper with its open door. "So you don't think nothing's gonna happen to the guy who did this."

Santo only shrugged.

Jeffrey waved and headed for his pickup where he wrapped himself in the blanket Jimmy had loaned him and stared out through the windshield. Jimmy's last words came back to him...

...said I ratted on him...sent someone to see him. I didn't rat...I think something got busted inside...

No, Jimmy, Jeffrey thought, you didn't rat. But Lugo thought you did...because of me. If I'd minded my own fucking business and gone back to my slab after I dropped you off, you'd be fine now. But no, I had to wander around until I found some asshole with a Navy logo on his place, an asshole who just happened to be sitting out front eating Fuegos when I passed. And okay, that would have been fine if I'd left it at that and kept driving, but no, I had to stop and talk to the fuck and leave him with the idea that you'd told me all about him.

Karma would have said "Tough shit" and let it go. Not his problem. People tended to get what they deserved, and Jimmy probably deserved what he got.

But did he? Jeffrey tried to find a way to make this Jimmy's own fault. Like he should have stood up to Lugo from the start and not let himself be bullied. But no, Jimmy was a scrawny little guy and not a fighter and the only thing that would have got him was a world of hurt.

And the worst part about all this was that Jimmy made damn good coffee and he wouldn't be making it no more.

Damn, that pissed him off.

This whole deal came to rest on Jeffrey's doorstep. All his fault. And that pissed him off even more.

He'd got the guy next door killed. Karma would shrug and walk away from that. But Jeffrey couldn't let that stand.

He removed GK from the glove compartment. Was this why she'd thrown it out the window? So he could use it to right wrongs instead of commit them? Lugo had done Jimmy wrong, and Jeffrey had been the cause. So it seemed only fair that he even the scale.

Yeah. The goddess would want that.

He slipped GK up his right sleeve, blade first, hopped out of the pickup, and started walking. Night had fallen but he remembered the way, and soon he was knocking on the door of Lugo's mobile home.

"Who's there?" said a voice from inside.

"We talked yesterday," Jeffrey said, looking around. Nobody in sight. "About Jimmy."

The door pushed open and Lugo stood there, glaring down at him. "I remember you. What you want?"

Jeffrey had his hands out, palms up. "Don't want no trouble, just gimme Jimmy's Fuegos."

"What?" Lugo said, making a face. "Are you outa your fucking mind?"

"Not a bit. He's dead and he left them to me in his will."

"He's dead? Well, ain't that too bad. I got dibs on his solar panels."

"The Fuegos?" Jeffrey said.

"Fuck off, asshole."

As Lugo reached out to close his door, Jeffrey charged up the three steps and shoved him back inside with his left arm while lowering his right and letting GK slip down into his palm.

"You wanna piece of me?" Lugo said.

Jeffrey made a backhanded stab, driving the blade into Lugo's liver and ripping across. Then two more backhanded jabs into the right side of his chest. He changed to a forehand grip and drove the blade into the heart area.

Then he stood back.

Lugo's eyes bulged as he clutched his bloody gut and dropped to his knees.

His voice was surprisingly soft as he said, "Not...fair."

"You got that right."

They say don't bring a knife to a gunfight, but it can come in real handy in a fistfight.

Lugo swayed on his knees, his mouth working, then his eyes rolled up as he pitched forward onto his face and lay still.

Jeffrey watched him for a while, waiting for him to breathe, but he didn't. He spotted a newspaper on the counter and wrapped GK in it. Then he jumped back outside, closed the door with the paper, and strode into the darkness. .

Quick in, quick out, then gone, leaving no prints.

Karma would have been proud.

SATURDAY—March 14

36

Someone knocking on his passenger window...Jimmy with some coffee?

No—couldn't be. Jimmy was dead.

Jeffrey bolted upright on the front seat and saw the guy from yesterday—what was his name? Santo. Right. He glanced through his rear window and saw the sun just clearing the peaks of the Chocolate Mountains.

"What's up?" Jeffrey said through the glass.

Santo made a rolling motion for the window. Instead Jeffrey opened the passenger door and got out.

"We need to talk," Santo said.

"So talk."

"I know what you did last night."

Jeffrey felt his insides go cold. What was going on here? What was this guy's play? He kept his expression and his voice flat.

"You mean sleep in my truck?"

"Hey, it's okay. I was hiding outside with a baseball bat, planning on breaking somebody's knees and then his head. I saw you go in and then come out. I know you was kinda friends with Jimmy so I wondered what was up. I peeked in the window."

"Yeah?"

Where was this going? Jeffrey wanted to kick himself for not spotting Santo last night. Yeah, it was dark, but still...

Santo stuck out his hand. "Thanks."

Jeffrey stared at it, not sure how to take this, then shook it, saying, "For what?"

Santo grinned. "If that's the way you want to play it, fine. Without mentioning your name—I haven't mentioned it to anyone—I told a friend I went over to give Lugo a pounding and found him dead. Together we took him and some of the carpeting under him out to the foothills and buried him. Then we left his car in Brawley with the keys in it."

"Won't somebody miss him?"

A slow shake of the head. "Nope. He's gone and no one'll look for him. We're going to have a celebration at the Range tonight. Most people won't know what it's about, but we will."

"What about his place?"

Santo shrugged. "We'll let it sit empty for a while, when maybe move somebody into it."

"And nobody's gonna say nothin'?"

"This is the Slabs, man. People come and stay, people come and go. There's no electric bills, no water bills, no property taxes, no nothin'. Lugo beat up Jimmy. When word came that Jimmy died, Lugo hauled ass outa here. That's all anybody needs to know."

He glanced past Jeffrey and his gaze fixed on something. Jeffrey turned and saw the newspaper he'd rolled up around GK lying on the passenger side floor.

"What?"

Santo said, "I'm figuring you've got some stains on that paper there. We have a trash fire on Saturdays now and again. You want that burned?"

Jeffrey grabbed it and GK fell out.

"Want me to take care of that too?" Santos said.

"No fucking way. That's a sacred knife. It's been blessed with the blood of a goddess."

Santos gave him a funny look. "Yeah. Okay. Maybe you better keep it then."

Jeffrey was about to hand Santo the paper when he saw the photo on the front page. Blurry, yeah, but re recognized her right away.

The goddess!

"I'll take care of this myself. Something I gotta read first."

"Have it your way, but I wouldn't keep it around too long. I—"

"Yeah-yeah-yeah. I 'preciate the offer but I gotta read this now. I mean like *right now*. See you later, okay?"

"Yeah, okay, whatever," Santo said. "Come over to the Range tonight. I'll buy you a drink."

He waved absently and paged through the paper. He'd heard about the Range—Slab City's open-air nightclub. No way was Jeffrey going to hang out there. He hadn't come here to make friends.

He found another photo on page 3. Nobody knew who she was but some people thought she was curing horrors patients. No one could cure horrors patients except maybe this mystery woman.

Maybe? Ain't no maybe about it. She was a goddess. If she could raise herself from the dead, she sure as fuck could cure a horrors patient or two—do it with her eyes closed and standing on her head.

It came to Jeffrey then that maybe the Goddess wasn't through with him. Because it sure as hell looked like she'd sent him a sign. It pieced together so nice: He uses GK to bring divine justice to Lugo and what's waiting for him there to see? A picture of the goddess. Really, how obvious could you get?

She was telling him he had a part to play in all this. But what? He couldn't ask her—she'd banished him.

Maybe his aunt would know. His mother's sister lived all alone out in the desert. He was pretty sure those two probably hadn't spoken since his mother ran off and got married to his asshole father. Now that those two were dead, maybe his aunt felt bad. He knew where she lived. Not far. Maybe she could tell him what to do.

Might be a good time to move on anyway. If Santo knew what he'd done, sure as shit others would know soon enough. People just couldn't keep their mouths shut.

Yeah, he'd just drive out of here like he was heading to the Buckshot for breakfast and keep on going. He'd been here less than a week and hadn't given his last name to anyone. Nobody'd miss him—most people didn't even know he was here—and only Santo would know he was gone.

Yeah, time to go find his Aunt Juana.

37

Lucy missed breakfast. She rarely missed a meal, but if she ever did, breakfast was the one. Usually because she'd been up extra late. So Tom ate alone this morning and was perfectly happy with that.

Breakfast was the one meal they didn't order in. Not that they actually went shopping. That would involve Lucy leaving the house. No, Lucy made a list—of course—and Instacart delivered the groceries every week.

Tom had finished his usual Wheaties and skim milk and was perusing the *Pasadena Star-News* when Lucy breezed in wearing a dark-blue kimono embroidered with a golden dragon. Well, damn, he should have moved to the den. Maybe he'd be lucky and she'd be in one of her blessedly frequent silent modes. At least she'd left her katana upstairs.

"Finally broke through that firewall," she said in her Minnie Mouse voice.

Oh, hell. She was going to gab.

Okay, he'd bite. "What firewall?"

She rolled her eyes as she popped two Eggos into the toaster. "We went over this: the Welsh clan out in the desert with the private fund and the incredible investing record."

Vaguely familiar. "You wanted to know their method but they were heavily encrypted, right?"

He remembered her furious expression: *They know something I don't know, Tommy.*

"Right. Very heavily encrypted. Had a tough time. I mean, can you believe it? Took me five whole days."

Well, color him shocked. Five days? As a rule Lucy could waltz through any firewall.

"And what did you find—insider trading?"

"Nope. Star trading. The clan uses astral configurations to guide their investments."

"Astrology?" He couldn't help but laugh. He didn't need an MBA to know astrology was not much use for investing. Not much use for anything, in fact. "That's crazy."

"What I thought, but you can't argue with results, which have been too consistently good to attribute to luck." She reached inside her kimono. "Here. I made a list of all—"

Lucy and her lists. He waved her off. "That's okay. I'll take your word."

The waffles popped up and he watched her slather them with butter, filling every indent, and then drown them in Mrs. Butterworth's Syrup, making sure every indent was suitably flooded. Tom considered mentioning her bulging waist under the kimono but thought better of it.

"What I didn't find was why they're selling off. They've consistently sold off before every major downturn so I'm taking it this means another."

"We're not in the market so what do we care?"

That furious expression. "They're hiding something and I'm going to find out what it is. I copied all sorts of stuff from their server. They've got a family history and this huge translation of some ancient scrolls."

"What could ancient scrolls have to do with the stock market?"

"Apparently that's the source of their investment advice—the star trading. The scrolls' official title is *Teachings of the Empty Places.*"

Tom turned to the obituaries. "Sounds fascinating."

"I'm going to start with their family history, because that's lots shorter. If that doesn't answer my questions, I'll have to plow into the Scrolls."

"Go for it, Lucy."

And she would. Part of her Asperger's spectrum thing—if indeed that was her problem—was relentlessness.

38

Jeffrey was glad for the high clearance on his pickup. The path that passed for a road out here in the Santa Rosa foothills was uneven as all hell. If you didn't take it slow you risked busting an axle.

Finally he found it: a tiny RV painted puke lime green. Two aluminum lawn chairs sat out front in the shade of a canopy strung from the door. He parked about fifty feet away and turned off the engine. He could hear a generator running somewhere in the back. Obviously the two solar panels on the roof didn't produce enough watts. She'd probably be better off living in Slab City than all alone out here. Safer, at least. Although, considering what happened to Jimmy, maybe not.

He got out but didn't approach. Instead he stood by the driver door and called, "Hello, inside!"

This looked like his aunt's RV but that didn't mean she still lived in it. And you didn't just stroll up to somebody's door out here. Some people lived alone for damn good reasons—either cooking some product they shouldn't, or bug fuck crazy. Either way, you didn't want to startle them.

The door opened and a vague shape stood in the shadow under the canopy. He couldn't make her out very well but no question about the big revolver she held waist high and pointed his way.

"Who goes there?"

"That you, Aunt Juana?"

"'Aunt'? I ain't nobody's aunt."

"It's me—Dominga's kid, Jeffrey."

The barrel dropped a little, angled more toward the ground now, but still pointed in his direction.

"Jeffrey?"

"Yeah. Jeffrey Kendrick."

"What do you want?"

Not exactly a big welcome but he hadn't expected one.

"I need some help."

"If you're looking for money—"

"No-no-no. Advice. I need advice. Mom always said you were the smartest sister and knew everything."

No harm in stroking the old gal, right? Couldn't hurt.

"I wouldn't listen to your mother. She never had a lick of sense."

"Well, I can't listen to her no more on account of she passed."

"Oh?" Softer..."Oh." Then, "Well, what do you need advice about?"

"This is gonna sound weird, but I met a goddess."

"You found yourself a girlfriend?"

"No, a real live goddess."

The pistol barrel lifted again. "You high on something?"

"No way. She's real as can be." He reached through the pickup window and grabbed the newspaper in the front seat. He held up the front page for his aunt to see. "And here's her picture."

Aunt Juana stared a minute, then stepped out of the RV and pointed her pistol at the pair of chairs.

"Sit. I want to hear how you know this 'goddess.'"

He did as she directed and took the chair nearer his truck. Aunt Juana sat in the other and laid the pistol in her lap, but still aimed at him. Big muzzle on that thing. Wouldn't do to have it go off on accident.

"I'd feel a whole lot better if maybe you could point that the other way."

She angled it toward her RV, which he noticed was studded with seashells. You could find them everywhere in the valley. What she do—dig them up and glue them to her home? His momma had said Aunt Juana was smart but she'd also said she was weird.

"Talk," she said, then jabbed a finger at the paper. "How do you know her? And is that blood?"

He glanced at the brownish smears from GK. "I was painting something."

During the drive out here Jeffrey had rolled this conversation over and over in his mind: How could he put this? How do you just up and tell your aunt you killed someone? And then how do you explain how that someone came back to life? But he finally figured since his Aunt Juana didn't know the goddess, he could just come out and say it—after swearing her to secrecy, of course.

"Okay. It's kind of complicated but you gotta promise me that what I tell you here don't go no farther."

She frowned. "Is it bad?"

"Well, yes and no. You promise?"

"Okay, okay," she said, looking annoyed. "I promise. Now get to it."

"Okay. Here's the thing: I was hired to kill her."

Aunt Juana's face got this real shocked look—*real* shocked. Not something you hear every day from your nephew, for sure, but she looked like a mother who'd just been told her kid had been killed.

"What?" she yelled, coming half out of her chair. "*What? Who*—who hired you?"

"Oh, I can't tell you that. I—"

"When are you supposed to do this?"

"I already did it, but—"

"You *killed* her?"

His aunt had the pistol up and pointed at him. The rage and grief in her eyes told him she was going to kill him. In desperation he swung his hand at the barrel and connected, just before it fired, sending the bullet over his right shoulder.

"What the fuck?" he shouted, ripping it from her grasp.

Damn, his ear was ringing like he had it pressed against a fire alarm.

But she wasn't through with him. She leaped at him with her fingers curved into claws that raked at his eyes. As he dropped the pistol and grabbed her wrists, it dawned on him:

"You know her? Goddamn, you *know* her!"

Shit, if he'd had a clue about that he never would have come here.

He shook her. "Calm down, calm down! She's still alive!"

But his aunt wasn't calming down a bit.

"You just said you killed her!" she screamed.

"Yeah, but she brought herself back from the dead!"

She froze and stared at him. "What?"

"You heard right: I stabbed her in the heart and killed her but she rose from the dead and threatened me with the worst kinda hell if she ever saw me again."

"Wh-when was this?"

"A week ago...early Sunday morning."

Aunt Juana stumbled back and dropped into her chair.

"A week ago? You stabbed her in the heart...and she didn't die?"

"Oh, she died all right. I know dead when I see it and she was dead. But she came back and knocked on my door and showed me how I'd spend the rest of forever if I didn't disappear. So I been sorta hiding out ever since. I mean till I saw this in the paper. How do you know her?"

She stared off at the horizon and spoke in a low voice. "I helped her set up her shop."

"Yeah? I never seen you there."

"I've been in and out. I was there yesterday and she seemed... fine." She looked at him now. "She's very important."

"Hey, tell me about it. She's a goddess."

"Goddess?"

"Hey, what else do you call someone who can rise from the dead? Plus she's curing the horrors."

"Yes...she is."

"So that's why I'm here. I didn't know you knew her, but maybe that's even better."

"You must tell me who wants to harm her."

Jeffrey shook his head. "Naw. Can't do that. I can tell you he's probably pretty pissed at me for not getting the job done."

"All right then, don't tell me. I have a pretty good idea who it is."

"Yeah?" No way she could know. "Who?"

She hesitated, then said, "Elis Pendry."

The words escaped before he could stop them. "Holy shit! How'd you guess?"

She shook her head slowly. "Not a guess. I know a lot about Elis Pendry, none of it good."

"But he can fuck off, y'know? I ain't harming a hair on that gal's head."

"You must do more than that. You must protect her. You must become her guardian."

"Is that what she's trying to tell me?"

"'Tell' you?"

He didn't think Aunt Juana needed to know about GK and

Lugo. He tapped the newspaper.

"This picture…I get the feeling she's sending me a message."

"Perhaps Pendry will try again."

"Well, if he does, he won't do it himself. He ain't the type that wants to get his hands dirty, and he ain't got many choices waiting around to do that kind of dirty work for him."

"But she's going to go public soon. Everyone will know her name. That will probably protect her from Pendry but not from the desperate and the deranged who will be drawn to her. Once her name is out there, you will have to keep watch."

"But I can't let her see me."

"When the time is right, I'll talk to her. Where are you staying?"

"I was up Slab City, laying low in my truck, but I moved out this morning."

"You can park here for now."

Jeffrey looked around and liked that idea. Nobody—not Pendry, not the goddess, not anybody from the Slabs—would ever find him out here.

39

("You're not opening today?")

"Nope." Daley said, shaking her head. "Not tomorrow either. Taking the weekend off."

She sat at the kitchen table sipping her morning coffee and chewing on a breakfast sandwich from the Coyote. She'd decided to take Arturo's suggestion and try his Taylor Ham special: thick slices of fried pork roll with cheese and a drippy, over-easy fried egg on a Kaiser roll. Pard sat opposite her, munching on a virtual version—so she wouldn't have to eat alone, he'd said.

"Damn," she said around a mouthful. "This is delicious. Why didn't anyone tell me about Taylor Ham before?"

("It's been an ongoing conspiracy to keep you miserable. But back to not opening: That's because…?")

"Because my picture is everywhere."

Not just her picture, but *movies*—CCTV footage of her walking down hospital hallways on every news show in

Southern California—maybe the world. Arturo had provided the icing on the cake this morning as he'd poured her coffee. He'd pointed to his little TV behind the counter where a news show was playing the footage with the insistent and recurrent plea for someone-anyone out there to identify this woman.

"You know," Arturo had said, "there's something really familiar about her. I almost feel like I know her."

Daley had abruptly changed her order to takeout and scooted back to her apartment.

"The more people who see me, the greater the chance of being recognized."

("So you're going to spend the weekend in hiding?")

"Yep, that's exactly what I'm going to do. I might even crawl back into bed."

("Why don't we simply go public?")

"And have Amber Seabolt labeling me a grifter? They'll run me out of town."

("Not after we start saving people from the horrors. Her accusations will hinder your credibility, but not my effectiveness. Once we prove ourselves—")

"But what if they believe her to the point where they won't let me near the victims?"

("Then we go straight to the families. I have no doubt we'll find plenty who'll do anything to help their loved ones. And once the irrefutable results start coming in, all doors will open.")

"Damn!" She wanted to kick something.

("What's wrong?")

"Oh, just everything. I thought I was so clever, running my little games, always one step ahead of everyone else. Now—just as you said—it's come back to haunt me."

("But it's not that cut and dried, is it?")

"What do you mean?"

("Think about it: If you hadn't run that car raffle scam in Coachella, Amber Seabolt and her friends wouldn't have unraveled your scheme and chased you into the desert—")

"—where I hid in a cave," she interjected, seeing where he was going. "A cave that just happened to house an alaret that dropped on my head—"

("—and merged with you, resulting in my becoming sentient and, by some long, strange, meandering route, our becoming the only way to cure the horrors.")

"So it comes down to…if I hadn't done bad then, I wouldn't be able to do good now."

("That's one way of putting it. Though not your original intention, your not-quite-legal scheme led—via an intricately circuitous route—to something good. I found an old saying in your head that seems to fit here: 'Oh, what a tangled web we weave when first we practice to deceive.'")

"So it all comes down to Amber Seabolt. If she hadn't sussed out my game, I'd be sitting alone in North Hollywood right now with no white patch in my hair, both my original hands, and plotting out my next scam."

Would she be better off that way? Happier? She didn't have an easy answer. In fact, she had no answer. For sure her life had become more interesting. But what was happiness, anyway? Had she ever been really happy?

("And I'd still be a non-sentient creature clinging to the roof of a cave. I guess I should say 'Thank you, Amber Seabolt.'")

"Is that…what? Irony?"

("I'm not sure what it is. More like unintended consequences.")

The cascade of events gave her an uneasy feeling.

"Are you *sure* they were unintended?"

Pard frowned. ("What are you getting at?")

A switch had flipped in Daley's head and she was seeing recent events in a whole new light.

"I mean the timing of everything we've been through is just so…so impeccable. I've run that car raffle scam a number of times in different towns and no one has walked away unhappy—clueless, yes, but nobody thought they'd been taken. Not this time, though. This time, in Coachella, a desert town, Amber not only figures it out, she chases me. But do I turn north toward where I live? No, I turn south, deeper into the desert."

("Well, I'd say it's smart not to lead someone's who's angry with you to your home.")

"Yeah, but then Amber and her posse get stuck at the Avenue 66 traffic light which gives me an opportunity to take a turn-off that leads me onto a desert side road toward the Santa Rosa foothills where my Jeep just happens to die. I look around for some shade and a vantage point, and gee, what's just a short walk up the slope? Your cave."

("Well...")

"Hear me out, Pard. I made a whole series of decisions along the way: turn north or south? I turned south. Continue on the 111 down the east side of the Salton Sea or bear right at the fork and take the 86 along the west shore? I took the 86. Stay on the 86 or get off? I chose to get off. I had my choice of a number of turn-offs, but the one I chose—just like every other choice I made—took me straight to you. *Me.* According to Juana, only one in a thousand can survive an alaret. I just happen to be that one. Doesn't that make you wonder, just a little bit?"

("This is how conspiracy theories get started. You've got some incidents or coincidences in your life you can't explain. So you ask yourself, 'What's going on here?' The honest answer is, 'I don't know.' But humans hate like crazy to utter those three words, so they start connecting the coincidences with speculations until they have what appears to be an explanation. They may not like the explanation, but at least the world makes some sort of sense again and, best of all, they don't have to speak that dreaded phrase, 'I don't know.'")

"Got it all figured, don't you?"

("Pretty much.")

"So, you don't get a feeling that something has started manipulating my life?"

("'Something' is awfully vague, don't you think?")

"I don't have a choice *except* to be vague, because it's just a feeling."

("Okay, let's accept for the moment that 'something' wants you here. Why here? Why Nespodee Springs?")

"That's what I was asking Juana. I think she really believes this is 'a place of power,' that some sort of 'lines of magic' crisscross here, but who knows?"

("Indeed. Who knows? In my reading I came across an approach to the unexplained called 'Occam's Razor.' It boils down to the position that the simplest and most direct explanation is usually the most likely.")

"What would Occam's Razor say about the Tadhak's windfarm? How would it explain a place that's bigger on the inside than it is on the outside?"

She still couldn't over get that monstrous space.

("Quantum physics,") Pard said in his everybody-knows tone.

"Tell me in terms I understand. I don't understand quantum physics."

("Nobody does, including me, that's why it makes for a perfect explanation.")

"Okay, wise guy, how would Occam's Razor explain what's been happening to me?"

("Probably 'feces abound.'")

Daley had to laugh. "In other words, 'shit happens'?"

("Precisely. We may have to deal with a certain amount of fecal matter when we go public tomorrow, but if we can locate the source of the horrors, it will all work out to everyone's advantage.")

"I just hope the fecal matter doesn't involve Amber Seabolt. Let's hope you never meet her."

("I have a feeling that's inevitable.")

Daley dreaded that confrontation.

40

"Our servers were hacked this morning," Rhys said as he moved his rook. "I'd been assured that no one could get through, but he did."

Cadoc countered with his bishop and said nothing.

Rhys threatened the bishop with his queen. "No comment?"

"I don't care about our servers," his brother said from the shadows. "I don't care that we were hacked. If it was a curiosity hack, so what? If it was a malicious, destructive hack, I'm sure Papa has everything backed up."

He had a point, but he sounded almost hostile.

"It wasn't destructive, but I think they copied pretty much everything."

"Well, then, you can hope they die of boredom reading through it." He slid his bishop three squares and said, "Checkmate."

Rhys leaned back and stared at the board—as usual, the only illuminated spot in the darkened room. Beaten again. But he'd seen that coming. He smiled.

"I can't tell you how good it is to hear you say that. Not that you won again, damn you, but that you're actually able to *say* it instead of just tapping my king."

His brother's voice had improved so much since Rhys had last stopped in on Tuesday night. Barely a whisper back then, but so much louder now with a tone that was virtually normal. Rhys hadn't heard him speak—truly speak—in more than a decade. His vocalizations had been pretty much limited to grunts since they were teenagers.

Cadoc chuckled and double-tapped the king. "I can still do that if you want. But I hope I never have to resort to 'Ungh' again."

"As do I, bro. Amen to that."

"Since we're on the subject of improvements, I've got something I want to show you."

He heard Cadoc rise from his chair and cross the room. Then, shockingly, the lights came on and he found himself staring at his brother.

Rhys shot up from his chair. "Cad! What's happened to you?"

His brother stood there in gym shorts and a T-shirt. By normal standards, his skin was a mess, but by Cadoc standards— Rhys remembered what he'd looked like when he'd gone into seclusion—he'd undergone a miraculous transformation. Much of his skin was still gray and peeling and barklike, but a good portion of it looked normal. Significant patches on his arms and legs and even his face had cleared of the Pendry Patch.

"I'm..." His voice sounded on the verge of breaking. "I'm clearing."

"Your voice *and* your skin! This is fantastic! Fucking fantastic! But how's it happening? Have you been getting treatments or something?"

"I haven't seen a doctor since I was a kid."

"Is it something you're smearing on? Some kind of supplement you're taking?"

"I'm not doing anything different to my body, not taking anything new."

"So...it's just happening?"

Cadoc hesitated, then said, "My only worry is that it won't clear all the way. Or worse, that it'll regress to where I was before."

"You can't think that way, bro. Gotta be positive." Rhys had an urge to hug him but held back, unsure of how he'd react. "So it's just...happening?"

"We live in wondrous times."

"Yeah, I guess we do. Look at the horrors. They came out of nowhere and now people are getting cured and no one knows why. Sort of like you."

"Sort of."

Speaking of the horrors...

"Hey, did you see that mystery girl from the medical center? She reminds me a little of Daley."

Cadoc started pulling on a light sweater. "You mean because she's slim and young? That would fit lots of women."

"Yeah, but they sort of move the same, you know?"

Cadoc pointed to Rhys's chair. "Sit down. I want to talk to you about Daley, okay?"

Daley? What did Cad have to do with her?

"What about?" he said as he settled.

"I've been in contact with her."

"Contact how?"

Cadoc left the lights on and took his seat on the other side of the board. So weird, after all those years sitting here in the dark, to be able to look at him like this. But he'd fixed his gaze on the board.

"I've been visiting her for a couple of weeks now."

"Visiting? But you don't let anyone see you."

"I would be outside her back door, she'd be inside, she'd talk, I'd write notes and slip them under."

"You never told me."

"You'd have thought I was being weird."

Yeah, he would have, because it was totally weird.

"She's never mentioned it either."

"I never told her my name. She had no idea I was your brother, and I asked her not to mention me to anyone."

"But why Daley?"

Cadoc shrugged, eyes still down. "I was drawn to her. Papa's fixation on her was part of it. And...I get lonely, Rhys."

Shit. Of course he did. How could he not? And Rhys spent—what? A couple of hours a week with a chessboard between them. He could have been a better brother all these years.

"Hey, I'm sorry. I should have—"

"No," he said, raising a hand and finally looking at him. "I chose to cut myself off and live this way. It's all on me. So don't you go beating yourself up. Anyway, she's..." His gaze dropped again. "She's wonderful, Rhys. You're very lucky to have her."

Oh, hell. My brother's in love with Daley. Well, why not? Who wouldn't be?

"Yeah, well, I don't know if anybody can 'have' her. She's pretty independent. But—"

"That's not why I sat you down, Rhys. That's just the preamble. I need to tell you that a week ago today, early in the morning, I sneaked Daley into the Lodge and started showing her the film."

Rhys wasn't sure he'd heard right. "You said 'the film'? As in *the* film?"

Cadoc nodded, still eyes down.

"You showed it to Daley?"

Eyes up again. "I only got through the first half."

Rhys could only stare at his brother. He'd just confessed to a major betrayal of the entire clan.

"Holy shit! Does Dad know about this?"

"He found out."

"He must have been...been..."

Cadoc's lips twisted. "Apoplectic? You could say so. Especially since he thinks I showed her the second half as well. He actually locked me in my room while you two were in San Diego. Like a bad little boy."

"Have *you* seen the second half?"

A nod. "Many times."

"Goddamn it, I haven't seen it *once!*"

Only Elders and prospective Elders like Rhys were allowed to see the second half of the film, and not until age thirty. Rhys still had two years to go.

"But you need to," Cadoc said. "You can't wait till Papa says it's okay. You need to see it *now.*"

"Why? And why would you show Daley?"

"I'm not sure. Probably because Papa thinks she's some sort of threat to the clan's destiny or mission or whatever delusions are driving him. And I think he may be right."

"About destiny?"

"No. About Daley. She's special, Rhys."

"You've obviously got a crush on her, but—"

"I'm very clear eyed about this. Daley is here, in this place, at this time, for a reason."

"Hey, you getting mystical on me, bro?"

"Not one bit, but there's more going on here than meets the eye. Papa is wrong about many things, but he's right about Daley: She poses a definite threat to his plans."

"A threat? She's a twenty-six-year-old shopkeeper without a mean bone in her body. What kind of threat can she pose?"

"I don't know. And she doesn't know either. She's totally clueless."

Rhys could believe that. Dad had been worried about her since the "pairing" message had come through, but Daley apparently remained oblivious to whatever role Dad expected her to play in his drama. If she had a part to play, someone had neglected to tell her about it.

Cadoc added, "But she needn't remain clueless. And neither do you. You both need to see the second half of the film."

"Well, show it to me."

"I can't. When Papa found out about Daley being here, he hid it away and I can't find it. Believe me, I've tried."

"All right then, tell me what's in it."

Cad shook his head. "You need to see it. You won't believe me if I tell you. You'll think I'm misremembering or I've gone crazy. You need to see it yourself."

"It can't be that bad, Cad."

"Really? There are reasons only the Elders are allowed to see it. Very *good* reasons."

Normally Rhys would write off a conversation like this as someone having too much to drink or too into drama. But Cad didn't drink and had always been anchored in reality. Plus... why indeed was viewing the second half of the film limited only to the Elders?

"Hey, Cad, if I can't see it and you can't tell me about it, what's the point of talking about it?"

Cad leaned forward. "There may be a way..."

SUNDAY—March 15

41

"Which is worse luck?" Daley said as she donned her Healerina ensemble. "Friday the thirteenth or the Ides of March?"

("I'm not going to have this conversation.")

"You said worrying about Friday the thirteenth was bogus and look what happened. Now we have 'Beware the Ides of March' and—"

("Julius Caesar was assassinated on March 15, but not because it was a bad-luck day. It was a religious holiday until Shakespeare fabricated the warning for his play. Bad-luck day for Caesar, yes, but not for the rest of us.")

"Every day's a bad-luck day for somebody somewhere, don't you think?"

("Not exactly a cheerful worldview, but the odds favor your being right.")

Daley grinned. "Hey! We agree on something!"

("Well, even a broken clock is right twice a day.")

"You've learned sarcasm."

("I've had an expert teacher.")

She checked herself in the mirror. Everything seemed in place. She wasn't opening Healerina today, but didn't want to present herself at ECRMC in jeans and a peasant blouse.

The Healerina ensemble…the outfit Pard had picked out for her before she'd opened the shop: a long-sleeved, scoop-neck black top, the black tights and skirt, the Cahuilla art stone Juana had given her tied around her neck. All that black made her white patch of hair seem to blaze.

She felt a need to look the part.

But really...what part was that? Pard was the actual healer but hers was the face, the image they'd present to the world. And *world* wasn't an exaggeration. She had no illusions about that. Once word got around that this chick could cure the horrors, everyone would want to know about her—*all* about her. All her past sins would be revealed. And forgiven, most likely. Someone who could cure the horrors would earn a pass on petty crimes and misdemeanors.

Everyone would want a piece of her. That was the part that scared the crap out of her.

But she'd decided to put her unique features out front—the white patch in her hair, the golden left hand. They would define her in the public eye. Hell, someone would be selling action figures of her before long. But she was counting on that very distinctiveness to help her hide when she wanted to. Put on a hat, glasses, and a pair of gloves and she became just another person.

("Nervous?") Pard said.

"A little."

("We'll do fine. You'll identify yourself as the woman they've been looking for. You'll admit you sneaked into the hospital and cured those three horrors patients. The medical folks will demand proof and you and I will give it to them. Pretty straightforward, right?")

"But then Amber Seabolt shows up."

("Won't matter. We'll have cured a clutch of horrors victims by that time and nothing anyone says can undo that. You'll be the toast of the town—the state...oh, hell, the *country*.")

"Right. And then we have to deal with that."

("We'll deal. The fact is, this plague needs to be stopped, and we're the only ones we know of who can do it. So let's do it.")

"But coffee first."

("Absolutely.")

Rather than walk all the way around the side, she cut through the store, back door to front, and stepped out onto the boards that passed for a sidewalk. A few doors up from her, Jason Tadhak came out of his office and waved as he strolled to his car and opened the trunk.

("For a man who's supposedly rich, he doesn't seem to mind working on a Sunday.")

How do you think rich people get rich? Not from taking a lot of days off.

("I wish you could ask him about that surreal storage area at the windfarm, but we weren't supposed to be there.")

As Daley stepped out into the street to cross to Arturo's café, she noticed a big SUV speeding downhill from the spa. The silhouette of the driver seemed to have his or her head down and the car was drifting to its right...toward where Jason was leaning into his trunk. She kept thinking the driver would look up but now the car was aimed directly at him.

"Jason!"

He looked up just as the SUV plowed into him, catching the rear of his car and sending him flying. He landed hard a good ten feet from the impact and Daley was rushing toward him before he stopped tumbling.

"Oh, God, Jason!"

A girl who couldn't have reached twenty yet jumped out of the SUV screaming *"Omigod!"* over and over. The phone in her hand explained why her head had been down.

Jason wasn't moving. Daley dropped to her knees beside him, calling his name. He was breathing but didn't respond.

("Make contact,") Pard said. ("I'll see if I can find what's wrong.")

Daley grabbed his wrist—his skin was cold—and hung on, still saying his name while the girl kept up her *"Omigod!"* mantra in the background.

Pard said, ("Okay, going in. I'll let you know when—")

His voice cut off abruptly which was unusual. Not alarming, just different.

Pard?

He didn't reply. Probably just busy. Daley gave Jason a quick visual check: He wasn't twisted into some crazy, unnatural posture; no blood, no obviously broken bones

The girl finally got a bit of a grip and said, "Who can I call? Who can I call?"

Daley thought about that. On a Sunday morning, Doc Llewelyn was very likely at home instead of in his office. The unconscious Jason was going to need an ambulance for sure, but that could take a long time to run from Brawley or El Centro.

Behind the girl she spotted the white Tadhak bus turn onto the street and roll their way.

"I think help is here now," she told the girl.

Perfect timing. They could take Jason straight to a hospital without waiting for an ambulance to drive all the way out here. She waved her free hand to flag them down but they kept on coming with no sign of slowing. She thought of stepping in front of the bus to make it stop but that would mean breaking contact with Jason, which would interrupt whatever Pard was doing inside.

The bus pulled past her, then made a three-point turn and came to a stop beside Jason. The side doors folded back and two men in gray coveralls, both with Jason's blocky build, stepped out and marched toward him.

"You're pointed the wrong way," Daley told them as they approached. "He needs to go to a hospital."

They didn't answer her—didn't acknowledge her presence let alone that she'd spoken to them. Without a word, one grabbed Jason under the arms, the other grabbed his ankles, and they lifted him.

"Hey, wait!" she cried, still clutching his wrist. "Be careful with him!"

She couldn't tell them that she was helping a separate consciousness explore Jason's insides and try to help him.

They ignored her and finally she had to let go.

Sorry, Pard.

She watched them carry Jason through the doors and lay him on the floor of the bus.

Pard?

No answer.

The side doors closed and the bus roared back upslope toward the Tadhak compound instead of down toward the towns and the hospitals. Did they have their own doctor up there? Some kind of infirmary?

Hey, Pard…

Still no answer. Where was he? Had something happened to him?

PARD!

42

Tom got a text from Lucy:
>*Got through the Clan history!*
>*They're planning the end of the world!*

Lucy liked exclamation points. Another recurrent annoyance.

He found her dressed in another of her kimonos and lying on the floor of her room, staring at her tablet. The tablet was bedizened with sticky notes containing her latest lists.

"What's this about the end of the world?"

She didn't look up. "Okay. So I decrypted the history of the Pendry Clan document, and dug into it, and am I glad I did. These folks have definite plans to bring on the end of the world—or at least the world as we know it."

Tom stared at her, looking for some sign she was kidding. But besides being literal and brutally honest, Lucy's totally flat affect didn't allow for humor. As in *zero* laughs. Because humor was an emotion, after all. Well, sort of.

"You've got to explain that."

She rose from the floor in a surprisingly fluid motion for one of her bulk and tossed the tablet onto the easy chair. "After we eat. I'm hungry."

"Hey, you're talking about the end of the world."

"Yeah, but that's not maybe gonna happen until long after lunch, and I'm hungry *now*."

He sighed. "What do you want to eat?"

"I'll make a list."

He had to wait for Grubhub to deliver from one of Pasadena's three KFCs before she'd talk. When it finally arrived, she dove into the Colonel's extra crispy—chewing with her mouth open, of course, another of her endearing habits. Eventually, after demolishing a leg and a thigh, Lucy got gabby.

"It all goes back to the British protectorate in Egypt," she said, swaying back and forth as she started on a breast. She often swayed when she sat.

"Protectorate? You've lost me."

"The Brits occupied Egypt after the Anglo-Egyptian War. From 1882 to 1956. Everybody knows that."

"Oh, right-right. Of course."

Tom hadn't the faintest what she was talking about. Lucy possessed a phenomenal memory crammed with all sorts of useless info. Probably from making all those lists. Tom figured he saved brain space by being choosy about what got filed away.

"So, anyway, lots of the upper-class types liked to vacation there—you know, see the Sphynx and the pyramids, ride camels through Giza, see all the old shit. The clan lived in Wales then, and one of the patriarchs went on one of those sojourns to Cairo in 1888 and was browsing a back-alley souq when—"

"Whoa. A back-alley what?"

"A souq. A bazaar. A marketplace."

"Then why not just say that instead of using a weird foreign word?"

She stopped in mid-chew to stare at him over the breast. "Everyone knows what a souq is."

He waved it off. "Go on."

"Okay, so this patriarch is browsing this *mar-ket-place*"—she said it slowly and carefully—"and comes across these battered old scrolls. On impulse he buys them and doesn't realize until he's back in Wales that he's got something special. The tip-off is a crudely accurate map of the world in the third scroll. He figures this is evidence that either the scrolls are fakes or its author had been granted knowledge unique among his contemporaries."

Tom said, "I don't get it."

Another withering look. "A map of the *world*, Tommy—the *whole* world. If the scrolls are as ancient as they're supposed to be, nobody was doing maps of the Americas and the Pacific Ocean back then, at least not until the sixteenth century."

"Oh."

"Alwyn eventually discovers that he owns the only existing copy of *Teachings from the Empty Places*—AKA *The Void Scrolls*."

That put Tom on instant alert. *Void* was a magic word for Lucy.

"So?"

"So I looked them up and there's not much info on them. No one knows where or when they originated. Legend has it the original set of scrolls had been written in Sanskrit but that those were a translation from an earlier, even more ancient language. From Sanskrit they were translated into Arabic, then Greek. In 48 BC the last set was presumed lost when Caesar burned forty thousand scrolls stored in a warehouse at the Library of Alexandria."

Really? Tom thought. How did one know how many scrolls were stored in an Alexandria warehouse in 48 BC? *How?* Whatever.

He said, "I'm gathering this set survived."

"You gather rightly. Apparently one of Titus Livius's flunkies had stolen a copy of the Greek translation before the fire. It got handed around down through the centuries with no one aware of what it was and wound up in this souq. The Pendry patriarch has it translated into English and what he reads changes his life."

Titus Livius...scrolls...Tom's eyes were glazing over. Lucy was unusually loquacious today. She could go for days with no more than monosyllabic responses or without speaking at all. Something had sparked her. But this was typical when she started talking on something she was into: on and on in stultifying detail. He didn't need all this background.

"What about the end of the world? Can we get to that part?"

"Relax. It's coming, it's coming. The scrolls tell of a time, four or five million years ago, when a race of alien beings occupied areas of the Earth. The Rymwyr—who called themselves 'the Lords of Creation' but are mostly referred to as 'the Visitors'— dwelled here during Earth's warmer days when ice caps were minimal and the oceans were higher."

This had an all-too-familiar ring to it.

"Let me tell you now, Lucy: The Scrolls are fakes. Someone's been reading too much of that Cthulhu Mythos shit."

She blinked. "You know Lovecraft?"

"Who doesn't these days? I've heard it all before and so have you. The maps and the whole tone of this scenario reek of a scam."

"Maybe we've heard it all before because people read these ages ago and remembered. And as far as a scam goes, according to the notes, the Scrolls were carbon dated back to BCE."

Tom shrugged. "I can go out and buy ancient blank papyrus and write whatever I want on it."

Her eyes lit with fury—there was that anger. "I know that, Tommy. Everybody knows that, which is why they had the ink dated and it's also BCE." She flashed a *so-there!* expression and went on. "The scrolls were written by an ancient group that worshipped the Rymwyr. Where the Rymwyr originated— another star, another galaxy, another dimension—no one can say, but one of their fave spots was an inland sea that ran from Palm Springs into the Gulf of California. When that dried up they decided to go elsewhere. Their return, if they come back at all, has to coincide with specific astronomical alignments."

"Let me guess," he said, urging her toward the point of all this. "Those alignments have occurred."

She held up a hand. "Don't rush me."

Damn.

Finishing the breast, she said, "The patriarch shared all this with his relatives and they started a cult that worshipped the Rymwyr. His son inherited leadership. For some reason—and I haven't ferreted this out yet—the San Francisco earthquake in 1906, combined with the flooding that created the Salton Sea in 1907, and then the two Imperial Valley earthquakes in 1915, persuaded the whole clan to move from Abereiddy, Wales, to the Salton Trough just a year later. They settled in a place called Nespodee Springs."

"Never heard of it."

"Nobody has. It's in a remote corner of the Sonoran Desert in Imperial County."

"A string of earthquakes *attracted* them? That would convince me to go just the opposite direction."

"I know, right? I get the impression the clan took the earthquakes and floods as a sign that the Visitors were coming back, but they haven't yet."

"Obviously. Well, this is all just riveting, Lucy, but once again I ask: What's any of it got to do with the end of the world as we know it?"

She'd grabbed a KFC biscuit and was slathering it with butter.

"Oh, that."

"Yeah, that."

"Well, the current leader of the clan keeps a digital diary of his progress toward bringing the Visitors back."

"And these Visitors are going to end the world as we know it?"

"If they're real." She jammed half the biscuit into her mouth and spoke around it. "Which seems highly unlikely."

Tom had to agree. Except...

In the past few weeks they'd experienced two quakes, a 3.6 and a 5.5, both originating in the Imperial Valley.

"You mentioned earthquakes attracted the original clan members back in the last century. And now we've got a couple of new ones. Connection?"

"I've been wondering the same thing. Most likely just coincidence, but I've got a lot yet to read. The clan scanned all their ancestors' papers into the server, and they were a verbose bunch."

Takes one to know one, Tom thought, but kept it to himself.

"Does this digital diary offer any clue as to how they plan to bring these Visitors back?"

She brushed off her hands as she rose from the seat. "It's currently on my reading list. I downloaded it to my tablet and was reading it when you stopped by. I'll let you know if I find something to worry about."

Lucy walked away, leaving him with the leftovers to clean up. Another hateful habit.

43

Y ou must protect her...You must become her guardian...

His aunt's words had haunted Jeffrey all night as he lay in his truck wrapped in Jimmy's blanket. Why should a goddess—one who could rise from the dead—need a puny human like him as her protector?

But Aunt Juana knew things most people did not. She said she knew a lot about Elis Pendry. Maybe he and his clan could find a way to kill the goddess so she'd stay dead. Maybe it was his job to get between them and the goddess. Maybe that was why she'd sent him that picture in the newspaper.

Putting it all together, he'd wound up back here in Nespodee Springs, parked downslope from her shop and apartment. He'd angled his pickup so he could keep watch on her place through his rearview and side mirrors.

He'd watched her come out the backdoor of her shop, go up the steps to her apartment, stay there for maybe ten or fifteen minutes, then come back down to the shop for about the same amount of time, then go upstairs again.

What the fuck was she up to?

44

D aley had spent most of the morning and into the early afternoon wandering through the aisles of her closed shop, then up to her apartment where she wandered from room to room, and then back down to the shop. All the while calling to Pard—usually in her head, but sometimes out loud.

Pard, where are you?

What could have happened to him? It had to have something to do with Jason Tadhak. Had he found Jason's nervous system more comfortable? A better fit? More welcoming?

Pard's voice had cut off in midsentence. Was that when he'd deserted her? If he'd left her...if he'd made the leap then, he wouldn't have been able to tell her because he would have been out of her system and into Jason's.

If he'd left her...
Would he do that?

He could be so annoying at times—no, make that *often*. More often than not. And he was always around. Always. She confessed that got on her nerves. How could it not? Did he sense that? She certainly hadn't made him feel welcome at first. And why would she? He *wasn't* welcome. Really, who'd welcome a second mind to their body? The whole situation was intrusive, invasive, bizarre.

And his obsessive-compulsive nature. She couldn't let herself get started on that. Like having Felix Unger or Sheldon Cooper living in her head—and constantly rearranging the furniture up there.

And yet...

And yet, against all odds she'd grown accustomed to his presence. She never thought she'd miss his annoying quips and constant corrections. No, wait. She didn't miss them. She'd just gotten used to them, like people living near train tracks got so used to the recurrent rattle that it stopped bothering them after a while. That was what he'd been: a noisy train rattling through her brain. And now that train had stopped running.

Not a bad thing...not a bad thing at all.

Three...no, three and a half weeks with Pard in her head, in her life. Not all of them bad, but maybe that was enough time together. He'd learned about humanity through her, and in return she'd learned a few things about herself. She might even be a better person now because of him.

Pard wanted to help humanity—well, at least those humans struck down by the horrors. Today was the day they'd planned to return to the medical center and see if they could do something meaningful about it, something beyond curing random cases.

So much for that plan. Up in smoke. Without Pard, she was helpless. No, make that *useless*. He was the essential ingredient; she was simply the transportation, the conveyance. If he preferred Jason, well, Jason could grab a victim's wrist just as well as she could, allowing Pard to go in and do his business. She was fine with that. Totally fine.

And yet...

And yet right now she knew she'd take a lot of comfort in the sight of Pard perched on his spot over there in the shop's front window.

"Goddamn it, *Pard!*"

A knock on the glass of the shop's front door interrupted her. She stepped to where she could peek at who was there and saw Rhys. He waved to her. She wasn't in the mood for company but she couldn't very well turn him away now that he'd seen her.

She unlocked the door and pulled it open.

"Is everything okay?" he said with a concerned look.

"Yeah, why?"

"I thought I heard you shouting at someone just now."

"Oh, that." What to say? "Just having a bad day. And when I'm having one of those I sometimes shout at the air. Makes me feel better."

His expression turned dubious. "You shout at…the air?"

"Do you see anyone else around? Now that you're here, I can shout at you. Want me to?"

"If it'll make you feel better."

Don't be nice to me, she thought. I'm too on edge for nice people.

"It won't." She stepped back and held the door. "Come in, come in so I can lock this again. I'm not opening today."

"Because of your bad day?"

"You got it. How can I scream at the air when there are people around?"

"Not the best way to encourage browsing, I imagine. But I'm glad you're closed today."

"Oh?"

"Yes. I had a little talk with my brother about you last night, and he told some surprising things."

Daley had known this was coming.

"Oh."

"Like Cadoc has been visiting you for weeks now."

"A nameless, faceless, voiceless stranger was visiting me. He never let me know anything about himself—least of all that he was your brother. And that was just a few days ago."

Rhys nodded. "Yeah, he told me. He also told me he'd shown you the first part of the film."

She was trying to read him, to suss out how he felt about that. She started to think the question at Pard but caught herself.

"It was...interesting, to say the least. I definitely want to see the second half."

"Very few people have. Including me."

"Cadoc thinks you should see it too. No, I think he said you *need* to see it. Something about learning 'hidden truths' about your family and its beliefs about its 'destiny.'"

Rhys sighed. "Yeah, there's that. Sometimes I wonder if I want to know these hidden truths. But...can't hide my head in the sand. My father's grooming me to take over his spot someday so I guess it's time to take the bit between my teeth and..." He frowned. "Why am I suddenly spouting clichés?"

For sure Pard would have had an acid remark.

Daley said, "I don't know, but you were on a roll there and I didn't want to interrupt. Anyway, the digital conversion company is in La Mesa and I have the number...somewhere."

Where? She'd been scattered after the Thursday night revelations at the windfarm, and then the Friday the thirteenth debacle at the hospital...where had she put the paper Cadoc had given her? Pard would remember...

The cash drawer. Yes. The *empty* cash drawer. She'd shoved Cadoc's note in there for safekeeping. She pulled it out and handed it to Rhys who immediately punched it into his phone. He listened for a few seconds, then ended the call.

"Closed on Sundays. Looks like we'll be heading over the mountains tomorrow. Unless you're opening the shop."

"I close on Mondays and don't plan to change the routine. According to your brother, the owner won't give a copy to just anyone. Has to be a family member."

Rhys smiled. "Someone with ethics. How refreshing. Looks like we've got a three-hour roundtrip road trip ahead of us."

"Can you get away? I thought—"

"Hired a new foreman yesterday. Or I guess I should say I promoted him from the ranks. I'm actually getting my life back. We can get the copy in La Mesa, have lunch there or in San

Diego, then come back here and have a watch party."

"I'll buy popcorn." She was trying to keep it light but she had a feeling from Cadoc's attitude that watching the film would not be a fun experience. "But my DVD player's back in LA."

"I'll have them put it on a flash drive and we can stream it on a laptop."

"Sounds like a plan."

"Hey, we still on for dinner tonight?"

Yikes. She'd forgotten about that. If she and Pard had followed through with their plan to go public with healing the horrors, she would have had to cancel. But now...

"Sure. Mama's Meatball, right?"

"That was the plan." He gave a little fist pump. "It's Sunday gravy night."

"Can we go early? I need a pasta fix."

"You got it. Pick you up at five thirty?"

"I'll be ready."

He headed for the door. "What are you doing the rest of the afternoon?"

"Gonna hang out here and scream at the air."

His look said he wasn't sure she was kidding. "Ooookaaay. See you later."

After she let him out the front door, she checked the front window ledge. No Pard.

"Pard?" she said to the empty shop. "Pard?"

She had a long afternoon ahead of her. Maybe she could find something on TV to pass the time. It had been a while since she'd been able to watch anything without a running commentary from the alien in her head.

She went out back and was halfway up the steps when she heard the voice behind her.

"Not so fast there, Daley."

Shit!

She turned to face Billy Marks.

"What are you doing here? I told you to stay away from me!"

"Now-now-now, Daley," he said with a placating smile, "before you go getting on your high horse again, give me a listen."

"Forget it!"

"I don't want to get in your way. You work your angle, I'll work mine. All I need you to do is, when you're finished with your marks, you send them to me for follow-up to prevent relapse. That'll be my specialty—no relapse under my guidance. That way we both wet our beaks."

"I won't be sending you anybody, Billy, because I'm out of it."

Not by her choice, but facts were facts. On her own she could do nothing for those people.

His smile disappeared. "Don't try to bullshit a bullshitter, Daley. Just 'cause you got yourself an angle, don't think you can keep it all to yourself."

"Listen and listen well, Billy. There's nothing to share. And like I told you Friday, we're done here."

As she turned to continue back up to her apartment, she heard a clatter on the steps behind her. A hand grabbed her and spun her around to put her almost nose to nose with Billy's furious face.

"Get this straight, you stuck-up little twat! You still belong to the Family and you'll do what I tell ya!" He grabbed her by both upper arms and bent her backward over the railing. "Don't fuck with me, Daley! Nothing I'd like better right now than to toss you over and break your scrawny little neck. But you're gonna come through for us, or goddamn it I'd do it!"

He shoved her onto the stairs and stomped back down to the ground. She lay sprawled on the treads as she watched him stride out of sight around the corner of her building.

Could things get much worse? Pard was gone, someone wanted her dead, and now Billy Marks was coercing her into preying on people who were already in dire straits.

She heard an engine start and saw a pickup truck down slope pulling away. It looked vaguely familiar, but then all pickups looked about the same to her. Probably someone renting down by the Thirsty Cactus. Maybe she'd be lucky and they'd run over Billy Marks like that girl had run over Jason Tadhak this morning.

If nothing else, she could look forward to dinner with Rhys tonight.

45

Jeffrey couldn't believe it. He'd sat stunned, paralyzed with shock as that guy had manhandled the goddess. It all happened so quick. Before Jeffrey could react, the stranger had shoved the goddess onto the steps and walked away.

He'd heard her call him "Billy," which meant he wasn't no stranger to the goddess. Jeffrey could tell from the git-go she didn't like him neither.

He'd wanted to chase after him but that would have meant getting out of his truck which would have allowed the goddess to see him. No way was he letting that happen. So he chose instead to drive out to the street and see if he could spot him there.

He eased to a stop in the alley between the Thirsty Cactus and the grocery store and checked the street—just in time to see Billy drive by in a Jeep Cherokee, heading out of town. Jeffrey gave him a long lead, then followed.

Billy led him to one of the budget motels on Adams Avenue in El Centro. Jeffrey parked at the opposite end of the parking lot and removed GK from the glove compartment. He hadn't had a chance to rinse the blade so it remained crusted with Lugo's blood. He slipped it between the buttons of his shirt and let it rest against his belly as he watched Billy step out of his Jeep.

He didn't have no plan. He was playing this totally by ear. Did Billy already have a room here or was he going to rent one? But he didn't head for the office, and he didn't head for one of the ten doors in the strip of rooms. Instead he hit the sidewalk and entered the bar next door.

Well, all right. Jeffrey wouldn't mind a brew or two himself right now.

He reached behind the front seat and grabbed the old Stetson he wore now and again. Might help keep his face hid in case he had to do some prolonged trailing of this dude. He adjusted it on his head, low on his forehead, and followed Billy inside.

46

"Want to tell me what's wrong?" Rhys said as they lingered over their coffees. Well, cappuccinos.

Daley held off answering because she didn't know what to say. Instead she stirred her cappuccino with an almond biscotti. Dinner had been delicious. Spaghetti and meatballs sounded so basic, but when made just right, few meals were better. The waiter had divulged how they made Mama's meatballs—a mix of veal, pork, and beef fried in lard—but no one would spill the secrets of her Sunday gravy.

"I'm sorry if I haven't been good company tonight."

"Something I said or did or didn't say or didn't do?"

She bit off the soggy end and began stirring again.

"Oh, it's not you at all." How could she put this? "I lost a friend."

"Oh, I'm sorry. How old was she?"

She forced a smile. "It's a he and he didn't die. He just up and took off without saying good-bye. One moment he's there, the next moment he's gone."

"Not very nice."

"No, it's not very nice. In fact it stinks."

She almost expected Pard to chime in with some sort of protest, but...nothing.

"It does. Big time. How close were you?"

She held up a pair of crossed fingers. "As close as you can get without sex."

She almost laughed at the look of relief on his face.

"When did you hear?"

"This morning." She bit another piece off the biscotti.

"Speaking of sex, you have no idea what watching you dunk and eat that cookie does to me."

"You mentioned that last week but you didn't say it makes you think of sex."

"But it does. Oh, yeah, it does."

She looked at what was left of the biscotti. "Come to think of it, it kind of makes me think of sex too."

His eyes practically bulged. "Really?"

"Totally. And you know what? I think we should stop thinking about sex and listen to Nike."

"You mean, 'Just do it'?"

"I do."

She didn't want to be alone tonight.

Rhys started waving his arms. "Waiter! Check please? Check!"

47

Finally, after sitting at the bar for hours and downing one beer after another, Billy stopped drinking and paid his bill. Jeffrey had seated himself in a corner and nursed a few Tecates. He wanted to stay clear and alert.

Billy didn't stagger out the door, but he moved with that careful walk of someone who's had too much to drink but ain't quite falling-down drunk. Jeffrey gave him a few seconds, then followed.

The sun had set but the clear sky still held light. He spotted Billy shuffling back to the motel parking lot. He wasn't actually thinking of driving somewhere, was he? No. He went straight to room five.

As he fumbled with the key, Jeffrey pulled GK from within his shirt and came up behind him, timing his approach to arrive just as the door swung inward. He body slammed Billy from behind, propelling him into the room and slamming the door behind him.

The drapes on the front windows were open, allowing in enough light to see faint details of the room as Billy stumbled forward and tumbled onto the bed. Jeffrey didn't go after him. He knew from experience that drunks could be unpredictable, so he held back to see what he'd do. He might stay face down on the mattress and start to snore, or he might bounce back up and charge.

Billy bounced, screamed, "What the fuck?" and charged.

Jeffrey held GK before him, waist high, and let Billy run straight into it. His eyes bulged with shock and pain as he staggered back, clutching his bleeding belly.

"Wh-wh-what?"

Jeffrey stepped in with the moves that had never failed him in the past: backhanded strike to the right lung, forehand to the heart.

"You put your hands on the goddess," he said as Billy flopped back on the bed and began a slow, wide-eyed slide toward the floor. "Nobody puts their hands on the goddess and lives. Except me. I was spared to take care of sinners who do."

Billy's baffled expression said he didn't know what the fuck Jeffrey was talking about. Well, Jeffrey had only just begun to understand all this himself. He was tempted to slash Billy's throat as a final punishment for his sin, but in the past he'd always regretted when he'd given into that temptation. Messy as all hell.

Billy stopped sliding but kept staring as his butt came to rest on the floor. Jeffrey looked around. Had he touched anything? No. He pulled back the bedspread and wrestled a pillowcase free. He used that to wipe the blood off GK, then wrapped it around his hand while he closed the curtains. He used it to open the door, then tossed it back inside as he left. Nobody about, so he strolled to his pickup and drove away.

Time to head back to Nespodee Springs and return to his guard post.

MONDAY—March 16

48

Cadoc winced as half a dozen plates shattered on the floor.
He had hoped to make a quiet entry into the dining room and simply take a seat while he waited to be served. But Maria ruined that. At the sight of him seated at the table her jaw dropped as did the stack of china plates she'd been carrying in from the kitchen.

"Señor Cadoc?" she cried.

Papa rushed into the room, drawn no doubt by the crash, and skidded to a stop on the tile floor as his jaw also dropped.

"Cadoc? Cadoc, what are you doing here?"

"I was hoping to have breakfast and save Maria the trip to my room."

"You can speak? You can speak! And your skin—it's almost clear!"

"How observant of you."

"I've got to tell your mother!" He hurried off, calling, "Hefina! Hefina!"

Maria approached him hesitantly. He remembered how beautiful she was before he'd gone into isolation. She'd aged but was still an attractive woman.

"I will fix your usual, sí?"

"Por favor. That would be wonderful."

As she bustled away he poured himself a cup of coffee from the carafe on the table.

He'd awakened this morning, taken a selfie—he had no mirrors in his suite—and decided he might be ready to face the world. Well, not the world, just his family. He'd already revealed himself to Rhys. He didn't give a damn about Papa, but his mother...she'd taken his self-imposed isolation hard, especially after losing Aerona to the miscarriage. She'd been left with one child when she should have had three.

He was ready to pour a second cup when his mother rushed in. She slowed to a stop halfway across the floor, then crept toward him with tiny steps, as if afraid she'd startle him and chase him away.

Over the years he'd watched her from the shadows—he watched everything from the shadows—as she'd sunk into depression and gained weight from the meds she took to ease the hurt from her unborn daughter's death and her firstborn's withdrawal from life.

He rose and went to her and enfolded her in his arms.

"Mom...I'm so sorry."

They sobbed together for a while, and then she pushed back and held him at arm's length.

"What's happened, Cadoc?"

"I've decided it's time to rejoin the human race. But slowly. By inches."

"But your skin, your voice...what's happening? How...?"

He'd promised not to associate his clearing to Daley. Not yet. He'd wait until she revealed her power to the world, then he'd give her credit. But for now he'd respect her wish for privacy.

"It's just seems to be happening, Mom."

"It's the Visitors," Papa said. "Their return is imminent and already it's having beneficial effects on the Faithful."

You're a monster and a madman, Cadoc thought, but he'd save his vitriol for a time when Mom wasn't around. For now he'd ignore him.

"Where's Rhys?" Mom said, looking around. "It's been so long since I've seen both my boys together."

"He'll be back later," Cadoc told her. "At the moment he's on a voyage of discovery...to San Diego."

49

The day went swimmingly until after brunch, and then it turned ugly.

The sex had been good last night, really good, lasting until the early hours of the morning when Rhys had left for home. Daley had wanted him to stay, but couldn't bring herself to ask. The town's tongues were wagging as it was and the sight of them walking across the street together for breakfast at the Coyote would trigger a blast of blather. So she'd lain in bed alone and lonely.

Pard's absence was a hollowness behind her eyes. She'd never thought she'd say it, but she missed him, damn it. Missed him terribly.

Rhys had picked her up not too many hours later at seven a.m. and they'd headed off to La Mesa in his Highlander. The trip over the mountains on the 8 had been an uneventful ninety minutes and along the way they'd discussed the first part of the film that they'd both seen. Rhys told her about the ancient scrolls—*Teachings from the Empty Places*—that were the basis of the Clan's religion and the film, and how his father had adapted them to a successful investment guide. He declared the content of the Void Scrolls as total bullshit, but couldn't deny his father's success with the stock market. Maybe he only thought the Scrolls were guiding him and his own innate savvy was the secret of his success. Whatever, Rhys was not a believer.

In La Mesa, after presenting suitable identification to verify his Pendryness, he was allowed to purchase copies of both films on flash drives.

When Rhys asked the owner, a chubby, nerdy Asian named Nozawa, why his father's disks could be played only on one machine, he explained that they might have been encoded for a different NTSC region or in PAL or SECAM format. Daley understood him about as well as she understood the parents in the Charlie Brown videos. She learned that the format on the flash drives would play on any computer with the proper software and that was enough for her.

Mr. Nozawa offered to sell them an all-region DVD player if they wanted to make a comparison but they passed, asking instead about a good place nearby for an early lunch. He recommended a Mexican restaurant down the street where they shared tacos and quesadillas.

As they were walking back to Rhys's car, they passed a convenience store with the latest *San Diego Union-Tribune* on display in a rack out front. The headline and accompanying photo stopped Daley cold.

HORRORS HEALER FRAUD?

Below that was a grainy photo of Daley in the ECRMC parking lot standing outside her car with Billy Marks.

Daley's heart clenched as she blurted, "Oh, no!"

"Hey, that looks like you," Rhys said, stopping beside her.

"It is."

No sense in denying it. Anyone who knew her could identify her from that photo.

He stared, wide-eyed. "You're the mystery woman everyone's been looking for?"

"Apparently, yes."

"Why didn't you tell me?"

"Because I didn't want anyone to know."

She grabbed the paper and opened to the story while Rhys peered over her shoulder.

Details were few. They'd yet to identify her at press time but her "companion"—Billy Marks—was well known to police as a career conman. The assumption was that if the mystery woman credited to the "miraculous" cures of the horrors—the significance of placing *miraculous* between quotation marks now wasn't lost on Daley—was associated with a known grifter, the two of them must be working up a horrors-related scam.

She jammed the paper back into the rack and walked on.

Guilt by association. Great. Just great.

The *Imperial Valley Press* would have the same story and photo, no doubt. Her cover was completely blown.

Rhys caught up with her. "I don't understand, Daley. You've got to explain this to me."

How on Earth could she do that?

"Let's wait till we're on the road."

She hoped that by the time they got back on the 8 she'd have an explanation, but she didn't.

"First off," Rhys said as they headed into the hills, "how do you know the conman in the photo?"

"His name is Billy Marks, some sort of a distant uncle on my father's side, who I'm pretty sure murdered my father on the day I was born but no one can prove it."

Rhys shook his head as if to clear it. "Wow. That is one loaded sentence."

"Did I mention I hate him?"

"You didn't have to. Your tone of voice pretty well carried the message. But if you hate him, why were you talking to him?"

"He won't leave me alone. He recognized me last week in that front page photo and came looking for me."

"Why?"

Here's where things get dicey, she thought.

"He thinks I'm working a scam at the hospital."

Rhys made a face. "A scam? Why would he think that?"

"Because his family—my father's family—that's how they live. They're all grifters. He thought I was setting up a scam with the horrors and he wanted me to butt out because he's claimed that for himself."

"Really? Ripping off horrors victims? How's he going to do that?"

"Don't know and don't want to know."

"But why would he come to you?"

"Because I was born into that family and left it to live with my Gram when I was thirteen. He wants me back in."

Rhys shook his head. "I'm realizing there's so much I don't know about you."

"I could say the same thing about you, don't you think?"

"Yeah, I guess so. We're both going to learn something about my people when we watch the rest of the film."

Good. The conversation was shifting away from her. She had to keep it moving.

"What do you think we'll see?"

Rhys shrugged. "I can't imagine what needs to be kept so secret, and frankly I'm a little scared. But my brother's seen it, and if he can handle it, so can I. We'll know soon enough, won't we. But back to you..."

Oh, damn. She wished he'd drop this. But how could he?

"Everyone thinks the mystery woman—and that would be you—cured the horrors. Don't think me crazy for asking this, but...did you?"

"No."

Pard did.

"But why do they think it?"

"I don't know. Can we drop this?" She tried to keep the annoyance out of her tone but didn't think she succeeded.

"If you want. I'm just curious about how you got saddled with this healing thing, especially since your shop is named 'Healerina.' I can't help wondering."

Healerina...Pard had hated that name. Daley wished now that she'd listened to him.

"I guess it's because they had these mysterious cures to explain and I was photographed just after they occurred."

He was nodding. "I get it: the *post hoc* fallacy."

"Well, I don't. What does that mean?"

"I remember it from a logic course in college. It's Latin. *Post hoc, ergo propter hoc*: 'After this, therefore because of this.' It means if B follows A, then A must have caused B. They saw you in the vicinity after the cures, so therefore you must have caused the cures. And the fact that they didn't know who you were only made the fallacy more attractive."

She nodded, seeing how easy it could be to fall into that trap. "Got it."

"It's how superstitions get started: 'I was burning incense during the storm when my next door neighbor got hit by lightning and my place didn't. I've burned incense during every storm since and have never been hit.'"

"Well, once the speculation started, I kept mum. You've

already mentioned that my shop's named 'Healerina,' and so if I identified myself I'd look like I was trying to cash in on the horrors."

He grabbed her hand and gave it a squeeze. "I'm proud of you for that. Integrity is a rare thing these days."

The thought of all the people she'd conned since high school soured the quesadilla sitting in her stomach.

You have no idea, buddy boy. No idea at all.

50

"Doctor Heuser!" Hendry said. "We've got P waves!"

Becky Heuser looked up and immediately spotted them on the monitor.

"Imperial Zone again."

She just happened to be in the data analysis room on the second-floor of Caltech's South Mudd Building. The not-so-big room was lined with computer stations. Large black letters high on the long wall announced it as part of the *Southern California Seismic Network*.

Two giant monitors were suspended beneath the words. The left monitor displayed seismic maps of Southern California, the western US, and the world. The right showed twenty or so feeds from seismic sensors set up all over the southern end of the state. The overall effect was like an EEG. A steady, staticky pattern was the rule, but now some were showing P waves—the faster compressive waves that precede the damaging S waves.

Her research assistant Mark Hendry was nodding. "The Elsinore fault."

"Did you notice any of those sine waves we saw before?"

"Nope."

Damn. The last two quakes from that area had been preceded by a weird sine-wave configuration she hadn't been able to trace or identify. All she knew was that it originated in the lower Imperial Valley.

"All right," she said, "issue a ShakeAlert."

"Will do."

The ShakeAlert Early Warning System gave people a heads-up to prepare for a quake. If they'd downloaded the MyShake app, their phones would let them know to get under a table or inside a door frame, or head for an exit before the building started shaking.

This didn't look major at all. But she wished she could get a line on those mysterious sine waves.

51

Daley wasn't sure what to expect on her return to Nespodee Springs, but she hadn't expected a sheriff's unit parked outside the shop. Sam Alvarez stepped out as Rhys pulled in next to it.

He touched the brim of his Stetson. "Morning, Daley. I suppose you've seen the papers."

"Yeah, Sam." She stepped out and leaned against the Highlander. "I have. I know it doesn't look good, but there's a simple explanation."

"You don't have to explain anything to me, Daley. Not now, not ever. I told you: You have a friend for life."

Daley felt her throat tighten. *A friend for life*...she had a feeling she'd need every friend she could find.

"Thanks. I appreciate that."

Rhys had come around the front of the car by then and introduced himself.

Sam turned back to Daley. "There are, however, some people at the medical center who have some questions."

"I'm sure they do."

"Who in particular?" Rhys said.

"Doctor Milton. He's chief of medicine."

Daley nodded. "Saw his press conference. What's he want to know?"

Sam's lips twisted. "He didn't share. But he's a good guy. You've been identified from the parking lot photos and he was wondering out loud how he could get hold of you. I told him I knew where I could find you and I'd pass on his request."

"Request for what? He wants to call me?"

"He'd like a face-to-face."

"Ohhh, I don't know about that."

"I don't either," Rhys said. "Sounds like some sort of inquisition."

Daley could sense him going into protective male mode. He definitely had her back and she loved him for it.

"I'd never allow that," Sam said. "There's nothing official about it. You don't have to agree, but I think you should. Just to clear the air."

"Of what?"

"Misconceptions, insinuations. That photo of you with a scam artist like Marks puts your reputation in danger of going down the tubes."

Anger flashed. Not fair! "I never took an ounce of credit for those cures!"

"*You* know that and *I* know that, but the papers want it to be something else and you with Billy Marks makes it a juicy story that'll sell copies. Showing up there could make it all go away."

"I think he's right," Rhys said. "And I'll go with you."

She looked at him, impressed. "You will?"

"Damn right, I will. I'm not letting you go into the lion's den alone. I'll be right at your side to dazzle them with my Latin." He winked. "You know—*post hoc* and all."

"You're serious?"

"Absolutely."

Well, she had these two on her side. Sam because he thought she could work miracles and would wow them with her magic. Little did he know that the magic had deserted her. And Rhys... Rhys and she had something brewing. He was solid, and he believed in her. She sensed they could go a long way.

She turned to Sam. "All right then. I'll meet Doctor Milton at nine tomorrow morning, if that works for him."

"I'll make sure it does," Sam said, grinning. "This is going to be great. I'll see you there."

"You're coming too?"

"You kidding? I wouldn't miss this for the world."

He waved, hopped in his unit, and rolled away.

"I think you've got a fan," Rhys said as he watched him drive off. "I heard his 'friend for life' remark. What's that supposed to mean?"

Daley repressed a smile. A little jealous, perhaps? Nice. But how to answer? She figured she could get away with the truth.

"His daughter had a brain tumor that miraculously disappeared, and he thinks I made it go away."

Rhys was nodding. "Yeah, well, I can see how that would make you a devoted friend. Did you?"

Here it comes.

"Did I what?"

"Cure the tumor."

"I wish I had that power. But no, it wasn't me."

Pard had done it...which started her thinking...

What if Pard had changed his mind and wanted to come back? He couldn't simply hop from Jason to Daley. He'd need contact. And even if he didn't want to come back, maybe he'd agree to a temporary reunion. That way she could go down to the medical center tomorrow and heal a few horrors victims... turn the doubters into believers.

Yeah, but then what? What if Pard wanted to go back to Jason? Where would that leave her? She'd have to come up with a reason she could no longer heal. Like maybe: the power burned out...or only so many cures in her...

She'd come up with something. The main result would be that the cures would be real and no one could call her a fraud or a fake.

Except for Amber Seabolt. But she was back in Coachella, and even if she opened her yap, no one would believe her then.

"I have to go visit the Tadhak compound," she said.

Rhys's eyebrows shot up. "Whoa! Talk about out of the blue! Where did that come from?"

"I was out here in the street when Jason got run down yesterday and I'd like to see how he's doing."

"I heard about that. He's in the compound? I assumed he was in a hospital."

"No, a couple of his relatives came by in the bus and took him away."

He shook his head. "Typical. They are the weirdest family."

Daley noticed a woman and her daughter from the Pendry clan coming out of the grocery store, both in long-sleeved, long-hemmed gingham dresses. Rhys followed her gaze and laughed.

"Okay, we Pendrys have some strange customs as well—I'm the first to admit that—but we're positively prosaic next to the Tadhaks."

"Still, I'd like to check on him before we settle down with the film."

"Hop in. I'll drive you up."

"It's not that bad of a walk."

"But it's all uphill—both ways."

She laughed. After what she'd seen at the windfarm, she wouldn't be surprised.

And then the ground started shaking.

"Oh, shit!" Rhys said. "Another one!"

But it was mild and lasted only ten seconds or so. The first thing Daley did when it stopped was check her front window: intact, no cracks. Good.

"That's the third one in as many weeks," Rhys said. "What's going on?"

"The end of the world. Come on. I want to get to the Tadhak place before there's another one."

So she let Rhys drive her to the compound—up almost to the Lodge and the spa, and then around to the left to the high beige wall that took up the whole end of the road. Everything that might have sported a hint of an angle or a sharp edge had been smoothed over. The result looked like a wall of coffee ice cream left out of the freezer too long. Beige meringue surrounding a single door and no windows, hiding whatever lay beyond.

"Wait here," she said, sliding out her seat. "I shouldn't be long."

"You don't want me to come with you?"

She waved him off. "It's okay."

She needed to ask Jason some pointed questions about a second consciousness he'd just acquired, questions Rhys wouldn't understand. He didn't need to know.

She walked up to the massive wooden door and looked for a

buzzer button. Finding none, she banged the thick iron knocker set in its center. She half expected the mustachioed guard from the entrance to Oz to open a tiny window and ask *Who goes there?*

But no. After a short wait, the door swung inward on silent hinges to reveal a dark-haired man with a familial resemblance to Jason. He was dressed in the gray coveralls that seemed to be popular with the workaday Tadhaks.

"Yes?"

"Hi. I'm Daley. I rent the—"

"I know who you are." His lips—only his lips—smiled. "Good day to you. Is there a problem?"

"Oh, no. Not at all. By the way, how did you fare in the quake?"

His brow furrowed. "Quake? What quake?"

"The one that rattled everything a few minutes ago. You had to have noticed it."

He shook his head. "We felt no quake."

No quake? Nobody was that oblivious.

"Is that why you came?" he said and started closing the door. "We appreciate your concern but—"

"No-no. I was down on the street yesterday when Jason was hit and—"

"Yes. We know. Thank you for trying to help."

"Don't mention it. How is he?"

She angled her neck to see if she could see past him and catch a glimpse of the inside but her view was blocked by another door identical to the first, forming some kind of vestibule. They must *really* like their privacy.

"He's healing, thank you for asking."

"Great. I was wondering if I could speak to him."

He shook his head gravely. "I'm afraid that's not possible while he's healing."

"Just for a minute? I have a question I need to ask him."

"No. Sorry. Not possible. Not while he's healing."

"Please? It's very important."

He started pushing the door closed. "Three more days. He'll be well enough to speak to you in three more days."

"But—"

The door thudded closed.

Damn. Three days meant Thursday...way too late for her purposes.

She stalked back to the car, hoping her frustration didn't show.

"Not exactly a warm welcome, I gather," Rhys said as she got in.

She sighed. "Not hostile or anything, but no way was I getting past that door."

"I've never heard of a non-Tadhak getting inside—ever. How's he doing?"

"He's 'healing.' That's all I got."

Three more days...something about that bothered her but she wasn't sure what.

Rhys backed them into a turn, saying, "Well, that's good. He's always seemed like a nice man."

Before yesterday she would have agreed. But he'd put her in an awful position by stealing Pard.

But *had* he stolen Pard? Four days to heal up with Pard on board? That didn't seem right. Considering how he'd grown her a new hand overnight, fixing up some internal injuries and a few broken bones should be a walk in the park—two days at most if the injuries were really serious. And today was already the second day. But Jason needed three *more* days before he'd be able to *speak* to her?

Something not right here.

"Why the troubled expression?"

"What?" Was she letting it show? "Oh, just thinking about that missing friend. I need to get my mind off him. Let's go see that film."

But if Pard hadn't switched over to Jason Tadhak, where was he?

52

"I know this is a far cry from the Lodge's A-V room," Daley said as they huddled before the 12-inch screen of her laptop, "but it's the best I can do."

She'd pulled the window shades for better viewing, and now she plugged in the flash drive with the second film.

Rhys grinned. "It's fine. And the company's certainly better."

"Cadoc couldn't risk playing the soundtrack when he showed me the first film, but I did fine with the subtitles. The speakers on this thing have been next to worthless since I dropped it a couple months ago, so I hope this one is subtitled too."

"Supposedly it was originally on one reel and shown only to the Elders. When my father had it digitized, he divided it in two. He thought the first part was useful as education for the clan's hoi polloi."

"And the second part...not educational?"

"We're about to find out, aren't we."

His expression was strange...a mix of anticipation and dread.

"You okay with this?"

"Not at all. Because I have no idea what 'this' is. I'll let you know when I do. Let her rip, Daley."

She found the file and hit *PLAY.*

As the screen lit with a panoramic aerial view of the Imperial Valley from the west—the green checkerboard of farmland south of the blue of the Salton Sea, all surrounded by the beige of the desert—the speakers accompanied it with bursts of static.

"So much for that," Daley said as she muted the sound.

"You must have damaged your sound card," Rhys said. "But we've got subtitles."

THE VISITORS CAN BE LURED BACK TO THEIR OLD PLAYGROUND BUT ONLY IF THEY FIND THE ENVIRONMENT HOSPITABLE. THAT CAN BE ARRANGED.

The view switched to a schematic of the Tesla tower, showing the superstructure as well as the steel shaft running to the bottom of the 120-foot shaft.

IT IS COMMONLY BELIEVED THAT NIKOLA TESLA

STOPPED EXPERIMENTING AND GAVE UP HIS DREAM OF WIRELESS BROADCAST ENERGY IN 1903 WHEN J. P. MORGAN CUT OFF HIS FINANCIAL SUPPORT. NOT SO. HE FOUND A NEW SOURCE OF FUNDING AND CONTINUED HIS EXPERIMENTS FOR ANOTHER THREE YEARS.

The scene closed in on the tower's cupola.

TESLA'S DREAM WAS TO BROADCAST POWER THROUGH THE AIR SO THAT IT MIGHT BE ACCESSED WITH AN ANTENNA. "ENERGY WILL BE AVAILABLE TO EVERYONE," HE ONCE SAID. "LIKE THE AIR WE BREATHE."

Animated waves of electricity fanned out from the cupola in all directions. Then the focus shifted to the subterranean section of the tower.

BUT TESLA ALSO BELIEVED HE COULD HARNESS THE TELLURIC CURRENTS IN THE EARTH'S CRUST TO "MAKE THE PLANET QUIVER WITH ENERGY...TURN THE EARTH ITSELF INTO A GIANT CONDUCTOR." HIS TOWER'S LOWER REGIONS WOULD CREATE TERRESTRIAL STANDING WAVES THAT WOULD TRANSMIT POWER THROUGH THE EARTH ITSELF FROM ONE RESONANCE TRANSFORMER TO ANOTHER.

More animation: sine waves radiating out from the central steel shaft into the surrounding earth. And then a light bulb in a socket with two prongs trailing from its base. The wires inserted themselves into the ground and the bulb lit.

"Hey," Daley said, "that looks like the contraption you had when they tested the tower."

"Exactly. Now we know where they got the idea."

"But where'd they get the idea only the Elders should see this? So far it's like an alternative energy lecture."

Rhys's lips twisted into a puzzled grimace. "It ain't over yet."

BUT THE TOWER WAS HAVING OTHER EFFECTS. EYE

WITNESSES AND LOCAL NEWSPAPERS AT THE TIME RECOUNTED BIZARRE STORIES OF FISH KILLS, BUILDINGS AND BOATS DISAPPEARING, AND STRANGE CREATURES NOT OF THIS EARTH. THERE WERE RUMOURS OF UNUSUAL INJURIES AND EVEN DEATHS, BUT LITTLE WAS VERIFIED IN OFFICIAL RECORDS.

The animation reverted to the superstructure where the animated waves of electricity still fanned out from the cupola.

ON WEDNESDAY MORNING, APRIL 18, 1906, TESLA FUNNELED THE FULL POWER OF TWO LARGE WESTINGHOUSE GENERATORS INTO HIS TOWER. ON THE OTHER SIDE OF THE ATLANTIC, IN THE TOWN OF ABEREIDDY ON THE COAST OF WALES—THE ANCESTRAL HOME OF THE PENDRY CLAN—ONE OF TESLA'S PEOPLE LIT A LIGHT BULB WITH CURRENT PULLED FROM THE EARTH ITSELF.

The animation of the socketed light bulb with the two trailing prongs inserting into the ground was repeated. Then the scene shifted back to the tower.

TESLA HAD PROVEN HIS THEORY AND MADE HIS DREAM A REALITY. BUT THE TOWER WAS CAUSING UNINTENDED EFFECTS. IT HAD BEEN BUILT NEAR A NEXUS POINT WHERE THE VEIL IS THIN AND IT CAUSED A BREACH, ALLOWING BEINGS FROM THE VOID ENTRY TO OUR WORLD.

The animation showed a gap in the air before the tower, a black space that expanded almost to the size of the tower. Dark, indistinct shapes began to ooze from it.

BUT THE TOWER WAS HAVING EFFECTS WITHIN THE EARTH AS WELL. THE STANDING WAVES IN THE PLANET'S CRUST EXTENDED EASTWARD ALL THE WAY TO WALES, BUT WESTWARD AS WELL. AND THOSE WAVES REACHED THE SAN ANDREAS FAULT AT A VERY

VULNERABLE TIME, TRIGGERING A 500-KILOMETER RUPTURE. THE RESULTING QUAKE, LATER ESTIMATED AT 7.9 RICHTER AND PERFECTLY TIMED TO TESLA'S EXPERIMENT, DESTROYED MORE THAN 80 PERCENT OF SAN FRANCISCO, RESULTING IN 3,000 DEATHS.

Grainy archival photos of post-quake San Francisco flashed on the screen.

FORTUNATELY THE GENERATORS BURNED OUT, CLOSING THE BREACH IN THE VEIL AND ENDING THE SEISMIC DANGER BEFORE MORE DAMAGE WAS DONE. WHEN TESLA REALIZED THE DEVASTATION HIS EXPERIMENTS HAD WROUGHT, HE SHUT DOWN HIS WARDENCLYFFE LAB AND ABANDONED THE TOWER TO HIS CREDITORS. HE RETURNED TO NEW YORK CITY A BROKEN MAN.

More archival photos followed, showing the tower being dismantled. Then the animated Tesla tower in the desert retuned.

BUT TESLA'S FALSE SENSE OF FAILURE OFFERS A VALUABLE LESSON AND OPPORTUNITY FOR THE CLAN. THE VISITORS CAN BE LURED BACK WHEN CONDITIONS ARE RIGHT...WHEN CELESTIAL BODIES PROPERLY ALIGN AND WHEN PROPER CONDITIONS EXIST IN THEIR DESTINATION.

"This is getting close to home now," Rhys said, sounding uncomfortable. "My father keeps talking about these mystical celestial bodies aligning with the next solstice."

"That's this week, isn't it?"

"No, that's the equinox, on Friday. Believe me, I know because it's always a big day for the clan. All five families come out for a massive picnic celebration every equinox, spring and fall. The solstice isn't till June. The start of summer? The longest day of the year, usually around the twentieth or so."

She always got them mixed up.

"That's just three months off."

He nodded grimly. "Tell me about it."

The animation again showed the Tesla tower creating a black opening in the air before it, only this time over a body of water.

THE SALTON SEA SHARES SPACE WITH A LARGE NEXUS POINT WHERE THE VEIL IS EXTREMELY THIN.

Hadn't Juana mentioned something about "lines of magic" converging at the Salton Sea? Could she have been talking about this nexus point?

THE VISITORS USED THIS POINT TO OPEN A PASSAGE THROUGH THE VOID FROM THEIR WORLD TO OURS. THAT IS WHY OSIAN PENDRY MOVED THE CLAN FROM WALES TO THE VALLEY. HE KNEW THAT IF AND WHEN THE VISITORS RETURNED, CHANCES WERE EXCELLENT THAT THEY WOULD ARRIVE AT THIS PLACE. AND SO OUR TASK WILL BE TO BUILD A TOWER THAT EXACTLY DUPLICATES TESLA'S STRUCTURE AT WARDENCLYFFE.

Daley looked at Rhys. "'Will be'? But the tower's already built."

"Don't forget, my grandfather had this film made in the nineties. My dad is the one who built the tower."

"Do you get a bad feeling about there this is going?"

He nodded, his expression grim. "Definitely."

The view on the screen shifted to the aerial view of the Imperial Valley but this time overlaid with a diagram of its various seismic faults, some labeled, some not. Daley noticed the southern end of the San Andreas in the Salton Sea, but the names of the others were unfamiliar. One thing was certain, though, even to her untrained eye: The Imperial Valley was *loaded* with faults.

THE IMPERIAL VALLEY IS HOME TO A NETWORK OF SEISMIC FAULTS. THE STANDING WAVES GENERATED BY THE TOWER'S SHAFT CAN DESTABILIZE THESE FAULTS. OF

PARTICULAR INTEREST ARE THE FAULTS TO THE SOUTH THAT RUN UNDER THE COLORADO RIVER DELTA WHICH DIVIDES THE VALLEY FROM THE PACIFIC OCEAN. SHIFTS IN THESE FAULTS, ESPECIALLY THE CERRO PRIETO FAULT AND THOSE IN THE GULF OF CALIFORNIA'S SEA BED, HAVE THE POTENTIAL TO OPEN A CHANNEL BETWEEN THE GULF AND THE VALLEY.

The animation shifted to the subterranean parts of the tower, showing smooth sine waves radiating from the steel shaft causing seismic shifts deep in the crust. Then the aerial view returned, showing a huge fissure opening from the Gulf of California, through Mexicali, and into the Imperial Valley. Seawater began to flood into Calexico.

"They can't be serious!" Rhys said in a harsh whisper.

SINCE THE IMPERIAL VALLEY IS BELOW SEA LEVEL—HUNDREDS OF FEET BELOW IN SOME AREAS—THE WATER OF THE GULF WILL RUSH INTO THE VALLEY OF ITS OWN ACCORD, SEEKING ITS OWN LEVEL. WITH THE WEIGHT OF THE ENTIRE PACIFIC OCEAN BEHIND IT, THE FLOW WILL WIDEN AND DEEPEN THE CHANNEL, ALLOWING IT TO INUNDATE THE VALLEY, GIVING THE PACIFIC DIRECT ACCESS TO THE AREA IT ONCE OCCUPIED FIVE MILLION YEARS AGO.

Animation showed the flood spreading north like a tsunami, inundating Calexico, El Centro, Brawley, and Westmoreland to merge with the Salton Sea. Then into the Coachella Valley and reaching toward Palm Springs.

MEANWHILE, THE ENERGY RELEASED BY THE TESLA DOME WILL OPEN A RIFT IN THE VEIL, ALLOWING THE VISITORS TO RETURN.

The aerial view descended toward the restored inland sea to show the large, blurry forms of the visitors floating on the water and gliding beneath—just like they'd been depicted in the first part of the film.

THE SALTON TROUGH WILL BE RETURNED TO ITS
NATURAL STATE, AS IT ALWAYS WAS, AS IT EVER WILL BE.
AND THE GRATEFUL VISITORS WILL HEAP GENEROUS
REWARDS UPON THE FAITHFUL.

The recording ended. Daley sat staring at the blank screen,
aghast.

"Did anyone think to mention the small matter of the
drowning of a couple hundred thousand people along the
way?"

Rhys sat with a stricken expression, his mouth working,
saying "I...I...I..."

Daley understood. "I know, right?"

"Now I know why only the Elders are allowed to see it," he
said, his voice rising. "It's fucking insane!"

Daley tried to calm him. "But your father can't really be
planning something like this...I mean, he just can't...can he?"

"He built the goddamn tower, Daley. He didn't spend
millions of the clan's money to do that just for fun. I can't believe
this! He's going to try to flood the whole fucking Imperial
Valley!"

"But that's crazy." She remembered how skeptical Pard had
been of Tesla's theories. "Besides, none of this has ever been
shown to be even remotely possible."

Rhys jumped to his feet and began pacing around the room.

"We just had our third quake in three weeks, Daley. I know
this is California, but that's an unusual number."

If Pard were here he'd want her to correct him that they
occurred over a three-and-a-half-week period, but she kept it
to herself.

"You don't really think your father is behind them, do you?"

"He could be. You know, test out the equipment before the
solstice. Makes sense."

"But you and I were out there the night they tested the tower.
Not only did it not send out wireless energy, it didn't cause an
earthquake either. That first earthquake happened hours before
the test."

"What date was that?"

"February twenty-sixth."

He gave her a skeptical look. "How do you remember that?"

"I'm good with dates, and that was the day after I opened Healerina. You and I climbed the tower in the morning and I helped you with the test that night. I remember being in the shop talking to Juana that afternoon when the quake hit."

Rhys stopped pacing and looked thoughtful for a few heartbeats, then started pacing again.

"The tower and the shaft are wired separately. He could have sent power only to the tower that night. And then...holy crap! He said we needed more power and the very next morning we made a deal with the Tadhaks to use their excess current."

"How much excess?"

"All we need."

After all those giant batteries she and Cadoc had seen in that bizarre windfarm warehouse, Daley figured the Tadhaks had plenty of power to spare. But she kept that to herself.

"And a week later," Rhys was saying, "we had an even bigger earthquake...the five-point-five that kicked us out of bed and broke your front window and messed up Mexicali and Calexico—which are right in the same area as the big fissure we saw in the film."

"You think he tested the shaft that night?"

"He could have done a lot of things that night and I wouldn't have had a clue. You and I were in El Centro learning to line dance—well, you were, anyway—and after that we were otherwise engaged. The tower gets more power...and a bigger earthquake follows. I don't like it."

"Except that today's wasn't bigger. It felt much milder than the last."

"Okay that's a point. But there's something else: The day after the first quake, when my father and I were in Jason's office looking to buy his excess power, a woman from the quake center at Caltech stopped by."

"Oh, I remember her. She stopped by Healerina asking about any sensations before the quake."

Daley remembered her because she came by right after Sam Alvarez's first visit.

"Yeah, something about tingling."

"Right. I felt it right before that one and the one a week later."

"How about today?"

She shook her head. "Nothing. You?"

"Nothing in any of them. But she said something else, something about their seismic sensor network picking up an 'odd signal' in this area before the quake. She was trying to track down the source."

"You're thinking that source could be the tower?"

"Well, according to the film, the shaft is supposed to create standing waves in the Earth's crust. Could the Earthquake Center's sensors have picked up those waves? She told us they occurred *before* the quake."

"Do you remember her name? We could call and ask her."

"Rebecca Something…" He pulled out his wallet. "My father asked if he could contact her and…" He extracted a business card. "Got it."

"She gave you a card?" Daley took it from him: *Rebecca Z. Heuser, PhD*. "She didn't give me one."

"Well, she and my father got into a discussion about earthquakes and…" He shook his head. "There it is: My father asked an earthquake specialist if he could contact her. And he seemed to know an awful lot about quakes. This is looking worse and worse."

"You've got to call her."

Daley read off the number and Rhys tapped it in, then opened the speaker on his phone. A guy who identified himself as her research assistant said Dr. Heuser wasn't available—tied up because of this afternoon's quake.

"Maybe you can help," Rhys said. "This'll only take a sec. Doctor Heuser came to our town after the February twenty-six quake asking about tingling before the shock."

"*Yes, we had scattered reports of various skin sensations before that quake and the March five quake the following week as well.*"

"Okay. She also mentioned 'odd signals' from the sensors in our area before the first quake."

"*Yes. Signals from the lower Imperial Valley sensors we couldn't account for.*"

"Did these signals precede the March five quake as well?"

"Yes. I saw them myself."

"What about today's quake?"

"No...nothing but the usual P waves. Why do you—?"

Rhys cut the call and tossed the phone onto the couch.

"Shit! Shit-shit-shit! It's him! Gotta be!"

His distress was palpable. What would Pard do here? Play the Devil's advocate, no doubt—because it all seemed so farfetched. Pard had explained false premises to her once— when they were arguing, of course. They'd spent a lot of time disagreeing. God, she missed those arguments.

"Maybe you're committing the same kind of fallacy you mentioned earlier—that *post hoc* thing. Maybe Tesla and your clan and you are all guilty of the same *post hoc* fallacy. Just because Tesla's experiment coincided with the San Fran quake doesn't mean it caused it."

"No, that's right. You have a point, but—"

"Let me finish. And you have no idea as to whether or not the tower was activated prior to either of those two quakes. So you don't even have a definite *hoc* to be *post.* Which means you might be basing everything on false premises." She ticked off on her fingers. "First premise: I don't know what these 'standing waves' are, but the truth is that neither you nor anyone else has any idea if the tower's shaft generates them or not. And second: Is there any proof anywhere that these standing waves, should they exist, destabilize seismic faults?"

Rhys stared at her, then started clapping softly.

"Bravo. You're quite the voice of reason, aren't you."

She curtsied. "I try."

It occurred to her that she never could have put together a refutation like that before Pard—or even known to call it a refutation.

Thank you, Pard. You taught me well.

Rhys wrapped his arms around her and hugged. "I know you're trying to make me feel better, but there's a very unpleasant—no, make that downright sickening fact I have to face, and it's got nothing to do with whether or not the Visitors are real, or whether or not the tower can create a passage through the Void—whatever that means—or generate standing waves in the Earth that will flood the whole damn Imperial Valley. The fact is my father believes it can, or hopes it can, and he went out and built the tower for just that purpose. Publicly he says it's to provide wireless power to the valley but, as the film confirms, the ultimate purpose of the tower is to flood it. And that means my father is not just a madman, but a monster as well."

He sounded close to tears. She tightened her arms around him.

"You're all wound up and tense."

"Wouldn't you be?"

"Of course. But you've got to put it aside for a while and then come back to it. It will all seem more manageable tomorrow."

"And how am I supposed to turn it off till then?"

"I can help." She grabbed his hand and tugged him toward the bedroom. "Come on."

She'd needed him last night, and he needed her now. It would be good for both of them.

53

"Hard to believe," Rhys said, licking his lips, "but this tastes pretty good."

"Told ya," Daley said.

He wore his T-shirt and boxer shorts, she had on her oversized Lakers T. After exhausting themselves in the bedroom, they'd decided they were hungry. So Daley had raided her supply of frozen dinners and microwaved a spicy beef and bean bowl for Rhys and a chicken and broccoli Alfredo for her.

"Never knew I was such a versatile chef, did you," she added.

"I do now." He leaned back and sipped from his vodka and OJ—all she could offer on the libation front. "I could get used to this."

She laughed. "My culinary skills?"

"No. Us. Like this. Just the two of us in our own little world. No crazy father to deal with."

"And no grilling by the hospital docs."

"You don't have to go."

"I know, but..." She shrugged. "I think Sam is right. I should clear the air so people will stop wondering and talking about me. You're sure you want to come?"

"I can't wait to be your consigliere."

She laughed. "I'm not a crime boss!"

"You know what I mean. My main purpose is to keep them from ganging up on you. I'll run interference, be your wing man."

That sounded good to Daley. Great, in fact.

"Well, if we're gonna be a team at the medical center, we can also be a team where your father is concerned. We have three months to see if that tower is capable of doing what the film says it can. If it can't, then it won't matter what his plans are, they'll fail. But if it can somehow really cause earthquakes..."

"What then?"

"We'll have to find a way to stop him."

Rhys stared at her for what seemed like a long time, then said, "Maybe my father was right to be obsessed with you."

"'Obsessed' with me? Why?" She wasn't all that surprised, but still didn't like the sound of it.

"He believes you're something called a 'Duad.' Don't ask me what exactly that means because the Scrolls are vague about a Duad's origin. The only thing he's sure about is that this mysterious Duad is a threat to his plans."

"But why would he think it's me?"

"Okay, I told you how we put images of the previous night's sky through our computers to guide the Pendry Fund's investments. Well, sometime around mid-February up pops this message saying, *A pairing has occurred.*"

Daley's gut clenched. "A 'pairing'...mid-February?"

Pard had entered her life in mid-February...the eighteenth, to be exact. She'd been a one before that, and then she'd become two...a pairing. And it had shown up on the Pendry computers? That was disturbing to say the least.

"Yeah. Seeing that message really set my father off because according to the Scrolls, the Pairing and the advent of the

Duad were a sign that celestial alignments were imminent for a return of the Visitors. And the Duad was destined to get in the way."

"That's no reason to think I was this...this Duad."

"Wait. You've only heard half the story. I don't recall the exact date in February, but I do remember that the 'pairing' notice showed up every morning for a few days in a row and then changed to *The Duad approaches.* I remember finding that on a Monday morning. And guess who shows up in town that very day to set up shop."

Daley swallowed. "Me."

"Right. That made my father suspect you were the mysterious Duad. And when the message changed the next day to *The Duad has arrived,* well he was absolutely convinced."

A sudden chill made her rub her upper arms. "You're giving me the creeps, Rhys."

"He sent me down to town to check you out."

"Is that why you showed up that day? Your father sent you?"

He nodded. "Yep. That was why I asked all those questions about whether or not you had a partner in the business."

"Checking to see if I was *paired* with anyone?"

If he'd only known.

"Exactly. I arrived as an investigator and came away smitten. I reported back that no way were you the Duad but my father couldn't be swayed. Once he fixes on an idea, that's it. He wouldn't drop it. That was when I began to suspect he might be going off the rails. And yet, here you sit, saying, 'We'll have to find a way to stop him.' Maybe he was right to be worried about you."

Worried enough to send Karma Kendrick after me? Yeah, probably.

"Except I'm not the Duad."

Not true yesterday, but true today. Too true.

Elis Pendry obsessed with her...not a comfortable place to be, but it explained a lot.

"Well," Rhys said, slapping the table and rising to his feet. "I'd better get dressed and get back to the Lodge."

"So soon?"

"I need to talk to Cadoc about what we saw on part two."

She put on her best offended expression and tone, and said, "Oh, fine. Is that it? Slam, bam, thank-you, ma'am, and you're off? What do you take me for?"

His jaw dropped, he looked stricken. "Oh, no. How can you think that? I would never in a million—"

And then she couldn't hold back the laughter any longer.

He threw up his hands. "You rat! Don't *do* that to me! I thought you were serious!"

In truth, she'd been kind of hoping he'd stay a while longer. She truly enjoyed his company. She'd never had any problem being alone before Pard—enjoyed it, in fact—but after weeks of his constant presence, she was finding the adjustment to a solo life difficult.

"You should have seen your face!"

"Well, you sounded really hurt!"

"I'm fine." She waved him off. "Go see Cadoc."

"Seriously, I think we need him on our team to counter my father. Cadoc wouldn't tell me about part two—said I had to see it to believe it. I thought he was just being coy, but he was right. If he'd tried to describe it I would have thought he was as crazy as my father. But now I know as much as he does."

Not even close, she thought. *Cadoc has secrets up the wazoo.*

Daley knew some of what Cadoc knew, but she also knew a lot that he didn't.

"Oh, by the way," Rhys added, "Cadoc probably told you that he stays in hiding because of a skin condition."

"He mentioned it. You've got that patch of rough skin on your back..."

"The Pendry Patch."

"Right. He told me he's got it all over."

"He does. Or rather he did. But it's started to clear."

She knew that, but put on a surprised expression.

"Wonderful! He found a cure?"

"No. He says it's just happening."

She'd made Cadoc promise not to connect her with any improvement and apparently he was keeping his word. Always nice to know who you could trust.

"Well, whatever the cause, it can't be a bad thing. Where

does the Pendry Patch come from anyway?"

He shrugged. "No one knows. It runs in the family. Been with us forever."

But according to Pard it *didn't* run in the family, it was acquired *after* conception. When she'd passed this on to Cadoc, he already knew. He'd described it as "an ugly secret known only to a very few" and when she'd asked him to explain he'd refused, saying the secret was "too awful." What could he have meant by that?

Clearly she had a lot to learn about the Pendry Clan. And oddly enough, so did Rhys.

54

Rhys knocked on Cadoc's door and was surprised to be admitted to a well-lit room. So weird to see his brother in full light.

"Your skin...it's even better than the other night." He'd last seen Cadoc on Saturday.

Cadoc smiled. He had a nice, even smile—and surprisingly white, considering he'd never seen a dentist. Must have done a lot of brushing and flossing over the years.

"A little more of it clears every day. Missed you at breakfast this morning."

It took a second or two for that to sink in.

"You went downstairs for breakfast?"

That had to be the first time in almost twenty years.

"Lunch and dinner too."

"How did Mom react?"

"We're both...very happy."

"This could be the best therapy for her."

"Enough about me. I assume your trip to La Mesa was successful."

Rhys checked to make sure the door was closed, then pulled a chair away from the chess table and dropped into it.

"Yeah. Daley and I watched it. I can't believe that travesty is part of our heritage. It's monstrous."

"You have no idea what's part of our heritage."

There it was: Cadoc's flair for the dramatic. He was always

saying things like this, and then refusing to explain.

"I suppose it will be a waste of my breath to ask you to elaborate on that."

A shrug. "You're the heir apparent. When you hit thirty you'll be privy to all our dirty little secrets."

Was he jealous? He was the older brother but when he'd gone into seclusion he'd given up all claim to being made an Elder. Had he changed his mind?

"You know, if you want to be an Elder, I'll step out of your way. I never wanted—"

He laughed—a bitter sound. "I don't want to lead this family anywhere—except away from the path Papa has chosen for it."

Rhys leaned forward. "That's what I want to talk to you about. If that tower can do what the film says it can—"

"I know for sure it caused the March fifth earthquake, and it most likely caused the one the week before."

The words struck like a punch to the chest. "Seriously? How do you know?"

"It's like I told you. I roam at night. I watch and see things, I listen and hear things. I *know* things. The February twenty-sixth quake occurred in the daytime, so I was here in this room. But a week later I followed Papa and the other Elders to the tower and watched them power up the deep shaft. I wasn't timing it, but less than half an hour later that five-point-five quake hit."

"Could have been coincidence," Rhys said, remembering his *post-hoc* remarks to Daley earlier.

"Could have been. But then why were all the Elders high-fiving each other once the ground started shaking?"

Rhys slumped back in his chair. "Shit."

"Exactly. But that's not all."

"Oh, great. There's more?"

"Unfortunately, yes. Remember the 'test' of the tower, when you and Daley were out in the desert plugging lightbulbs into the sand?"

"Sure. Quite the light show."

"Well, apparently the real show was elsewhere. While Papa worked the tower and sent the sparks flying, one of the other Elders took a boat out onto the Salton Sea."

"Really? I had no idea. Why would...?" And then he remembered part two of the film. "The nexus point?"

Cad smiled again. "Good boy. You were paying attention. I couldn't be out on the water spying on them, so I kept Papa in sight. Whatever they were looking for out there, they must have found it, because Papa got a phone call that made him very happy."

"But what...?"

Cad leaned forward and lowered his voice. "I think they saw a breach into the Void at the Salton Sea nexus point. The Veil is thin there, so if the tower was to create an opening, it would happen there."

Rhys stared at his brother. "Do you hear yourself? Nexus points, the Veil, the Void, breaching the Veil into the Void... what the fuck are we talking about?"

"Ancient secrets, brother. Things the average everyday Jane and Joe know nothing about—and they're better off being left in the dark. Their religions present a tidy, comforting, ordered cosmos, when in truth reality is a chaotic, inimical mess. Other realities impinge on ours and sometimes the barriers between them rupture, allowing an exchange. Thus, the Visitors."

"Then they're real?"

A nod. "Very real."

"Then Dad's not crazy?"

"Rhys, he's totally insane. No one who wants to bring back the Visitors can be sane. They will totally fuck up our reality."

"Okay, but wanting to do it and being able to do it are two different things. *Can* he do it?"

A big shrug. "How can I say? He can create earthquakes. But can he cause enough slippage in the right faults to create a fissure between the Gulf of California and the Imperial Valley? Who knows? Even he doesn't know. He hopes he can. And he'll give it his best shot—which is what scares me the most."

Rhys saw where he was going. "Because even if he fails, the amount of destruction he'll cause along the way will be..." He searched for the word.

"Incalculable?" Cad said.

"Yeah. Incalculable. We've got to stop him, Cad."

"We've got a tad over three months to figure out a way."

"Short of killing him." Rhys added.

"I'm not ruling that out either."

Rhys started to laugh, but it died when he saw the look in his brother's eyes.

"You're kidding, right?"

"I'm deadly serious. Two hundred thousand people live in that valley. It also supplies food to the entire country. If there's no other way, I'll do what has to be done."

Staring at him right now, Rhys believed he would. But he was sure beyond any doubt that they could find another way.

"We'll see that it doesn't come to that." He rose. "We'll talk on this more tomorrow. Right now I'm off to get some shut-eye. Need to be on my toes tomorrow."

"Oh?"

"I'm taking Daley down to the medical center first thing in the morning. The medical people want to talk to her."

Cadoc frowned. "You think that's wise?"

"She wants to clear the air of all this fraud talk. And if she's going, I'm going with her."

"If you really want to help her, you'll talk her out of it."

"Well, the deputy who brought her the invitation thinks it's a good idea too."

"I don't," Cad said. "I don't see anything good for Daley coming out of tomorrow."

TUESDAY—March 17

55

"I've got to admit I'm a little scared," Daley said as Rhys parked the Highlander in the visitor lot.

"I can see that," he said. "I mean, who wants to be suspected of fraud? But it's pure guilt by association. You can't choose your relatives. You've got nothing to hide."

That's what you think, she thought. *If only that were true.*

She wished Pard were here. They had no secrets between them.

Rhys unplugged his phone from the in-car charger and checked the screen.

"Fully juiced. Let's go."

She'd left the black Healerina getup back at the apartment and dressed in the jeans, peasant blouse, and floppy sun hat she'd worn on her first trip to the hospital, hoping that would send a message that she had nothing to hide. She'd skipped the big sunglasses, however.

As they headed toward the front entrance, Daley noticed a crowd of about twenty people—men and women of all ages and shades, and even a few kids—grouped under the portico leading to the front entrance. Someone spotted her and pointed and whatever conversations they were having stopped as they stood and stared.

"That's her," she heard someone say in a hushed tone. "That's the healer."

They moved aside, leaving a path for her. Daley couldn't

meet their needy gazes, so she kept her head down and quickened her pace.

"Can you help us?" a woman said. "Please, help us?"

No, she thought, not looking up as the glass door opened automatically ahead of her. I can't help anyone.

In the lobby she noticed bright green shamrocks on the walls. St. Patrick's Day—she'd totally forgotten. She'd have to give Gram and Seamus a call when she got back home.

Rhys left her side and strode to the security desk.

"Ms. Daley is here for a meeting with Doctor Milton. He's expecting her."

The security man checked a list in front of him, nodded and picked up a phone. After speaking a few words he hung up and said, "Someone will be right out to see you in."

Sure enough, a middle-aged woman with very short black hair and a neutral expression appeared and came straight toward them.

"Ms. Daley? I'm Doctor Sandoval's assistant. Follow me, please."

"Who's Doctor Sandoval?" Daley said as they fell in step behind her.

"She's the medical center's CEO. She'll be at the meeting."

Daley glanced at Rhys who shrugged, but looked concerned.

She led them down a hall past a door labeled *Alfred Milton, MD—Chief of Medicine*.

"Aren't we going in?" Daley said.

The assistant nodded. "Doctor Milton is in the conference room."

She opened another door and led them into a crowded meeting space. The buzz quickly died upon Daley's entrance.

"Where's Doctor Milton?" Rhys said into the quiet.

A man in a white coat rose from a seat halfway along a large oblong table. "Right here."

"Ms. Daley was under the impression she was meeting with you."

"She is. That's why I'm here."

Rhys gestured to the rest of the dozen or so people present. "Then who are these folks and why are they here?"

"I'm not sure," he said.

A short, red-haired woman in a dark suit two chairs farther down rose. Her frown seemed at home on her face. "I'm Doctor Sandoval. They're from various departments in the hospital who wished to sit in on the meeting."

Rhys's head gave an emphatic shake. "That won't do. Ms. Daley agreed to a sit-down with Doctor Milton, not a circus."

Sandoval looked offended. Her frown deepened. "I beg your—"

Rhys jerked a thumb toward the door. "They go or she goes."

Daley wasn't keen on letting him speak for her but she agreed with his sentiment. This crowd wasn't what she'd been expecting. And she had to admit she was impressed by Rhys. She'd never imagined he could be so forceful. And since he seemed to be enjoying himself, she let him run with it. Besides, she found it kind of sexy.

"You're being unreasonable," Sandoval said.

He gripped Daley's upper arm. "Come on. We're walking."

They were only halfway into their turn toward the door when Sandoval said, "Very well, we'll clear the room. Just give us a minute."

Daley moved back against the wall and Rhys followed, speaking low out of the corner of his mouth. "If they were looking for a gangbang, they're not gonna get it."

They watched Sandoval's assistant usher people out. Some looked indifferent, some a bit huffy. Finally only Milton, Sandoval and her assistant remained.

"There," Sandoval said with a sour expression. "Happy?"

"The point is not to make Ms. Daley happy," Rhys said. "The point is to stick to the agreement."

"Very well. Let's all sit down, shall we?"

"'We'?" Rhys said. "When Deputy Alvarez conveyed the invitation, he did not mention anyone else."

Sandoval gave him a level stare. "Well, Mister...? I never caught your name."

"Pendry...Rhys Pendry."

"Are you her attorney?"

"No, just a friend looking out for her interests."

"Well, as chief executive officer, I'm looking out for the medical center's interests, and so I'm staying, as is my assistant. Marguerite will be taking notes."

The woman radiated hostility and Daley sensed she wasn't going to budge. So, apparently, did Rhys.

"Fair enough, I guess," he said, pulling out his phone. "And I'll be recording the proceedings to make sure any comments that come out of this are accurate. By the way, I know Doctor Milton is an internist. What is your specialty?"

"My doctorate is in health administration."

Okay, Daley thought. A business woman, not a physician.

"Where is Deputy Alvarez?" Daley said. "He said he'd be here."

"He was here earlier," Marguerite said, "but he got called away. Something about a dead body at one of the motels. He said he'd be back as soon as he could."

Daley wished he were here. She trusted Sam, and someone from law enforcement present and on her side couldn't hurt.

Dr. Milton glanced at his watch. "Can we get started? I still have rounds to finish."

"Excellent idea." Rhys said.

He and Daley moved around the other side of the table until they were opposite the other three and took their seats. She kept her hands out of sight in her lap. She had her white patch hidden under the hat. She didn't want that or the discoloration of her left hand to become a topic. Rhys started his phone recording and pushed it toward the center of the table.

"Before we get started, I'd like it made clear for the record that Ms. Daley is here voluntarily and solely at your request. She has not connected herself nor taken credit in any way for the cures of the horrors patients that occurred in this hospital. Now, Doctor Milton…I believe you had questions?"

Milton held up a copy of the *Imperial Valley Press* front page splashed with the same photo as yesterday's *San Diego Union-Tribune*: Daley standing by her car talking to Billy Marks.

"The woman in this photo was identified as you. Is that indeed you?"

Since her face was plainly visible, Daley saw no use in denying it. "Yes."

"You're dressed as a scrub nurse, even down to the surgical mask. Why is that?"

Oh, hell. She'd expected questions about her connection to the cured patients, not how she was dressed.

"I'd intended on visiting the hospital to see an acquaintance and I had a cold. I didn't want to pass it on to any patients." Lame-lame-*lame*! "At the last moment I decided not to risk it and turned back at the door."

Sandoval looked like she was about to follow up, but Milton cut her off by holding up another issue—Friday's *Press* with the front-page photo of a woman in scrubs and the same flowered surgical cap caught in a hospital hallway.

"This woman's face isn't visible but she has the same build and is dressed identically. Is that also you?"

Once you'd seen the later photo, this one was obviously the same person.

"That's me."

Sandoval interrupted again. "Why were you impersonating a nurse?"

"'Impersonating'?" Rhys made a slashing motion with his hand, a karate chop at the air. "If you're going to start making wild accusations, we'll just call it quits right now."

The CEO backed down immediately. "Perhaps 'impersonating' is the wrong word. I meant—"

"Not only the wrong word," Milton said in an acid tone, "it's off-topic. I'm asking the questions here and I'm not interested in what she was wearing. I'm more interested in her whereabouts on certain days."

Obviously these two had clashed before.

"Then let's stick to that, shall we?" Rhys said.

Sandoval leaned back in silence, her perpetual frown deepening even further.

Milton said, "Did you also visit the hospital on Monday of last week? We have security footage of a woman built very much like you and dressed exactly as you are now in the hallway outside the room where the first patient recovered from the horrors."

Right. Timothy Blaine. She was here to clear the air, so might as well go for it.

"That was me."

Pard, of course, would have wanted her to say "That was *I*."

"Did you visit Mister Blaine?"

"I did."

"But his wife said he had no visitors that day."

"She wasn't there when I stopped by—just him and his roommate."

She'd been the center of attention up until now, but suddenly the attention deepened. All eyes, including Rhys's were locked on her.

Milton leaned forward and tapped the eraser end of a yellow pencil on the table. "Now we're getting somewhere. *Why* did you visit Mister Blaine? Is he a friend?"

"He came down with the horrors in Nespodee Springs on Saturday afternoon."

Milton nodded. "I'm well aware of that."

"Well, I live in Nespodee Springs and have a small shop there. I happened to be standing in the shop's doorway when this middle-aged tourist staggered into the street, holding out his arms like he was blind and screaming his lungs out. A number of people, me among them, ran to him as he collapsed in the middle of the street. We were trying to help him when this guy who said he was an EMT took over."

"What did you think was wrong with him?"

"Well, we all assumed he had the horrors. What he was showing was what had been described."

"And you didn't do anything to help him then?"

"We were all trying to comfort him and his wife. But as for Timothy himself, the EMT guy wouldn't let anyone near him."

"How did you know his name?"

"His wife kept shouting it."

More pencil tapping. "So you had no contact with him between then and the following Monday afternoon?"

"None."

I was murdered early Sunday morning, but I don't see a need to go into that now.

"So what prompted you to visit on Monday?"

Daley shrugged. "I'd never seen the horrors before. I wanted to know how he was doing. I called the hospital to find out but they wouldn't tell me anything, so I came down."

"Just to visit...with no intention of healing him."

"Healing? I can't heal anyone."

I left that to Pard.

"And yet your shop is named Healerina."

Daley plastered on a smile. "I try to help people heal themselves. The body can work wonders on itself if you'll simply let it."

Milton's smile was genuine. "I don't disagree, Ms. Daley. Not one bit. But you don't claim to do any healing yourself—no herbs or potions or magic spells or the like?"

"Not a bit.

"And you gave nothing to Mister Blaine while you were in his room."

"Not a blessed thing."

"And how was he while you were there?"

"He was starting to get restless so I left."

"And you gave him nothing and did nothing to him while you were there."

"Nope."

"Yet Wednesday morning you returned in scrubs, and two more horrors victims were cured. Did you visit them as well?"

"I don't even know who they were."

"Then why did you return?"

Time to fabricate.

"To check on Timothy Blaine but someone else was in his bed."

"Yes, someone who was also cured of the horrors, along with his roommate."

"The same room as before?" Rhys said in a hushed tone. "And they were roommates?"

Milton nodded. "Yes. We never mentioned that publicly. You look suitably surprised, Mister Pendry. Ms. Daley, however, does not."

She didn't know they hadn't released that info.

"I'm no scientist," she said, "but it seems to me that if all the cures happened in the same room, the room should get the credit."

Milton's expression turned dubious. "If so, then why does the room work its miracles only when you are in the building?"

Daley spread her hands in a plaintive gesture. "I wish I could help you, Doctor Milton, but I don't know what to say." True. "If I could heal the horrors, I'd march straight upstairs with you at my side and go from room to room curing one after another."

Also true—so very, very true. But no longer possible without the missing ingredient: Pard.

Obviously frustrated, he tossed the pencil on the table. "Still no answers! I can't prove it, and the doctor part of my brain doesn't buy it, but I know in my gut that you're somehow at the bottom of all this."

"Which is just what she wants us to believe," Sandoval said, smiling for the first time all morning. Daley decided she preferred the frowns.

"And what's that supposed to mean?" Rhys said.

Sandoval whispered something to her assistant who hopped up and headed for the door.

"Just be patient a moment and all will be made clear."

Still smiling, Daley thought. This can't be good.

56

Juana had borrowed a chair from Arturo's café and seated herself in front of Healerina. Deputy Sam had told her about Daley's meeting at the medical center this morning and she'd stationed herself here to await her return and get a first-hand report. Jeffrey had driven out to her trailer and was catching up on some sleep.

She hadn't been here long when a brand new Maserati Ghibli pulled up before the shop. It had probably been a gleaming black when it started out this morning, but now had a generous coating of desert dust.

If I ever win the lottery, Juana thought, that's what I'll buy. My need for speed.

A tall, good-looking black man in an expensive suit unfolded himself from the car and strode toward the shop's front door. He stopped abruptly at sight of the CLOSED sign.

"I'm looking for Stanka Daley. I was told she runs this shop."

"She's out of town today," Juana told him.

He looked vaguely familiar. Where had she seen him before?

"I really need to see her."

"She's down at the medical center in El Centro."

His face showed instant concern. "Is she all right?"

I sure hope so, Juana thought, but said, "Just talking to some folks."

"Do you know when she'll be back?"

"No idea."

He thought a moment. "How far is El Centro?"

"Half an hour in a normal car." She pointed to the Maserati. "Probably twenty minutes in that."

He smiled. "The medical center, you say?"

"El Centro Regional Medical Center."

"Got it. Thanks."

He jumped back into his car and roared off.

"Now who on Earth was that?" she muttered. "Why do I know him?"

And then she remembered: Dr. Stabler from St. Michael's... the doc who amputated Daley's ruined left hand. What was he doing down here?

57

"While we're waiting for Marguerite," Sandoval said, still smiling, "let me ask you about this Billy Marks you were photographed with in the lot. The authorities have identified him as a conman. Why are you associating with a known conman?"

This was one of the areas Daley had wanted to clear up, and something she could be perfectly honest about.

"I am not now and never have associated with Billy Marks in any way. Why would I have anything to do with the man who murdered my father on the day I was born?"

This brought the expected startled looks from Sandoval and

Milton. She'd told Rhys about it yesterday so it was old news to him. Sandoval's smile had slipped.

"My only relationship with that man is blood," Daley added. "He's supposedly a distant uncle on my father's side."

"But you were seen discussing something with him," Sandoval said.

"We weren't 'discussing' anything. I was telling him that I want nothing to do with him and that he should leave me alone and never speak to me again. If you want to hire a lip reader you'll see that's exactly what I told him."

"I considered that, but I was told the frame rate is too slow to allow for lip reading, otherwise—"

The door opened and Marguerite reentered, followed by a big, gray-suited man Daley didn't recognize, who was in turn followed by an apple-shaped, bulldog of a woman who was the last person on Earth Daley wanted to see this morning.

"That's her!" Amber Seabolt cried as soon as she spotted Daley. "That's the cheating bitch!"

Sandoval's smile returned as she said, "Now, now, Ms. Seabolt. I must insist on a modicum of decorum. But whatever do you mean? Are you saying that Ms. Daley was involved in something illegal?"

"Damn right! She was running a car raffle scam in Coachella last month. She made off with thousands. I chased her out of town but lost her in the desert."

In the old days, the pre-Pard days, Daley would have been on her feet, fronting straight up, and right back in Seabolt's face. But now she felt only shame, especially with Rhys here.

Sandoval put on a shocked expression. "Is this true, Ms. Daley?"

"Don't answer that," Rhys said, but his expression said he wanted an answer himself.

But Amber Seabolt wasn't through. She raised hands curved like claws. "If I'd gotten hold of you—"

"That will be enough, Ms. Seabolt," Sandoval said.

"Oh, listen, lady, I'm just getting started."

"No, you're finished. You've served your purpose. My assistant will show you out."

As Marguerite tugged her toward the door, Seabolt jabbed a finger toward Daley. "I'll see you outside."

"What an unpleasant woman," Dr. Milton said after she was gone.

Yeah, Daley thought. I sure know how to pick my marks.

"Are we through here?" Rhys said.

Sandoval shook her head. "Almost. We tentatively identified Ms. Daley on Sunday. I immediately contacted Mister Decker here. He's an investigator who does background checks for the medical center and I asked him to look into Ms. Daley. Mister Decker, what did you find?"

An investigator? No way could this be good.

Daley turned to Rhys. "Maybe we should go."

Rhys shook his head. "No, let's hear this."

Crap!

Decker pulled a folded sheet of paper from his breast pocket.

"I could find almost no background on Stanka Daley's childhood. No school history until high school so I assume she was home schooled until then. Her—"

"Recent history only, please," Sandoval said. "Say the past two years. That's where it gets interesting."

Obviously Sandoval had already read the report.

Decker cleared his throat. "Okay. Over the past two years I found evidence that Stanka Daley ran numerous car raffle scams in Santa Monica, Venice, Pasadena, and Palm Springs as well as Coachella."

"What the hell is a 'car raffle scam'?" Rhys said.

Decker looked up from his notes. "It's a bait-and-switch scam. You sell raffle tickets on an expensive new car but the prize turns out to be something worth far less. You apologize, reimburse the winner for his or her ticket, then drive off in the switched car with the proceeds from all the other tickets. It's almost foolproof because the winner has had the price of his ticket returned, so he's out nothing and doesn't feel cheated."

"Amazing!" Rhys said, staring straight ahead.

Decker went back to his notes, saying, "I've also determined that she's been running an ongoing fake invoice scam for years." He explained without waiting for Rhys to ask. "That's when you create a fake business and barrage unsuspecting companies with bogus invoices for services rendered. A certain percentage can be counted on to pay without question."

Rhys looked at her and whispered, "This is you?"

The shock and disappointment in his voice cut like a knife.

"We can talk about it later."

"Thank you, Mister Decker," Sandoval said. "I think we get the picture." As Decker headed for the door, she looked at Daley and rubbed her hands together. "Well, well, well. A few minutes ago Doctor Milton said he knew in his gut that Ms. Daley was somehow at the bottom of all the mystery cures. To which I replied that that was just what she wants us to believe. And you, Mister Pendry, wanted to know what I meant by that. Now you know."

Fighting a wave of nausea, Daley rose to her feet. "I've had enough."

"I hope so," Sandoval said, also rising. "I hope you've had enough of El Centro Regional Medical Center to last you the rest of your born days, enough to take your lowlife schemes somewhere else and never darken our doorway again. Really. Trying to connect yourself to our patients! I don't know what you were planning, but it's not going to work here, not on my watch."

Decker had just opened the door to leave when a tall black man pushed in, Marguerite close behind.

"Sir, you can't go in there now. Sir!"

But the man kept coming. "I'm Doctor Caleb Stabler from St. Michael's in Burbank and I must see Stanka Daley!"

Oh, hell. The hand surgeon.

"What now?" Rhys said, sounding exhausted.

Daley wanted to shrivel up and die. She looked around for an escape route but the room had only one door and Stabler was standing in it.

Now Dr. Milton was on his feet as well. "Cal? What are you doing here?"

Dr. Stabler's eyes lit. "Alfred! God, am I glad you're here. Tell these people I'm not some crackpot."

"It's okay, Marguerite," Milton said. "I know Doctor Stabler from the state medical society. He's one of the finest hand surgeons around." He pointed to Daley. "There's the woman you want to see, although for the life of me I can't imagine why."

"There you are," Stabler said, striding around the table toward her. "Let me see your left arm."

Daley held her hands behind her. "I'd rather not."

"Please."

Daley shook her head. No good could come of this. "What's this all about, Cal?"

Stabler's eyes bored into her. "When I saw the photo of the mystery woman in the parking lot, I didn't connect her to you, but one of my nurses did. She said, 'Hey, there's that patient that ran off.' I looked and said it can't be. She's got two hands and she couldn't have a working prosthesis by now. But I studied the pictures and became convinced it was you."

"I'm not following you," Milton said.

"Just a few weeks ago Ms. Daley was an emergency patient of mine. Her left hand had been crushed by a big pavement roller. The hand was unsalvageable, so I had to amputate."

She heard Rhys gasp behind her. *"What?"*

"And yet," Stable said, "you appear to have a working left hand. May I see it, please?"

He was blocking her path to the door. She'd have to push him out of the way to escape, and that would involve using her hand and revealing it. She saw no other choice.

She held out both her hands. Dr. Stabler made a sound, a sharp intake of breath. His hands trembled slightly as he reached out and took her left hand in both of his.

"It's *not* a prosthesis," he said, his voice suddenly hoarse. "It's flesh…warm…real flesh. How? I removed this hand…it went into the incinerator." He looked up at her, his expression pleading. "How is this possible?"

How could she explain that Pard had rebuilt a new one from scratch? They'd have her on the loony ward in a straitjacket. She saw no choice but to turn the tables and make him look loony.

"I think you're mistaken, Doctor…what was your name?"

"You know damn well it's Stabler," he said, his voice growing louder. "How did this happen?"

All innocence: "How did *what* happen?"

"You grew a new hand!" He was shouting now.

She forced a laugh into her voice. "Doctor Stabler, I don't know about where you come from, but where I come from, when a person gets a hand cut off, they don't grow a new one."

She moved to get by him but he blocked her way.

"But you've just become the exception."

The Family had taught her: When backed into a corner, Deny-deny-deny.

"Please let me by. You've obviously got a case of mistaken identity here."

He grabbed her arm. "I've got to know!"

From behind her Rhys said, "If you don't let her go right now, *you'll* need to grow a new hand."

He released her and stepped aside.

"Please," he said as she passed by, "tell me the truth."

She felt sorry for him. Seeing her with a new hand must be turning is whole world upside down, but what could she tell him? The truth? That an alien intelligence had invaded her and was conscious down to the molecular level. A new hand was among the least of the changes it had made in her body. Sure. Like he'd jump right on board with that. And by refusing to accept the truth he'd be left knowing no more than he did now.

Deny-deny-deny.

She was almost to the door when Deputy Alvarez burst in.

"I'm glad I caught you," he said. He looked stressed.

"I missed you. We were just leaving."

"When did you last see Billy Marks?"

Something in his voice...something wrong.

"Sunday afternoon. He came out to Nespodee Springs to bother me again. I told him to get lost, same as I'd told him that morning."

"And that was the last time you saw him?"

"Yes. Why? What's wrong?"

"A housekeeper found him dead in one of the Adams Avenue motels."

Daley was shocked—he'd seemed pretty fit—but couldn't say she was sad. Not even a little.

"What happened to him?"

"Multiple stab wounds. He was murdered."

58

Sam convinced Sandoval to get everyone out of the conference room except Daley, Rhys, and himself. He'd wanted to question Daley alone but Rhys would have none of it.

Sam sat down with an old-fashioned notebook before him.

"Okay, you last saw Marks on Sunday afternoon. When, exactly?"

"I'd say around two o'clock."

"And where, exactly?"

"On the back steps to my apartment. I told him I wanted nothing to do with him—ever—and he stomped off. That was the last I saw of him."

"Where were you Sunday night?"

Daley had a terrible thought. "You don't think I had anything to do with this, do you?"

Sam shook his head. "No. We figure it was another male, but you were seen with him Sunday so I have to fill in the blanks."

"I can help re Sunday night," Rhys said. "I picked her up at five thirty and we drove into Brawley for dinner at Mama's Meatball."

"And after dinner?"

"I drove her back and we hung out at her apartment for a few hours. When was he killed?"

Alvarez leaned back. "As best we can determine at this point, sometime early Sunday night. He drank quite a few beers at the bar next door, then left. The bartender remembered because he said he hoped the hell he wasn't going to drive anywhere. He also remembers another customer following him out, but his description fits half the middle-aged males in the Valley."

Daley said, "Well, we were in Mama's Meatball until eight-thirty or so."

"Why do you say the killer was a male?" Rhys said. "Just curious."

"The wounds were the work of someone pretty strong, who

knew his way around a knife."

A knife...Billy had murdered her father with a knife. Maybe there really was such a thing as karma.

"No sign of defensive wounds," Sam said. "So it looks like Marks never had a chance, especially with all that beer in him."

"Well," Daley said, still unable to muster any sadness for him, "he ripped off a lot of people in his day..."

Sam nodded. "That's our thinking: a disgruntled mark. Might be hard to track, though. I'm sure he didn't keep any records." He flipped the notebook shut. "Well, that does it for me. How'd your meeting go?"

"Couldn't have gone worse," Daley said. "But at least it's over." She looked at Rhys. "Take me home?"

He nodded and led her out of the conference room. Sandoval was waiting outside.

"I don't ever want to see your face again, Stanka Daley," she said.

It's mutual, Daley thought, but held back. A reply would only dignify the remark.

Dr. Stabler hovered beside her. "Please, Ms. Daley, if I could just—"

She held up a hand—the right one—but kept moving. "I've had enough for one day. Just...let it be and leave me alone."

The crowd around the front entrance had grown, numbering maybe thirty now. As Daley passed through the doors a voice yelled, "There she is now, the cheating bitch! Phony! Fraud! Liar! Fake!"

Amber Seabolt. Of course.

Daley ignored her but couldn't ignore the faces that had been full of need on her way in were now twisted with anger. And now they took up a chant.

"Fake! Fake! Fake! Fake!"

Daley quickened her pace through the gauntlet. Toward the end an old woman spit at her, landing a glob on her sleeve. She wanted to cry.

"Fake! Fake! Fake! Fake!..."

She hurried out from under the portico where the sky was

contemptuously clear and the late morning sun intolerably bright as the chant followed her into the parking lot, fading only slightly with distance.

The car...the car...where was the car?

A Highlander off to the left chirped and it took all Daley's will power to keep from dashing for it. She jumped inside and slammed the door, shutting out the chant...at last, at last.

"Not fair!" she said, fighting unexpected tears—she'd always thought she was tougher than this. "I never said I cured anyone. Never! So how can they call me a fake?"

Rhys started the car and got them rolling. She found a tissue and wiped away the spit.

Get me away from here, she thought. As far and as fast as possible.

"What else can they think?" Rhys said.

The question took her by surprise. "What do you mean?"

"All that stuff they said about you in there—that woman about the bogus car raffles and the detective—was it true?"

Oh, crap.

"Well...kind of."

"'Kind of'?" he said, keeping his eyes straight ahead. "What's that mean? Something's either true or it's not. Something either happened or it didn't."

"I'm saying it used to be true but it's not anymore."

"Daley...either you did that stuff or you didn't."

"Okay, I did it, but I don't do it anymore."

Rhys didn't respond. They passed the El Centro city limits sign and he remained silent. Daley figured she knew why.

"I guess you're a bit shocked by what you heard."

"'A bit' doesn't even come close. I had absolutely no idea I was involved with a professional con woman."

A professional con woman...was that what she was? Or rather, what she had been? Yeah, probably. That fit.

She sighed. "That's the way I was raised."

"I don't know a damn thing about how you were raised. You know all my family's dirty secrets but I know nothing about yours. You've always shied away from the subject."

"With good reason. The Family is not something you brag

about, at least not to the straight world. It's not a pretty story."

Rhys didn't ask to hear the story so Daley decided to tell him anyway.

"Grift was all I saw growing up. After my father's death, his family—which was also Billy Marks's family—insisted on taking me in. My Gram and Pa were still on the East coast back then, so my mother had no other support system. So I was raised in my father's family. They had no standards of behavior other than fooling people who weren't in the Family into handing over their money. The world was divided into the Family and everybody else: *us* and *them*. I can't call it a loving family, but you got approval—you *earned* approval, I should say—by getting *them* to fork over money to *us*. I remember when I was little, my older sisters used to tie my foot up behind my butt so I could play an amputee child."

A disgusted shake of the head. "Oh, great."

"They made a game out of it at first. They'd take me out on the street and I'd use my innocent face and waif eyes to induce passing kindhearted souls to drop their change in the bowl. When we had a good day, I'd be heaped with praise. These folks were uneducated—illiterate for all intents and purposes—but believe me, they knew all about positive reinforcement.

"By the time I was thirteen I'd learned how to cold read a mark and cheat at three-card monte. We never went to school and were never allowed to have friends outside the family, so I never learned how to make friends. That left me pretty much isolated in high school. I didn't exactly help myself by using my three-card-monte skills to cheat my classmates out of their lunch money."

"This is getting better and better."

She let it slide.

"After she'd get home from work—my mother refused to take part in the Family's scams—she taught me to read and tried to instill some sort of moral compass in me, but she worked full time at a straight job while I was left all day with my father's relatives, absorbing their values. So despite spending my teen years with my Gram, who's a real straight arrow, I entered adulthood as someone with no standards in the realm of separating other people from their money."

"People overcome their upbringing all the time," Rhys said.

"Sure they do. But it's not easy. Two very different historical figures said that if they had control of a child in their formative years, they could shape them for life."

"Yeah? Who?"

"Lenin said, 'Give me four years to teach the children and the seed I have sown will never be uprooted.' And then Francis Xavier, founder of the Jesuits, said, 'Give me the children until they are seven and anyone may have them afterward.' Polar opposites in their philosophies, but they knew the truth about permanently shaping young minds."

More residue from Pard—she'd never read anything by either of those two.

"So it felt totally natural for me to fall into the grifter life. Then I came in contact with someone who had all sorts of standards—positively lousy with them—managed to be a total pain in the ass about them."

"Is this the close friend you mentioned, the one who up and took off?"

Yeah...Pard.

"That's him. An obsessive-compulsive goody two-shoes. He considered sending out phony invoices or running car raffle scams beneath me...thought I was too good for them. Can you imagine that? He had a higher opinion of me than I did. We wound up spending a lot of time together." As in like every freaking minute. "And through all that contact I began to look at myself in a new light and didn't like what I saw. Gradually he wore me down and brought me around.

"So, yeah, I used to be a professional con woman— emphasis on 'used to be.' I'm not the same woman I was then. I've got standards now. I've got self-respect. I really am too good for those scams. Instead I want to do something *real* with my life."

Pard...it banged home now how much he'd changed her. She hadn't realized or appreciated it until she'd been forced to vocalize it. Shocking, in a way, how much of an effect he'd had.

"But you could have told me," Rhys said.

"Yes, I could have. Easy to say. But maybe I couldn't bring myself to do that. And maybe I didn't *want* to. How could I tell you that I used to support myself by cheating people? And *why* should I tell you when that isn't me anymore? I wanted it all behind me. The old life in the rearview mirror, something new and better ahead."

He shook his head again. "I thought we had something—or at least we were starting to have something."

His use of the past tense was not lost on her.

"We do have something, Rhys. I would have told you eventually, but I wanted you to get used to the new me first before you heard about the old me. Nespodee Springs could have been a clean start, but now, with all the bad publicity that's going to come out of this, that's ruined."

"It sure is."

His bitter tone stung.

"You don't think people can change?"

"I think people should be honest with each other if there's going to be a relationship."

A non-answer. She sensed he was hurt more than anything else, but he wasn't going to admit that.

"The last thing I wanted to do was cause you pain." And that was true, very true. "But you've got to realize I've spent most of my life hiding things from people. It's a hard habit to break. But I'm trying."

"I just wish I'd had some clue before we went into that meeting. Do you know how I felt as they're saying all these terrible things about you and you're not denying even one of them? Can you imagine what that's like? Here I am, there as your friend, and I'm totally clueless. I felt like an idiot."

Oh, he was definitely hurt. And rightfully so.

"All I can say is I'm sorry."

"But that CEO, that Sandoval, I mean that woman is one tough cookie, and she very obviously believes you've been laying the groundwork for a scam."

"Yeah…a horrors rip-off."

"Well?"

"Well, what?"

"Is she right?"

Daley stared at him. "Are you seriously asking me that? First off, do you really think I'd stoop that low? And second, I just told you that crap is all behind me."

"Yeah...but that's just what a con woman would say, wouldn't she?"

Daley felt her jaw drop. "You actually think...?"

Her words dried up as the hurt washed over her. At least Karma had stabbed her in the front. If they weren't in the middle of the desert now, she'd tell him to pull over and let her out. But then what? Probably no cell signal out here.

Rhys seemed oblivious. "That meeting left me with so many unanswered questions. Like, why were you dressed up like a scrub nurse?"

Daley folded her arms and stared out her side window. "I think it's better if we stop talking."

He looked surprised. "What? No—"

"You'll only think I'm lying so why bother?"

"Seriously, Daley. I—"

"Stop. Talking. Now."

"But—"

"*NOW!*"

He finally shut up.

59

Daley wandered about her living room. The rest of the ride back from El Centro had been...quiet. By now her anger had dissipated somewhat, but not completely. And the hurt, well, that still...hurt.

Okay, she'd pulled her share of cons, but they'd been inconsequential affairs. Most of her marks hadn't even known they'd been conned. Did Rhys actually think she'd take advantage of the families of victims of the horrors? The very idea appalled her. Didn't he know her at all?

Well, to be fair, in his mind, he *didn't* know her. He'd thought he did, but all those revelations during the meeting had morphed her into some bizarre, lowlife stranger.

And who did she have to blame? No one but herself. Oh, how smug she'd been back in the day. Stanka I-got-all-the-answers Daley. So contemptuous of the straights. They weren't middle-class people working long hours for their money, they were *marks*—low-hanging fruit waiting to be harvested. No matter what plans they might have had for *their* money, she'd made it *her* money.

Pard had warned her how her cons could some someday circle back and bite her in the ass. Not that he'd used those words. How had he put it?

...these kind of things don't go away entirely. They're always out there, waiting to come back and haunt you...

So right—as usual. But her old life wasn't content with a mere haunting, it had circled back to torpedo and sink the new one. Maybe she deserved it. What goes around, comes around, and all that crap.

Juana was the only one she could think of around here who might know the real score and give her the benefit of the doubt. Daley had come home to find a note from her saying she'd been waiting here for her return but had to leave for the reservation on some tribal business. She'd be back tomorrow.

Which left no one to turn to. She was on her own. She'd always liked her alone time. Maybe alone was the answer. Alone meant no one around to stab you in the back.

Listen to me! Enough. Enough about me. I'm sick to death of me.

She grabbed the remote and switched on the TV. She needed a distraction. A rerun of *Law & Order* or one of its variations had to be playing somewhere. Lose herself in a murder case.

But as she surfed the channels she saw a female reporter holding a microphone in front of a goateed man in a garish suit. The banner below him read: *Markus Gruber—author of "The Mind of the Con Artist."* When she recognized the front entrance of ECRMC, she stopped for a look and a listen.

REPORTER: *—ointed out that she took no credit for any of the three cures, in fact she denied credit. How can you be working a scam if you don't take credit for past successes?*

GRUBER: *Ah, you've already taken a great leap. Let's back up a step and ask: Were those* genuine *horrors victims? What if they were faking the illness?*

REPORTER: *But the doctors said—*

GRUBER (waving a hand): *The horrors are uncharted territory. There's no definitive test, just symptoms. People involved in the con could be faking those symptoms and the doctors would have no test to say otherwise. As for denying credit, that tells me that we're dealing with a highly sophisticated scammer. The con artist plays on what is known as the mark's "will to believe." They need to believe they'll win the raffle, they need to believe they're getting a great deal on resealing their driveway, they need to believe they've just spoken to their dead wife. And once they accept that belief, God himself can't change their mind.*

REPORTER: *But if the scammer denies credit...*

GRUBER: *...they become all the more believable. I know it sounds like a contradiction, but it's true. If they tout themselves as the healer, they'll trigger skepticism. People will say "Prove it." But if the con artist simply puts himself in the vicinity of the cures when they happen, he or she becomes* connected *to the cures. They become a person of interest in regard to the cures. And then by denying it, they become credible. Repeated denials only increase their credibility. People will say, "Well, if he was really a con artist, he'd be hogging the credit. But if he's walking away...he's hiding his miraculous abilities." As a result, he doesn't have to prove anything. He hasn't asked for a leap of faith because he doesn't need to—the lemmings are leaping all on their own.*

REPORTER: *As you said, the will to believe.*

GRUBER (grinning): *Exactly! And who in the world wants more to believe in a cure than someone whose loved one has an incurable condition?*

Sickened, Daley turned off the TV and dropped onto the couch.

They thought they had it all figured out. They'd retrofitted a con to support what they thought were the facts. This Gruber knew his stuff. He might even have been a grifter himself at one point. Yeah, the will to believe...tap into that and people will buy into anything.

But the press was painting her as a monster...someone plotting to prey on panicked, grieving families.

She bounded to her feet again. Unbelievable! She'd pulled off dozens of scams and everyone believed her. Now these cures, *real* cures, the one true thing she'd been involved in her whole life, and no one would believe her. What was that—irony? Or just a fucked-up world?

She had to get out of here—out of Nespodee Springs, out of the whole damn Imperial Valley. Back to her place in North Hollywood. That sounded good. She'd pack up a few necessities and hit the road.

60

"What are you doing here?" Rhys said when he opened his bedroom door.

His face registered the profound shock Cadoc had expected.

"It's my home," Cadoc said.

"I'm well aware of that. But you haven't visited my room since...since..."

"The last time I had a meal with the family?"

"Yeah, that would be it."

Cadoc smelled the tequila on his breath. Rhys tended to need a reason to drink—stress, usually. "You okay?"

"Yeah. Fine."

Like hell. "Can I come in?"

"Sure-sure-sure." He backed away to make room for entry. "Want a drink?"

"No. I want to talk about Daley. Some nasty stories about her floating around."

"That she's a professional con woman and a grifter?"

"Those would be the ones."

"They're all true."

The bitterness in his brother's tone spoke volumes. Cadoc couldn't hide his shock. "They're *true*?"

A slug from the Patrón bottle, then a nod. "Told me so herself." A sidelong glance. "She ever give you any clue?"

"No. I'm flabbergasted. It just doesn't seem like her."

"Well, it is. She says she was raised that way. The hospital CEO seems to think she was planning a scam on the horrors victims."

Cadoc fought a surge of anger. No one had a right to talk about Daley like that.

"Do you believe that—I mean, do you believe she's capable of something like that?"

"She said she'd never stoop that low, but who can believe a word she says now?"

"Oh, come on."

"I don't know what the fuck to believe, Cad! I was really into her—really, really into her, and then I find out she's got a secret life. A petty crook! A con woman!"

"Did she ever take credit for those cures?"

"No…not that I heard."

"Well, she should have."

The Patrón bottle was on its way back to his mouth but stopped in mid-journey.

"What did you say?"

"She has a power, Rhys…a healing power."

"Bullshit."

Cadoc rolled up his sleeves. After all those years of sleeves down to his wrists, no matter what the season, he felt exposed with anything shorter. He rotated his arms back and forth.

"You saw only my hands when we played chess, but my whole body was like that. Look now. You've seen how I've been clearing."

"Yeah, some kind of miracle. I'm so—wait. You're gonna tell me Daley did this?"

"That's exactly what I'm telling you. That Sunday night you returned from San Diego with Papa and we had our delayed chess game. I doubt you remember, but you told me then that Wynny Baughan's Pendry Patch had cleared and she was blaming Daley."

"Yeah. I got stuck listening to Elder Baughan because his daughter was being shunned because she wasn't a real Pendry without the Patch."

"You might remember I called off the second game. After you'd left, I went straight to Daley's place and asked her if she'd cured Wynny's Patch."

"I'm not sure 'cured' is the right word. It's not a disease, it's—"

"It's *exactly* the right word, Rhys, but I'll get to that in a minute. Daley hemmed and hawed but finally admitted that she'd fixed Wynny's Patch while trying to help with the blood clot in her lung."

Rhys blinked. "'Help with the blood clot'? What—?"

"Stay focused on Sunday night, okay? I pressed her and finally got her to admit that she can, in a way, under certain conditions, heal certain things."

"Total bullshit, Cad. She's a con artist."

Cadoc held out his arms again and rotated them. "Is this a con?"

"A coincidence, then."

"There's a woman out there who's convinced Daley healed her intractable stomach ulcer and saved her from surgery."

Rhys gave a dismissive wave. "Yeah, and a sheriff's deputy who thinks she cured his daughter's brain tumor. Which she denies, by the way."

Yes...here was the problem.

"She publicly denies all healings, yet when I backed into a corner she admitted she could heal certain things."

"Don't be taken in, Cad. It's all part of her game. How much did she charge you?"

"For clearing my skin? Her price was seeing the second half of the film."

He watched Rhys digest that.

"That's all? No money?"

"Not a cent. I truly believe she has a power to heal. Not to cure everything, just certain things. I think she wants to work her magic or whatever it is without being branded a miracle worker, because we all know nothing good can come of that."

Rhys stared at him a while, then said, "What did she do to you, exactly?"

"She invited me in, we sat at the kitchen table, and she held my hands for maybe a minute, probably less."

"That's it?"

"That's all of it. By Monday morning I could already see signs of improvement, but I thought it was just my imagination—I *wanted* to see improvement, so that's what I saw. But by Tuesday there was no question that my skin was starting to clear."

"Placebo effect maybe?"

"You're reaching, Rhys."

He stalked around the room. "You're asking me to believe in magic, Cad! In miracles!"

"'There are more things in heaven and earth, Horatio'—"

"Yeah-yeah, I know the quote. In fact Dad used it before he took me out to the desert to give me my first view of the porthors."

"Which you thought were a fiction until then. So why are you holding back here?"

"Because I saw them with my own eyes. I saw what they did to that empty shop. But I can't buy into faith healing. I *can't*! It's not in me!"

The porthors...that gave Cadoc an idea.

"Of course it is. You believe in the Pendry Patch don't you?"

He stopped and stared. "How can I not? Like the porthors, it's not a matter of faith. I've got one on my back. And you..."

"Right. I had it all over, so I should know it best of all. My point is that you've taken what you've been told about it on blind faith, and everything you've heard is a lie."

"What are you talking about?"

Cadoc checked his phone for the time. Yeah, the sun was well down and it was probably late enough. He crooked a finger at Rhys.

"Follow me. Just as with the film, you must see to believe."

61

Daley yawned as she turned onto Burbank Boulevard and cruised toward her apartment. Clouds obscured the night sky and it felt like rain. When was the last time she'd seen rain? Not a single drop in Nespodee Springs during her stay there.

Her place sat over a bookstore. She noticed the store's lights were still on, then remembered Tuesday was reading club night and they stayed open later than usual. She pulled around the corner where she found her usual spot taken. No surprise. She hadn't been back in weeks. She'd have to hunt up a spot on the boulevard, not always a sure thing this time of night.

As she turned around and pulled up to the stop sign at Burbank, she noticed someone sitting in a parked car across the street. A perfect spot. She waited for them to pull out but they never budged. The street lights showed a woman behind the wheel. She seemed to be involved with her phone, either texting or playing a game. But every so often she'd look up and stare across the street—straight in the direction of Daley's apartment.

Or am I just imagining this? she thought. Paranoia was always Pard's department. That doesn't mean I have to sub for him. But damn it, there she goes again, looking directly at my apartment. Or was she watching the bookstore...waiting for someone attending the book club?

Daley couldn't recognize her from over here, but maybe those miracle-cure-hunting women from the medical arts building who'd chased her last month had posted one of their number to watch her place.

Ridiculous. Crazy. Absurd. Yet there she sat, right across the street, keeping an eye on the place.

If I go in now, and she's watching for me, she'll call her friends and my place will be surrounded again.

Only one thing to do: call the lady who always had her back.

She picked up on the second ring.

"Hey, Gram, it's me. Can I crash there tonight?"

"Oh...well...it's gettin' on late, you know."

Tarzana was only a dozen miles west.

"I'm just a hop and a skip away."

"Oh...well...I guess so."

"Great. I'm heading there now."

Daley hit the gas and pulled out onto the boulevard. Gram didn't sound quite herself. She hoped she was all right.

Twenty minutes later Daley rolled through the entrance of Entrée, Gram's retirement community, and parked before her unit, a tiny ranch with stucco walls and a barrel-tile roof. Gram answered her knock. She'd always been lean and lanky, but she somehow looked more frail than when Daley had last visited. Her blue eyes were red-rimmed.

"Come in," she said and walked away, leaving the door open.

What?

Brendan, Uncle Seamus's Jack Russell terrier, gave his usual greeting, pawing at her leg, tail wagging. But Gram...

Daley stepped into the familiar overheated, tobacco-smoke-laced air and closed the door behind her.

"Gram, are you okay?"

"Just fine," she said without turning.

Something definitely wrong. She hurried after her.

"Gram, what's wrong. Is it Uncle Seamus—?"

She whirled. "No, it's you!" she said in her thick Irish accent. "I'm after spending the whole day listening to terrible stories about you."

Daley sagged. No escaping it, not even here.

"And you believe them?"

"Not at first. They say you'll be making your living running confidence games, just like those people I took you away from after your mother died. And then they'll be showing a picture of you with that awful Billy Marks. What am I supposed to believe then? You told me you wanted nothing to do with him."

"I don't. I wasn't with him because I wanted to be. He tracked me down."

"They say you're after cheating people with phony car raffles. You've been telling me you're doing car *sales*. Which is true?"

Daley had told her she was in car sales as a half-truth. How to explain this?

"I haven't been entirely honest with you about some things, Gram."

He eyes widened. "Then it's true?"

"Hardly any of it is true. I can ex—"

"But you lied to me!" she said, her voice filled with hurt. "Your own Gram!"

Oh, you're killing me, Gram. Tearing my heart out.

"Listen—"

"I'll be going to bed now. I'm tired of this day and I want done with it." Shaking her head, she turned away and headed for her bedroom. "I thought I'd done a good job raising you."

"You did, Gram," Daley said, feeling the tears start. "You were the best. You still are."

"If that were true, you wouldn't have turned out a guttersnipe...a lying guttersnipe."

With that she closed her door behind her.

Guttersnipe...to Gram's mind that was about the worst you could think of someone.

Daley crept up to her door. She had to tell her, had to explain. She was about to knock when a voice said...

"You're best off letting her be for now." Uncle Seamus stood in the kitchen doorway with a finger's worth of whiskey in his hand—had to be Jameson's since he'd drink no other. "She's hurt something terrible. Crying all day—on Saint Paddy's day, of all days."

"But I can explain—"

"There's no explaining livin' like that," he said. "She tried so hard to undo what your father's people had taught you. She thought she'd shown you how to be a good person."

"But she did! She succeeded!"

"If she had, do you think you'd be spending your days cheatin' people?"

What could Daley say to that? She couldn't think of a damn thing.

"I'll be hittin' the hay meself, I think." He downed the last of his whiskey. "Come on, Brendan."

"I'm sorry, Unk. All I can say is I'm sorry. I'll make it up to her."

He stopped in his bedroom door and turned to her. "Too late for that I'm afraid." He gave a sad shake of his head. "You broke her old heart today, dearie. Broke her heart, you did. Clean through."

He closed his door, leaving Daley alone in the main room. She turned in a slow circle, taking in the excess of furniture and the array of Gram's religious statuary.

Broke her heart...

The last thing in the world she'd ever want to do...break the heart of the woman who'd taken her in when she was orphaned and raised her and nurtured her and loved her and made her feel safe. She'd rather die than be responsible for breaking Gram's heart.

Rather die...there's a thought.

Who was left? Who could she turn to? Who hadn't she turned against her? What bridge had she left unburned?

What did tomorrow offer but more of the same shit? And the day after that? And the day after that? Where did she go from here? She wouldn't go back to the grift, even if she could.

Let's face it, girl: You're a pariah. You've got no friends in this world, so why hang on? Tomorrow's gonna suck so why not just cancel tomorrow? And all the tomorrows after that? Really... who the fuck is going to miss you or be sorry you're gone?

She couldn't think of one lousy person.

She stood there for she didn't know how long, staring at the wall, trying to think of one person who needed her, and couldn't come up with one. And slowly it came to her what to do.

She stepped to Seamus's door and put her ear against it. She could hear him snoring on the other side. She eased the door open, slipped through, then left it open a crack behind her so she could see. As she tiptoed toward his nightstand, Brendan's tail started thumping on the bed as he lifted his head.

Don't wake him!

She eased open the nightstand's bottom drawer where he kept the Webley. She felt around and found it under some papers; she'd forgotten how heavy it was and almost dropped it. Clutching it to her chest, she hurried back to the main room where she examined it in the light. The eight-chamber, weirdly sculpted cylinder was fully loaded. Unk had always said an unloaded pistol wasn't worth a damn. He'd taken her to a gun range in the hills a number of times during her teens, so she had some idea of how to use it.

Okay. Now she just had to decide the best place to put an end to all this...

62

"Leave your shoes here," Cadoc said.

"What? This is crazy, Cad."

He and his brother stood before a heavy, bolted door in the antechamber of the entrance to the Lodge. The door opened onto the stairs down to the Nofio pool. Rhys had been down there countless times. Why was Cad taking him down now?

"I know it seems crazy, but just humor me for the next five minutes and you'll see something you'll never forget."

"But—"

"Five minutes, Rhys." He was sounding testy now. "Five lousy minutes."

"Okay, okay."

He could spare him five minutes, he supposed, even though Cadoc was acting a bit loony tonight.

I truly believe she has a power to heal...

Seriously? Daley has magic powers?

Maybe Cad had been cooped up in that room for too long. But Rhys would go along for now. He removed his shoes.

"Now," Cadoc said, stepping out of his own, "if this is going to work, we have to be go down those steps in the dark and in complete silence. *Complete* silence. Not even a whisper. I'm serious about that. The slightest noise will ruin it."

"Ruin what?"

"Everything I'm trying to show you. Ready?"

"I guess."

"I'll lead. Hold onto the railing with one hand and keep the other on my shoulder so we stay together."

"Got it."

Cad turned off the antechamber overhead light and eased the door open, revealing deeper blackness within the darkness. Humid, slightly sulfurous air wafted around them. Rhys put his right hand on Cad's shoulder as he began to move down, found the railing with his left, and followed him onto the steps.

The Pendry family lodge had been built over a hot spring. The area was full of them. The spring trickled downhill under the foundation and pooled in a roughly square depression running twenty feet on a side. The runoff flowed into a subterranean channel that took it who knew where.

Not the most pleasant place. Ventilation had been added but it wasn't enough to combat the constant moisture. As a result the walls were slimy and moldy. The place had been lit by oil lamps in the old days, but the grotto had been equipped with electric lights for the last thirty years or so.

Why all the trouble? The Nofio—another inane clan ritual. Every three months all the pregnant women in the clan would trek down here to immerse themselves for an hour or so in the hundred-degree, mineral-rich spring water. During the immersion the head of the clan would read a passage from the Scrolls invoking a blessing from the absent Visitors upon the unborn.

After they were through, the women would dry themselves off, go back home, and no one would visit or give another thought to the pool until the next Nofio.

Rhys didn't remember there being so many steps, but finally Cadoc stopped. He felt him lean forward and twist slightly to the left, and suddenly the grotto was ablaze with light. That was when Rhys realized they weren't alone down here.

A dozen dark figures occupied the pool. And they weren't human.

After a frozen heartbeat during which Rhys's mind tried to comprehend what his eyes were telling it, the tableau dissolved into thrashing movement as the figures dove into the runoff channel and disappeared.

Rhys found his voice. "Porthors? Were those...porthors?"

"Give the man a prize!"

"No, seriously, I thought they lived in the desert."

"They do. But apparently a certain number of them—I don't pretend to know how they decide whose turn it is, but there's a group soaking here pretty much every night."

"But-but-but—"

"You sound like motorboat, Rhys."

"But how do *you* know? How did you find out?

"This was one of my earliest discoveries. When I first went

into seclusion, I used to sleep in the day and wander the Lodge at night—raid the fridge, watch movies...and skinny dip. The minerals in the spring water made my messed-up skin feel better. One night I decided to take a nap down here, so I turned off the lights, stretched out on that bench over there, and dozed off. I awoke to sloshing sounds in the pool. Scared, I turned the lights on and—*whoa!*—got the fright of my life."

"I'll bet!"

According to the Scrolls, the Visitors took early hominids or proto hominids, and transformed them into something else—something that doesn't die but has limited intelligence and cannot speak—and left them behind when they returned to wherever they came from. Rhys had always considered them bullshit, some sort of boogie men, imaginary beings to frighten children. *The porthors'll getcha!* was a familiar phrase around many a clan home.

"Why didn't you tell me, bro?"

Cad shrugged. "I didn't want you to know I was wandering around the Lodge at night. Little brother would want to come along and I didn't want company. It was my time. I had the place to myself. I was undisputed Master of the Lodge at night."

"But what's this got to do with the Pendry Patch?"

"They're the source of the Patch."

Rhys could only stare at him. Cadoc had lost his mind.

"No," Cadoc said, "I haven't lost my mind."

"But the porthors live out in the desert. Our clan has been here only a little over a century, while the patch has been in the family forever."

"Ah, but that's where you're wrong. If you go back to the nineteenth century in Wales, there's no mention in the family records—not a single one—about a rough, discolored patch of skin on anyone. I know. I've looked. Only after we moved to the desert does it get mentioned. I know that too. I've done the research and the first mention was on a child born in 1919 and almost every child thereafter."

That was a shocker. The patch being part of the family had always been one of those everybody-knows things.

"But that still doesn't mean—"

"I don't know how it started. Maybe a hot mineral spring was such a novelty when we first moved here and the clan was small enough so that everyone soaked. And then the pregnant ones began to give birth to kids with the patch. Somehow it became part of clan lore that the patch will mark us as makers of the way for the Visitors, and as such we will be exalted upon the Return. And so began the Nofio ritual: every three months all the pregnant women soaked here. After a couple of generations, the patch was everywhere."

"But how? How does it happen?"

Cadoc shrugged. "I've got no scientific studies to back me up, but my theory is that when the porthors soak here they leave their 'essence' in the water."

Rhys grimaced in revulsion. "You don't mean..."

Cadoc laughed. "No, not semen. They're sexless, remember? But they leave *something* behind that causes the patch."

"But you..."

"I had an exaggerated reaction, I guess. Instead of a small patch it spread over my entire body. Could have been worse, I suppose. I mean, I could have been born without the patch."

That was a shock.

"I thought every Pendry had a patch."

"It happens."

"Who do we know who doesn't?"

Cadoc gave him a level stare. "No one."

"Then what are you saying?"

"A Pendry child born without the patch is reported stillborn to the parents and put up for adoption. There's no shortage of childless couples out there looking for a lily-white child they can raise as their own."

"Bullshit!"

"It's the truth. It's rare and only the Elders know that there's nothing inside that little closed coffin when it goes into the Pendry crematorium."

Rhys slowly sat down on a bench. "Not Aerona. Don't tell me...please, don't tell me our little sister is being raised somewhere by another family."

"I wish I knew. I've tried to find out if she really died or was adopted, but it's been beyond me in my previous condition. I've combed the files and the computers for some kind of record but came up empty time after time. And since all Pendrys are cremated, an exhumation is impossible."

"But if she is alive...then what?"

"It would be just enough to know she's safe and well. It would be no favor to let her know what kind of family she was born into."

Rhys felt his gorge rise. The possibility was monstrous... inconceivable.

"I can't believe Dad would tell Mom Aerona was dead when she wasn't. He wouldn't let her live all these years blaming herself...would he?"

Cadoc's voice was flat. "It's the Pendry way."

"No. I can't buy it. I know Dad's become unbalanced lately, but he'd never do something like that."

Cadoc bent at the waist and got in his face. "You've seen the film," he said when they were almost nose to nose. "The man who hopes to make that a reality is capable of anything."

63

"Where the fuck you think you're going?"

Cadoc jumped at the unexpected sound of a voice, then froze. He'd made it only to the third tread on Daley's back stairs. He turned slowly but could see no one in the dark.

"Who's there?" he said.

"I asked you a question."

He didn't see why he should answer to anyone, but the undeniable menace in the voice made him wary. Might be better to humor this one.

"Going up to the apartment. Why?"

"You know her?"

"We're friends."

"I ain't seen you around before."

"I'm not terribly social."

Why am I explaining myself?

"Easy to say you're a friend, even if you ain't. Kind of late to be bothering a friend."

"I felt she might need friendly company tonight." Rhys had refused to come along and Cadoc didn't think Daley had many friends left. "Who are you?"

"Her watchdog. Every goddess needs a watchdog."

Goddess? Interesting...

"She stationed you here?"

"She don't know nothin' about it. And you might as well save yourself some steps because she ain't here."

Cadoc glanced at the empty spot where she usually parked. He hadn't thought to check that first.

"Where'd she go?"

"If she don't know I'm here, she ain't about to tell me, is she?"

"Good point. So you spend the night out here watching her place?"

"I got her back."

Something about the way he said it made Cadoc believe him.

"Well, I'm glad someone does. And since she's not here, I guess I'll be going."

"Good idea."

That could be the oddest conversation I've ever had in my life, Cadoc thought as he walked away. *All with a man I couldn't see.*

At least he seemed sincerely devoted to Daley. As was Cadoc. Despite all that had happened, she still had friends. She might be glad to know that.

64

Daley didn't want Gram or Seamus finding her body so she'd looked up the nearest branch of the LAPD and made the short drive to the West Valley Police Station. She parked in a non-spot across the street and pulled out the pistol. Someone in the station would hear the shot and come to investigate.

Whenever Seamus had taken her to the gun range, his Webley-Fosbery always caused a stir because invariably there'd be a gun collector there who'd spot it and beg to buy it. Unk's response had always been the same: "It was me Da's and I'll not be selling it for any price."

Daley didn't want to think about this too much more. She'd mulled it plenty on the drive over and hadn't changed her mind. So just do it and get it over with.

She pointed the barrel at her face and opened her mouth but couldn't stick the muzzle inside. Something just so *wrong* with that. Pard must have read up on suicide by gunshot because somehow she knew that the surest way to succeed was to put a bullet through the brainstem. Plenty of people had survived a bullet in the brain but the brainstem controlled bodily functions like breathing and there was no coming back when you blew that out the back of your head.

She closed her mouth and pressed the muzzle against the top of her throat. With the proper upward angle, she'd hit the brainstem.

Oh, wait. She had to undo the safety. One of the features of the Webley-Fosbery that caused all sorts of oohs and aahs at the range was its safety at the top of the grip. Apparently revolvers don't have safeties. This model was an exception. She flicked the little lever on the left side to off and repositioned the barrel, hooking her thumb around the trigger.

Ready.

She hesitated.

"Okay, Pard," she said aloud. "This is where you make a miraculous return and say, '*Stop! Don't do it! You'll be killing me too.*' Pard? Hey, Pard, I'm waiting."

Shit. He really was gone. She truly was all alone. Which was the whole problem, wasn't it. The whole reason she was here.

And yet...

Why had she been expecting Pard to stop her—no, wait: *wishing* Pard would stop her? Didn't that mean she didn't really want to do this? Yes, that could *only* mean she didn't want to do this.

She lowered the pistol.

Cancelling tomorrow...all tomorrows...

What had she been thinking? She'd pulled some dumbass

stunts in her day but this took the proverbial cake.

When did I become so goddamn pathetic?

People think I'm a crook, a fraud. Well, that's true in the past tense, and well deserved. I'll own that.

People distrust me. I deserve that. Some people even hate me enough to spit on me. I don't think I deserve that, but it's hardly the end of the world.

I'm the pariah of the moment. But haters will hate and people have short memories. The haters will soon find someone new to hate. And if they don't, so what?

Fuck 'em.

Fuck. Them. All.

She'd come through a dumbass moment but she wasn't a total dumbass. Yeah, she was down—way down—but she wasn't out. Not nearly. She had options. Didn't know what the hell they were just yet, but she'd figure them out. She would.

She flicked the safety back on, lay the pistol aside, started the car, and headed back to Gram's for a night on a couch.

Let tomorrow bring what it would. She'd be there to face it down.

65

("W ake up, Daley.")
     Daley bolted to a sitting position on the couch.
"Pard?"

("Hold it down. Don't want to wake the old folks.")

You're back!

She wasn't sure how she felt: Happy? Mad? Relieved?

("Never left.")

What? What kind of a game are you playing?

("No game. I've been paralyzed. Mute. Powerless.")

I can barely hear you.

("Still very weak...low input to your nervous system.")

What happened?

("Jason Tadhak is what happened. He's not human.")

"What?"

("Shhh!")

Hey, I couldn't help it. You can't be serious.

("Dead serious. When I tried to enter him to see what I could do, I was hit with this unimaginably fierce neural blast that knocked me unconscious.")

Wait-wait-wait. Jason's not human? *Then what is he?*

("No idea. Didn't get far enough in to find out. He's not a robot or android, I can tell you that. He's organic but not like any organism I can imagine. What you see is not what you get. Merely looks human. Inside he's entirely something else.")

Daley closed her eyes and tried to fathom this. Totally out of left field. And yet...maybe not all that far out.

He knocked you out?

("Don't know if it was deliberate or a reflex or just the way he's built.

When I finally came to I realized two days had passed. But I was merely aware, otherwise I was still paralyzed and voiceless.")

Oh.

So…you were aware when I was…

("Toying with the Webley? Yes.")

I wasn't "toying." You weren't scared I'd pull the trigger?

("Horrified. When you stuck that muzzle against your throat and angled it up at your brainstem, I thought it was all over. And I couldn't do a damn thing about it. Please, don't ever do anything like that again.")

No worry. I'm over it.

("Glad to hear it. I became aware again during your morning meeting in the hospital—which, by the way, couldn't possibly have gone any worse.")

Tell me about it. If I'd known that CEO, that Sandoval, was planning a character assassination…

("I think it's time we resurrected your character.")

You mean…?

("Yes. Time for Doctor Sandoval to develop a taste for crow. But I'm not ready yet. Getting stronger by the minute but I won't be up to battling the horrors for a while yet.")

How long is "a while"?

("I need a few hours, at least.")

Daley hadn't realized how much she wanted this until just now…when it became a real possibility.

It's a good three-hour drive from here…how about we leave now and you recuperate along the way?

("Let's go.")

66

"How do I look?" Daley said.

Pard, dressed in his usual jeans and boots and flannel shirt, leaned against the stove. This was the first time he'd become visible since the incident with Jason on Sunday. Earlier he'd said he hadn't had the capacity to create an image for her. He'd kept silent for most of the ride down from LA, gathering his strength, reintegrating with her nervous system and all her physiological functions, and now seemed ready to go.

("Exactly as you did Sunday morning when we were also

readying to head to the medical center.")

The Healerina outfit...all that black and the shock of white hair on top...

"I think this makes a statement."

("They're not going to recognize you at first. They've never seen you with your head bare. But after we're through today, they're never going to forget you.")

That was the way she wanted to play it. They'd had a field day screwing with her reputation. Front page, all the way. But retractions tended to get relegated to the bottom corner of an inconsequential section. Not this time. She was going to be so damn photogenic they couldn't *not* put her on the front page.

Pard added, ("Are you sure you want to cut such a highly recognizable figure?")

She nodded. "I do. Because that'll make it easier for me when I *don't* want to be recognized. Put on a mousy brown wig, sunglasses, and ordinary baggy clothes and no one will even see me, let alone recognize me."

Someone knocked on her door. She stepped to the kitchen window and saw Arturo—greasy apron, backward Padres cap, and all—standing outside on the landing, holding a paper sack. Strange...

When she opened the door he grinned, saying, "Hope I'm interrupting something."

"Not a bit."

"Oh? I thought I heard you talking."

This was happening more and more.

"Oh, I just finished on the phone."

He held up the sack. "Breakfast."

"You're kidding."

"Nope. You told me how much you liked the breakfast special so I made you another."

("Oh, yum. Taylor Ham with egg and cheese.")

"Thanks so much, Arturo." She stepped back. "Come on in. This is so unexpected."

"Well, I thought I'd save you the trip over. Especially after, you know..."

"The wonderful things being said about me?"

"Yeah. Don't matter. You got friends here, Daley."

She turned away as her eyes filled and her throat tightened. She could barely speak, but managed, "You don't know how much I've needed to hear that."

"Well, it's true." He placed the sack on the kitchen table. "This one's on the house, by the way."

She turned back to him. "You're really working hard on making me cry, aren't you."

"Nah. Hate to see a woman cry. Hey, you got your work clothes on. That mean you're opening today?"

"Nope. Heading for the medical center."

"Really?" His expression said he didn't think that was such a good idea.

"Yep. They haven't seen the last of me yet."

The grin returned. "Gonna give 'em hell? You go girl."

She lifted the sack. "I'll eat this on the way."

He followed her down the back stairs to her car, she found Juana standing at the bottom. Arturo left with a wave to go back to work.

Juana said, "I waited for you as long as I could yesterday. I wanted to see how it went. I had to leave but I heard about it later."

"Yeah, a disaster."

"I'm so sorry. A lot of bad feelings out there."

"How do *you* feel?"

She grinned. "You don't get rid of me so easy."

Another rush of emotion. Damn!

("You've touched a lot more people than you realize. And you're about to touch a lot more.")

Juana pointed to the Cahuilla art stone dangling at Daley's throat. "I see you've put that to good use."

"Well," she said, fingering it, "you said it's me. Might as well wear it." She moved toward her car. "I've got to get moving..."

"I'll just be a minute," Juana said. "There's someone here I think you should know about."

Daley looked around and saw no one. "Who?"

"My nephew." She turned and called out, "Jeffrey!"

A burly man wearing a battered Stetson stepped around the corner. He looked vaguely familiar but Daley couldn't place him.

"Why do you want—?"

("That's Karma Kendrick,") Pard said. ("He's shaved off his beard.")

She took an involuntary step back. "Karma! Didn't I warn you—?" She swung on Juana. "He's your *nephew*?"

"My sister's boy," she said quickly. "Look, I know what he did—"

"You have no idea!"

She lowered her voice. "He told me he killed you."

The words jolted Daley. So surreal to hear someone say that.

"That's exactly what he did."

It seemed to take Juana a while to absorb that—as if something she hadn't truly believed had just been confirmed. After a pause, she said, "He also told me you came back from the dead. Is that true?"

Daley hesitated. "In a way..."

Juana stared at her. "He says you're a goddess and I'm beginning to believe he may not be too far off."

Me, a goddess? Me?

("I gave him a taste of the horrors I'd seen in Timothy Blaine, remember? It may have unhinged him a little. Well, that and seeing someone he'd stabbed in the heart rise from the dead, of course.")

Daley slashed her hand through the air. "Get him out of my sight. I never want—"

Kendrick bowed his head. "My life is yours, goddess. I'm here to protect you."

"*What?* This is crazy!"

"Maybe," Juana said with a shrug, "but he's totally devoted to you. He says you could have banished him to hell but you let him go. He says you gave him a second chance to earn his way back into your good graces."

Where'd he get *that* idea?

"If I need to be protected, it's *from* him, not *by* him."

Juana's gaze bored into her. "If you're going to El Centro to do what I suspect, you will be attracting all sorts of people. You will need someone to fend for you. I am worried for you and I will vouch for him."

("Maybe she's got a point.")

Not you too?

("That's Karma Kendrick saying his life is yours. The old Karma couldn't fake that. This is someone new.")

You really think I should give him a chance?

("Look at him. You can't buy that kind of devotion. He's obviously undergone a sea change.")

In the desert?

("Apparently.")

She trusted Pard's judgement and she knew Juana was on her side...

"Okay, Karma," she said. "We'll give it a try."

He backed up a step but still kept his head down. "Thank you. But it's not 'Karma' anymore. You told Karma you never wanted to see him again, so Karma Kendrick is dead. It's Jeffrey now."

"If you say so. But you stay here."

I hope I don't regret this.

67

On the road to El Centro, Daley said, "Maybe if I'd run into Arturo yesterday, I wouldn't have felt the need for that pistol."

She prayed today would turn out better—*lots* better—than yesterday. Back in Tarzana she'd left a note for Gram promising to make things right. She hoped this would do it. She couldn't bear the thought of Gram hurting because of her.

Pard, in the passenger seat, said, ("It seems you've made real friends here, Daley. People who'll stick by you.")

"I also had people I thought were friends let me down when I was counting on them."

("You mean Rhys.")

"Who else?"

("The sting of those nasty words hasn't left you. You're still hurting. I can feel it.")

"Let's not talk about him."

As she pulled out the foil-wrapped sandwich—still warm—a totally unrelated thought hit her.

"Holy crap!"

("Now what?")

"You weren't around Sunday afternoon—it happened after your encounter with Jason Tadhak—but Billy Marks tracked me down here and got a little rough with me when I refused to play ball with his horrors scam. Grabbed me and shoved me down on the back steps."

("I had no idea. I'll find the memory when I have time.")

"But here's the thing: Billy was murdered in his motel room that night. Stabbed to death. The theory is that a disgruntled mark got even with him, but you and I know from experience how handy Kendrick is with a knife."

("Ah, I see. You're thinking that if your self-appointed protector had been watching and saw this happen, he would have taken matters into his own hands. You're a goddess after all—*his* goddess—and no one is allowed to defile a goddess.")

"Exactly what I'm thinking."

("We should ask him when we get back.")

"Maybe we shouldn't. I want as little contact with him as possible. And frankly, I'm not sure I want to know."

Not that she felt anything at all for Billy Marks. He'd been a cold-blooded killer who'd murdered her father. What goes around had finally come around...and landed squarely on him.

As they entered El Centro she spotted an auto parts store and on impulse pulled in.

Pard said, ("What...?")

"I guess I can't tell you to wait here, but this'll only a minute."

She hopped out and hurried inside where she bought a pair of black leather driving gloves.

("Completing the ensemble, I see.")

She wriggled her fingers into them and got the car moving again, saying, "Can't have too much black, right?"

("I'll treat that as a rhetorical question.")

"Sounds like you're back to your old self."

("I'm fairly close to some semblance of what might be called 'normal,' and I should be able to stay that way as long as I don't have another encounter with Jason Tadhak.")

"I did some thinking about Jason on the drive from LA."

("Thinking...always a dangerous thing.")

"Oh, you are back, aren't you. Anyway, aliens in Nespodee Springs...it boggles the mind. I mean, why there?"

("My guess is it's connected to the Visitors.")

"I thought we didn't believe in the Visitors."

("We didn't believe in aliens among us either, but...")

"I see your point."

("So maybe they're an advance team for the Visitors. According to Rhys, the Tadhaks are practically giving away the extra energy Elis Pendry needs for his tower.")

"That reminds me: You need to see the film."

("I have your memory of it. That's fine for now.")

"Jason being an alien explains why his family wouldn't allow him to be taken to the hospital after the accident. I'll bet all the Tadhaks are aliens."

("I think you can count on that. It also explains how that building on the windfarm is bigger on the inside than the outside—alien technology.")

"But it doesn't explain why he's stockpiling all that energy."

("Like I said: Maybe to enable the Pendrys. Then again, maybe they're following the hallowed immigrant tradition of working hard and sending the excess home.")

"You have any idea where their home might be?"

("I can't even imagine.")

Daley hesitated bringing it up, but since they were on the subject of Jason...

"Don't laugh, but I thought you left me for him."

("Jason? Well, first off, I don't laugh. Have you ever heard me laugh?")

"Come to think of it...no."

And she decided right then she didn't want to...ever. She imagined it an appalling sound.

("Secondly, why would I want to do such a thing?")

She shrugged, a little embarrassed now. "I don't know. Maybe you found his nervous system more attractive or accommodating. You know...better suited to you."

Pard made a disgusted face. ("Really, Daley? After all we've been through? If I had feelings they'd be hurt.")

Well, yeah, they had been through a lot. He'd pretty much brought her back from death, but still...

"I thought maybe you were tired of me and wanted to try someone new."

("I am not some sort of neurological lothario. As I told you back at the start—I guess you weren't listening so I'll tell you again: I *can't* leave you, Daley. You and I are stuck with each other. And even if I could leave, I wouldn't. We make a good team. I happen to like you and I enjoy being with you.")

To hear this after all the rejection and name-calling and... and spittle she'd experienced in the last twenty-four hours... Daley's throat constricted again and wouldn't allow her to speak right away. So she threw a thought at him.

I missed you.

("Of course you did.")

That brought her voice back—real quick. "'Of *course*' I did? That's a helluva thing to say."

("I think it's an obvious thing to say. Why wouldn't you miss your best friend?")

Daley found no answer for that. She'd never had a best friend. Until Pard.

68

As the medical center came into view, Daley said, "Are you sure you're up to this, Pard?"

("What? Curing the horrors?") Much to her dismay, Pard shrugged. She wanted cocky confidence, not a noncommittal shrug. ("I can't know for sure until I merge with someone and block that pineal-amygdala pathway, but I'm pretty sure.")

*Pretty sure...*not exactly brimming with confidence.

("I sense hesitation, Daley.")

"Well, right now I'm ECRMC's bête noire and—"

("Delighted to see you making use of your augmented vocabulary.")

Yeah, two months ago she would have had no idea what that term meant, which was great and all, but...

"If you're through patting yourself on the back, I'll continue."

("Go right ahead.")

"Okay: As the official least-favorite person in there, it won't take them long to recognize me. And if I go in and just hold hands with a patient and nothing happens, I'll be demoted from just plain old run-of-the-mill scam artist to mentally deranged scam artist."

("I will do my damnedest to prevent that from happening, but I can't swear it won't.")

She pulled into a parking spot in the visitor lot.

"Well, that's certainly reassuring."

("The best I can do, I'm afraid. The only way we can know for sure is to try.")

She sat and stared through the windshield at the medical center.

"Wow. You know, I went to sleep last night thinking things can only get better, but that's not quite the case, is it."

("As long as you're breathing, things can always get worse. But they can also get better. That place is full of people who need help, and we're the only ones who can provide it.")

"*Maybe* provide it."

("True enough. But they need us and that means we need to try.")

She looked at him. "Anybody ever tell you you're a good person?"

("Of course not. No one even knows I exist. Which means that when we walk in there, it's *your* reputation on the line, not mine. And I happen to know you've already decided to go. Which makes *you* the good person.")

Yeah, she had indeed decided to go, hadn't she. Ah, well...

"I'm thinking we go in through the emergency room. I'm pretty sure I can find my way to Doctor Milton's office from there."

"What makes you think he'll want to get involved?"

"Because he's convinced I'm connected to the three cures we did. He doesn't know how, he doesn't know why, but he said it right to my face: 'I know in my gut that you're somehow at the bottom of all this.' If he thinks I can answer his questions, he'll help."

("Then let's find him and make these bozos eat their words.")

Daley laughed. "That's the spirit! We just have to watch out for Sandoval. She's got it in for me."

("She's only doing her job, which is to protect the hospital, and she thinks you're trying to pull a fast one on the patients. We simply have to change her mind.")

"Then let's get to it."

Feigning supreme confidence, Daley stepped out and strode toward the emergency entrance where an ambulance was just pulling away.

("I'm going to disappear so you don't start talking out loud to me. Not exactly a confidence builder.")

Good idea.

As the automatic doors slipped open to admit her, she was assaulted by a man's piercing screams. Sounded like the horrors.

That ambulance must have brought him.

("Should we?")

Daley wondered about that. Who knew if they'd ever make it to Milton's office before a security guard recognized her and ejected them? An opportunity had presented itself.

Let's see if we can help.

She followed the screams to a curtained-off alcove where a middle-aged Hispanic man lay limp on a gurney, staring slack-jawed at the ceiling. Every few seconds he would tense and let loose a howl of terror. An IV ran into his left arm while a slightly younger Hispanic woman stood on his right side, tearfully clutching his hand. Daley moved opposite her.

"Los horrors!" she moaned. "Los horrors!"

"Marido?" Daley said, pulling off her left glove. Her Spanish was rudimentary at best but she knew a few words.

A nod. "Yes."

She held up her golden hand. "May I touch him?"

The woman looked confused but said, "I guess so. Who are you?" Her English was undoubtedly better than Daley's Spanish.

Daley grabbed his wrist. "Just trying to help."

Okay, Pard. Do your thing.

He waited the necessary ten seconds or so to establish contact, then said, ("Going in.")

And do not *pop out of his chest.*

She prayed Pard could work his magic in there. If not—

"Excuse me," said a male nurse as he pushed through the curtains. "Are you a member of the family?"

Daley didn't bother answering that—the briefest glance made it pretty obvious she was not.

"I'm here to help."

"He's got the horrors. I'm afraid there is no help for—"

The man screamed again, an agonizingly terrified sound, and Daley's heart went to him and his devastated wife.

"Just let me hold his wrist for a minute, okay."

The nurse's eyes widened. "Hey, wait. You're her, that phony. Get outa here right now!"

He started moving toward her but the wife grabbed his arm. "It's okay. She's not—"

"She not supposed to be anywhere near here, ma'am."

Come on, Pard. Finish up. We're busted.

And then Sandoval stormed in with two security guards behind her.

"It's really you! When they told me they'd spotted you on the security cams I didn't want to believe it, but it's you!"

The nurse pulled Daley's hand free.

("Damn,") Pard said. ("I haven't finished.")

Daley took a step back.

"Don't you move!" Sandoval said, jabbing a finger at her. "I'm calling in police and—"

"What's going on here?" the wife said. "He has the horrors."

Sandoval turned on her. "Oh, no! Don't start that with me!" Back to Daley. "Do you think we're all idiots? You send a plant in here so you can pretend to cure him and expect us to buy it?"

"A plant?" the wife said, looking from Sandoval to Daley. "What does she mean?"

Sandoval grabbed the husband's shoulder and shook him. "Okay, mister, you've got a good scream, I'll grant you that—I heard you all the way down the hall—but we know you're a fake, so you can cut the act."

The wife stared at her. "Act?" she said as she came around the gurney and got in Sandoval's face. "He collapsed and started screaming in front of our children and you call it an *act*?"

"That's exactly what I'm calling it." She pointed at Daley. "She hired you two to fake—"

The woman's face twisted in rage. "Fake?"

She slapped Sandoval across the face with a resounding smack! Then followed it up with a barrage of punches.

As the guards tried to pull the woman off their CEO, Pard said, ("I think that's our cue to exit.")

But Daley was already easing around the far edge of the curtain. Once out of the alcove, she made a beeline for the hospital hallway and then quick-walked toward the hospital offices, pulling her glove back on as she moved just short of jog speed.

I think Doctor Milton's office is right down this hall here…yep.

She stopped before the door labeled *Alfred Milton, MD— Chief of Medicine*, knocked, then pushed inside without waiting for a response.

Leave this to me. No interruptions or distractions, okay?

("You have the floor.")

A startled Dr. Milton looked up from his computer as she entered and shut the door behind her.

"Yes?" Then he frowned. "Wait…aren't you—?"

"Yes. Daley. From yesterday."

His expression turned angry as he rose behind his desk. "You're not supposed to be here."

"Not even if I'm here to cure horrors patients?"

"Especially not. As I recall, you told me yesterday you weren't able to do that."

"That was yesterday. Today is different."

He reached for his desk phone. "I'm calling security."

Daley raised a hand. "Wait. Listen to your gut."

He frowned, his hand resting on the receiver. "Pardon?"

"Yesterday you said you knew in your gut I was somehow at the bottom of the cures. Give me a chance with one patient— any patient of your choosing, with you standing right beside me."

She could see him wavering—at least he seemed to be—then he lifted the receiver.

"Sorry."

"What have you got to lose, Doctor Milton?"

"How about my reputation and self-respect. You told me flat-out yesterday that you did not cure those three cases. Now you're saying you did?"

She spread her hands. "It's really, really complicated."

"Fakery is fakery. Nothing complicated about that."

"Think! If there's a possibility—even the most remote possibility—that I can cure even one more, with no downside, how can you refuse?"

"No downside? There's always a downside. Just what do your supposed 'cures' involve?"

She held up her left hand. "I remove this glove and wrap my fingers around the patient's wrist."

"A laying on of hands? That's it?"

She nodded. "That's it."

"Hocus-pocus bullshit."

"But no risk to anyone. Don't you have an obligation to do everything you can for your patients? I repeat: you choose the patient and you stay right on top of me."

He slammed the receiver down. "Okay, damn it. One patient, and I know just the one."

Pard, who'd been standing off to the side, clapped his hands but they made no sound. ("Yes!")

Daley opened the door and Milton followed her into the hall. "Stay close to me," he said. "We may run into flack."

They made it to the elevator without a problem, but then Sandoval and her two security guards rounded the corner. An angry red welt graced her left cheek.

"There she is!"

"She's with me," Milton said, "and we're headed upstairs."

"Oh, no. This one's headed straight out the door where the police will—"

Milton took Daley's upper arm and propelled her into the elevator, then turned and held up his hand.

"Your sphere is administration, I believe. This is a medical matter. You can wait down here until we're done."

The doors pincered closed, cutting off the CEO's glare.

("No love lost between those two.")

I'll say.

Milton turned to Daley. "It appears you have strange effects on people."

"Oh?"

"Doctor Sandoval, for instance. Usually she's just irritatingly officious, but you've managed to turn her into..." He hesitated.

"A harridan?"

"I wouldn't go that far. And then there's Doctor Stabler, a well-respected surgeon, who is convinced you've grown a new hand. And now me...I'm taking an admitted con artist up to see one of my patients." He shook his head. "Bizarre."

"Speaking of this patient...is there something special about her?"

"Amelia Horowitz...I will tell you only that she was one of our earliest horrors patients and I happen to know her personally."

"Good. So there's no chance she's a plant."

"Absolutely none."

"Let's just hope she's light on her sedation."

Milton frowned. "Oh. And why is that?"

"If she's knocked out, how will you know whether or not my 'hocus-pocus bullshit' worked?"

His lips twisted. Suppressing a smile?

"I deal in science, Ms. Daley. I owe it to my patients to recommend only therapies that have been proven to work."

"So you're not into alternative medicine, I take it."

"When 'alternative' precedes a therapy it means the therapy has not been proven to work. Once we know a therapy works, it stops being 'alternative.'"

Pard had been leaning against the rear wall of the cab. ("I think I like this fellow.")

Daley said, "Well, you've got to admit that what I'm about to do is alternative as all hell."

"I do admit it. And I also admit that I'm desperate as all hell. I can't see how a laying on of hands will do a damn bit of good, but *primum non nocere*—it will do no harm—so, for Amelia's sake, I'm placing my rationality on hold and going with it."

("Yep. Definitely one of the good guys.")

The elevator deposited them on the second floor and Dr. Milton led the way down the hall. Pard trailed along. Somewhere along the way he'd switched to surgical scrubs.

As Milton passed the nursing station he slowed and said, "When's Amelia due for her next dose?"

The nurse checked a sheet. "Right about now."

"Come with me and bring it along."

They continued to the last room on the left where Milton stopped next to the window bed. A sixtyish woman lay propped on her side, out cold.

"Here's your patient."

The nurse said, *"Her* patient? But she's—?"

"Yep," Daley said as she pulled off her left glove. "The fraud. The con artist."

("A designation we hope to change,") Pard said.

Let's not waste any time.

Daley grabbed Amelia's wrist. After the necessary pause, Pard dove in for the merge. Daley prayed he could still do this.

Milton said, "I'm holding off on Amelia's sedation for now. But at the first sign of distress—which is inevitable, I'm afraid—I'll have Nurse Ames here dose her. We won't mention this in the chart. You simply visited the patient. And then I'll deliver you to Doctor Sandoval."

"Not an optimist, ay?" Daley said.

With every passing second she edged closer to pessimism herself. Pard seemed to be taking a long time. Or was it just her nerves?

"I consider myself a realist," Milton said.

"Where's the fun in that?"

This earned another hint of a smile.

Pard reappeared at last. ("Did it. At least I hope I did.")

Hope?

("I think it'll work. I did what I could to clear some of the sedative from her system but she'll be under for a little bit longer.")

Daley released Amelia's wrist. "There. Done."

Milton blinked. "That's it?"

"That's it."

"She's just the same as before," Ames said. "You did nothing."

Daley turned on her. "Thank you for stating the obvious. She's still sedated. When that wears off, we'll see."

Ames said, "This is nonsense, Doctor Milton."

He sighed. "Most certainly, yes."

What's taking so long?

("The damn sedation...I hope.")

Hope...that word again. Daley could feel her muscles bunching with tension. If they failed...

I can't stand this. What do we do while we wait?

("Well, she's got a roommate. Let's give her a try. If Amelia doesn't come around, maybe this one will.")

This was torture.

"And it isn't right," Ames was saying. "If Amelia gets too light and starts screaming..."

"I appreciate your concern, Ames, but if we're going to give this a fair shot, we have—"

"Hey!" Ames cried. "Stay away from her!"

While those two were talking, Daley had slipped over to the wall bed and grabbed the much younger occupant's wrist. As Ames rushed over, Daley held up her free hand to stop her.

"No harm being done," she said as Pard slipped in for the merge.

Milton stepped to Ames's side. "This wasn't part of our deal, Ms. Daley."

"Just putting the wait time to good use."

"I think you'd better—"

"Alfred?" said a croaking voice. "Alfred, is that you?"

All eyes turned toward the window bed where Amelia was up on one elbow and looking around with a dazed expression.

"Oh, Alfred," she sobbed. "It was awful, just awful!"

She'd come out of it. She was conscious!

A few feet away, the tray with the syringe that Ames had been holding clattered to the floor as she cried, "Oh, my God! Oh, my God!" and ran out of the room.

Weak with relief, Daley sagged against the wall bed. She felt like crying.

Milton rushed to the bed, saying, "Amelia! You're back? Really back?"

Daley could have done a happy dance, but stayed in contact with the roommate because Pard was still merged.

Dr. Milton and Amelia threw their arms around each other and sobbed together.

Pard suddenly reappeared.

You did it!

("So it would seem. Look at that clinch. Now that's what I call a close doctor-patient relationship.")

How'd you do with this gal?

("Same as with Amelia—blocked the pathway. Give her some time.")

Daley retreated to the side wall as Nurse Ames rushed back in with two other nurses and they crowded around Amelia's bed with cries of wonder. Then the twenty-something in the wall bed rolled over. Her voice too was hoarse.

"What—what's going on? And can I have some water?"

One of the new nurse arrivals squealed, "Kathy! Kathy, you're awake?"

Kathy's confused expression said she had no idea where she was.

Daley used the ensuing chaos to step out into the hall and gather herself.

Pard leaned against the wall by her side, grinning. ("Success! I've still got it!") He held up a hand. ("Slap me five!")

I don't high five.

("All humans high five.")

Not this one. Only pitiful, needy souls in constant search of affirmation. And that's not even a real hand.

He kept his hand up. ("You gonna leave me hanging, babe?")

Babe?

He brought it down to thigh level. ("Low five then?")

If you insist.

She jabbed her index finger at the center of his palm. Of course, her finger went straight through.

("A *one*?")

That's as far as I go.

("What's bothering you?")

I'm thinking we just put an end to the life we used to live.

("Yeah, I'm afraid so. Now we've got to figure out a way to adjust and make the best of the new one. But the important thing is we did it!")

You *did* it.

("I'm useless without you. We're a team, Daley. Never forget that.")

Nurse Ames stepped out of the room and approached Daley as if walking barefoot on broken glass.

"Ms. Daley," she said in a small voice, "I...I don't know what you did or how you did it, but this...this is a miracle and I just want to apologize for, you know, doubting you."

Daley shook her head. "Please don't apologize. You were only looking out for your patients, which is exactly what a good nurse should do."

"Doctor Milton's such a good man and you brought his sister back. He thought she was lost forever."

"Amelia is his sister? He never let on."

("I guess that explains the warm embrace.")

As if he'd heard his name, Dr. Milton appeared at the door to the room and stared at Daley with damp eyes and a dumbfounded expression.

"How?" he said in a hushed tone. "How did you do this?"

What do I say?

("Not the truth—he'll never believe the truth. Make up something close to the truth.")

He won't believe that either.

("Who cares? We're not here to create believers, we're here to kick the horrors' ass.")

You have such a way with words.

("I've had a great teacher. Oh, yeah, and don't forget: We're also here to find out where the horrors comes from.")

Daley looked from Milton to Ames and said, "Do you really want to hear this?"

They both nodded, and Milton said, "Desperately."

Recalling—though not fully understanding—what Pard had told her, she said, "The horrors victims have a neural pathway running from their pineal gland directly to the amygdala. The horrors feeds through the pineal gland and travels along that pathway to the fear center in the amygdala."

Milton frowned. "'Feeds' from where?"

"That's the big mystery. I'd love to find out. By the way, if you don't have that pathway, you're immune from the horrors."

"Okay...accepting this pathway exists, what do you do?"

Here's where we lose him.

"Well, if you block the feed you stop the horrors. So I send a part of me into the victim and block the pathway."

Milton spoke slowly, in a halting tone. "You send part of yourself inside..."

("Look at him...you can see him shutting down.")

But check Ames: She's totally buying it.

"You go *inside*?" she said, eyes wide and sounding breathless. "Like with your mind? Can you teach me?"

"I wish I could," Daley said. *You have no idea.* "But it's simply not possible. You either can do it or you can't."

Milton shook himself, obviously far out of his rational comfort zone. "Okay, explanations aside, you gave those two women back their lives and for that I—and everyone here—is eternally grateful. Can you cure more?"

"Sure," Daley said.

The more we do, the better your chances of tracking the source, right?

("Right.")

"How many more can you manage?" Milton said.

"How many y'got?"

He stared at her. "You're serious?"

"I'm here. Put me to work."

"Damn, did we ever misjudge you. But anyway, I can't give you an exact number off the top of my head. It's constantly growing. More than half the hospital's beds are filled by horrors patients and the steady influx is threatening to take over the rest. Our resources are so stretched we're thinking about moving some of the healthiest ones—younger victims with no

complicating medical issues—to an intermediate-care facility."
He gestured down the hall. "But for now they're all under
one—uh-oh."

Daley followed his gaze and felt her heart sink.

Sandoval was marching their way with two sheriff's
deputies in tow. One was Sam Alvarez who did not look happy
to be here.

Dr. Milton stepped between Daley and the newcomers.

"What's going on?" Milton said.

The CEO was wearing that smug smile. "Taking out the
trash."

Daley bit back an angry retort as Milton shook his head in
disgust.

"Is that really necessary?"

"I've reported her as a disorderly person. These two fine
officers of the law will remove her from the premises."

Milton said, "You might want to look in the room we just
exited first."

"No, that won't be nec—"

"You will check out the two horrors patients in that room,"
he said, his tone hardening. "And until you do, I don't care if
you bring in the goddamn National Guard, this young lady is
not going anywhere."

("Told you he was a good guy,") Pard said.

Obviously taken aback, the CEO glanced uncertainly at the
two deputies.

Sam gestured toward the doorway. "Be easier if you did."
The other deputy nodded agreement.

Sandoval's expression said she loathed the idea of lowly
deputies calling the shots, but she couldn't remove Daley from
the hospital without their cooperation.

"Go ahead," Milton said. "There are two nurses in there
tending to the patients."

Squaring her shoulders, Sandoval marched past them and
into the room. Less than a minute later she stumbled out with a
slack expression.

"Amelia's back? She's awake...they're both awake...they're
both talking..."

"Knew it!" Sam said softly with a little fist pump.

Sandoval looked at Daley. "You?"

Daley nodded but said nothing.

"I...I don't understand."

"Neither do I," Milton said. "But I know what I see. And Ms. Daley has agreed to bring back as many as she can."

"But how?"

"How doesn't matter. And you're wasting her time. People need her." He ushered Daley toward the next room. "Shall we?"

"I didn't know," Sandoval said, taking a hesitant step forward as Daley turned away. "If I'd known I-I-I'd never..."

On impulse Daley went back to her.

("Daley? What are you doing?") Pard sounded worried.

Gonna pretend I'm a grown-up.

She thrust her hand out to Sandoval and said, "It's okay. You couldn't have known. Maybe we can we be friends now?"

The CEO's mouth worked but no words came out. She did manage to nod as she grasped Daley's hand in both of hers.

"Great." Daley pulled free, saying, "Gotta go. Work to do."

("Her expression,") Pard said. ("If I laughed, I'd be in hysterics right now.")

Sometimes I like to do the unexpected. And besides, Gram says that being nice to an enemy is like heaping hot coals on their head.

Dr. Milton's expression mimicked Sandoval's. "You are something else, young lady. What planet are you from?"

"This one." She lowered her voice and jerked a thumb over her shoulder at Sandoval. "But she's from Uranus." As Milton burst out laughing, Daley said, "Okay, let's do this."

69

("How are you holding up?") Pard said as he emerged from the last of the victims.

Daley released the guy's wrist. Already he was stirring. How long had she been at this? Hours and hours that seemed like days.

A little pooped—more emotional exhaustion than anything else, I think. You're doing all the work.

("But it's not physical for me. Nor emotional. Just frustrating.")

Because you can't find the source?

("Exactly. The images they're experiencing are emanating from somewhere outside their bodies, but they seem non-directional. They appear to be all around us but only those with that neural pathway can perceive them.")

So we don't know any more now than we did this morning.

("We know that a private life may be a thing of the past for you from now on.")

Sam Alvarez stood guard at the door to the last two patients' room to keep out the curious and the obnoxious. After the Sandoval confrontation this morning, his fellow deputy left to resume his regular duties, but Sam had appointed himself her personal bodyguard. She'd thought that unnecessary at first, but as the day had worn on, she was glad he'd stayed.

"Ready to move?" Sam said.

"How's the crowd?"

"Even bigger, I'm afraid."

The news that someone was curing the horrors victims at ECRMC had flashed through the valley like lightning. Victims' relatives swarmed the lobby and soon overwhelmed the security resources, flooding through the building to all the patient areas.

It didn't take them long to realize that the slim young woman in black with the white patch of hair and the golden hand was the source of the miracles. The Hispanic families called her "La Curandera." Those with loved ones she had already seen wept with joy. Those with relatives still lost to the world prayed she would be able to work her magic on them. And an obstreperous few demanded that their loved one be next.

Daley tried to remain above it all, simply going from one room to the next. Often she had to wait for a room to be cleared so she could do her thing. Sometimes the relatives refused to leave and so she simply moved onto the next without entering. The lesson was quickly learned: Clear the area for La Curandera or delay the miracle.

Daley took a deep breath. "Get me out of here, Sam."

Dr. Milton had left her in Sam's care to take care of medical issues elsewhere in the hospital. Sandoval had morphed from and enemy to an advocate and had assigned her two of the hospital security guards—Marcus and Elena. So, with Sam leading the way and a guard on each side, they began to push through the crowded hallway.

News that she had cured the last of the victims present had spread through the crowd and a cheer went up as she appeared. They made way for her, their cellphones held aloft to record her passing, and many hands reached out to touch her as she passed.

What a difference a day makes. They were spitting on me yesterday.

("Fear appears to lower the IQ, but what it really does is blunt the capacity for critical thinking. They're afraid, so they emote instead of think. They don't know who the horrors will strike next. And with no cure, the fear ramps up and up.")

Now they have a cure—me. But I'm it? No one else can do this? That's scary.

("And a huge responsibility.")

Finally they reached the elevator where Sam would allow only Marcus, Elena, and himself on with Daley.

"Give me your car keys," he said as soon as the doors slid closed.

Daley wriggled a hand into the pocket of her skirt. "What for?"

"I'm going to drive you out of here in a sheriff's department unit. That should discourage any of your new fans from following. Elena will take your car and we'll all meet at the Old Eucalyptus Schoolhouse."

"Schoolhouse?"

"Actually it's a banquet hall, west of town on S80. You can switch to your own car there and I'll drive Elena back."

"You really think that's necessary?"

He shrugged. "I could be overreacting, but if I've learned anything from this job is that a certain percentage of people are crazy—not psycho, necessarily, but filled with crazy ideas. Most of those aren't bad people, but they can cause harm without meaning to. You're not Ms. Daley anymore, you're La Curandera, and if somebody out there thinks they can use your magic or somehow share it, things could get strange and maybe even dangerous."

Seems like overkill.

("Might be. But he's given this some thought, and he's got your best interests at heart. Go with it.")

"Also," Sam added, "to some warped person's mind, it's only a slight sidestep from 'La Curandera' to 'bruja.'"

Daley knew the word: *witch.* Some of the Pendrys had already slapped that label on her, and wasn't there something in the Bible about not allowing a witch to live? She shuddered. This could turn ugly.

She described to Elena approximately where she'd parked her Crosstrek and gave her the license-plate number. And then the elevator doors opened on a madhouse. The hospital lobby was *jammed* with people. A cheer, much louder than upstairs, went up as they spotted her and surged forward. Cell phones were raised everywhere, some on sticks as people leaned in to catch a selfie with La Curandera. Sam, Marcus and Elena had to push hard against them to move Daley toward the entrance.

Luckily, El Centro PD had sent a number of officers to aid with crowd control and they helped clear a path to the outside. Once more, people were reaching for her, touching her, calling out "La Curandera! La Curandera!"

I take back what I said about overkill.

Sam's unit was parked right in front of the main entrance portico. He quickly ushered her toward it, avoiding a reporter with an extended mic. Daley caught a passing glimpse of a panel truck labeled *K-something-TV* with a dish on its roof. Sam pushed her into the passenger seat, then got them rolling. He hit the flashers and siren and roared north on Imperial Avenue. Cars pulled over to let him pass.

"Made it," he said, checking the rearview. "Nobody following."

"Thanks for all your help," she said.

She leaned back. It felt so good to sit. She'd been on her feet for hours.

"*You're* thanking *me*? After what you just did back there? The whole town—the whole *state* should be thanking you. And after what you did for Araceli...you will admit now that you did it, right?"

What do you think, Pard?

("The cat is, as they say, out of the bag now, so why not?")

She nodded. "Yeah, I did."

He pounded the steering wheel. "Knew it! Knew it! Knew it! So it's not just the horrors you can cure."

"I can't cure everything, Sam. Just a few things. A small brain tumor that hasn't spread just happens to be one of them."

"But why wouldn't you tell me? Why keep saying Araceli cured herself?"

She looked at him. "We just waded through the reason."

"Oh...right. But where did you get this power? Were you born with it? Did someone teach you?"

Here was the second time today she'd been asked if it could be learned. She recycled the answer she'd given Nurse Ames this morning...which seemed like an age ago.

"You can't learn it. Either you can do it or you can't."

You'll notice I'm trying not to lie these days.

("I *have* noticed, and I'm duly impressed with how, with that one simple statement, you managed simultaneously to avoid lying and avoid answering the question.")

Think I might have a future in politics?

("I thought you promised to give up scams.")

Sam said, "I've known in my heart all along that you cured Araceli. It happened when you gave her the pink quartz. You put her hands around the stone and your hands around hers. That's when it happened, right?"

Daley nodded. The contact had allowed Pard to go in and strangle the tumor's blood supply.

"That was it."

Another bang on the steering wheel. "Knew it! You know, even though I was totally sure of it, I never mentioned it to anyone, even Araceli's mom, because I knew they'd think I was crazy. But now—"

She put her hand on his arm. "Please don't. Leave it a mystery miracle."

"But—"

"Like you said: Some people get crazy ideas. If they hear I cured one tumor, they'll think I can cure all tumors."

"And you can't?"

"Definitely not. I'm still learning about this. There are so many things I *can't* cure. People won't understand that. I'll tell them 'I can't help you' and they'll hear 'I *won't* help you' and get mad and maybe even violent. So please, let's leave Araceli our secret, okay?"

"Anything you want, Daley. I'm on your side forever. If that's the way you want it, that's the way it'll be. Mum's the word."

70

Rhys answered the knock on his bedroom door and found Cadoc standing on the threshold.

"My room," his brother said in a clipped tone. "Now."

Before Rhys could respond, Cadoc was on his way down the hall. Well, he had nothing better to do, so he followed him to where his brother held the door and shut it behind him as soon as he'd entered.

"What—?"

"You need to see this," Cad said, grabbing the TV remote. "I recorded it earlier."

The flat screen on his wall came to life with a freeze frame of a crowd outside the medical center in El Centro. Then the people started moving and the camera focused in on an African American female reporter holding a mic before a tearful young woman.

WOMAN (sobbing): —e's back! I can't believe he's back!

REPORTER: *Who's back?*

WOMAN: *My dad. He got hit with the horrors last week and all they've been doing for him is knocking him out to keep him quiet. Then we hear—I mean, my uncle calls us up and says he heard there's someone down the hospital curing the horrors.*

REPORTER: *Did you believe it?*

WOMAN: *Well, no. I mean we heard about this con artist they caught and I figured it was her.*

Rhys groaned. "Is this going to be a rehash of Daley's—?"

Cadoc held up his hand and made a shushing sound. "Listen."

REPORTER: *You mean the woman who—?*

WOMAN: *Yeah-yeah, but my uncle, he says, No this sounds like something's really happening—something big. So I come down here and—* (puts hand over her eyes and sobs again)

REPORTER: *Go ahead.*

WOMAN: *So I come down here and there's this whole crowd of people—I mean, the place is totally mobbed, you know? I can't barely move. But then my uncle—he's my father's brother—he finds me and drags me up to the second floor where—*(breaks down again) *where my dad's sitting up in bed—I mean he's sitting up in his* (beep) *bed talking! It's a* (beep) *miracle!*

REPORTER: *What happened?*

WOMAN: *This girl—woman—she's like my age, you know? She's all in black and she's got this white splotch of hair up here* (touches her crown) *and she's going from room to room curing the horrors!*

Rhys said, "She's describing—"

Cad nodded. "Yes, I know."

REPORTER: *Did you get her name?*

WOMAN: *Everyone's calling her "La Curandera."*

REPORTER (nodding): *"La Curandera"—the Healer.*

WOMAN: *Right! I took a picture of her—* (holds up her phone)

REPORTER: *Thank you. We have smartphone video we've acquired.* (looks toward camera) *Is it loaded? Okay, we're ready. This was recorded by someone in the medical center just a short while ago.*

Some static on the screen and then a shaky video of a slim young woman all in black with a white patch of hair exiting a doorway and being escorted by a sheriff's deputy a short distance through a crowd of onlookers into another room.

As the visual returned to the reporter, Rhys could only stare in awe. Daley...Daley had returned to the medical center.

The screen went dark as Cad turned it off, saying, "Believe in her now?"

"But she flat-out denied that she'd cured those first cases."

Cad dropped into a chair. "Yeah...I couldn't understand that. But you know, after seeing the crowd she attracted down in El Centro, maybe I do."

"You've got no doubt that she cleared up your skin?"

"Not the slightest."

"And the horrors? *The Horrors?* Nobody's been able to do a damn thing for the horrors."

"Until now."

"How many did she...?"

"According to the news, all of them. Sixty-two, to be exact."

Rhys found a chair for himself and stared at the blank TV screen. Daley could heal people...cure the horrors. His Daley...

His? That was debatable now.

"I've really blown this. If only she'd told me."

"Well, she didn't and it's easy to understand why. I know you're hurt, but—"

"It's that obvious?"

"It oozes out of you. But it's all over and done with. You need to pull up your big-boy pants and put it behind you."

"Easier said than done, I'm afraid."

"Uh-oh. What did you do?"

This was hard to talk about.

"The hospital's CEO thought Daley was planning to scam the horrors patients' families. She said she'd never stoop that low and swore to me that her scamming days were over...that she'd put all that behind her."

"I'm afraid to ask: Your response was...?"

"I said something like, 'That's exactly what I'd expect a con artist to say.'"

Cad leaned back with a pained expression and closed his eyes. "Oh, shit!"

Exactly: Oh, double-shit.

"Yeah, I think I hurt her."

"You *think*? You flat-out called her a liar—*to her face!* She hurt you so you had to hurt her back. Not to mention that when she hurt you, it was by *omission*—something she *didn't* do—but you had to go and punch her in the gut. Forget what I said about putting on your big-boy pants—they won't fit."

His brother's words struck a nerve deep within Rhys—he knew he could be a dumbass at times but he'd been a real jerk yesterday—but something else struck him.

"You really care about Daley, don't you. You're really into her."

"Goddamn right I am." He pulled up his sleeves to bare his clear skin. "She gave me back my life."

"Do you love her?"

The question seemed to startle Cadoc, but he answered almost immediately. "I probably do. But I'm not looking for a relationship—with anybody. Frankly, I don't think I'm capable of one yet. Not sure I'll ever be. But she's special, Rhys. I knew that from the start." He held his arms in the air. "I didn't know just *how* special."

"She's the Duad our dear father's been obsessing about, Cad." In response to Cad's bewildered expression, he added, "Look, I don't pretend to know what a Duad is, but it's pretty obvious she can do things no ordinary human can. I thought Dad was crazy for worrying about her messing up his plans, but now I think she may be the one to do it."

"How?"

"I don't know. And neither does she. She doesn't know what a Duad is either."

"Well, that's all well and good, dear brother, but we're talking about a woman who'll probably never speak to you again."

Rhys remembered their last exchange in the car. Her words came back to him in a searing rush.

I think it's better if we stop talking...You'll only think I'm lying so why bother?...Stop. Talking. Now. NOW!

"Yeah, that's a real possibility."

71

The sun had slid well below the mountain tops by the time they reached Nespodee Springs.

(Oh, this isn't good,") Pard said as they drove into town.

Daley knew immediately what he meant: The main drag was crowded with cars and even a few RVs.

"Crap. They've connected me with Healerina."

("Well, you're a celebrity now.")

The last thing she wanted.

She turned off into the alley between her building and its neighbor and pulled to a stop near her usual parking space. A small, ragtag group of people were clustered around the bottom of her back steps where Karma—no, make that Jeffrey Kendrick stood with his big arms folded across this chest, blocking the way.

("Well, well, well. A dragon is guarding the gate to your castle. I'm not sure whether that's good or bad. I hope this doesn't get ugly.")

As long as he can prevent trouble without inciting it, it could be a good thing.

The crowd recognized her as soon as she stepped out of the car. A sound, almost like a sigh, went up and they started to flow toward her.

Kendrick raised his voice and said, "Everybody stay put!"

Most of them obeyed but a couple kept moving forward.

"That means *you*, assholes!"

They froze, then moved to the side to clear the way.

("This might work out after all.")

"Can we talk to you?" said a man as she passed.

Daley slowed but kept moving.

"Look everyone, I've had a long day. I can only do so much and I can't do anymore today. It's just not in me."

"My wife has MS," he said.

"I'm sorry for her, but I can't help."

Right?

("Right. I couldn't begin to repair the damage.")

His tone turned bitter. "If you can't heal people, you shouldn't call yourself 'La Curandera.'"

She stopped and turned on him. Time to put a stop to this.

"Get this straight: I don't call myself 'La Curandera' or anything else. The crowd at the hospital stuck that on me. I'm just one person who can help with one thing—a one-trick pony."

She moved on to the back stairs where Kendrick moved aside, but kept his head down and his eyes averted. As she started up, people surged after her but Kendrick pulled a red aluminum baseball bat from beside the staircase. He made no threatening gesture with it, simply tapped the head against his palm. The people held back.

She lowered her voice and said, "Don't hurt anyone."

"Who me?" he said, keeping his eyes on the crowd.

Pard led the way up, taking the steps backward. ("Not exactly true.")

What?

("The one-trick pony remark.")

I know. But we've already got too many people hanging out here. Imagine if they knew I—or rather, you—could heal things like lung and brain tumors and such. Even Kendrick couldn't hold them back.

She hurried to the top and into her apartment, locking the door behind her without turning on the lights.

("Home sweet home.")

"I never thought I'd ever be so glad to see this place."

Leaving the light off so she wouldn't be backlit, she moved to the front picture window and peeked through. So weird to see so many cars in Nespodee Springs. Even weirder to see the lights on across the street at the Coyote Café, which usually limited itself to breakfast and lunch.

"Looks like Arturo's staying open."

Pard came up beside her and pretended to inspect the scene below. ("Doing what any good businessman does: responding to the increased demands of a suddenly expanded market.")

"Coffee and a sandwich sounds awfully good right now."

("Don't tell me you're thinking about going out there.")

"No way. I was thinking of sending you. Oh, wait..."

("Very funny. There's always your stock of frozen dinners. What gourmet delight awaits tonight?")

"I'll check the fridge as soon as I check my phone."

She'd turned it off in the hospital and hadn't turned it back on. She didn't need a light for it so she lit it up in the dark and noticed she had unread texts.

("Four messages from Rhys.")

The first said: *I want to apologize. Can we talk?*

The rest were just follow-ups:

Can we talk?

We need to talk

Please?

Was he kidding?

"Well, isn't this just wonderful?" she said. "When my name was being dragged through the mud, he threw me under the bus. But now when I've risen from the ashes...suddenly he's singing a new tune."

("You do realize you're mixing metaphors.")

"Look at this face—does this look like the face of someone who cares?"

("I can see only what you see, so unless you're looking in a mirror—")

Grrrrrr!

She erased all four texts.

("I'm guessing you're not in a talking mood.")

"Not with him."

("You're sure?")

"Totally."

("You forgave Sandoval.")

"Did I?"

("Okay, you pretended to. I note she's still on your shit list. But—")

"Rhys and I spent a lot of time together—in bed and out of bed—and he could call me a liar when I said I'd never rip off horrors victims?"

("I wasn't there, so I can go only by your memory, but maybe he was just being a jerk.")

("Well, he can go on being a jerk all by himself. And fuck himself while he's at it.")

Pard backed off a step and raised a placating hand. ("Okay. I'm going to stop talking now.")

"Excellent idea. Oh, and tonight's agenda: food, bath, bed. In that order. Any objections?"

("None...none at all.")

THURSDAY—March 19

72

Breakfast with Lucy could be a challenge for Tom. He liked to eat but also liked to watch his weight. Lucy liked to eat too, but didn't worry about her weight. Still, ordering half a dozen sausage Egg McMuffins delivered for breakfast was excessive, even for her.

"Six, Lucy? Really?"

"I'm celebrating," she said, taking a huge bite out of her first.

What? he wanted to say. Adding another inch to your waist?

But instead he pasted on a smile and said, "What's the occasion?"

"You know that clan I was taking about?" She was chewing with her mouth open, as usual. Disgusting. "The ones that want to bring back alien Visitors from another dimension?"

"Oh, right, right." He did remember, vaguely. "End the world as we know it and all that."

"Those are the ones. Well, I finished going through the head man's digital diary. What a nutcase."

"Does this digital diary offer any clue as to how he plans to bring these Visitors back?"

"Yeah." Lucy stuffed in the end of the McMuffin and mumbled, "Interdimensional breach."

"Sorry. I thought you said, 'Interdimensional breach.'"

She swallowed convulsively. "I did."

Tom couldn't suppress a chuckle. "And he's going to accomplish this how?"

"Something to do with a tower. His entries are the equivalent of quick scribbles, like he's jotting down a timeline he can return to later and flesh out. Right now he's worried about something called 'the Duad' interfering and he's got to deal with her."

Tom had never heard of a Duad and never would have guessed it was female, but he didn't want Lucy to get sidetracked.

"Why are you telling me all this?"

She really seemed into this.

"Don't you think it's interesting? Fascinating? I mean, we've got this cult living just a few hours from here down in the Sonoran Desert working to transport aliens from another dimension. Isn't that cool?"

"No, dear sister, bat-shit crazy isn't cool. It's...crazy."

Tom studied her as she reached for her second McMuffin. Her eyes were bright and her expression animated and he hadn't heard her so involved since the Bitcoin episode. She'd become damn near manic.

"Lucy," he said. "Lucy, look at me." She stopped chewing and stared directly into his eyes. "Truth now: What is it about this that's got you so all fired up?"

"The Void, Tommy. The only way this clan can reach the Visitors is to pierce the Veil and open a channel through the Void."

And there it was. The Void...Lucy was obsessed with the concept of a big empty nothingness that spawned all humans. Tom knew better than to argue its existence with her. Once an idea took root in her mind, it stayed. Only she could dislodge it. Any challenges to that idea sparked instant hostility and shutdown.

He had to tread carefully here if he wanted to keep an open channel. Couldn't challenge the Void itself, only the method or the possibility of reaching it.

"Do you think this head guy can do that?"

"*He* thinks he can and he may have found secret knowledge in those scrolls that'll open a gateway."

Ah...Secret Knowledge...the old standby.

"Yeah, Lucy, he may well know stuff nobody else does. But I still don't get the attraction." Tom was being perfectly honest here. "Why are you so fascinated with the Void? By definition it's nothing. Vacuum."

She grinned. "Exactly! Where we could be pure intellect—our original state of being. We all once existed in another form. In the Void you can be nothing and yet still *be*."

"And that's a good thing?"

"Better than being trapped in this decaying meat sack."

It took a second or two for him to realize she was talking about the human body. Her anti-natalism thing again.

"'Decaying'?"

"Of course. The decay starts the instant we're conceived. We were free and formless intellects in the Void until we were thrust into the physical world and trapped in these spoiling fleshy prisons. It's all downhill from there, all entropy until the meat dies and takes our being along with it.

"Wouldn't you think we'd all return to the Void when we die?"

"You wish! That's the sin of being born! It makes us mortal! If we'd been left in the Void we'd live forever. But once we're flesh our days are numbered."

Tom backed off here because she seemed to be getting worked up.

"Okay, so this clan leader—"

"Elis Pendry."

"Okay, so this Pendry guy thinks he's going to open a channel into the Void. But what if he's just a crazy guy?"

"But what if he's *not*? What if he's right and succeeds?"

"I think we can lay money that he won't."

"But if he does, Tommy, it'll happen at the equinox, and I want to be there when it does."

He laughed. "You do realize, don't you, that that would require leaving the house?"

"Yeah, that's the downside, but if he does succeed, the trip will be so worth it. And you'll be so glad you took me."

Wait...

"Me?"

"Sure. We're heading down to Nespodee Springs in time for the equinox tomorrow. And you're driving."

73

Coffee in one hand and Coyote Café breakfast special sandwich in the other, Daley watched the street below from her front window. Arturo stood beside her. He'd made another breakfast delivery, and brought an extra for Kendrick who remained on guard below.

"Crazy down there," he said.

Daley, dressed in jeans and a lightweight V-neck sweater, shook her head. The cars and RVs had multiplied overnight. "What do they want?"

"Ain't it obvious? You."

"But what do they expect from me?"

"Miracles. And that's not just a guess. I hear them talking in the café and they think you can heal anything."

This was so frustrating—and so scary.

"Where'd they get *that* idea?"

"Best I can tell—from each other. They start off talking about what they *hope* you can do and then somebody adds what they *heard* you can do, and before you know it, that becomes what they *know* you can do." He started to turn away, then snapped back. "Well-well, what's this?"

The Tadhaks' white bus was pulling to a stop in the street in front of Healerina.

Daley waved her breakfast special in the air. "They must have heard how good these are."

Pard, sitting cross-legged on the couch is a semi-lotus position, said, ("Alien invasion.")

Under different circumstances, that might have been funny.

("I have a feeling Jason is well enough to meet with you now.")

Yeah, but did she want to meet with him?

"I'm glad you like it so much," Arturo said. "As for the Tadhaks, I love Jason. He's a great guy. But no Tadhak has ever bought a thing at the café, so it's a good bet they're not here for me. But even though they're not, I'd better get back. I left Pete working the grill. He'll be eating up all the profits."

"Hey, let me pay you for this. Kendrick's too."

"No way. I'm gonna have the best week since I opened the place and it's all because of you. I can sure as hell spare a couple of thank-you sandwiches."

She watched two Tadhaks exit the bus and walk toward Healerina. Both wore the gray coveralls that seemed to form the alpha and omega of Tadhak fashion. Jason was the only member of that clan she'd ever seen in a suit.

I think you're right. They're looking for me.

Daley wasn't so sure she liked that.

She followed Arturo out the door and stood on the landing. A murmur and a few cheers rose from a crowd of about twenty people below. Immediately smartphones were raised on high.

Just to be polite, Daley gave a non-committal wave as she finished her sandwich. Arturo descended to where Kendrick stood guard at the bottom, holding the crowd at bay. Had he been there all night?

She watched Arturo slip through the crowd and disappear around the corner just as the pair of Tadhaks pushed in from the other direction.

Pard appeared next to her. ("I wonder why Jason didn't come himself.")

Maybe he's still hurt.

Words were exchanged as Kendrick held his bat in bunt position and blocked their way. Finally he turned toward her but kept his eyes down.

"They say Jason wants to speak to you."

"Is Jason all right?" Daley said to the newcomers.

"You will want to speak to him," said one of the Tadhaks.

I will?

("I think that's their way of saying he has something to tell you.")

But do I want to hear it? I mean, you say he's not human.

("All the more reason to hear what he has to say, don't you think?")

I suppose.

As she started down the steps, the crowd below began to stir excitedly.

"You're going with them?" Kendrick said.

"Yes. But I'll be back."

"I should go with you."

She did *not* want him as a traveling companion.

"I'll be fine. Better if you stay here."

The pair of Tadhaks flanked her and escorted her through the crowd. As in the hospital, people reached out and touched her. Whoever was driving the waiting Tadhak bus had turned it around so it now pointed uphill. The blackened windows gave her pause, though.

Is this such a good idea?

("Jason's never been less than a good friend to you.")

But he isn't human.

("Yes, there's that, but you say it like it's a bad thing.")

What's that supposed to mean?

("Oh, like all the humans you know are wonderful?")

Billy Marks immediately came to mind. And Karma Kendrick, of course.

Point taken.

The people gathered in front of Healerina got busy with their smartphones when she appeared but made way for her. The two Tadhaks had an implacable way of moving that discouraged anyone from impeding them. The side doors split as she approached and her escort let her enter first, then followed.

The interior was like any other bus except the windows weren't tinted—at least from this direction.

("Sort of like a one-way mirror,") Pard said. ("Light passes through in only one direction.")

As the doors *shoosh*ed closed, Daley took a seat somewhere near the middle while her two guides seated themselves in the rear. The bus followed the usual route—up the hill and to the left to the high beige meringue wall at the end of the road. The bus slowed only slightly as the massive door swung open, then stopped before the second door, which opened only after the first had closed behind them.

Reminds me of the entrance to the warehouse at the windfarm.

("With good reason,") Pard said as they entered a wide

courtyard with tall, slim pine trees soaring beyond.

Daley's ears popped. The smooth meringue wall of the compound had become a high wooden plank fence. The bus stopped, the doors slid open, and the first thing Daley noticed as she stepped out was that the air was different—cooler, thinner—and the sun was higher in the sky. A huge, rustic, two-story, log-walled building with a green roof lay straight ahead.

("I believe those are ponderosa pines,") Pard said. ("If you'll pardon the paraphrase, Daley, I've a feeling we're not in California anymore.")

Then where on Earth are we—I mean, we are on Earth, aren't we?

("The sun looks like ours but a good hour higher, so, my best guess? Colorado.")

After what she'd seen at the windfarm, this didn't come as a shock. Okay, a bit of a shock, but not terrible. It explained why the Tadhak who'd greeted her at the door on Monday knew nothing about the earthquake that had rattled Nespodee Springs just moments before.

Her two escorts plus the driver exited behind her.

"Jason's in the main house," one of them said. "We'll take you to him."

He moved off toward the big building. Daley followed him inside. In contrast to the log-cabin style of the exterior, the interior was sleek and modern, with stark white walls totally free of decoration. Jason stood waiting in the center of the high-ceilinged great room.

"Welcome to our humble abode," he said.

His right arm was in a sling; he wore a brace on his left knee. Other than that, he didn't look much worse for wear.

"I'm glad to see you up and about," Daley said. "You look a lot better than the last time I saw you."

"Yes, well, my injuries were more extensive than originally thought. Please," he said, indicating two easy chairs by the cold fireplace. "Have a seat."

When they were settled—with Pard leaning against the mantle—Jason offered coffee or tea but she declined.

She said, "Pretty obvious now why no one from the town has ever been allowed through the gates."

"Well, you already know more than any of the townies, more even than Cadoc Pendry, and that nosy bastard knows too much." He gestured around. "Where do you think we are?"

She remembered what Pard had said. "Colorado?"

Jason inclined his head. "Very good. Yes, not too far from Pueblo."

Daley was confused. "That storage area was bigger on the inside than the outside, but this is like teleportation?"

"No. They're both the same. It's a special pairing of doors: when the first one closes, the second opens into a different place. You people aren't ready for it yet. You came very close to developing something similar not too long ago when the Americans put a German physicist named Osterhagen to work for them after World War Two. He called his project *'Lange-Tür'* which translates to *'Long Door.'* A clever name, but that was as far as the cleverness went. They never got it working, and the idiots probably never will."

This was a different Jason from who she was used to: bitter, verging on hostile. The *real* Jason Tadhak?

"What else do you know?" Jason said.

Daley glanced at Pard. *Tell him?*

("I don't think you'll be telling him anything he doesn't already assume we know.")

Jason must have noticed her glance. He pointed with his free hand toward the fireplace. "Is your symbiont's avatar over there?"

("Oh, yeah. Assume he knows everything.")

Daley nodded. "You know about him?"

His eyebrows lifted. "'Him'? I'd assumed it would have adopted its host's gender. But no matter. It must be quite an experience, having a sentient symbiont."

"Yes. Quite."

("Don't be snarky.")

"A little frightening at first, I imagine."

"Try terrifying. But you can get used to anything."

He gave her a hard look. "No, Daley. You can't." He seemed to catch himself and leaned back. "So...you're the Duad."

"You know about that too?"

"There's damn little we don't know. We keep close watch

on the Pendrys and know that Elis has been concerned about the coming of a Duad, which I'd assumed was you when you arrived with Juana."

"Is that why you were so generous with the rent-free shop and apartment?"

He shrugged. "It cost me next to nothing and I wanted to keep you in town to see what effect you had on Elis. Call it an experiment, if you will. You people are nothing if not predictable, and he didn't disappoint me. His behavior became increasingly desperate but I still wasn't completely sure about you until your symbiont attempted to invade me."

"He was only trying to help."

"I realize that, and appreciate it, I suppose, even though he was grossly underqualified to be of any use. I assume he was damaged when he was so forcibly rejected."

"He was out of commission for a couple of days, but he's okay now."

"So I gathered. What did he have to say about the experience?"

Daley hesitated, then, "You have no idea how weird it is to say this to someone, but he says you're not human."

Jason gave a quick nod, said, "Correct," and then let it hang there for a few heartbeats before adding, "but you might have suspected that after Cadoc Pendry showed you our storage space at the windfarm."

"You know we were there?"

"Of course. That perimeter patrol is just for show. We know what transpires on our properties at all times."

"We suspected alien technology but never dreamed..."

"That we had it because we're aliens?"

"Are we talking space aliens? Like with UFOs and the like?"

Jason barked a very human laugh. "Not at all. By 'alien' I mean 'not from here.' We didn't cross interstellar space to get here, we crossed layers of the multiverse."

"But why?"

So surreal to be sitting here casually discussing interdimensional travel with a member of an alien race that had invaded Earth.

"Believe me, we're not here because we want to be. You humans are wholly barbaric and your civilization is dreadfully primitive. Every day among you is an imposition. We're here because the environment of our home world was rendered uninhabitable by the beings the idiot Pendrys call the Visitors."

Daley couldn't hide her shock. "Wait...the Visitors are real? I thought they were just some crazy ancient myth from those Scrolls the Pendrys have."

"*The Teachings of the Empty Places*—the so-called *Void Scrolls*—are full of lies, but that part is true. The Rymwyr—that's the closest the human tongue can come to pronouncing the name of their race—once occupied areas of Earth, the Salton trough being one of them. The alaret—the source of your symbiont—is a leftover from those dim past times. In fact they were the equivalent of ticks or lice on the Rymwyr."

("Oh, wait a minute now—wait just a—")

"You've upset him," Daley said.

"Isn't that too bad? I'm supposed to worry about the feelings of a former cave slug? Just stating a fact."

I used to like him. Is this the real Jason?

("I'm thinking so.")

Daley said, "Are you having a bad day?"

"Every day here is a bad day. Does your symbiont have a name?"

"Pard."

"'Pard'...interesting."

"You mean 'hokey,' don't you?"

("Are you still carping about my name?")

Jason turned toward the mantle. "Well, Pard, as for your feelings, I doubt you have any, so don't take this as an apology. It's not." Back to Daley: "But you, young lady, you're rather well-spoken these days—improved from the uncommunicative and largely inarticulate girl who arrived here."

"Well, if that's a compliment, it totally sucks. But be that as it may, I have Pard to thank."

Not to mention rescuing me from certain grievous injuries.

Pard inclined his head. ("De nada.")

Jason said, "The symbiotic relationship has obviously

benefitted you both, but it also forms a bridge between the Rymwyr and humanity."

Daley wasn't so sure she liked that. "I'm connected to the Visitors?"

Jason made a face. "The Visitors...such a benign name for a vicious, destructive, parasitic race. Call them the Rymwyr."

*Vicious...destructive...parasitic...*and Elis Pendry wanted to bring them back?

"Does *your* race have a name?"

He tilted his head. "Why...'Tadhak,' of course."

("Of course.")

"So...the Rymwyr left Earth and ruined your world, driving out the survivors. Is that why you chose to move here? Because they'd already come and gone?"

Jason shook his head. "No. Because they'll be back."

That didn't make a whole lot of sense.

Daley said, "I saw this film the Pendrys made. It referred to the Visitors—the Rymwyr—as 'the Lords of Creation.'"

Another laugh, bitter this time. "The Rymwyr are lords of *nothing*! They can manipulate minds and matter, but they create *nothing*! As formidable as they may be, they're just minor players in a drama unfolding on a cosmic stage. They didn't leave Earth on their own accord—they were kicked out by vast entities that dwarf them and are far more powerful than they could ever be. But they never relinquished the hope of coming back. They migrated to our planet and remade it to their liking—virtually wiping out one of the most exalted civilizations in the multiverse."

("No problems with self-esteem here.")

Well, yeah, but still...

"All? An entire race? That's horrible. I'm so sorry. But why'd you come here if you know they'll be back?"

"First off, we don't need your sympathy. And second, we've been waiting for them. They plan to return and repopulate Earth with sympatico creatures that will transform the planet into a nightmare for humans—just like they did to our world. But when they arrive, we'll have a little surprise for them."

"How...how long have you been here?"

"A long, long time. Our patience is frayed, frankly. We adopted this bizarre and clumsy human form and made lives for ourselves here while we await their return. *We* wrote *The Void Scrolls* as part of a long-term plan to influence feeble minds and trick gullible humans into aiding the return of the Rymwyr."

"And those gullible humans happen to belong to the Pendry clan."

"They do. And most recently the spread of what you people call 'the horrors' is proof that the return of the Rymwyr is imminent."

"They're connected?"

A nod. "Very much so."

("I never would have guessed. Mainly because I never would have guessed the Visitors had any basis in reality. But I knew the images were emanating from somewhere. Now I know where.")

"What's the connection?"

"I don't know if your infantile minds can understand the situation, but let's start by presenting you with a harsh fact: We are property. Humans, Tadhak, the Rymwyr...all property, all pieces in a game we can never fully comprehend, all playthings of vast, incomprehensible entities."

What's he talking about?

("Why don't you ask him?")

"What entities?"   ·

"I can't give you their names because they don't have names."

"They've got to have names."

"You humans love to name things. You somehow feel a thing is manageable then because once it's labeled and pigeonholed you can stick it in a box and put it away for safekeeping. Well, not when you're dealing with beings so vast and so few. The only names you have are those made up by your fellow pets— names like 'the Ally' and 'the Otherness.' The best you can expect from the so-called Ally—or any of the entities, for that matter—is indifference. The Otherness, however, is vicious and destructive. Both collect sapient worlds. Currently Earth is in the pocket of the Ally but that's about to change. I believe the

Otherness is pushing the Rymwyr to return here to act as some sort of vanguard. Thus, the horrors."

"I'm not following."

"The horrors emanate from the Rymwyr to susceptible human minds and place them in a state of constant terror. We learned on my home world that the Rymwyr take sustenance from fear. Thousands of humans spending every minute in abject fear provides a very tempting and sustaining environment."

"Do the Pendrys know this?"

"There's no way for them to make the connection. But you, Daley...by healing the horrors, you deny the Rymwyr a source of strength."

That's why he wanted me here...why he made me an offer I couldn't refuse.

("The light dawns.")

Odd stories and strange theories she'd heard during the past few weeks were beginning to come together.

"Juana says Pard and I became paired for a reason, that my 'coming' was foretold. She even gave me an ancient art stone with a drawing on it that looks an awful lot like me. Pard and I come along just when the horrors starts ramping up. This can't all be coincidence."

Jason looked like he'd bitten into something rotten. "You don't actually believe in coincidences, do you? The entities make moves and countermoves. I have little doubt that events were manipulated to maneuver you into a circumstance where you came in contact with an alaret and the two of you formed a Duad."

Manipulated...I hate that idea

("I fear we might have to get used to it—especially if we are all, as he says, 'property.'")

A thought struck Daley with the force of a blow.

"Wait a minute. You said the Rymwyr ruined your planet and killed off your race, and yet, according to Rhys, you're helping his father's plans by providing all the extra power he needs to run the tower. We humans have an expression for that sort of thing. It goes: What the fuck?"

"You humans have an expression for everything, don't

you. If your critical thinking faculties were even rudimentally developed, you wouldn't have to ask. But very well, now we get to the crux of why I brought you here today. Now that you and the two Pendry boys know the clan's plans regarding the Rymwyr, you feel compelled to stop them. I brought you here to tell you to do nothing."

"Nothing? Did I hear you right? Just let it happen?"

"This is correct. Go on curing the horrors, by all means, but hands off the tower."

"But you're talking about earthquakes taking thousands of lives."

"I'm well aware of that. But here's the situation: If you do something radical and decisive—say, dynamite the tower—"

I hadn't thought of that.

("I did.")

"—you will certainly put an end to Elis Pendry's plans."

"Which is just what we want."

"But you won't put an end to the Rymwyr. They found a way here before and they'll find one back again. We—the Tadhak—can and will, once and for all, put an end to the threat."

"How?"

"By putting an end to the Rymwyr."

("Okay, that sounds even better.")

"Again, how? No offense, but it doesn't seem like there are enough of you."

Jason rose and limped to the mantle where he stood next to Pard. "It's not a matter of numbers. Elis Pendry must be allowed to open a passage for the Rymwyr, one that runs through the Void from my world—or rather, my *former* world—to this one. They will travel en masse, but before they arrive here we will trap them between planes."

"But that will leave them just that much closer to us. If they break out of there—"

Jason stood shaking his head. "Try to wrap your feeble human mind around this. 'Void' is a misnomer in this case. It should mean an empty, neutral space. But it's not empty. It's hungry. You can pass straight through it and remain unharmed. But you can't stay. If you linger, you will be absorbed. The

Rymwyr will not survive the Void once we trap them there. It's the permanent solution. But one that will never happen if the Pendrys don't open the passage."

Pard said, ("It remains to be seen whether they can open a passage at all. If they can't, then we don't have to do anything.")

Good point.

She said, "But *can* they open a passage?"

"They already have. That night at the end of February when they ran that very public test of the tower—"

"The light show."

She remembered helping Rhys test lightbulbs for wireless power via ground and air. The test had failed but the night had marked the starting point of their relationship. A relationship he'd pretty much ended on Tuesday.

"Yes," Jason said. "Very primitive but it got the job done. While all eyes were on the tower, a Pendry Elder was afloat on the Salton Sea where he observed a small breach in the Veil. Too small to entice the Rymwyr through, but a breach nonetheless. They'd proven they could do it, but they needed more power to enlarge it. So, the next day they came to me to work a deal. This was an opportunity we'd been waiting for. I was more than happy to offer them all the power they needed and more."

"Sounds like a very risky opportunity. What if your trap fails?"

"Failure will prove risky for you, certainly, but not for us. Shortly after the passage is open, I'm going to send a power surge. You've seen our storage facility. We have tremendous capacity. I'll send a surge strong enough to melt the cupola on that tower. The passage will collapse, the Rymwyr will be trapped, and their threat eliminated. Forever."

I'm suspicious. Why should he want to do this for us when they so obviously hold us in contempt?

("Oh, I'm pretty sure it's not for us. It's obvious he wants revenge.")

Revenge…is that what this is all about? Should we trust him?

("Revenge is very single-minded, and that's a good thing—if it's true.")

What do you mean?

("How do we know a single word he's told us is true?")

Well, he is an alien, right?

("Absolutely.")

Well, if that's true then why can't the Rymwyr be real?

("I'm now pretty well convinced they are. But what is the Tadhak agenda? Do they have designs on us—'us' being humans?")

I'll ask.

"Is that your true goal: destruction of the Rymwyr?"

Another disgusted look. "Why else would we put ourselves through the degradation of coexisting with you? We want them extinct. The Tadhak must be avenged."

"That's your *only* goal?"

A small, barely tolerant smile. "You shouldn't project your species' base inclinations on ours. We are not an acquisitive race."

Daley couldn't let it go at that. "You've hidden among us for who knows how long...are you going to go on hiding indefinitely?"

"Surely you are joking. Oh, no. Once we are sure the Rymwyr are destroyed, we'll destroy ourselves."

Okay, she hadn't expected that.

"You're kidding, right?"

He seemed surprised that she would question him. "Our planet is uninhabitable, our people are virtually extinct, our sole purpose has been the elimination of the Rymwyr. After we accomplish that, what else is left for us? What other course is there to take? Stay here? Among you savages?"

("Well, if you put it that way...")

"Seems awfully extreme. If you hate this place so much, there must be another—"

His expression turned vicious. "There is *no* other world like ours. There will *never* be another civilization as magnificent as ours. We cannot accept second best." His expression softened—just slightly. "We're all tired of this pretense and don't want to keep it up any longer than we have to." He limped past her toward the center of the room. "And now that we've had our talk, I'll send you back to town."

That's it?

"Wait a minute. You want me to stop Cadoc and Rhys from interfering with their father? I don't see how I can hold them off unless I tell them about your plan."

He stopped and turned. "Don't even consider it. The Visitors cannot—*must* not get wind of our presence here. They know what they did to us and what we will do to them if we get the chance. If they have the slightest suspicion that we are involved, they will never return. You must keep our true natures a secret."

"But we're talking about three months—how can I possibly stall them for that long?"

He frowned. "Three months?"

"Yes...until the solstice, right?"

Jason thought about that for a few seconds, then said, "I can't believe I must depend on a human and her symbiont to come up with a workable plan, but there it is. I don't care what you do, as long as you don't kill them."

Did he just say—?

"'Don't kill them'?"

"Absolutely not. Yes, I know that would be the surest way to protect the tower from the Pendry boys, but it would cause major disruptions in their family which could very well distract Elis from opening the passage. And he *must* open the passage. So, no killing of the Cadoc and Rhys, no matter how tempting a solution it might seem."

"Tempting..." Daley felt dazed. He was serious. "No killing..."

He smiled. Sort of. "I'm glad we understand each other. Elis Pendry must be fully willing and capable of opening that passage when the time comes. Your entire world and all your fellow humans are depending on you."

74

Your entire world and all your fellow humans are depending on you...

Daley watched the crowd out in the street below her front window—she'd spent much of the day standing here—and wondered how so many people, both human and non-human, had come to count on her.

She was still recovering from that surreal meeting with Jason. The phrase *The man is crazy* kept running through her head, even though she knew he wasn't a man at all, and probably not crazy by the standards of his species.

Oh, yeah, and keep Rhys and Cadoc from interfering with their father's plans, and do it without killing them, as "tempting" as that might be...

"I think I know how we can do this."

Pard had resumed to his lotus position on the couch. ("Do what? Keep the Pendry boys—I've grown rather fond of Jason's designation—away from the tower? I don't think we can.")

"Neither do I."

He frowned. ("Then how—?")

"I thought about it all the way back from Colorado."

("That sounds impressive, Daley, but I happen to know it's just a short jaunt up the street.")

"Still, I think I have a solution."

("I'm all ears—avatarly speaking, that is. What is it?")

"I'm going to scam them."

His eyebrows rose. ("I thought that was all—")

"In the past? As a lifestyle, yes. But just hear me out. I've got three months I've got to fill with delays and setbacks—"

("You can always kill them as per Jason's suggestion.")

"Jason...what a weird encounter. I always liked him—until this afternoon. Talk about a...a..." Words failed her.

("Let me try. How about an arrogant, imperious, condescending—")

"—asshat."

("That fits. No love lost for humans there.")

"Yeah, but despite those shortcomings, we've wound up on the same side, looking for the same result. And to that end, I think I've worked out a long game that will put us where we want to be. We work from the premise that none of us believe the Visitors are real—"

("'Believes.'")

"What?"

("'None' is a singular noun so the verb must agree, thus, 'believes.'")

She turned on his image. "I'm going to go back to Jason and have him zap you again."

He waved his hands. ("Don't even joke about that!")

At last she had a threat she could hold over Pard. He'd been impervious to any sort of intimidation until now.

"Who's joking? Now, can I finish uninterrupted?"

("Please. I'm truly interested.")

"Okay. They don't believe the Visitors exist. Neither did you or I until Jason straightened us out, so—" She saw his lips move. "Did you say something?"

("No. No, nothing.")

"Your lips moved. Spill."

("It slipped out.")

"What slipped?"

("'Nor.'")

"*Nor?*"

("Yes. 'Neither' is followed by 'nor,' not 'or.' But I didn't say it to you, just to myself.")

Daley ground her teeth. "Am I ever going to finish telling you my idea? *Ever?*"

Pard nodded, holding a finger up to his lips and saying nothing.

"Okay. One last time. Since Rhys and Cadoc don't believe the Visitors are real, I'll keep reinforcing that, which will make it possible to convince them that the upper part of the tower doesn't matter, and that we must concentrate our efforts on disabling the lower portion—the part that causes the earthquakes, since those will do all the harm. That will leave the top intact and able to open a passage."

Pard stared at her a moment, then said. ("That is *brilliant*, Daley. And 'brilliant' is not a word I use lightly. You can further push the plan by telling them that we can find a way to disable the subterranean portion without leaving any evidence of tampering. As a result, their father will have no clue that his tower is functioning at only half-capacity until it's too late. The bottom is dead but the top can still enable cross-dimensional transport. Genius, I say! *Genius!*")

She'd never experienced such effusive phrase from Pard. It made her suspicious.

"You're serious? You're not just trying to make up for the grammar torture you put me through?"

("Daley-Daley-Daley! You can take the girl out of the scam but you can't take the scam out of the girl. You are one of a kind! I can see only one downside.")

"Oh?"

("To make this work, you're going to have to swallow your pride and deal with Rhys.")

Daley couldn't help but smile. "That side is not as far down as you might think. He thinks of me as a soulless con artist—he so much as said so to my face. So it will be *such* a pleasure to con him into doing exactly what I want."

THE EQUINOX

Tom

Lucy never learned to drive—no surprise there—so Tom had the wheel of their rented Hummer. He'd wanted to get a driver but she refused to be in a car with a stranger.

He'd tried to talk her out of this fool's journey, but no one can talk Lucy out of anything. He knew damn well the Visitors were a figment of some ancient nutcase's imagination. No passage was going to open, and Lucy was doomed to disappointment. But he wasn't about to call it off and be the one to deprive her of an encounter with her precious Void. Ohhhh, no. She'd never let him forget it. She'd never buy that it didn't happen. She'd rage that it *did* happen and she'd have been there to witness it if Tom hadn't let her down.

No one outside their little household could even begin to understand what a pain in the ass she was. She inspired a very specific version of anti-natalism in Tom: He wished she'd never been born.

So they left before dawn for the long, long drive. He took the 10 down to Indio where he switched over to the 86. And then onto the 111. Kind of surreal down here, passing through desert, then through towns like Coachella and Indio, past farms crammed with thousands of palms, and then back into empty desert—*really* empty desert. No Joshua trees or Saguaro cacti or even chaparral, just miles and miles of bare sand and scattered sagebrush. And then, out of nowhere, he found himself outpacing a two-mile-long freight train running south on their left.

To add to the pleasure of the trip she provided a droning commentary from memory as they traveled. No, he didn't know that the San Gorgonio Pass is the windiest place in the United States. Or that snow birds triple the population of Palm Springs every winter. Or that Coachella was supposed to be called "Conchilla"—*conch* is Spanish for shell and the soil is full of fossilized seashells from when the ocean covered the area—but the original map maker screwed up and printed it as 'Coachella' and the name stuck.

Yeah, a running travelogue.

After three hours or so, he spotted something shimmering to the right. It wavered in the sunlight peeking over the Chocolate Mountains, like a giant heat mirage. Everyone has times they think they see a big puddle on the road ahead but when they reach it they find nothing. Only this wasn't a mirage, this was real. They'd reached their destination. Well, one of them. Their target destination was Nespodee Springs by way of Slab City, so they still had a ways to go.

"Behold the Salton Sea," he said.

Lucy looked up from her tablet. She'd hooked into the Hummer's Wi-Fi after they'd passed Coachella and hadn't come up for air since. For the trip she'd arrayed herself in a bizarre ensemble of red harem pants and a yellow T-shirt. Perfect desert wear.

"Hardly a 'sea,'" she said. "More like a lake—a giant puddle on the fault."

"Which fault?"

"The big one—San Andreas. The Salton sits on its southern end."

How comforting. He'd had no idea it ran this far south.

He said, "Those last two quakes originated down here, right?"

"Yeah. In the Imperial Valley. But not in the San Andreas."

Oh, good.

"Okay, so, when exactly is this equinox?"

"It's when the plane of Earth's equator intersects with the center of the Sun."

"I don't care about the astronomy. I meant the *time*—the hours and minutes on the clock."

"Ooh, cranky."

"I'm not a morning person, dear sister. You know that. Stick me behind the wheel at four a.m. and you can count on cranky or worse."

"We'll get you another cup of coffee. As for the equinox, it's today, March 20, at sixteen-twenty-one hours. Or four twenty-one this afternoon for the numerically impaired."

The dashboard clock read *6:56.*

"Well, hell, why did we leave so early? What do we do till then?"

"*Explore,* dear brother. There's things I'd like to see before I die and since I don't get out much, here's a chance to see a couple. Enjoy. We're two-hundred-some feet below sea level here. We're travelling through another world."

He couldn't argue with that. Here was this lake in the middle of a trackless low desert sunk between two mountain ranges. The air felt thick, *looked* thick. He knew people lived here, but damn, it felt empty. Desolate. Deserted.

She said, "We need to get the lay of the land so we know the best place to be when the Void is revealed."

Tom didn't want her getting her hopes up too high, because when they were inevitably dashed she might very well crash. And guess who would have to deal with her.

"You need to consider the possibility that this'll never happen, Lucy. I mean, this is all pretty far out."

"So you've said. And said and said. I'm well aware of that. But there's so much more cooking beneath the surface here." She tapped her tablet. "I've been reading scans of Osian Pendry's journals, and it's clear they didn't move here on a whim. He had a connection with Tesla and—ooh, look. The visitor center. Turn in."

"They're not open at this hour." *Nothing* was open at this ungodly hour.

"Oh, I don't care about that. It's on the list of stops."

"I need coffee."

She started waving a sheet of paper. "It's on the list! It's on the list! We have to stop!"

"It's closed!"

"I don't care. I want to go down to the beach."

"You brought a swim suit?"

"I want to see the shore. Turn in! Turn in!"

Grinding his teeth, Tom made the turn and wound along a palm-lined road, through an unmanned gate, and down to a low-slung building on the shore of the Salton Sea. He pulled into in the empty parking lot and Lucy jumped out as soon as he stopped.

"Come on!" she said.

What the hell. But when he opened the door the stink hit him and he almost gagged.

"What is *that*?"

"Algae bloom," she said, leaning into the backseat where she was fiddling with the duffel bag she'd brought. "Happens every spring. Stop being a drama queen."

If anyone was into drama, it was Lucy. Proof was the katana she removed from the duffel and slung across her back. Tom couldn't believe this.

"You're kidding, right?"

"Marauders," she said, slamming the car door.

He gestured around at the empty parking lot. "We're the only ones here."

"Appearances can be deceptive. Always prepare for the worst. Let's go."

He followed her off the pavement and onto the curiously granular sand that made a funny, crunching sound under his soles. Lucy picked up a handful of the white pebbles and was flicking through them with a finger.

"So cool!" she said.

Curious, he did the same. Took him a second to realize—

"Hey, these are bones!"

Her eyes were bright. "Right. Bits and pieces of the skeletons of the hundreds of thousands of fish and birds that have died from the toxins in that water."

"I assumed it was all rainwater."

"Nah. The Colorado River overflowed its banks and flooded the valley a hundred-plus years ago. Left the Salton Sea behind. Since then it's been collecting the pesticides and fertilizer in the runoff from all the farms nearby. But would you believe it's still got fish in it?"

"Mutant fish?" His stomach turned. "Imagine what that tastes like."

"Mostly tilapia. *If* you can catch one. I mean, imagine how tough a fish has gotta be to survive here. If you hook one it'll probably pull you in and mug you."

Tom stared at her. Part of Lucy's on-the-spectrum thing was she didn't get jokes, didn't process humor. And yet...

"Did you just make a funny?"

She frowned and cocked her head. "Did I? I didn't hear you L-O-L."

"Not all humor gets a guffaw."

A shrug as she dropped the crushed bones. "Whatever. I've seen enough. Slab City is next on the list."

Elis

"I've assembled you this morning in this rather unorthodox fashion on a matter of momentous importance," Elis said to the four other Elders of the clan.

"*Rather* unorthodox?" Iwan Gwynn said from where he was squeezed between Kyle Mostyn and Maddox Baughan in the backseat of Elis's Land Rover. Bran Llewelyn had been assigned the roomy front passenger seat because of his bulk. "I'm bloody crushed!"

"I know it's uncomfortable but it couldn't be helped. I can't risk anyone but you four hearing this."

Elis had picked them up one by one at their homes this morning and driven out here to the desert east of the solar array. He could not allow a word of this to get out.

"What is it then?" said Baughan, testy as usual.

Elis twisted in his seat. "Today is the equinox."

"Tell us something we don't know," Llewelyn said. "The wives have been preparing for the fest for weeks."

As the others muttered about that being all they'd heard about day in and day out all month, Elis dropped the bombshell.

"Today is also the day we welcome the Visitors back to our world."

Dead silence for a few heartbeats, and then a shocked cacophony, mostly revolving around the fact that Elis had told them again and again that the Return would occur during the coming summer solstice.

But he'd lied. He'd lied to everyone about the date for the simple reason that he mistrusted everyone. Not that he thought his fellow Elders would deliberately betray the clan, but they hadn't achieved Elder status through accomplishment. They'd arrived at the position simply via their rank in their respective families. Discretion was not a prerequisite. Llewelyn and Baughan, in particular, could be classified as blabbermouths where their wives were concerned.

When the hubbub finally died down, Elis lied again, saying, "The astral configurations have suddenly shifted in their prediction and indicated that this year's vernal equinox offers us an opportunity to create a passage that will not be matched for at least a decade, maybe more. As clan Elders, we have a solemn duty not to let this slip away."

If they'd studied the Scrolls a mere tenth as closely as they studied the monthly P-and-L reports Elis sent on the Pendry Fund, they'd have known he'd been feeding them a fiction all along. Pierce the Veil during a solstice? A *solstice*? Whether winter or summer didn't matter, a solstice was an extreme and asymmetrical alignment, entirely unsuitable for any sort of dimensional conjunction. But an equinox...ah, well, everything was aligned in perfect symmetry during an equinox. Gateways fairly begged to be opened during an equinox.

Before the hubbub could begin again, he added, "We must continue to keep our plans secret from the clan. We will be ending the world as they know it. As we are all aware, the Pendrys will gain an exalted status in the new world order after the return of the Visitors—the Pendry Patch each one of us carries will guarantee that—but it will indeed be a *new* world. We must present the change to our families as a fait accompli. And obviously, because of the enormous collateral damage entailed in the process, we must remain discreet about our involvement. No one can know." He looked each in the eye. "*No one.* Not even those closest to us."

As Elis paused to let that sink in, Baughan said, "Are we sure we want to go through with this?"

He'd expected this question and was ready for it.

"I've asked myself the same thing many times, Maddox. Do I want to be the architect of such destruction? The answer is a resounding *no.* But the Visitors *are* coming back, with or without our help. Maybe not today, but soon. It's in the stars. And once they're back, *they* will make those same changes. But if *they* make them, they will be beholding to no one. And we, the Pendry Clan, will share the same status as every other human on Earth. But I don't want us to be like everyone else. I refuse to stand idly by and watch that happen. I want us to be exalted. And that is what we shall be if we pave the way for them, and if we are there to greet them as the Lords of Creation that they are."

Elder Gwynn chimed in, saying, "We are merely doing what will be done anyway. The damage will be the same either way."

Elis silently thanked him for the backup.

"But here's the important thing," Elis said. "The ground will shake today like we have never felt it shake before. We must make sure every member of every family is outside in the safety of the festival between three and four o'clock this afternoon—*everyone.* We have done what we can to make our homes as earthquake safe as possible, but we don't know what magnitude we will be dealing with. This is uncharted territory. The elevation of our properties will mitigate the tremors, but we still might suffer damage to our loved ones. Houses can be rebuilt, but we can't replace our loved ones. So I repeat: Every clan member outside at three o'clock."

"Will you be needing Rolf?" Gwynn said. His son was the clan's chief engineer and he'd wired the tower.

Elis shook his head. "Tell him to stay with his family. The five of us will start off at the celebration. I'll leave extra early to prepare the tower. You four stay till two thirty or so, at which time you'll excuse yourselves to join me for an 'Elder Conference.' But instead you'll all head to the Salton."

"What? All of us?" Llewelyn said.

"More than enough room aboard. The clan must provide the Visitors with a proper welcome."

"I'll have to get the boat ready," Mostyn said. "If I'd known, I would have had it gassed up and ready to go."

Mostyn had been out on the Salton Sea during the late-February test of the tower when he'd witnessed the breach in the Veil.

"I'm sure you can accomplish that in the six or seven hours you have before you shove off. Just make sure you have the satellite phone along, and all of you wear wrist watches. If the tower works as well as we expect it to, those of you who've come to depend on your phones for telling the time will be out of luck. I don't anticipate many cellular towers still standing after the quakes."

Baughan said, "Are we sure the breach will occur over the Salton?"

Elis gave a vigorous and sincere nod. "That's where Mostyn witnessed it. And it makes sense that it should appear over the only body of water in the area. Any questions?"

"Do we know what magnitude quake we're expecting?"

Elis shook his head. "There's no way to tell. This is not an exact science."

"Well, isn't that irresponsible? Causing a quake without knowing how destructive it will be?"

Elis couldn't believe his ears. His patience suddenly ran out.

"What are you saying? That causing a quake would be somehow *responsible* if I knew the magnitude in advance? Do you hear yourself? Do you ever actually listen to yourself when you talk?"

Idiot!

He'd had enough of this. He'd have been so much better off acting alone, but tradition saddled him with these dolts. He put the car in gear and headed back to town.

He felt a wave of satisfaction, of exaltation engulf him as he passed the countless panels of the Pendry solar farm. Despite an array of encumbrances—which reached all the way into his own family—everything was falling into place. He just wished his sons could be involved in this momentous day, but Cadoc had betrayed him and Rhys had proven not only ineffectual, but an ally of the Duad.

The Duad...he'd been worried about her, but his misdirection via Rhys about the true timing of the Visitors' return had rendered her a non-factor. She was tied up now with the horrors so he could put her out of his mind.

Elis had removed all obstacles, leaving an unobstructed path to the Return.

Daley

D r. Milton called Daley at around nine thirty.
"*We had a bizarre uptick in our horrors cases overnight.*"

"'Bizarre' in what way?"

"*So many. We've never had this sort of influx in a twelve-hour period. Not that we've had that much experience with the syndrome, of course, but this is unique. A little scary too.*"

"Any idea what might be behind it?"

"*None at all. Can you come in and...do whatever it is you do?*"

She smiled. "Work some of my 'hocus-pocus bullshit,' you mean?"

A beat, a sigh, then, "*You know, you left on Wednesday before I had a chance to formally thank you. And to apologize for doubting you.*"

"*Doubting* me? It's your responsibility to doubt outliers like me. And you don't have to apologize for doubting something that's totally outside everyone's experience. Hell, it was totally outside my own experience until last week. As for my abrupt departure, I was emotionally fried and the crowd was growing bigger by the moment. I had to get out of there."

"*I understand. And I'm asking you to come back today. Will you?*"

How could she say no?

"Of course."

"*Wonderful. Sam Alvarez is on the way to either escort you in or drive you in his sheriff's car, which ever you'd prefer.*"

"'On the way'? You were that sure of me?"   ·

"*Absolutely. I saw you in action on Wednesday. I had no doubt.*"

"Okay. I'll be on the lookout for him."

As she ended the call, Pard said, ("My how opinions change.")

He'd abandoned yesterday's lotus position and was now stretched out supine on the couch.

"Don't they, though?"

She couldn't put her finger on it, but something felt...off.

("What's bothering you?")

"Don't know. Maybe this upsurge in horrors victims."

("The Rymwyr are probably just compensating and making up for all those we cured the other day.")

"Yeah, maybe. Probably."

("My explanation seems to have left you less than convinced.")

"Maybe it's got something to do with Jason's worldview. We're 'property'? That's a hell of a way to go through life."

("Well, you have to admit it's an eyes-open approach, one I find oddly acceptable since I became aware of the unearthly origin of Jason and his kin. They've been here a long, long time and no one had a clue. And the notion that the best you can expect from the cosmos is indifference certainly seems more realistic than the belief that something out there has got your back and is watching out for you.")

Daley sighed. "Yeah, maybe. Be nice though, wouldn't it?"

("Having a cosmic guardian angel? Depends on how you want to live your life: free or as a pet.")

"Well, when you state it in those terms..."

("You're still bothered by something.")

"I can't put my finger on it but...something about the way Jason reacted when I asked how I could possibly stall them for the three months until the solstice. Part of being a grifter is learning to read people. I couldn't read his expression—and who knows what the spontaneous expressions of an alien in human disguise might mean—but he almost seemed surprised. And now this uptick in the horrors..."

("You're thinking that if the date of the Return is three months away, why a surge in horrors victims now?")

"Yeah. Could it mean the Return is happening sooner?"

("Like at the equinox instead? That's today.")

"Today?" Why did that make her uneasy? "Oh, right. Rhys mentioned a 'massive' celebration by the entire Pendry clan every equinox."

("Well, it sounds like they'll be engaged in something other than bringing aliens in from another dimension.")

Daley shrugged. "Yeah, I guess so."

But she still couldn't shake this vague, uneasy feeling.

Tom

After driving the length of the east shore of the Salton Sea, they arrived at the tiny town of Niland and had to wind their way through it to reach Slab City. Lucy's purpose in visiting the area was to see Salvation Mountain, and Tom had to admit he was glad they'd stopped. A cotton-candy-colored dune decorated with spiritual sayings and quotes from the Bible. All the work of a now-departed fellow named Leonard Knight. Lucy and Tom weren't raised with any religion, but she was speechless and he found himself moved by the monomaniacal devotion of a single eccentric to get this done. He died in 2014 but his dream lived on.

He was probably on the spectrum too. A kindred spirit to Lucy.

Next they toured the East Jesus sculpture garden, just a short walk away. Everything in the garden was fashioned from junk. Tom found the Bottle Wall especially interesting.

He'd feared Lucy's katana would cause a stir as they wandered about but the place was all but deserted at this hour, and the few locals they passed didn't give it a second glance. Eccentricities seemed the rule here.

Okay. He was seeing things he wouldn't normally see, even though they'd existed here for years, just a few hours from where they lived. At least this wasn't going to be a completely wasted trip.

He really needed to get out more.

The reason he didn't was walking beside him. His therapist had told him he harbored deep resentment toward her. He couldn't argue with that.

After the Slab City area they headed back to Niland where Tom bought them a couple of sandwiches and Pepsis at the Buckshot Deli & Diner. They ate in the car, of course. God forbid they ate inside, even though the place was deserted.

And then it came time for Tom to take Lucy to the next place on her list, their ultimate destination: Nespodee Springs, home of the nefarious clan that supposedly was going to end the world as they knew it.

If only, he thought.

Daley

Daley hadn't realized how hungry she was.

Dr. Milton had forced her to take a break and come down to the conference room where he'd had an assortment of sandwiches and soft drinks from the caf laid out on the big table.

After Milton's call earlier, she'd changed into her Healerina outfit, now so identified with La Curandera, and let Sam transport her in his sheriff's unit. It had made for a slightly easier exit from town, but what neither of them had anticipated was the whole Nespodee Springs crowd hopping into their various vehicles and following them into El Centro. The arrival of the ragtag caravan only exacerbated the already chaotic situation at ECRMC. The streets around the hospital had been jammed through the night with relatives of the newly stricken. Then word got out that La Curandera was coming back, and that drew a flood of the curious. And sprinkled among all those was an especially devoted subset: former victims who had been cured by La Curandera.

Even with his lights blaring and siren wailing, it had proved a long, slow process to wend their way to the front entrance.

"This really hits the spot," Daley said as she chowed down on a ham-and-Swiss on rye. "Thanks for thinking of it."

Dr. Milton paused before biting into his club. "Well, I don't know what your nutritional requirements are for this sort of work, but I wanted you to keep up your strength."

They sat side by side, with Pard across from them as he

munched on a virtual sandwich identical to Daley's.

("I think I'd prefer a little more mustard,") he said.

Mine's fine, Daley replied, smiling as she gave the mustard jar a little push toward him. *But feel free to help yourself.*

He made a face. ("A veritable Fanny Bryce.")

The name sounded vaguely familiar but didn't click.

Who?

("'Funny Girl.'")

Who?

("Never mind.")

"It looks like we put a good dent in the new cases," Daley said.

"Those are just the ones who've been admitted. The ER's packed with new victims and more coming in all the time."

Daley leaned back, feeling overwhelmed. "Will I ever catch up?"

"It's a daunting prospect, I'll admit. If only there were another like you." He glanced at her. "Is there?"

"I wish."

Do you know of another Duad, Pard?

("Not a clue, I'm afraid.")

Milton said, "The horrors acts a little like an infection, but on the whole its occurrence is far too random, and besides, no one's been able to identify an etiological agent or vector. You mentioned a neural pathway running from the victim's pineal gland to the amygdala. If I could find a medication that blocks that pathway..."

"First you'll have to identify it." She recalled what Pard had told her. "It's not a discrete bundle of fibers, just a pathway among the fibers."

He leaned toward her. "Here's what I want to do. I'll guide you around for a while longer, then I'll have one of my associates take over while I sit down with our chief radiologist and go over the various PET scans on record and look for evidence of this pathway. If we can identify it, we can start experimenting with ways to block it. If we can find that med, we can break the back of this epidemic or whatever it is by treating all the patients in all the centers at once."

"And then you wouldn't need me." Wouldn't that be a relief. "Sounds like a plan. In the meantime, I'd better get back to work."

Elis

Elis spent an hour or so at the equinox festival and then made his excuses about overseeing some work on the tower. As he drove down through town he saw Jason Tadhak standing in front of his real estate office, his shoulder in a sling. Elis had heard about his accident and worried that his injuries might interfere with the availability of the extra voltage needed for today, but it looked like business as usual for Tadhak. Good. Couldn't let anything interfere with the Return.

He gave a neighborly wave as he rolled past. *Have a nice day. Tomorrow will be different...very different.*

He'd given all the workers at the solar array the day off with pay. No need for extraneous personnel hanging around. He didn't want anyone observing his activities, especially what he was about to do now.

He pulled to a stop before the gate in the tower's fence. He'd festooned it with DANGER and NO TRESPASSING signs. They'd serve another purpose today. He'd brought a jar of water from the Nofio pool and began using it to paint arcane symbols on the sheet metal of the signs.

Once he'd completed that, he removed the blanket-wrapped porthor horn from the Land Rover's rear compartment. He put it to his lips and blew. He heard no sound, but he wasn't the intended audience. He blew three times, then put it away.

The porthors would come. The water-drawn symbols contained their essence and commanded their actions. The commands were simple: allow no one to pass.

Elis felt secure knowing the porthors would become his personal security detail.

Tom

Nespodee Springs proved not the easiest place to find. They got lost despite Waze and various map services, first around the south end of the Salton Sea, winding past fields of broccoli and lettuce and cauliflower—no wonder they called the Imperial Valley "America's Salad Bowl." West of there they got lost in the desert, wandering from one cracked and crumbling two-lane blacktop to another. Tom was trundling along something called Huff Road when he saw a sign with a red arrow pointing west, telling them they were "almost to Nespodee Springs!" Woopty-doo.

They followed the arrow and turned even deeper into the desert toward a small mountain range.

"Those hills have a name?" Tom said.

Without looking up, Lucy said, "According to the map they're the Sawtooth Mountains, part of the Peninsular Range."

About ten miles later another sign welcomed them to Nespodee Springs itself. The pavement improved as they passed neat rows of mobile homes lining both sides.

"The clan all left Wales for *this*?" he said. "I can see wanting a better climate but this is nowhere."

Deep in her tablet, Lucy made no reply.

A windfarm rose on the right—small compared to the one they'd passed in the San Gorgonio Pass, but still impressive. And then a vast array of solar panels gleamed to the left. Talk about energy independence. But how did they put all this power to use? And further south, beyond the panel farm, a tall, skeletal, mushroom-capped tower poked into the sky.

Tom jabbed Lucy on the arm. "Hey. Check out the Tesla tower."

She surfaced from cyberspace and said, "You know Tesla? I'm impressed."

"You're not the only one with a trivia arsenal."

As she followed Tom's point, her eyes snapped wide. "Oh. My. God. They built one—actually built one. The clan keeps mentioning a tower in their notes, but I had no idea. Tesla's was almost two hundred feet tall and that looks like it's built exactly to scale." She looked at Tom, her face shining with wonder.

"They're really serious about this. They're really going to try to breach the Veil and open the Void."

He could see her hopes soaring. The higher she flew, the harder she'd crash.

"Hey, easy now. The key word there is 'try.' That doesn't necessarily mean—"

"I've got to talk to Elis Pendry!"

Tom couldn't believe what he was hearing.

"You? Talk to a stranger?"

"Well, no. You'll talk to him. I'll tell you what questions to ask."

Okay, that was more like it.

They entered something that resembled a town. A row of one- and two-story buildings lined each side of the road. A planked boardwalk acted as a sidewalk, giving it an Old West look. A sign pointed ahead toward the Nespodee Springs Hotel and Spa, farther up the slope.

"Where would we find the Pendrys?" she wondered aloud as they passed a market—not super by any stretch.

Here and there among the scattered pedestrians Tom spotted a pair of young girls in long-sleeved, high-collared, low-hemmed gingham dresses, worn over tights. Though varied in color and pattern, both dresses were uniform in style.

"I bet they belong to a clan," Lucy said. "Ask them."

He slowed and stuck his head out the window. "Do you happen to know where I can find the Pendry clan?"

They squealed and ran away.

"Was it me or just mentioning the Pendry clan?"

"Definitely you," Lucy said.

Moving on they passed a café, a bar, a liquor store, a doctor's office, a place called "Healerina," and then—

"Here we go," Tom said as he spotted *Tadhak Realty* on the left. "If anyone knows, the local realtor does."

He'd just nosed in to park when a stocky man with his arm in a sling stepped through the door and onto the boardwalk.

"I'm looking for Elis Pendry," Tom said from the Hummer.

The local's expression was grim, and he looked as if was going to ask why Tom wanted to know. Instead he pointed up the slope.

"He lives up there but he's not home. He's down at his tower."

"The Tesla tower?"

His expression stayed grim but added a soupçon of suspicion. "You know about that?"

"Just saw it for the first time."

"Well, stay away. He's cranking it up and things are going to get nasty around here."

So saying, he swiveled and limped to an old station wagon with *Tadhak Realty* on the side.

"Not exactly a friendly sort," Tom said as his window slid up.

"Did you hear that?" Lucy said. "He said he's 'cranking it up'! That means the game is on!"

"The game? What game?"

"The Void game. The clan is going to try to open a passage." She jabbed a finger at the dashboard clock. "It's almost two. We've got to get back to the Salton Sea. Pronto."

"We just came from there."

"But that's where the passage is going to open."

"How can you possibly know that?"

"I just put it together. The Visitors like water. They left here millions of years ago because the water dried up. If the clan is going to bring them back, there has to be water. And where's the only water around here?"

All very logical, but all based on shaky premises. Tom figured if he were an alien crossing over from another dimension to frolic in water, the Salton Sea did not have the kind of water he'd be looking for. But then again, maybe the Visitors liked toxins.

Not that any of it mattered. No breach would occur, no transdimensional beings would arrive, Lucy would be crushed, Tom would pick up the pieces and cart them home. He consoled himself with the knowledge that this whole fiasco would be over in a couple of hours when the equinox passed. Until then he'd simply keep playing along.

Elis

Elis stared at the switch that would power up the base of the tower. He'd been chafing to throw it but had needed to give the other Elders time to reach the Elmore area where the boat was docked. He'd dialed the power feed to MAX. All the voltage from the solar array plus the excess from the Tadhak windfarm would funnel down into the Earth with a simple flip of that switch.

Now the time had arrived—three o'clock on his phone—but he couldn't pull it. His hands had gone sweaty and shaky.

He *had* to pull it.

The last century-plus of the clan's existence had pointed toward this moment, leaving its entire future resting on his shoulders.

But pulling the switch was like stepping into an abyss. No turning back, no undoing.

But it's going to happen anyway, he told himself for at least the thousandth time today. He wasn't changing the big picture, only the details. The Visitors were going to return no matter what, and when they were back they would flood the whole Imperial Valley. So Elis's doing it for them changed nothing but the timing…and the clan's future. They would be linked to the Visitors, be part of the coming new order.

"Damn it!" he shouted and pulled the switch.

Done. Flashes from below lit the shaft as the resonant transformer—a large Tesla coil around the base of the shaft—began to spark in the depths, generating standing waves in the Earth's crust.

We need a big one, he thought. Really big. But not so big as to bring down the tower itself. He'd closely overseen its construction, steel-bracing it to within an inch of its life, quadruple bolting each support to the foundation, and fitting each support with isolators to reduce the severity of any shaking it suffered. It must *not* come down. That would bring all his plans to an abrupt halt.

And he prayed the all clan was outside as he'd instructed.

Because now it begins…

Becky

Mark Hendry fairly lunged through Becky's office door. He sounded out of breath.

"Doctor Heuser! Those weird sine waves are back!"

Dr. Rebecca Heuser leaped up from behind her desk and started toward him.

"Show me."

Immediately prior to the February 26 and March 5 quakes, the seismic sensors down in the Imperial Valley had picked up odd sine waves running through the desert floor. Their origin was unclear and the sensors couldn't localize them to a specific fault. Yet on both occasions they were followed by significant earthquakes of 3.6 and 5.5 intensity. Monday's quake had shown no sine waves, however. Yes, it had been a minor tremblor, but still…a baffling situation.

She followed Hendry to the data analysis room where the big seismic network monitor high on the wall showed three lines of sine waves running through the lower feeds—large sine waves.

"Did you up the gain on those feeds?"

Hendry shook his head. "I did nothing. As soon as I saw them, I ran for your office."

These waves were so much bigger than the last two incidents. Did that predict a bigger fault slip?

As other members of Caltech's seismology lab crowded in behind her, she said, "Issue a ShakeAlert."

"But it's not showing P waves," Cheatham said.

"I'm well aware of that. But these same waves appeared before the five-point-five on March fifth and I held off until the P waves showed. I could have given folks lots more warning if I'd listened to my gut. So I'm going with my gut today. I'll take full responsibility. ShakeAlert—now!"

Daley

A couple of hours after lunch, as a pair of security guards were making a path through the second-floor hallway for her and Milton and Nurse Ames, Daley's skin began to tingle.

"You feel anything?" she said to Ames. "On your skin?"

She shook her head. "No. You?"

"Yeah. A weird tingle."

("This is similar to what you felt before the first two of the three recent quakes,") Pard said.

I remember. Is it me or is it stronger this time?

("It's not you, but—say, isn't that...?")

Daley was surprised to see Juana standing in the crowded hallway outside one of the patients' rooms.

"What are you doing here? Is someone sick?"

"A cousin came down with the horrors. They brought him here last night. I just got here."

"How'd you get through that traffic?"

"Almost didn't. Had to leave my sidecar at a gas station."

Daley pointed to the room. "Let's get to it then. I—"

A faint alert signal began to sound from a number of directions. Ames pulled out her phone and thumbed the screen.

"Oh, shit! The MyShake app. It's sending an alert. We've got a quake coming—a big one, from the looks of it—right in this area!"

She wasn't the only one with the app. Lots of phones were chiming, and the hallway filled with cries of dismay as people rushed for the stairwells.

"How long have we got?" Daley said.

Ames shook her head. "It doesn't say. Get in a doorway or get outside."

Dr. Milton grabbed Daley's arm and pulled her toward an exit sign.

"I want you out of here. We can't have you getting hurt. You're not replaceable."

"But the patients—"

("Do as he says, Daley,") Pard said.

You're sure you don't just want to save you skin?"

("I don't have any. I want to save yours. I definitely don't want to be on the second floor of this building during 'a big one.' I want even less to be on the first floor. I want to be outside.")

"Let us worry about the patients," Milton said. "We go through drills for this." He pointed straight ahead. "That door there will take you to an outside stairway down to the rear parking lot by the emergency room." He pulled off his white lab coat and wrapped it around her. "Cover up with this." Then grabbed a surgical cap from the head of an OR tech hurrying by. "And this. I don't want you mobbed out there."

"But—"

"Go." He pushed her toward the door. "Please."

So Daley went, Juana beside her—out the door and onto the exposed, external metal-frame stairway. As she hurried down, a thought occurred to her, but Pard said it first.

("Do you think this could be Elis Pendry's doing?")

Just wondering that. The equinox could have been his target date all along.

("I'm willing to bet it was. And what better misdirection than to make us believe it was the solstice, leaving us to think we had three months to stop him.")

He scammed us. The bastard! I can't believe I fell for it.

("You didn't, exactly. You got a clue from Jason who knew the truth but let us go on believing the lie. But then, he was been pretty up front about wanting the same thing as Elis.")

But only up to a point.

Daley reached the ground with Juana close behind. She tightened Milton's coat around her black outfit and kept her head down as she wound her way through the milling crowd in the parking lot to an empty spot between two cars near the carport.

She'd just turned to Juana when the ground heaved and jumped, rocking the cars around them, literally bouncing a couple of the smaller ones. It would have knocked them off their feet had they not been able to brace themselves against the cars. And then the ground began to shake, knocking them almost to their knees. The crowd screamed as many of them were thrown flat. Some jumped up and ran only to be knocked down again. People were thrown from the crowded external staircase as some of the facing on the hospital's main building began to crack and fall off. Then part of the staircase pulled free of the wall and tilted at a crazy angle, dumping dozens of people onto the ground.

"This is a big one!" Juana shouted.

No kidding, Daley thought.

Finally, after a seemingly interminable interval, the ground settled down. And Daley knew immediately what she had to do.

"Juana—I've got to get to Nespodee Springs."

"What? Why?"

"I'll tell you on the way."

("Really?")

Well, as much as she needs to know.

"I don't have my side car."

"That might be a good thing. I'll sit behind you. But we've got to get there fast. I'll need you to drive more like a maniac than you usually do."

Juana grinned. "Flattery will get you anything. I'm parked over near the carport. What's the rush?"

"I've a very bad feeling that this one is just the first in a series of quakes."

"Then why go to Nespodee?"

"That's where they're originating." As Juana opened her mouth to speak, Daley pushed her toward the carport—its roof had fallen onto the vehicles it had been sheltering from the sun. "I already told you I'd explain on the way."

Tom

During the hour-plus drive back to the Salton Sea, Lucy located a small motorboat to rent in Salton City at a place called the Western Shores Marina and RV Park. Of course, she handed the phone to Tom to make the arrangements as they drove. God forbid she spoke to a stranger, even on the phone.

They approached Salton City from the south on 86. Tom

didn't know what he was expecting, but this was no city. Hardly a town, it seemed. From the highway he saw lots of streets but not many houses on them. And what houses he saw looked like converted trailers. So…a city that wasn't a city on the shoreline of a sea that wasn't a sea.

And suddenly something jolted the car, knocking it off course. Luckily no one was coming the other way because the Hummer veered into the oncoming lane before Tom could straighten it out.

Lucy said, "You hit something."

Tom was pretty sure he hadn't. He looked in the rearview mirror and saw nothing in the road, but then the Hummer started jittering and bumping along.

"More like a blowout," he said. "Feels like we've got a flat."

He pulled to a quick stop on the shoulder but the car kept shaking.

"It's a quake," Lucy said like someone else might say it's raining.

A bad one. They had to cling to their grab handles to keep from being banged about the interior. It seemed to last twenty minutes but probably less than one. As a lifelong California resident, Tom had been through a lot of quakes, but never one like this.

Finally the ground stopped moving and they sat there, catching their breath, staring at each other.

"That was bad," he said. "Lucky we're in a car. If we'd been home…"

Lucy nodded. "We might be *under* the house now."

Tom said what he was pretty sure they both were thinking: "You don't think the clan's Tesla tower did that?"

She shrugged. "I don't know. They're supposed to be breaching the Veil into the Void. What's an earthquake got to do with it?"

He pointed to her tablet. "Get online and see what you can find. Meanwhile…"

He tuned Sirius to its news channels and landed on HLN. The newsreader said a major quake had shaken California's Imperial Valley. Well, hell, they already knew that. He wanted details. Maybe he'd tuned in too early. It had just happened. He dialed up and down in the news channels but wasn't finding much.

"Here's something," Lucy said. "Found the SCEC website. They say it was a seven-point-eight magnitude quake in the Mexicali region. They're blaming the Cerro Prieto fault." She looked up from her tablet. "We need to get to our boat."

"You can't be serious."

Now she looked at him. "What?"

"There's just been a major earthquake. There'll be aftershocks—big ones."

"So? We'll be safer on the water than on land."

"Did you happen to see our swimming pool during the last quake—all the waves and the water sloshing out?"

"The Salton Sea isn't a swimming pool, dear brother. It's thirty-five miles long and fifteen wide and fifty feet deep. And for sure nothing can fall on us if we're out there."

"You're crazy!"

"If you don't want to go, I'll go alone. Just get me to the marina. You said you'd take me to the Void. A deal is a deal."

Shit-shit-shit! He'd figured this would be just a sightseeing trip. They'd drive around aimlessly while the equinox came and went, then head back to Pasadena. He hadn't figured on a fucking earthquake.

He got the car rolling again.

Cadoc

He watched from the second-floor dining room as his mother walked toward the Lodge from the equinox festivities. She carried what looked like a plate of food.

Cadoc had intended to attend the celebration—make his debut as a Pendry adult, so to speak—but had lost his nerve at the last minute. He'd be going from living in the dark and never being seen to the center of attention. The Pendry no one knew existed. The freak. The recluse. The hermit.

I'd heard rumors he was too ugly to show his face. I'd heard he was a hunchback. But he doesn't look so bad, just pale. Awfully pale. Let's cluster around him and gawk and ask him a million questions.

No thanks.

Had to admit though, he *was* awfully pale. When had he last exposed his skin to the sun? Age eight, maybe?

His mother disappeared below as she entered the Lodge, and soon he heard her on the stairs.

"Oh, there you are, dear," she said, proffering a paper-napkin-covered plastic plate. "I brought you a sandwich."

"Thanks, Mother. You didn't have—"

"Hot corned beef on rye. I know you love it."

Well, yes, he did. His mouth started watering as he caught the fragrance.

She placed a hand on his arm. "You really ought to come down. I'd love to show off my two handsome boys."

"Maybe some other time."

She gave a little squeeze. "Reconsider, Cad. Just show your face. A flyby, just enough to prove to everyone that you're more than a rumor. And then you can come back here."

"I'll think about it. Where's Papa? I thought I saw him drive off."

"Oh, you know your father. Always something going on. He had to meet someone down by the array, and then there's an Elders meeting."

"Did Rhys go with him?"

"No, he's out there trying to avoid Fflur Mostyn. He needn't worry. Like everyone else, she's heard of his trysts with that Healerina woman from town, and she seems just as happy to avoid him."

The Mostyn and Pendry families had "promised" Fflur and Rhys to each other to be married when he turned thirty, but Cadoc couldn't see that happening now, not after Rhys's very public affair with Daley.

His mother headed toward the rear of the house.

"Where are you going, Mother?"

"I just want to lie down for a minute. I need a break from the other Elder wives. I can take only so much of their chatter."

Half a minute later a thundering *Boom!* shook the house as if a bomb had gone off, knocking Cadoc onto his back. The building shifted and shook and rattled, bouncing him off the floor, making it impossible to regain his feet. Despite all Papa's retrofitting of the Lodge with wall braces, foundation bolts, and base isolators to keep the place from shaking too much, his first thought was getting to the shelter of a doorway. The second was...

"Mother!"

From the rear of the house rose a cacophony of rattles and rumbles and the cracks of lumber snapping and splintering

"Mother!"

Fighting the jumping floorboards, Cadoc had just struggled to his hands and knees when something crashed onto his back, knocking him flat again as dishes and glassware shattered all around him. Pain shot down to his wrist and up to his shoulder as something cracked in his left forearm. The damn China cabinet had tipped off the wall. The house stopped shaking as he tried to worm out from beneath it but his clothing was tangled in it.

Rhys stormed up the steps then.

"Cad!"

He rushed over and lifted the cabinet enough to allow Cadoc to slither free.

"Are you okay?"

"My arm's been better but never mind me—"

"The whole rear of the house collapsed and—hey, where's Mom?"

"That's what I'm trying to tell you. She went back to her bedroom."

"Oh, shit!"

Rhys took off at a run. Cadoc struggled to his feet—damn, he hurt all over—and raced after him. They both skidded to a stop when they found the hallway choked with debris.

"No!" Rhys cried. "No-no-no-no!"

Cadoc shouted, "Mother!"

Then Rhys: "Mom!"

They were answered by a high-pitched groan from beyond the rubble.

"She's still alive! Dig! We've got to get her out!"

Becky

"I need aerial recon," Becky said. "Any way there's a satellite in range? Get hold of our contact at NRO. See if they can feed us some images."

A major slip and spreading in the Cerro Prieto fault had triggered a massive 7.8 multi-fault event in the lower end of the Imperial Valley with the epicenter just west of Mexicali. Seismic waves had propagated south through the isthmus to the Gulf of California and north through the valleys—definitely rattling Pasadena and the South Mudd Building here at Caltech—and into the Los Angeles basin where they gained velocity and destructive power. Very preliminary reports cited extensive damage.

And because the epicenter was in Mexico, and SASMEX neglected the Baja area, Becky was not getting anywhere near the data she needed.

Hendry said, "One of the Yuma TV stations has a chopper in the air over Mexicali. I've got it on my monitor."

Becky and the other members of the seismic lab crowded in behind him. The feed from the chopper said they were just west of Mexicali.

"Shit!" Cheatham cried. "That looks like a surface rupture!"

"Nah," said Pryor. "Can't be. It's too big."

Becky strained to focus on the jittering image.

The Cerro Prieto complex involved a major spreading center so no surprise that the surface had split, but she agreed it was awfully damn big. Had to be some sort of camera artifact.

Then the chopper closed in on it, leaving no doubt that they were looking at a huge surface rupture. The data collection center fell silent as the chopper followed it south. Though it stayed over the fissure, Becky could make out few details.

"If they'd only get closer we could—"

Just then the camera changed angle to the east where smoke and flame belched into the air.

"Something's caught fire," a voice behind her said—Pryor. "That's where they'll spend their time now. Fire's much more interesting than a crack in the ground."

But the smoke and flame weren't coming from ground level. It seemed to be originating from a mound that had to be seven- or eight-hundred feet high.

"But what's burning?" Cheatham said. "It looks like a mountain's on fire."

"Holy shit!" Hendry gasped. "That's a volcano. I've been down there. That's the Cerro Prieto Volcano. The last time it erupted was during the Halocene!"

Someone on the other side of the room shouted, "We've a satellite view coming in!"

Like stampeding cattle they all rushed to the new monitor. A few people gasped, but then they all stood and stared in silent awe. A huge surface rupture ran from Mexicali to the Gulf of California.

Becky had never seen anything like it...had never dreamed she ever would. Water from the gulf was rushing into the fissure. Good thing it didn't extend through Mexicali into the Imperial Valley, otherwise they'd have an unimaginable catastrophe on their hands.

"Hey, you know," Hendry said from his station, "those sine waves are still running."

Becky walked over to the data monitor on the wall. Now that the other seismic activity had simmered down—at least until the next aftershock—the sine waves were still present. They'd probably never stopped. They didn't look natural. Was someone creating them?

"I've got a bad feeling about those sine waves," she said. "Someone get hold of Homeland Security. This could be a terrorist act."

Hendry looked at her. "You're serious?"

She pointed to the monitor. "Look at those waves." She'd spent most of her adult life monitoring seismic feeds and had never seen anything like that. "Those do not originate in nature. Those are manmade. I'll stake my career on it."

And they meant that whatever was going on wasn't over yet.

Tom

This could still work out, Tom thought as he piloted the Hummer toward the Salton Sea. The quake could have disrupted things enough down at the marina that they wouldn't be able to rent a thing.

Marina Drive sounded promising so he turned onto it and followed its curving course past scattered houses; many looked like converted double-wide trailers, although some were fairly nice with Spanish-style stucco walls and tile roofs. A lot of the houses showed quake effects ranging from cracked stucco and fallen tiles to being knocked off the foundation. One had a roof cracked like an egg. Eventually he found the marina and RV park. It had a big parking lot, a motel, and a corrugated steel building billing itself a "Johnson's Landing Café & Bar." A couple of RVs lay on their sides. This was looking better and better for no rental.

He parked and walked toward the water. The stink hit him again. He spotted a crusty bearded fellow in a camo boonie hat standing at the waterline with an aluminum outboard runabout nosed onto the sand.

Damn.

"Are you Zeke?" Tom called.

"You the fella that phoned?"

Double damn.

"Yeah."

"Still want the boat?"

He glanced back at Lucy who was vigorously nodding from inside the car.

"I guess so," he said, walking down the gentle slope toward the water. "Are we going to have a problem out there with the aftershocks?"

"The water got a little rough during the quake, but this thing's damn near unsinkable, especially on the Salton."

"How so?"

"High salinity—maybe a dozen times saltier than the Pacific. Increases the buoyancy. You'd have a tough time drowning out there."

"That's good to know, I guess."

"Yeah, you should be all right. I been listening to the FEMA channel. They said it was a seven point eight. That's a big one."

"Didn't know FEMA had a channel."

He gestured to a little battery-powered radio on a nearby cinder block. "Yeah. Shortwave. I ain't got cable and my dish just got knocked off my roof, so the shortwave keeps me in touch. Anyway, FEMA says it mighta been just a foreshock."

"Foreshock?"

"Yeah. A smaller quake that occurs before the mainshock. Pretty common with bigger quakes running above seven. And, like I said, this one was seven point eight. Knocked me right off my feet. So you've got to consider that could've been a foreshock."

This was looking worse and worse. Tom turned to Lucy again but she was out of the Hummer and strapping her katana across her back. She walked past Zeke without looking at him.

"Get that radio," she said to the air.

Then she stepped into the boat, seated herself near the front with her back to the shore, and started swaying back and forth.

Zeke grinned. "Looks like your lady friend's made up her mind."

"That's my sister."

He stuck out his hand. "I'll take the hundred up front."

One hundred bucks for a few hours rental. Seemed steep, but what did Tom know? He pulled out his wallet.

"How much for the radio?"

He shrugged. "I got a backup. I guess I can part with this one for fifty."

"For that little thing?"

"Take it or leave it."

He took it. No biggie. He had the money and Zeke was the only game in town at the moment.

"Been a while since I was out in one of these," Tom said as he handed over three fifties. "How about a quick run-through?"

In truth, he'd never piloted a boat—not even a rowboat.

He got in and handed Lucy the shortwave, then started his boating lesson. Zeke showed him how to unlock the outboard engine, the starter button, and the combined throttle-gearshift with its simple F-N-R positions. Piece of cake.

"Your fuel tank is full," he said, pointing to the red plastic container in the stern with a tube running to the engine. "Twelve gallons will last you hours but keep an eye on the gauge. You run out, well, no one's gonna come for you."

Tom didn't like the sound of that. "What do we do if something happens? I mean, like, if the engine fails?"

"That's why you've got oars. You'll have to start paddling."

Fair enough. Note to self: Do not go too far from shore and do *not* run out of gas.

Zeke pushed them off. As they drifted away Tom turned to Lucy and gestured to her katana.

"No marauders out there on the water, Sis."

"There are water marauders, you know. Ever hear of pirates?"

On the Salton Sea? Ah, well. What can you do?

He dropped the propeller into the water, hit the starter button, and they were off. It had a car steering wheel and drove like one—except no brakes. Tom supposed you could reverse the propeller to slow down, but no worry: his was the only bloody boat on the water.

"You'd never know we just had a seven-point-eight quake," he said, waving an arm at the placid surface perfectly reflecting the sky.

Lucy had the radio on but he couldn't hear it over the outboard motor.

"What's it say?"

"They say the Cerro Prieto Fault created a huge fissure into the gulf."

"What gulf? The Gulf of California?" Tom was picturing the big spur of the Pacific filling the space between the Baja Peninsula and the Mexico mainland.

Lucy made one of her *must-I-explain-this?* faces that he hated. "No, the Gulf of Mexico."

Her tone irked him. "Don't be a wiseass. It's just that I've never heard of a Cerro Prieto fault."

"Neither have I. But apparently it's associated with a volcano that's started erupting."

"The shit's really hitting the fan, isn't it."

"Big time".

Lucy turned the radio off and swiveled to face front, scanning ahead. Tom checked his phone for the time—3:52.

"Almost half an hour till the equinox," he said. "Plenty of time to position ourselves. Where do you think best?"

"Welllll," she said slowly, drawing out the word, "that Tesla tower is to the south so maybe we should head down that end."

She was swaying again. As if the boat weren't rocking enough by itself. Usually Tom could ignore it, but the two out-of-synch motions were making him seasick.

He shifted his attention to the placid water. "Sounds like a plan."

Hardly a plan, but at least they had a direction.

Daley

As they roared toward the windfarm, Daley could see that the quake had hit it hard. Half the turbines were either down or leaning against each other. The rest were still turning however—and still in synch.

Juana had driven her Harley like a mad woman, winding between and around the jammed cars in El Centro, then opening the throttle once they broke free. They raced along the desert roads at speeds way past Daley's comfort zone, but she couldn't lose a second getting to the windfarm.

As they rode Daley had given her a version of the situation which she'd simplified down to Elis Pendry using the tower to create earthquakes and open a passage to bring the gods of his religion back to Earth. Juana seemed to have no trouble accepting that.

"Drive by the front gate," Daley told her.

"But don't you want the tower?"

"I'm sure Elis has got it surrounded by clan men to keep everyone away. I'll never get past." The gate stood open with Jason's car and the Tadhak bus parked outside. "Drop me here."

"Then we should have brought the cops."

Daley hopped off. Damn, it felt good to be off that seat. She adjusted her skirt which had ridden way up during the trip—not designed for hog riding, by any means. She pulled off the helmet and shed Dr. Milton's lab coat. With fewer turbines turning, the noise wasn't as gratingly loud as when she'd last visited with Cadoc.

"Think about how long it would have taken me to explain this situation. And even in the unlikely case they semi-bought it, they're dealing with a town shaking itself to pieces. How could they spare anyone to come out here? And one cop isn't going to hack it."

Juana gestured toward the gate. "What do you expect to do in there, then?"

"Make an end run around Elis. Wait for me here."

"You're going in alone?"

Daley glanced at the maze of fallen towers inside. Looked like a forest after a hurricane. Or tornado, maybe. No way the Harley could get through.

"Some stuff there you probably shouldn't see. I'll be fine."

She took off at a run, ducking under some fallen towers, sliding over others.

("Reminds me of Tunguska,") Pard said.

"What's Tunguska?"

("A place in Siberia.")

"You've never been to Siberia."

("I've seen photos.")

A black-and-white image sprang into her mind: What was once a forest with all its trees—*all* its trees—flattened like matchsticks, all pointing in the same direction.

"Hey. This isn't *that* bad. A fair number of these are still standing."

("They won't be after Pendry's next quake, I'll bet. That's our destination straight ahead.")

The central tower was still standing, its turbine's blades turning. The door to its base building stood open.

("Not much reason to lock it today, I guess. By the way, what do you hope to accomplish here?")

"Stop any more quakes."

("Do you really think Jason cares about that?")

"If you've got a better idea I'm all ears."

("Unfortunately...no.")

Daley entered, crossed the empty front room to the rear door—also unlocked—and entered the short anteroom, closing the door behind her. Without hesitating, she pulled open the next door and stepped into the huge warehouse space Cadoc had shown her before. A few of Jason's fellow Tadhaks moved among the putty-colored, boxcar-size blocks that stored all his voltage.

I don't see any damage in here.

("It's probably located outside any seismic zones.")

A couple of the Tadhaks spotted her and started hurrying toward her, but Jason, standing by an open panel to her right, waved them away. They backed off, but not far.

"I suppose you're in a snit because I didn't tell you it was the equinox instead of the solstice."

Like yesterday, his insufferably superior attitude put her on edge, but she wasn't going to let him know.

"I don't get into snits. And besides, you were under no obligation to jeopardize your agenda for mine. I would have done the same were positions reversed."

"My, aren't we rational today. Such a rarity for your species. I'm impressed."

("So am I.")

Trying to get on his good side.

"Are you ready to melt down Elis's tower?"

"Ready and waiting for the exact moment."

"Do it now."

Jason shook his head. "Too early. We wait until the exact moment of the equinox—four twenty-one Pacific Time—and then we wait just a little longer until the passage is stabilized and the Rymwyr are in the Void. *Then* we send the surge."

"No. Send it now. People are dying out there."

"It's called collateral damage."

"It's called people's *lives.* If he succeeds in flooding the valley, hundreds of thousands could die."

He gave her a cool look. "There are nearly eight billion of you out there. What do a couple hundred thousand matter?"

"It sure as hell matters to them! And it matters to *me*!"

"But it doesn't matter to me. The only lives that matter to me are those of the Rymwyr. And those are lives I want to *end*."

"Please. I'm begging you."

A pitying smile. "And now the façade slips and the sentiment pours through, scouring away the patina of rationality. I've told you our history with the Rymwyr, I've told you how long we've waited to balance the scales, and yet you stand there thinking an emotional appeal at the last minute will convince us to put all that aside, to weigh a few hundred thousand of your species against billions of ours and decide on your behalf. How pathetic."

She took a step forward. "Please!"

He gestured to the nearby Tadhaks. "Remove her."

Daley lunged for him but two of the Tadhaks grabbed her under the arms, lifted her off her feet, and marched her out the door. She struggled and kicked but they remained implacable as they carried her into the little anteroom, and then ejected her from the outer door into the base of the wind turbine. She leaped back to the door but it found it locked.

"Damn you!" she shouted as she pounded on it.

("What's this going to accomplish?") Pard said.

She stopped and leaned against the door.

"Nothing. Absolutely nothing."

("And when you leaped at him back there...what were you going to do if you managed to reach him?")

"Hell, I don't know. I lost it. I just wanted to do some damage."

("Well, now what?")

"We head for the tower, I guess, and hope we can get past anyone he's got guarding the place."

("And then what?")

"We *interfere*, damn it! I've never wanted to own a gun, but I wish I had one now."

("I don't see you shooting someone.")

"Well, neither do I, but I could sure as hell make them believe I would. Let's get back to Juana."

She stepped out into the sunlight and the noise and hadn't

gone ten steps before the ground heaved beneath her and tossed her off her feet. She hit hard, knocking the wind out of her. She groaned in pain as the ground bounced her around like a pinball.

This is no aftershock!

("A new one! Pendry's still at it!")

She tried to rise but was knocked flat again. A shadow fell over her and she looked up to see one of the towers falling toward her. She screamed and rolled out of the way as it landed against another fallen shaft with a deafening crash. The turbine blades broke off and went flying in three different directions.

Still the ground shook.

And then it eased a little, although it still jittered. Another tower crashed to earth behind her.

("You've got to get out of here!")

Ya think?

She forced herself to her feet and started moving. She wanted to run but couldn't find an open stretch long enough to allow it—duck under one tower, hurry ten feet to the next fallen shaft and slide over that. Her knees would buckle slightly as the ground rose and sank under her. And still the turbines tumbled, seeming to fall in slow motion only to buckle and shatter on impact and send their massive blades pin-wheeling through the air. More than once she had to duck to keep from losing her head.

Finally she reached the front gate and bolted into the clear to where both Juana and her Harley lay on their sides in the dirt.

"Are you okay?" she panted as she skidded to a stop beside her.

Juana nodded and held up a hand. "Help me up." Daley pulled her to her feet and helped dust her off. "I tried to get up a few times but kept getting knocked down, so I stayed down. I'm gathering from this new quake that your end run failed."

"Miserably."

"What now?"

"Get me to the tower."

"But I thought you said—"

"The tower, Juana. Before he triggers another."

Daley had a feeling Elis would keep pushing right up till the equinox, and maybe even after—until he got his flood.

She helped right the Harley but when Juana got on and hit the pedal, it wouldn't start. After numerous tries, she got off, leaned it on the kickstand, and started messing with the cowling.

"Something must have shook loose while it was bouncing around on the ground."

Daley couldn't wait.

"Catch up to me if you get it going."

"But it's miles away!"

She started running.

Becky

"We need to get someone from maintenance up here," Becky said. "And someone from IT as well. We need that monitor working—now more than ever."

The mainshock had clocked in at 8.2 Richter and knocked one of the big wall monitors from its moorings. The data collection center was chaotic at the moment.

Pryor, hunched before her monitor, said, "The epicenter was the Cerro Prieto like before but it propagated southward into the Gulf. We've got a significant upheaval in the Wagner Basin."

That made sense. The Wagner Basin sat underwater at the southern end of the Cerro Prieto fault and connected to the East Pacific Rise. The whole Gulf was a hotbed of seismic activity due to its being home to the Gulf of California Rift Zone, the spreading center that was slowly taking the Baja Peninsula farther and farther from the mainland. She didn't like what she was hearing, though.

"How 'significant' an upheaval?"

"We're working on it."

"Do we have any DART stations in the Gulf?"

Pryor swiveled to face Becky. "No. All the DARTs are deep ocean. You worried about a tsunami?"

"Worst case, we could have a big wave funneling north."

Pryor made a face. "Oh, crap. You're not thinking a Tafjord scenario?"

"Exactly what I'm thinking."

"Well, shit, it's possible." She turned back to her monitor and began banging on the keyboard.

Hendry turned to her. "Tafjord scenario?"

"Long time ago," she said. "Norway in the 1930s. Part of a mountain collapsed at the end of a fjord and created a tsunami that roared down the channel to devastate the town of Tafjord with fifty-foot waves. If the rockslide had happened on the ocean, or even on a big lake, the waves would have spread out in all directions and dissipated. But because it occurred in a fjord, the force of the wave was concentrated and focused straight ahead as it funneled down the channel. A lot of people died."

"So you're thinking the Gulf of California—"

"Yeah. Also a narrow body of water, and most narrow at its northern end. The force of any wave traveling north will be funneled straight ahead—just like in Norway."

Cheatham shouted from his monitor, "Fishing boat just called in an eighty-foot rogue wave rolling north in the Gulf."

"Eighty feet!" Becky said. "That's no rogue wave. That's the tsunami."

Hendry said, "But tsunamis don't rise that high."

"They do when they get channeled. What's the coastline like at the north end?"

"Marshy desert. The Colorado Delta Bioreserve takes up most of the area and it's, like, maybe ten feet above sea level."

"Plus the surface rupture ends right there," Becky said.

This was looking bad, very bad. A 7.8 foreshock with a huge surface rupture into the Gulf, followed by an 8.2 mainshock combined with a sea-floor upheaval sending a tsunami up the Gulf toward the rupture. That eighty-foot wave was going to hit with tremendous force and have nothing in its way, leaving it free to plow right into that rupture.

What would happen then?

It was probably hitting the coast right now.

"Get the NRO back on the line," she shouted. "We need an eye in the sky!"

Rhys

"You're looking a little better," Cadoc said. He wore what looked like some cloth napkins tied into a makeshift sling for his arm.

Rhys was feeling a bit better himself but kept the ice pack against his scalp. His head hurt like a bitch. At least it had stopped bleeding.

They'd spent a long time on the second floor trying to free Mom. Cadoc could use only one arm, but his back was fine and he helped drag debris from the pile clogging the hallway. When they finally reached the bedroom, Mom was trapped under a fallen ceiling panel. They'd pried her free and hauled her downstairs just in time. The rear of the house was pretty much uninhabitable now.

They'd been just carrying Mom from the house when the mainshock hit, knocking Cadoc and Mom, who were going out the door ahead of him, forward onto the walk. Rhys, though, had been rocked back into the house where his head met with a falling four-by-four. Damn near knocked him out. It might have been a lot worse if Cadoc hadn't used his good arm to grab his wrist and drag him out before more debris came down.

Cadoc leaned closer and lowered his voice. "This is Papa's doing."

"No shit," Rhys said. "He lied to me about the solstice being the target date. Lied to everyone."

Cadoc said, "We've got to stop him."

Rhys forced himself to his feet. The world swayed a little but he held himself rigid.

"Not we. You need to take care of that arm and one of us has to stay with Mom."

"Maria can—"

"Seriously, Cad. Mom needs one of us here and maybe I can get Dad to listen to me."

"A fool's errand. No offense, but that man listens to no one, only his vaunted scrolls."

"Maybe so, but he'll listen to me more than you. He's still

pissed at you for showing Daley the film." Which reminded him: "Hey, speaking of Daley, do you have any idea where she might be?"

"Down in El Centro. It was on the news that 'La Curandera' had returned to the medical center." He smiled as he shook his head. "Our Daley...La Curandera...who'd'a thunk, huh?"

"'*Our* Daley'? Damned if I know whose Daley she is now, if anybody's, but she sure as hell isn't mine anymore."

Cad gave his shoulder a gentle punch. "You can worry about that later. Right now we have a madman to deal with. Be careful down there. And be prepared: Talk may not be enough."

Talk may not be enough...

The words followed Rhys to his car. The Elders had all wandered off a short while after Dad's departure. Supposedly for a little conference. He wouldn't be surprised if he'd find them all gathered at the tower, pumping their standing waves into the ground to cause these quakes.

What then? Would they try to keep him from his father? They were all older men, but hardly frail codgers. He wouldn't be able to bull his way through all four of them if they wanted to stop him.

Dad had a gun...a .32 he kept in his bedroom. That would be a handy option to carry right now, but thanks to the mainshock, the second floor of the Lodge was totally inaccessible.

He raced down the hill but slowed as he entered town, aghast at the destruction. The Tadhaks had built the town and it was obvious now they'd done little to earthquake-proof the buildings. Most of them were in shambles—Jason Tadhak's own real estate office was no exception. In fact, that whole block of wood-frame buildings had been reduced to kindling, Daley's Healerina included. A few people wandered here and there in a daze.

Rhys stopped and stared at the wreckage. The second-floor apartment had collapsed into the store beneath, leaving the store destroyed and the apartment uninhabitable. If Cadoc hadn't told him Daley was in El Centro, Rhys would be charging into the rubble looking for her. The wreckage across the street was only maybe half as bad, but Arturo wouldn't be serving meals again for a while. Maybe never.

Shaking his head in dismay, Rhys gunned his Highlander ahead. He passed the trailer park where a lot of the units had been knocked off their foundations. Some lay on their sides. Lots of dazed looking people here. Wanton destruction...but this didn't even scratch the surface of what his father had to answer for.

He found the gate to the solar array locked but unguarded. Well, Dad had given the workers the day off, supposedly as part of the clan's equinox celebration. Rhys had thought it a generous gesture at the time, but now he knew the real reason: no witnesses.

The tower loomed in the sky at the far end of the array. The copper fittings on the cupola glittered in the sun but no high-voltage arcs split the air. Soon they would, but for now all the current was flowing into the earth's crust. Something vaguely different about the tower. Did it lean ever so slightly to the south? And some of its struts and trusses appeared to be missing. Shaken loose by the tremblors?

He had a key to the gate, and since the only way to the tower was through the array, he wound his way around the panels until the base of the tower came in sight. Close up now he could see definite signs of damage but nothing too severe. The steel braces and isolators had done their jobs better here than back at the Lodge.

Only one vehicle parked by the open gate—his father's Land Rover. No sign of any Elders or their cars. They couldn't all have arrived in the Land Rover. Did that mean his father was alone? Maybe this wasn't such a fool's errand after all. Then again, simply talking to Dad was a long way from persuading him.

He parked, jumped out, and hurried toward the gate. The ground beyond it was sprinkled with fallen bits and pieces of the tower, but no Elders in sight. No father in sight, but he could be around on the far side of the central shaft.

Rhys was maybe two steps from the gate when something closed around his leg. He yelped and jumped but it held him fast in a viselike grip. He looked down and saw a gray-brown hand clinging to his ankle. And then, all around him, porthors began climbing form the sand. A dozen or so. The grip on his ankle was released and he was pushed back from the gate. Then the porthors surrounded him, enclosing him in a tight circle.

And then they stopped moving.

They stood straight and silent, shoulder to shoulder with their arms at their sides, eyes staring, their rudimentary, humanoid features expressionless. Rhys tried to push one out of his way but it wouldn't budge. Tried to squeeze between two but again, they wouldn't budge. Utterly immoveable.

Rhys faced the tower and shouted, "Dad! Dad, what's going on here?"

His father came around from the far side of the shaft, wiping his hands on a cloth. He smiled.

"What do you think is going on? You're being contained."

"We need to talk. Please! You've got to stop this!"

"Talk? You want to talk? It's a little late for that now, isn't it? You've been doing all your talking—and a lot more than talking, from what I gather—with the Duad. But none of that matters now. I neutralized her, and I neutralized you, and everything is proceeding as planned."

That implacable tone in his voice. Not a shred of doubt.

"But people have died in these quakes, Dad. Died because of you. It's murder plain and simple. Don't make it any worse. Please!"

"At the risk of sounding clichéd and heartless, Rhys, I'm making an omelet—a *cosmic* omelet—and that requires the breaking of some eggs."

Cadoc was right: They were dealing with a madman.

"What happened to you, Dad? How did you get to this point?"

He didn't seem to hear. He pointed to a portable shortwave radio on a nearby bench. "See this? It's tuned to the FEMA channel. When I hear what I need to hear, I'll cut the power to the shaft and kill the standing waves. I'll wait until four sixteen—exactly five minutes before the moment of the equinox. And then I'll power up the dome and open a passage through the Void to the Visitors' realm."

More madness. Rhys doubted anything of the sort was possible, but that wasn't the point. The earthquakes had already done their damage. No reversing that. He pounded against the porthors but they wouldn't budge…gave no sign that his blows even registered.

Kendrick

Jeff crawled out from under a pile of broken and splintered boards that used to be the back stairs up to the goddess's home. In fact, the rest of the place was in pretty much the same condition. Her Healerina store was flattened, completely collapsed under the upstairs apartment which had landed on it. Definitely not livable but you could still tell it had once been an apartment.

Fuck! Broken wood everywhere. That last shaker had come out of nowhere and bigger than anything before. All the other buildings in sight from here had taken a beat down, some worse than the goddess's.

After the she'd gone off this morning, Jeff hadn't had nothing to do, what with all her devoted followers trailing after her. He'd hung out at Arturo's for a while, then came first shock and that had done some damage, loosening the staircase from the rear wall. He'd been trying to fix it when the bigger one hit, collapsing everything around him.

He picked his way through the wreckage toward the street to get an idea of what was left of Nespodee Springs. Turned out not a whole lot. The café looked wrecked. He noticed a few people about, but most of the town—Jeff included—had places in the trailer park. He walked down to check on the Thirsty Cactus and found its roof all caved in. Well, shit. He and Benny had downed a lot of beers there, but now the Cactus was dead as Benny.

As he turned around to head back up to the goddess's place he spotted an SUV stopped in front of it. Looked like the Pendry kid's. Jeff crouched behind some rubble and watched. Old man Pendry didn't have to know he was back in town.

After the kid drove on, continuing past without seeing him, Jeff quick-walked back to his truck. The kid could be heading out to find the goddess. He might be worried about her. Jeff wasn't worried a bit. No earthquake could harm her, but that didn't mean she couldn't use a little help if people started bothering her.

When he reached his truck he realized he'd have to drive over a shitload of splintered lumber to reach the street. He could easily blow out a tire in the process and he wasn't sure his spare was inflated.

Fuck!

Well, better get started shifting the shit.

Becky

NRO was feeding a series of satellite photos to one of the desk monitors at Caltech's data collection center where everyone waited breathlessly for each new image to appear.

One after another showed further progression of the tsunami as it hit the lowlands of the bioreserve at the northern end of the Gulf and washed away everything in its path, including a small desert town in Baja called El Indiviso. It blasted into the Cerro Prieto surface rupture, widening it and then disappearing into it.

"It's a miracle!" Pryor said. "The water's being swallowed by the fault. That's going to minimize the damage."

Not to a place like El Indiviso, Becky thought. The little town had been wiped off the map.

The next few photos showed the remnant of the tsunami receding.

"If everything will just hold like this," Cheatham said, "there should be no more damage."

Becky wandered to the opposite side of the room where the fallen screen with the seismic sensor network feed had been leaned against the wall. The mysterious sine waves were still running through the lower Imperial Valley. She had a feeling this wasn't over yet.

And then Hendry called from the station receiving the NRO

images. "Doctor Heuser! Something happening here!"

Becky rushed over to where Hendry was pointing a shaky finger at the latest image.

"What is *that*?"

He was indicating the northern end of the Cerro Prieto Fault's surface rupture, just west of Mexicali. What—?

"Oh, Christ! Is that water?"

The next image left no doubt. Water was breaking through the surface, extending the fissure northward. Successive images showed the rupture widening and lengthening until the water was flowing freely across the border into the Imperial Valley.

Pryor came up behind her. "What's happening?"

"The force of the tsunami extended the rupture. The Gulf of California is flowing into the valley toward Plaster City and Dixieland. We've got a major disaster on our hands."

Hendry looked up at her. "How major?"

The repercussions and consequences were just dawning on Becky. "It's a downhill ride from there. The whole central part of the Imperial Valley is below sea level. That water's not simply flowing from a higher level to a lower level, it's got the weight of all the water in the Gulf of California behind it, and the Gulf has the weight of the entire Pacific Ocean behind *it*! That flow is going to pick up speed and start carving out the sides and the bottom of the rupture. That's not bedrock it's flowing through, that's loose sediment laid down by the Colorado River for ages. The flow will chew it up and spit it out the other side. And the wider and deeper the channel, the more seawater it can deliver."

Hendry's voice lowered to a whisper. "They're fucked!"

"Damn right they are. This could be catastrophic. Calexico and El Centro are next because they're below sea level—El Centro is way below. We've got to let FEMA know. They're going to have to start evacuating a large part of the Imperial Valley—unless someone can figure out a way to block that channel."

As people rushed to phones, Becky turned back to the wall monitor and stared at those damn sine waves. Never in all the seismology group's worst-case scenarios had they imagined a compounding of disasters like this. No one had. And, against all reason and science, she knew those sine waves were somehow involved...somehow *behind* everything that had happened.

Tom

Tom had piloted the outboard about a mile along the mirror surface when it started to become agitated, first with wavelets, then with definite chop.

"Aftershock?" Lucy said, frowning.

"Unless the last one was a foreshock and this is the main—holy shit!"

The water to the south was rising in a huge swell and racing toward them, a wave from a surfer's dream.

Tom didn't know what to do. His first instinct was to turn the boat and flee, but he didn't think they could outrun it, and even if they could, they'd eventually come to a shore. Or what if it broke on them as they ran?

"Whatever you do," Lucy said in her flat tone, "don't turn the boat. Keep us moving and pointed straight at it."

"But that thing's gotta be ten feet high!"

"Nose on, we'll slide right over it. But if it catches us broadside, we're sunk—literally and figuratively."

How could she be so calm?

Since he didn't have a better idea, Tom followed her directions and kept the bow pointed at the wave. As it came at them, he took a deep breath and prayed his bladder would hold. The unflappable Lucy busied herself turning on the shortwave.

And sure enough, just as she said, they slid right over it. Another smaller wave followed close behind but they slipped over that too, like surfers paddling out to where they could wait for the Big One.

The waves then became disorganized, sloshing this way and that as they ran into one another while the quake continued. Out here the water acted as a sort of shock absorber, so he could only guess at the severity of the current tremors on land, but he did notice how some of the graffiti-soaked walls of the abandoned buildings scattered along the shore were tipping and falling. They'd withstood the 7.8 of a while ago, but now they were crumbling. Did that mean this one was even bigger?

He headed for the center of the Salton, figuring the water would be deepest there and harder for the tremors to roil, then idled the engine and waited for calm.

Lucy turned up the radio and they listened. As the waves subsided, the FEMA channel announced that the earthquake center at Caltech had just pegged this new tremor's magnitude at 8.2.

"That's huge," Tom said. "Could this be the Big One?"

Lucy shrugged. "Could be."

That was when the air changed. No, make that the atmosphere. It filled with a sense of foreboding, of portent. An augury of impending...what? Tom looked around. Nothing had changed—the sun was still high and bright, a gentle breeze rippled the water—yet he was filled with this unaccountable sense of imminent doom.

Lucy said, "We're moving, you know."

"Just drifting," he said. "The breeze—"

"The breeze is coming *from* the east and we're drifting *toward* the east. Does that compute?"

No, it didn't, and yes, they were definitely moving toward the eastern shore.

"Then it's a current," he said.

What was her point here?

"Really?" Another of her patented disdainful looks. "We're floating on a giant, landlocked puddle, Tommy."

He got it. "And puddles don't have currents."

"Unless somebody's stirring it," she said.

Something about her tone. As Tom processed it he noticed how they'd angled to the left and were now drifting north, though the breeze remained from the east. Weird.

And then came this loud, sucking gurgle from somewhere off to the left. He saw nothing. When it came again, he stood for a better look and spotted what appeared to be a hole in the water. But what—?

"Whirlpool!" he cried.

"As I suspected," Lucy said.

"You suspected? How could you *suspect*? And why didn't you say something?"

He dropped back into his seat and jammed the gear/throttle into fast forward. The engine died. Tom screamed. Not a girly scream. A guy scream. But a scream nonetheless.

"You did it too fast," Lucy said. "Be calm."

Calm? Easy for her to say. She was never anything *but* calm.

"What's happening?" he shouted as he jammed his finger on the starter button.

"I'm just guessing, of course," she said, adopting that infuriating lecture tone, "but the Salton Sea sits over the southern portion of the San Andreas Fault. It's not surprising that a high-magnitude quake like the one we just had would involve multiple faults. When I noticed we were moving against the breeze, and in a counterclockwise direction, I figured the San Andreas had opened down below. No surprise a whirlpool formed. They rotate counterclockwise in this hemisphere, by the way."

The starter was cranking but the engine wasn't catching.

"I don't want to get flushed down the San Andreas Fault!" Tom cried.

The engine still wasn't catching so, logically, he pressed the starter button harder.

"You're going to drain the battery if you keep that up," Lucy said.

"Really? *Really?*" Sudden fury roared through him. They were picking up speed and revolving faster and faster toward the whirlpool's empty center—circling the drain, as the expression went. The vortex had grown wider and Tom no longer had to stand to see it. "Do you have any better ideas?"

"Well, the first thing I might do is return the gearshift to neutral."

What? Oh, right. The handle was still in the "F" position. He pulled it back to "N" and mashed the starter button again. The engine caught right away. Their stern was almost to the whirlpool's sucking maw. They had to *move*. But, remembering what had happened last time, Tom restrained himself and eased the lever forward. He almost wept when the boat lurched into motion.

As he gunned away from the vortex, he realized that while he'd been so intent on the starter, the surface of the Salton had shrunk and sunk. Significantly. The water's edge sat lower on the shoreline which was much closer than before. A wide expanse of glistening, vile-looking mud now showed between the sand and the water's edge.

"Maybe you should slow down, Tommy," Lucy said. "We don't want to—"

They were both abruptly thrown forward as the prow crunched against something rough and gritty that stopped them dead.

"—run aground."

"Sorry!"

The engine was making horrible noises so he threw it into neutral. The water drained away all around them leaving flopping fish and crawling crustaceans and a stench Tom couldn't believe. He'd thought the ambient odor of the area was awful but this went light years beyond. He tried breathing through his mouth but he could *taste* it.

"I can't stand this," he said, gagging

"Just hang in there. Your nose will adjust after a while."

"It will never adjust to this." He pointed toward the near shore. "Let's go. We can walk."

"Go ahead. I'm not going anywhere."

"Lucy—"

"Number one: I'm not stepping in that disgusting mud. Number two: I came here to witness the Void. We still have ten minutes to go before the equinox."

"There won't be a Void to witness, Lucy! The Clan—they're psychos! Delusional! They're—"

"Oh, look. That's where all the water's gone."

He followed her point to a massive crack in the sea floor, running north and south as far as Tom could see. No wonder the water had disappeared so quickly. Steam rose from the fissure as dying fish flopped all about on the glistening, puddled mud under a bright blue, cloud-flocked sky. The effect was positively surreal, like a Dali landscape.

But that didn't cancel out the growing sense of doom.

"Oh, listen to this," Lucy said. "Something about an evacuation."

She turned the volume knob on the shortwave but nothing happened. She hit it with her palm but still nothing. "Batteries must be shot."

She held it up to her ear, frowning at first, then her expression growing slack with shock.

Lucy...shocked? What the hell?

In a hushed tone she said, "They're ordering the evacuation of the whole Imperial Valley. Remember that fissure from the Cerro Prieto Fault that ran into the Gulf of California...the mainshock widened it northward all the way into the valley. The water's pouring through...the Pacific...it's flooding the valley."

Tom fought to process it. "How can that be?"

"I'm thinking this is all part of the plan."

"What plan?"

"The Clan plan. It's brilliant in a way—sick, but brilliant. The Visitors left because the trough was drying up. If you want them back, you've got to make the place inviting again. So you flood it."

Tom liked to think of himself as unshockable, but...

"They're behind these quakes?"

"I think you can bet on it."

"But there's gotta be a zillion people living down here, all below sea level!"

"Yeah, there's that." Totally unfazed.

And then he realized...

"Oh, shit! Nobody's farther below sea level than we are right now. We've got to get to higher ground."

"Yeah, we do...eventually. But it's only eight minutes to the equinox, and the water's got to flood forty miles through El Centro and Brawley before it gets here. So we've got time."

"You can't be serious! The car's over there in Salton City. We need to slog through this gunk to get there, then drive—"

"How do we get around the San Andreas?" she said, the radio still pressed to her ear.

He stared at the long, thirty-foot-wide fissure stretching between them and Salton City on the west shore.

"Oh, shit!" Just then a deep rumbling echoed up from the fissure and vibrated the hull of their beached craft. "Now what?"

Lucy didn't answer as they both stared at the fissure. Another quake? An aftershock?

But no. Water began bubbling and gushing from the opening.

"It's spitting it back!" Tom couldn't help a hysterical laugh that sounded scary even to him. "Must not like the taste!"

But this was good. They could motor back to Salton City.

"I don't think that's the same water, Tommy."

"What? What other water can it be? You don't think it's ocean water, do you?"

"If it is, it's not from our ocean. Look at those *things* in it."

Elis

E lis couldn't help a triumphant smile as he cut the power to the subterranean section of the tower.

"There!" he called to Rhys, still imprisoned by the loyal porthors. "Any new quakes after this will not be my doing. Happy?"

Rhys shouted back, "I'd be happier if *no* quakes were your doing. Let me out of here!"

"Not yet, my boy. Not yet."

Word had come via the FEMA channel that the quakes plus a tsunami had opened a waterway between the Gulf of California and the Imperial Valley. A tsunami! Not only had he caused earthquakes, he'd caused a tsunami. FEMA was recommending evacuation of Calexico and El Centro residents to higher ground until the flow of seawater could be stopped. Rhys was so damn worried about loss of life down there, but it wasn't a terribly big deal to travel just a few miles outside of town to put yourself above sea level.

But the flow wouldn't be stopped. Once the Void passage opened and the Visitors came through, they'd take over and see to it that the flooding continued.

He checked his watch: just coming up on four sixteen. Five minutes to the exact moment of the equinox. Time to pierce the Veil. He opened the circuit to feed full power to the dome.

Let the fireworks begin!

Kendrick

Jeff cursed steadily as he drove. It had taken him too damn long to clear the rubble blocking his pickup from the street and now he'd lost any hope of following the Pendry kid. He had a feeling the kid knew where the goddess was. Those two were tight. He'd seen that. The goddess had told him not to come along, but he'd find a way to keep watch from a distance, far enough away so she wouldn't be any the wiser, and close enough to step in should any shit hit the fan.

As he was passing the access road that ran south to the solar array he saw someone jogging along it. He was already past when it struck him: a jogger...all in black...in a skirt. A skirt? Reminded him of the goddess.

He slammed on the brakes.

Naw. Couldn't be. What would she be doing running through here? Still...only take him a sec to check. Stupid to go all the way to El Centro if she was already here.

He hung a U and headed down the side road. The closer he got, the surer he became that she was the goddess. Then he saw that white patch on top of her head and all doubt disappeared. When she turned and stuck out her thumb, he skidded to a halt.

She was panting when she leaned on his passenger door. "Hey, can you give me a lift—?" She made a face. "Karma?"

"It's Jeff now."

"Whatever. You're supposed to be back in town watching Healerina and the apartment."

"Ain't no Healerina no more. Ain't no apartment neither. Quake took care of that."

She looked shocked. "Really?"

"Yeah. Pancaked. Where you need a ride to?"

"No way I'm riding with you."

"But—"

"You're aunt's going to be along to pick me up."

He looked around. "I ain't seen no one on the road."

"Then maybe she needs your help. Her bike broke down back by the wind farm."

"She'll be okay. Where you need to go?"

"Forget it. I'm not—"

Just then the sky lit up. The sun hung high and bright in the west over the mountains but not as bright as the giant bolts of lightning shooting from the top of the Pendry tower.

"No!" she shouted as she stared that way. "Damn it, no!" She pulled the door open and climbed in. "Take me to the tower. Fast!"

"You got it."

Big one-eighty change of mind on a dime. First it's *I ain't getting' in with you* and then it's *Get me there fast*. She might be a goddess but she was still a woman.

Tom

Lucy had been right about the "things" gurgling up from the fissure. Creatures of varying amorphous shapes and sizes writhed and wriggled in the spewing water, mostly football-sized bodies with tentacles sprouting everywhere.

Tom heard her mutter, "My-my-my...how Lovecraftian."

"Octopi? Squid?"

She shook her head. "You wish."

Whatever they were, they seemed hungry, because they immediately latched onto the beached fish—the *normal* fish—and started ripping them apart and devouring them.

Water spewed in massive fountains ten feet high, and as the surging outflow spread toward them, Lucy moved to the stern and watched over the edge.

"Start the engine but leave it in neutral. As soon as the propeller's off the bottom, I'll give the signal to start us moving."

"Got it."

Tom hit the starter button and the engine caught. He understood the need to wait: If the propeller was on the bottom, it might break off, and then they'd have to row.

The water swirled around them, and so did the polypoid creatures. Good thing they didn't have a V-shaped hull or they'd be on their side and taking on water instead of starting to float again.

He watched the water continue to gush from below, and as it deepened, larger shapes began emerging from the depths. He could feel his heart hammering and his hand sweating as he gripped the gear lever. They had to *move*.

"Ready?"

Lucy shook her head. "Not yet."

Tom really, really, really wanted to start moving. Shapes in the water were coming their way. The boat shifted...floating free of the sandbar that had caused them to run aground? Or pushed from below?

"N-now?"

"Almost...wait...wait...okay, put her in reverse—*gently*."

He did just that, and they started to move—at last—but he noticed an unusual vibration from the engine.

"Are you sure we're clear?"

"Clear of the bottom, yes, but what you feel is the propeller making chum of those ugly things."

The water around them was starting to change, showing swirls of dark color.

"What color's their blood?"

"Black. Maybe real dark blue. Hard to tell. Keep going. It's not the little ones I'm worried about, it's their big brothers. And here comes one now."

She reached behind her head and unsheathed her katana. The blade gleamed in the sunlight.

"Wh-what are you doing?"

She'd moved to the middle of the boat and stood with her legs spread and the katana held vertically in a two-handed grip before her right shoulder.

"Preparing to defend our rotting meat."

Aw, shit. She'd lost it.

"Please, sit down."

"I warned you about marauders, didn't I? Well, you're about to meet some."

"Really, Lucy—"

She gave him a look. "Marauders come in all shapes and sizes, Tommy. Put us in forward and keep us moving."

"Where to?"

"Stay in the deeper water. We don't want to run aground again. Not too fast, just keep us moving. I'll—"

A long, smooth, slim, tentacle, glistening black, emerged from the water and darted toward her. Her katana flashed and severed it, the top piece flying one way, the spurting stump retreating below the surface.

Damn, that blade was sharp.

Tom shifted the engine to forward and steered them into a wide turn. He fought the urge to go full throttle because it would topple Lucy overboard. She might be the bane of his existence but she didn't deserve that.

As they chugged along, more tentacles darted from the water, sometimes in twos and threes. He crouched behind the steering wheel, kneeling on the flooring and keeping his head just high enough to see over the prow. But Lucy stood her ground, ducking and bobbing and slashing left and right, chopping through those tentacles in silence. A grim smile lit her face. She was having fun, damn her!

Were it anyone else, Tom might have felt admiration, but she was his personal royal pain in the ass who'd got them into this mess. And he was going to go down with her.

All he could think of was how fucked they were. And yet... still that looming sense that things were going to get worse.

The tentacles were coming thick and fast now and he heard Lucy start to pant from the exertion. She wasn't in the best of shape. He was worrying about how long she could keep this up before one of them got to her and then he realized he had something else to worry about: the smaller tentacled horrors were pulling themselves up onto the gunwales.

Remembering what they'd done to those beached fish, he was going to point them out to Lucy, but she was pretty near overwhelmed with the long tentacles. Tom left the steering wheel—they had only empty open water ahead of them—and grabbed one of the oars from its rack on the side and started smashing.

They squished easily. Reminded him of Whac-A-Mole. But these weren't cute harmless rodents, and for every one he killed, two or three replaced it. The situation was growing desperate and he was silently cursing Lucy and her scatterbrained obsessions when the little horrors began jumping back into the water and the long tentacles abruptly withdrew, retreating below the surface and leaving the floating severed segments as the only evidence of their existence.

"What happened?" Tom said, eying the water for their sudden return. "Where'd they go?"

"Scared," Lucy said as she swished her katana blade in the water to rinse off its coating of dark blood. She was spattered head to toe with more of the same.

"Hey, you're good," he said. "I'll even be the first to say you're great with that blade. But I don't think those things are scared of anything."

"Yeah, they are." She pointed the tip of her katana at something behind him. "That."

Tom whirled…and there it was…the doom he'd sensed.

A mind-numbing sight. A hole in the air, a perfectly round six-foot wide pit of black emptiness hovering maybe a dozen feet above the surface of the water. The boat was gliding straight for it.

He grabbed the wheel and quick pulled them to the left. But as they coasted around its side, it still appeared as a circular hole in the air. It looked like a sphere from every angle but remained an opening. A two-dimensional spherical hole seemed self-contradicting…all wrong…but here it was.

The hopelessness and despair flowing from it engulfed him, claimed him. He idled the engine and they both stared in silence.

Daley

As Kendrick raced his pickup through the solar array, Daley worked to catch her breath as she watched the wildly flashing tower—damn, she was out of shape. The huge bolts of energy arcing into the air made the test run of a few weeks ago look like a July Fourth sparkler.

("What are we doing here?") Pard said.

I'm not sure anymore.

The electrical display could mean that Elis had stopped doing whatever he did to cause the quakes and put all his voltage into the dome. If so, she could turn around now. All she cared about were the quakes. She hadn't brought all those people back from the horrors just to have them crushed in collapsed buildings.

("Do we care whether or not he opens a passage into the Void—assuming he can?")

Not really. Because even if he can, Jason's going to take care of that.

("And soon…if that dashboard clock is accurate.")

She tapped the clock and asked Kendrick, "Is that the right time?"

He shrugged. "Close, I guess. I ain't been too worried about the right time lately."

It read 4:18.

What had Jason said? *We wait until the exact moment of the equinox—four twenty-one Pacific Time—and then we wait just a little longer until the passage stabilizes. Then we send the surge.*

("We've got maybe five minutes before the tower blows. I'd prefer to watch that from a distance.")

I'm with you.

"Slow down," she told Kendrick.

"You said you wanted to get here fast, but okay. Sure."

The pickup slowed as the base of the tower came into view at the end of the road.

("We should be going in the other direction.")

Yeah, you're right.

She was turning to tell Kendrick to head back the way they'd come when she caught sight of a familiar-looking car parked by the tower.

"Hey, isn't that…?"

Kendrick nodded. "Yeah, the Pendry kid's Highlander. Saw him drive by earlier."

He's here to stop his father.

("And doing a bang-up job of it, I see.")

Rhys might have hurt and offended her, but still…

We've got to get him out of there.

("Then you'd better move fast.")

"Pull up by the Highlander," she told Kendrick.

When the pickup stopped next to it, Daley reached for the

door handle and froze. A crowd of...what...creatures? Whatever they were, a dozen or so of them stood in a tight circle with Rhys at the center.

"What are *they?*"

("They look like hominid Ken dolls.")

"Don't know," Kendrick said. "Want me to have a look?"

"I'll go with you," she said.

"You should stay here, goddess."

She hopped to the ground. "Stop calling me that."

Kendrick pulled his aluminum baseball bat from behind his seat and they approached together.

"Rhys!" she called.

He spun and saw her. "Daley! Get out of here! He's totally out of his head."

She stopped about a dozen feet away. "What are those things and can you get away? Because you need to get away—like now."

"They won't let me pass. And they're immovable."

"What are they?"

"They're called porthors. Remember the night somebody wrecked that empty shop next to Healerina? They did it. My dad sent them."

("I recognize them now. They're the 'lizards' we saw in the desert that night.")

"But—?"

"Well, well, look who's here," said a voice from under the tower. Elis Pendry stepped out into the sunlight. "The Duad arrives. And look who's with her. The traitor."

"What are you talking about, Dad?"

Kendrick said, "I tried, but she can't be killed. She's a goddess."

Rhys stood there with his mouth hanging open.

Elis laughed. "A goddess! Is that so? Well, the goddess arrived too late." He waggled a phone in the air. "Just talking to the Elders out on the Salton Sea."

Daley said, "Who're you kidding? Phones are useless. You've seen to that."

He waggled it again. "Satellite phone. They just told me

that the passage is opening. They're approaching it now. All the dominoes are tipping just as planned. We've reached the point of no return."

What he doesn't know can hurt him, but I'm not telling him.

("But it can hurt Rhys too if he stays here. Maybe your dragon can free him.")

Worth a try.

"Karma," she said. "Get Rhys out of there."

"It's Jeff now," he said, shaking his head. "And I stay by you, goddess. My duty is to protect you."

She didn't need Jeff right now, she needed Karma.

"We have to get Rhys out of there."

Another stubborn head shake. "I'm not here to protect him, I'm protecting you."

"That's the way you're playing it? Okay…then protect me."

She broke into run toward the tower.

"Goddess, no!"

Tom

"The Void," Lucy said, eyes wide, her voice a whisper.

He'd have to take her word for it. Whatever it was, it didn't come from their world or their reality. And that realization brought everything crashing down around him. He'd been writing off all this Visitors crap as just that: crap. But if this clan could open a gateway into the Void or whatever that blackness was, then everything else surrounding their mythology might be true. And that meant reality wasn't what he'd always assumed it to be.

"Get closer," Lucy said.

Every cell in his body screamed *NO!*

"I can't, Lucy. Absolutely not. If those monsters that came out of the fault are afraid to come near it, we should be too."

"I think those 'monsters' are here as snacks for the Visitors. Someone's stocking the pond, so to speak. Closer, Tommy. Please. I've waited all my life for this."

Still, he held back. Couldn't she see the opening was expanding?

"It's getting bigger, Lucy. It could swallow us up!"

"Would that be so bad?"

"Damn right it'd be bad! If you're right, that's pure nothingness in there!"

It spanned eight feet, maybe nine now, and had lowered to within a few feet of the water. He could feel air flowing past him into its maw. In fact, their stern was drifting around as they started to float toward it.

"I'm moving us away," he said, reaching for the gearshift.

"*No!*" she screamed in a singular display of emotion. "I need to see! Just a glimpse. You can throw it into gear and race away on an instant's notice, but just let me *see!* Just once! Please, Tommy!"

The naked need in her voice reached deep inside him. She was feeling something. As much as he resented her for putting him in this spot, he left it in neutral...but kept a tight grip on the gearshift.

The katana clattered on the aluminum hull as she dropped it and pulled a folded piece of paper from within her harem pants.

"Take this."

"What—?"

"Just hold onto it and read it when you have a chance. I would have texted it to you but I didn't know if texting would work out here."

He took it and promptly dropped it as she moved to the stern. There she leaned on the engine, stretching over it on tiptoe to peer into the blackness.

"Careful!"

Suddenly faint, frantic voices echoed across the water. Tom looked around and saw a white fiberglass, inboard runabout approaching. Four older men stood at the sides or leaning on the windshield, all waving frantically.

Their words became clear as they neared.

"Get away from there!"... "Stay back!"... "You don't know what you're doing!"

"I know exactly what I'm doing," Lucy muttered as she leaned even farther.

"They act like they own it," Tom said. "They must be from the clan."

Lucy said, "Tell them to fuck off."

"We're fine!" Tom shouted back.

"No!" one of them called. "It's dangerous. You're in the way!"

Lucy cried, "I see something!"

"If it's truly a window into the Void," Tom said, "you shouldn't see anything."

"The Visitors, they're coming this way, coming through."

Was she really seeing anything? Was it possible?

What was he thinking? Of course it was possible. If this hole in reality was possible, so were the Visitors.

The clansters had idled their engine and were drifting about thirty feet away, still calling warnings.

"Maybe we'd better move away," he said. "Maybe they know something."

She shook her head. "No. Stay. The Visitors are still far off."

"What do they look like?"

He envisioned lots of tentacles, like their "snacks."

"They're just blurs."

They'd drifted too close for Tom's comfort. "I'm going to move us away."

"No! I'm not finished!"

"Finished what? I'm sorry, I—"

Lucy cried out as the stern suddenly lifted into the air. A chorus of wails and shouts from the runabout echoed her. The bow stayed in the water but the stern hovered three feet above the surface. Lucy clung to the engine but Tom noticed her ponytail had drifted off her back.

"I feel weightless!" she cried. "I *am* weightless. There's no gravity by the passage!"

Nonplussed, he pushed the gearshift to "F" and the engine howled as the propeller spun in the air.

"Stop that, Tommy! You'll burn out the engine and then you'll be stuck out here!"

He couldn't argue with that so he idled again...

...and watched in horror as his sister let go of the engine and floated free in the air.

The shouts from the clansters increased in volume.

Baffled, Tom cried, "What are you *doing*?"

She rotated toward him and her expression was beatific as she drifted toward the opening. "Heading home."

"No-no-no! Stop!"

As he scrambled uphill toward the stern, he grabbed the oar he'd used against the little horrors. He almost dropped it as he entered the no-gravity zone or whatever it was. His insides lurched and he had to clutch the engine cowling to keep his feet on the deck as he extended the oar toward her.

"Grab this! I'll pull you in!"

She folded her hands as if praying. "It's okay, Tommy," she said, her voice and expression maddeningly calm. "I'm right where I want to be. I've been aimed toward this all my life. I couldn't be happier."

"Lucy, please! You're happy now, but you don't really know anything about what's in there! It's just a guess! The Void is a myth! A hope! Wishful thinking! And if it *is* real, it's a Void, Lucy—a fucking *Void*! It's empty by definition! Nothingness! You'll die in there! You won't be free—you'll be *nothing*!"

Her mouth twisted. "I already am nothing."

The bow of the boat was angling around in the breeze but the stern remained fixed in the air. Cries from the clansters in the runabout had reached the point of hysteria by now. What was their *problem*?

That was when he noticed thin, postage-size flakes of red and yellow drifting off Lucy's back and flowing into the blackness of the sphere—her harem pants and T-shirt. Her back and buttocks were quickly exposed, and soon pieces of her flesh began floating into the opening.

He pointed a finger that shook like he had Parkinson's. "Lucy! You're flaking away! Dissolving!"

She was disappearing into the void, being *absorbed*. Tom had such mixed feelings. He'd wanted her gone from his life but not this way.

"Am I? I don't feel anything."

In no time she was half-gone and kept flaking away. But her expression remained serene.

"Lucy, my God!"

"I'm all right with whatever's happening, Tommy. I've been wishing for this my entire life, it seems, and now that wish is coming true. I—" Her beatific smile died, turning to a frown. "Wait..."

"No, *you* wait! Think this over!"

The frown became an open-mouthed, horrified grimace. "It's not empty!"

"What are you talking about?"

"The Void! It's full of hunger and-and-and malice and-and—" She grabbed the oar, clutching the blade with both hands. "It wants me, Tommy! Pull me back! I can't go there! *Pull me back!*"

For a second Tom was tempted to push instead of pull. How long had he listened to her yammer on and on about the wonderful Void and her awful flesh-trap body? She'd dragged him down here to face his "irrelevance" and suddenly he was to be her savior? Fuck that.

But he didn't have it in him. He couldn't be the one to push her into that black hole. So, damn her, he pulled. But he had no weight here, no purchase. Gravity had been suspended and so was he. He released one hand from the oar and wrapped his fingers around the gunwale for anchorage. He pulled but the blackness wouldn't let go. Aloof and relentless, it kept swallowing her, *absorbing* her, bit by bit—and in the process, pulling the boat and Tom closer and closer.

"Oh, Tommy, please don't let go! Don't let it have me!"

He wasn't going to let go, but Lucy's legs and torso had been swallowed. All that remained visible were the front of her head and her arms. Then her ears went away, leaving only her terrified face. Her mouth moved, forming a word with no sound. He could read her lips though...

"*Tommyyyyyyyyyy!*"

When her face disappeared her fingers spasmed, going rigidly straight as they released the oar.

And then Lucy was gone, gone like she'd never been. Tom screamed her name, shoved the oar through the shrinking blackness, and fought a crazy impulse to tie the anchor rope around his leg and go after her.

Daley

Daley ran toward the left flank of the—what had he called them?—porthors and straight toward the tower gate, hoping some would make a grab for her. That would break their ranks and maybe give Rhys a chance to make a run for it. And if they went for her, Daley was counting on Kendrick and his bat to go for them.

As she neared the pack, three of them broke away and grabbed for her. From behind her came a hoarse cry.

"Hands off, assholes!"

And then Kendrick was among them with his bat. As he sent one after another flying, Daley waved to Rhys as he struggled with the suddenly disorganized creatures.

"Get out of here!" she shouted. "It's going to blow!"

She glanced toward the tower and froze as she saw Elis standing within the supports, aiming a pistol at her.

"I should have done this right at the start."

Daley ducked as he fired but knew even as she moved that she was too late. But almost simultaneously she heard Kendrick's aluminum bat *conk!* against a skull and a porthor was flung between her and the tower. The creature grimaced but made no sound as the bullet tore into its back and it fell against her, knocking her flat.

Suddenly Kendrick was rushing the tower.

"You shot the goddess! You shot the goddess!"

Elis's eyes widened as he raised the pistol again and fired off another round. Kendrick bucked and half-turned, but kept coming. Elis shot again, and again Kendrick bucked and stumbled a little this time, but he wasn't stopping. He ducked in under the supports and threw the bat at Elis who was backpedaling too furiously to get off another shot. Kendrick launched himself at the older man and the two of them went over the low wall around the shaft. Elis's panicked cry echoed up and then stopped abruptly.

Daley jumped to her feet as the porthors froze and Rhys said, "Dad?"

He started toward the tower but Daley grabbed his arm. "We've got to get out of here now!"

"But my father—"

"Is a goner and you will be too—we'll both be if we don't leave now! I may be just a lying con artist who can't be trusted, but you'd better listen to me this once. Out of here now or you're dead. *NOW!*"

Another look toward the tower, then, "Shit! Okay!"

They raced to the Highlander and jumped in.

"Don't even turn around," Daley cried. "Just put it in reverse and back up. The thing's gonna blow!"

"Blow?" he said, but started the engine and hung over the back of his seat at he reversed down the path. "How's it gonna blow?"

"Jason's sending a monster surge to—oh, God!"

The electric bolts brightened and multiplied and swelled as the copper fittings on the cupola began to glow white hot.

"Move-it-move-it-move-it!" she screamed.

The giant bolts lanced into the ground all around the tower, and seemed especially drawn to the two cars parked before it. The Land Rover and pickup rattled and shook with the impacts and even glowed a little before they exploded.

And then the entire tower ignited like a match head and flared with intolerable brightness. The heat blistered the paint on the Highlander's hood and washed through the windshield.

Rhys took his foot off the gas and stared. He spoke one barely audible word.

"Dad?"

Tom

He stood there screaming his sister's name, praying to whatever power that controlled these things that the aperture would spit her out and they could laugh about how even the Void couldn't tolerate her for very long. But the opening remained empty.

Finally he quieted and waited, ignoring the cries of *We-told-you-so* and *We-warned-you* from the runabout. Fuck 'em. He'd wait right here for her to come back.

As he drifted he spotted her note where he'd dropped it by his feet. He unfolded it. She had written him a letter. On her computer, of course. In a handwriting font, no less.

Tommy...

I was never right for this world. In the Void I can leave this rotting meat sack and return to pure being. I'm so tired of this flesh. Exhausted. Remember the last line from A Tale of Two Cities? "It is a far, far better rest that I go to than I have ever known."

This fleshy life is nothing—all nothing. I've faced my irrelevancy, Tommy. My life has always been a sort of void, so I'm not really losing anything. I'm going home. I'd be happy about this if I knew how to be happy but I don't, so you'll have to be happy for me, okay?

I know I've been a drag on you. I know I've been a terrible burden, and you've been a better brother than I've been a sister. I'm sorry to leave you here to face your irrelevance alone, but miss me just a little, okay, Tommy? Just a smidge?

Your sister,

Lucy

Yeah, she really signed it, *Your sister, Lucy.* Like he had another sister or might think it was from someone else. So typical. Typical, too, how she could never bring herself to say this out loud. But he had to admit he was touched. Even a little choked up, to tell the truth. This was a side of her he hadn't known existed.

Poor Lucy.

He stared at that goddamn flat spherical hole hanging in the air—and noticed irregularities along its edge, a shimmer and ripple along its surface, areas of which arched out in offshoots of blackness, like coronal mass ejections on the sun.

What was happening to it? Some sort of inner disturbance?

The clansters in the runabout were making concerned noises now. They'd opened the passage. Maybe they were having trouble sustaining it.

And now wild convulsions wracked the flat sphere's surface, expanding it briefly into a bizarre, tortured shape before it winked out.

That was what it did—winked out. No noise, no blinding flash. One second it hung in the air, and then, in the space of an eye blink, it vanished, taking with it all hope of seeing Lucy again.

The stern slammed back into the water with a bang and a splash. Gravity had reasserted itself. And now, with the aperture gone, the surface of the water began to ripple with deeper activity as tentacles started to break the surface, cautiously, as if testing the air.

Total panic among the clansters as tentacles darted toward them. One wrapped around the neck of the guy at the helm and pulled him overboard.

Tom spied Lucy's katana lying near the stern and tried using it. He managed to chop a few tentacles, but they became increasingly aggressive and he didn't have her skills, so he started the boat moving.

The clansters weren't so lucky. They had no defenses and the tentacles were all over them. Tom didn't know how to help them and wasn't all that sure he wanted to. One by one, they were all pulled overboard and dragged below the surface.

He kept up his speed and cruised in circles, never moving too far from where the opening had appeared, but it never returned.

Water still gushed from the fault, roiling the surface in steady waves that rocked the aluminum hull. The tentacled things were becoming bolder by the minute. He couldn't stay, couldn't outfight them, but he could outrun them. He felt guilty about leaving…as if he were abandoning Lucy. But she was beyond his reach now—beyond anyone's.

Some of the things followed him a ways toward Salton City but couldn't keep up when he maxed the throttle.

What had happened? He'd brought Lucy here on the premise that everything she'd read in those scrolls was a fantasy, and that they'd get nothing out of the journey beyond an interesting day trip. But turned out the clan had indeed opened some sort of interdimensional passage. But then what? Hadn't they been able to sustain it? He wasn't complaining. An influx of interdimensional beings wouldn't be good for anyone.

He couldn't help remembering how the natives had North America all to themselves before the white man came. Now look at them.

The Visitors' arrival had been cancelled—good.

Lucy was gone—bad. Very bad.

But what of Lucy? Did she no longer exist? Or had she found that state of non-corporeal being she'd longed for? Tom hoped for the latter.

But whatever her state, he was headed back to an empty house—assuming it was still standing. Their folks had built it to earthquake codes and it sat a good two hundred miles from the quake's epicenter down near the Mexico border.

He was free and Lucy would never tie him down again. But that big house was going to feel strange now. They saw each other only at meals—their usually silent meals—but the rest of the time, even though she tucked herself away in her upstairs hidey-hole, he'd known she was there, and that had made the house seem less empty.

Tom had dreamed of life without her—craved it—but he never imagined she'd leave such a...void.

Daley

Daley and Rhys stood as close as the heat from the smoking remnant of the tower would allow. The copper cupola had melted, leaving the canted tower with a flat top.

Looks like a burnt matchstick.

("If not for the steel shaft running up its center, it surely would have collapsed.")

The Pendry Land Rover and Kendrick's pickup lay in smoldering pieces around them.

Daley said, "I'm sorry about your dad," though she really wasn't. The bastard had shot at her—might have killed her if that porthor hadn't got in the way. But, at this moment, it seemed like the thing to say.

"Yeah," Rhys said, his expression stony as he stared at the tower. "I don't know what to feel. If this were a week ago, I'm pretty sure I'd be devastated. But now...after what he's done...

the death and destruction..." He turned to Daley. "Did he really hire Kendrick to kill you?"

She nodded. "Yeah."

"But Kendrick was here protecting you."

"Long story."

"Well, they're both gone now and you're still here. What goes around..."

"So it seems."

The porthors or whatever they were called were gone too. Back into the sand, she guessed.

Rhys sighed. "No one will be able to retrieve those bodies for a while yet, and I've got to go break the news to my mother and brother."

Daley didn't envy him that. She knew nothing about the mother but she'd sensed Cadoc had only contempt for his father.

"Can you drop me at my place?"

"Absolutely. It'll give us a chance to talk. And we do need to talk."

I don't want to talk to him, Pard. I heard enough of his talk on Tuesday. I'm done talking to this man.

("I understand. But it's a long walk.")

And then she heard the rumble of a Harley hog. Juana was coming down the road.

("Cavalry to the rescue!")

"Thanks anyway," she told Rhys. "Juana will give me a ride."

"But we need to talk."

She turned to him, trying to keep her tone level. "You need to talk to your family and I need to talk to Juana. Karma was her nephew."

He blinked. "He was? I had no idea. Yeah, of course. Go ahead. We'll catch up later."

"Yeah."

Don't hold your breath.

Rhys was gone by the time Juana had parked and kickstanded her bike.

"I've got bad news," Daley said as she approached. "About Karma—Jeff."

She stared a moment at the charred remnant of the tower, then back to Daley. "Gone?"

She nodded. "He was protecting me. Took a couple of bullets for me, then took Elis Pendry with him."

"A good death, then?"

"Yeah. A good death."

They stood in silence for a moment, then Juana said, "I'll take you home."

But where was home anymore?

On the road to town they passed the wind farm where not one turbine remained standing—which gave Daley a thought.

"Make a stop at the Tadhak compound first, okay?"

They roared through the deserted and devastated town to the meringue walls of the compound. The front gate stood open. Daley hopped off and found the inner gate open as well. Beyond it lay nothing but an empty courtyard. The interior had probably always been empty. The Tadhaks had deactivated their long door after they'd all returned to Colorado. To do what? Commit mass suicide? She'd probably never know.

Back down the street to the crushed Healerina. Looking at the wreckage gave her a twinge of regret, but no big deal. That phase of her life was over.

The remains of her apartment sat almost at ground level, the interior a shambles but intact enough to allow her to fill her duffel with toiletries and a couple of changes of clothes. She grabbed her laptop and her cash candle and took inordinate pleasure in the recovery of her battered Dodgers cap before rejoining Juana outside.

"Do you have a place to sleep?" Juana said.

Daley shook her head. "I may drive back to LA."

Juana frowned. "Now? After the day you've had? Stay at Jeffrey's."

That did *not* sound like a plan...

"Oh, I don't know about that..."

"He'd want you to. I'd stay with you but I've got to help out at the reservation. Lots of damage there."

Someone had cleared a path from the rear area to the street—Kendrick? Daley and her Subaru followed Juana down to Kendrick's double-wide. It had survived the quakes mostly intact, though one end had slipped off a crumbled support, leaving it on an angle.

It felt weird stepping into a dead man's home, especially one with a tilted floor. Roomy, though. Forty feet long and twenty feet wide, with two bedrooms. And the electricity still worked. The trailer park had been supplied by the Tadaks so she supposed the monster batteries were still online. The first thing she did was open all the windows. She closed them again after Juana left, and threw the bolt on the front door.

"Okay, Pard," she said. "Just one night. I don't see me sleeping too well here."

From his position on the La-Z-Boy, Pard morphed into Jason Statham again. ("I'll stand guard.")

"As if. I don't need a guard as much as I need a shower—good, long, hot one. But forget it. I'd feel totally creepy getting naked in Karma Kendrick's digs."

She decided to head for LA in the morning and shower in her North Hollywood place. She did change out of her black Curandera outfit though.

Her phone didn't work. Doubtful that a single cell tower in the valley remained upright. As for food, nothing in the cabinets but some stale Fritos and a fresh tube of plain Pringles; the fridge was empty except for half a six of Bud. Though she'd have preferred something other than beer, she settled down in front of the TV with her dinner of Pringles and brewskis and turned it on. The trailer park had its own dish that apparently still worked.

The big news was that the seawater gushing from the Gulf of California into the Imperial Valley and been blocked and the flow stopped. Two MOABs had been deployed, straddling the channel and collapsing it at the Baja-Sonoma line south of the devastated desert town of El Indiviso. The Mexican government was all sorts of outraged by the dropping of bombs on Mexican soil, but the US President didn't seem to care. He hadn't been about to let Calexico and El Centro and "America's Salad Bowl" be flooded with seawater.

The other big story was that the horrors had disappeared.

All its victims had experienced spontaneous cures somewhere around four thirty that afternoon.

"Jason's power surge must have worked," Daley said.

("Well, it would seem that way. He said the Rymwyr were feeding the horrors into the area. If the Tadhaks trapped them in the Void, it stands to reason that the feed would stop.")

Another story of local interest concerned strange tentacled creatures that had invaded the Salton Sea, but the bizarre fauna seemed to be dying off, killed by the toxins stirred up from the sea bed by the quakes.

And then an all-too-familiar image appeared.

"Uh-oh."

Daley's face filled the screen. The newsreader gave a recap of the day's events at the El Centro Regional Medical Center and said that La Curandera was being credited with the universal cure.

"Me? That was Jason."

("But he's gone—maybe gone in every sense of the word. That leaves you. You're officially a miracle worker. They'll be fitting you for a halo soon.")

The story concluded with a statement that the mystery woman had disappeared and no one knew where to find her.

("Let's work at keeping it that way.")

"I'm with you. I say we sneak out of here *real* early tomorrow."

("Excellent idea.")

"**R**HYS! RHYS! RHYS! RHYS!"

Rhys watched the crowd and wanted to block out their chant.

Cadoc stood at his side, saying, "You've got to do it."

"I don't want it!"

The front end of the first floor of the Lodge had suffered only mild damage, so Rhys and Cad had spent the night on couches in their father's office. Mom had stayed at her sister's place.

In a single day the clan had lost all five of its Elders. Elis at the tower, and the boat carrying the other four had been found drifting empty on the Salton Sea. The verdict was they'd fallen victim to the monstrous creatures that had invaded the water.

Against all reason, the sentiment had quickly spread through the clan that twenty-eight-year-old Rhys Pendry was the man to take the reins. And now members of all five families had gathered outside the Lodge to elect him by acclaim.

Cad said, "You're the only one who knows enough about the workings of the Pendry Fund to take it over. The clan depends on it. And that gives you a golden opportunity to lead them away from this insane religion that's hamstrung us for generations."

Forgetting about the Visitors...what a concept.

"And the nofio," Cadoc added, his words picking up speed. "You can end that practice. For good. And no more clan kids put up for adoption. And-and-and we can find Aerona if she's alive."

Learn what happened to their long-lost sister...absolutely.

"How about you give it a year, Rhys? Just a year. You can do so much good here in a year."

A year? Yeah, maybe he could handle a year. Why not?

"Okay, Cad. You win. A year. But no more."

"Great! Go out there and tell them right now. Because I can't stand listening to them anymore."

Rhys stepped outside and shouted that he'd accept the job—without mentioning the time limit—and then sent them all home.

"I think I'll head into town," he said when he and Cad were finally alone. "See if I can help. It's about time we became more involved with the locals."

Cad grinned. "And maybe check to see if Daley's around?"

He had to laugh. "Am I that transparent?"

"Like polished glass. Mind if I come along?"

"Not at all."

Cad might provide a mollifying element. Rhys sensed that those two shared a certain rapport. Something she'd once shared with Rhys before he'd trashed it.

They decided to walk. Rhys had seen the ruins of the town yesterday, but the destruction was all new to Cad.

"Will they ever rebuild?" he said.

Rhys shrugged. "I hope so. That'll be up to the Tadhaks, but they all seemed to have disappeared. Jason included."

They found a crowd of people standing before the remains of Healerina.

"This is the first time I've ever seen the store during the day," Cad said. "But who're these?"

"Her followers. They clogged the entire town Thursday night after she returned from the hospital, and followed her back to El Centro yesterday morning. Looks like some are back." Rhys stepped into the group. "What's going on? Have you seen Ms. Daley?"

"No, señor," said an elderly Mexican woman with a black mantilla draped over her silver hair. Tears filled her eyes. "La Curandera is gone."

"She'll be back!" said a twenty-something woman all dressed in black, a patch of her dark hair bleached white. She waved her left hand—painted gold. "She's watching over us!"

Rhys stared at her. She'd made herself up like Daley. He spotted a guy beyond her—also in black with a white patch of hair. What was this all about?

Backing away, he turned to Cad and lowered his voice. "They're like pilgrims to a holy place and Daley's a saint."

"'La Curandera,'" Cad said. "That's a scary thing to have to live up to. Especially when you can really heal."

Especially when you can really heal...

Each word was a red-hot knife jabbed into his skin.

...really heal...

And he'd called her a liar.

"I'd been hoping to find her poking through the wreckage," he said. "But I've got this feeling she won't be back."

"Not with these...worshippers about."

"I've got things I need to say to her."

"You'll get your chance...maybe."

"Yeah? When?"

"Can't say for sure, but she'll be back."

"Where? Here? In Nespodee Springs?"

"No, not here. Just...back. Out of hiding. She'll resurface when we need her. And I have little doubt we're going to need her again before too long."

Rhys sure as hell hoped so.

About the Author

F. PAUL WILSON is an award-winning, bestselling author of seventy books and nearly one hundred short stories spanning science fiction, horror, adventure, medical thrillers, and virtually everything between.

His novels The Keep, The Tomb, Harbingers, By the Sword, The Dark at the End, and Nightworld were New York Times Bestsellers. The Tomb received the 1984 Porgie Award from The West Coast Review of Books. Wheels Within Wheels won the first Prometheus Award, and Sims another; Healer and An Enemy of the State were elected to the Prometheus Hall of Fame. Dydeetown World was on the young adult recommended reading lists of the American Library Association and the New York Public Library, among others. His novella Aftershock won the Stoker Award. He was voted Grand Master by the World Horror Convention; he received the Lifetime Achievement Award from the Horror Writers of America, and the Thriller Lifetime Achievement Award from the editors of Romantic Times. He also received the prestigious San Diego Comic-Con Inkpot Award and is listed in the 50th anniversary edition of Who's Who in America.

His short fiction has been collected in Soft & Others, The Barrens & Others, and Aftershock & Others. He has edited two anthologies: Freak Show and Diagnosis: Terminal plus (with Pierce Watters) the only complete collection of Henry Kuttner's Hogben stories, The Hogben Chronicles.

In 1983 Paramount rendered his novel The Keep into a visually striking but otherwise incomprehensible movie with screenplay and direction by Michael Mann.

The Tomb has spent twenty-five years in development hell at Beacon Films.

Dario Argento adapted his story "Pelts" for Masters of Horror. Over nine million copies of his books are in print in the US and his work has been translated into twenty-four languages. He also has written for the stage, screen, comics, and interactive media. Paul resides at the Jersey Shore and can be found on the Web at www.repairmanjack.com.

Repairman Jack*

The Tomb
Legacies
Conspiracies
All the Rage
Hosts
The Haunted Air
Gateways
Crisscross
Infernal
Harbingers
Bloodline
By the Sword
Ground Zero
The Last Christmas
Fatal Error
The Dark at the End
Nightworld
Quick Fixes—Tales of Repairman Jack

The Teen Trilogy*

Jack: Secret Histories
Jack: Secret Circles
Jack: Secret Vengeance

The Early Years Trilogy*

Cold City
Dark City
Fear City

The Adversary Cycle*The Keep

The Tomb
The Touch
Reborn
Reprisal
Nightworld

Omnibus Editions

The Complete LaNague
Calling Dr. Death (3 medical thrillers)
Ephemerata

Novellas

*The Peabody-Ozymandias Traveling Circus & Oddity Emporium**
*"Wardenclyffe"**
"Signalz"
*

The LaNague Federation

Healer
Wheels Within Wheels
An Enemy of the State
Dydeetown World
The Tery

Other Novels

*Black Wind**
*Sibs**
The Select
Virgin
Implant
Deep as the Marrow
Sims
*The Fifth Harmonic**
Midnight Mass

Collaborations

Mirage (with Matthew J. Costello)
Nightkill (with Steven Spruill)
Masque (with Matthew J. Costello)
Draculas (with Crouch, Killborn, Strand)
The Proteus Cure (with Tracy L. Carbone)
A Necessary End (with Sarah Pinborough)
*"Fix"** (with J. Konrath & Ann Voss Peterson)
Three Films and a Play (with Matthew J. Costello)
Faster Than Light – Vols. 1 & 2 (with Matthew J. Costello)

The ICE Trilogy*

Panacea
The God Gene
The Void Protocol

The Nocturnia Chronicles
(with Thomas F. Monteleone)

Definitely Not Kansas
Family Secrets
The Silent Ones

Short Fiction

Soft & Others
The Barrens and Others
Aftershock and Others
The Christmas Thingy
Quick Fixes—Tales of Repairman Jack*
Sex Slaves of the Dragon Tong
Secret Stories
The Compendium of F (Three Volumes)

The Rx Mystery Series

Rx Murder
Rx Mayhem

The QUAD Novels

Double Threat
Double Dose

Curious about other Crossroad Press books?
Stop by our site:
http://store.crossroadpress.com
We offer quality writing
in digital, audio, and print formats.

Made in the USA
Middletown, DE
22 September 2023

39062923R00227